Judy Corbalis was born and grew up in New Zealand but now lives in London. A former Hawthornden Fellow and Visiting Scholar at the Centre for Women Leaders at Lucy Cavendish College, Cambridge, she has an MA in Creative Writing from the University of East Anglia and was the inaugural Royal Literary Fund Fellow at the Courtauld Institute of Art where she currently holds the post of Academic Support Tutor.

She has adapted her own work for radio and has written and fronted television programmes for children. Her children's books have been published by Deutsch, Hodder and Scholastic — children love them for their humour and the fact that no character behaves as expected. Her new children's book, *Get That Ball*, illustrated by Korky Paul, will be published by Andersen Press in 2016. Her adult novels include *Tapu*, and *Mortmain*, shortlisted for the 2009 Encore Award.

She is married to the sculptor Phillip King, PPRA, and makes frequent visits to New Zealand.

A Crooked Rib

JUDY CORBALIS

VINTAGE

VINTAGE

UK | USA | Canada | Ireland | Australia
India | New Zealand | South Africa | China

Vintage is an imprint of the Penguin Random House group of companies, whose addresses can be found at global.penguinrandomhouse.com.

Penguin Random House New Zealand

First published by Penguin Random House New Zealand, 2015

1 3 5 7 9 10 8 6 4 2

Cover and text design by Sarah Healey © Penguin Random House New Zealand
Cover photograph © Lee Avison/Trevillion Images
Author photograph by Phillip King © 2013
Printed and bound in Australia by Griffin Press, an Accredited ISO AS/NZS 14001 Environmental Management Systems Printer

A catalogue record for this book is available from the National Library of New Zealand.

ISBN 978-177553-826-4

creative nz
Arts Council of New Zealand Toi Aotearoa

The assistance of Creative New Zealand towards the production of this book is gratefully acknowledged by the publisher.

penguinrandomhouse.co.nz

For

Penelope Hoare	*&*	*Phillip King*

With fondest love

Fool'd and beguil'd, by him thou, I by thee,
To trust thee from my side, imagin'd wise,
Constant, mature, proof against all assaults,
And understood not all was but a shew
Rather then solid vertu, all but a Rib
Crooked by nature, bent, as now appears,
More to the part sinister from me drawn.

— Adam to Eve: John Milton, *Paradise Lost*, Book 10

I

AOTEAROA

Tihe mauri ora.
The breath of life.
Tihe mauri ora.
All life is breath.

The wind, the breath of the sky; the tides, the breath of the sea. I saw the pulse in his tiny chest rise and fall with his first gulp of air.

Tihe mauri ora.

Listen to my words. I was there. I saw it all. How quickly a man is made a hero; how easily a woman is reviled and cast out. Only I know the truth of what took place. Listen to my story. Listen to my breath.

NEW ZEALAND, 1845

The figures on the jetty blurred and dwindled. The coast of Western Australia swam slowly away. It had been ten years since I had first seen that shoreline, its sands gleaming white and unwelcoming as tombstone marble, the barren little settlement huddled above them.

I heard again Lucy's angry voice: 'How *can* you have brought us to this horrid place?' And, abruptly, I had an unbidden image of the convict women, released from the hold and manacled two by two, herded together at the far end of the *Buffalo*, their faces turned towards the fresh sea breeze. The same wind blew around me now. I shuddered a little, seeing once more the stronger of the women in one of the pairs suddenly hauling at her companion and attempting to fling them both from the *Buffalo* into the swirling waters. And I remembered how, restrained by the guards, she had shrieked and cursed like a madwoman as she and her companion were dragged back below.

High on the hillside in the distance I glimpsed the flutter of the White Ensign above Uncle's grave, a final signal of farewell. Beneath my genuine sorrow at parting was euphoria: I was twenty-one years old, in possession of a comfortable income and answerable to no one but myself. Throughout our stormy passage across the Tasman Sea, I experienced neither fear nor regret; instead, the nearer we approached New Zealand, the more I felt a rising sense of elation. Very soon, I was going to see Lucy again.

Many souls stray almost nowhere from their birthplace, spending their entire lives in the serenity and security of a landscape in which every pathway and corner, each wall and stone is known as intimately as a loved friend. Some, like my own dear papa and Uncle Spencer, travel far from home to fulfil their duty to Sovereign and Country; thousands of these lie buried in foreign soil or rest only as bleached bones scattered across the floors of the world's great oceans. Others, condemned by circumstances and fortune, go where their fathers and husbands choose to transport them. Educated women without income or protectors may become governesses, but the poor are obliged to go into service to earn their bread and lodging. I was startled to discover that on our ship are five women, two with a child each, who have engaged themselves in binding contracts to be married in New Zealand to men whom they have never seen, and of whom their only knowledge is that they are in want of wives. It seems there is such a dearth of marriageable women in the colony that any woman, no matter how ill-formed or impecunious, may secure for herself a tolerable husband.

One of these women has a daughter, seven years old, whom she has brought with her from Scotland in search of a new life. Already she wears a wedding ring, which was placed on her finger by a proxy bridegroom in a ceremony in a chapel in Fife. Her unknown husband is a carpenter, devout, and a steady earner, who has agreed to adopt her daughter as his own and has already built a small house in preparation for their arrival. She says she was widowed while carrying the child, but I suspect she was betrayed and abandoned, and that even this course of uniting her future with an unknown man, thousands of miles from her native land, seems less bleak than her former life. She is not so pleasing in appearance, having a rather stern countenance and a manner with her child neither tender nor gentle. For the little girl's sake, I hope that the new father will love her as he has promised. I asked the mother if her husband would be in Auckland to meet them from the ship but, no, she replied, they must take another boat to Wellington and, from thence, yet another to Dunedin in the far south.

Something in her demeanour recalled to me the sad resignation of a woman I saw as a child when Papa, Mama and I made a rare visit to Dorchester. The streets of the town were thronged with people, and as we stood in the clamour and confusion we heard the rattle of a cart on the cobbled road. In it stood a woman in chains, clad only in a shift, her hair shorn, her head bent in misery or shame.

'What is it, Papa?' I asked, puzzled by such a sight.

'The hangman's cart,' he said. 'She is being taken through the streets to the gallows and the public spectacle of her miserable end.'

I shrank against him. 'How cruel. Everyone is jeering at her.'

'It is but simple justice,' said Papa. 'She smothered her infant and afterwards savagely murdered her husband with a butcher's knife. She knows her own guilty heart. See how calmly she awaits her fate?'

Child though I was, it seemed to me that the murderess was already half-dead to the living world and its savagery, that she bowed her head like an ox to the weight of her yoke, and that all that was left to her was to move slowly forward to whatever unknowable thing awaited her.

The nearer we drew to New Zealand, the more difficult I found it to contain my exhilaration. Six years earlier, Lucy had sailed as a bride from Australia; I had not seen her since. At first, there had been regular letters, though often, in true Lucy fashion, written in breathless haste. She had met her husband's large family and *loved them all*, London was *a delight* and though she had not yet returned to Lyme she had *great hopes of doing so in the near future*. Then came the letter that contained the news that her husband had been posted to Adelaide as Governor and they would be sailing very soon, *before my confinement, which it seems will now be at sea*. For months following, there had been silence. At the arrival in Western Australia of the rare ships carrying mail, Aunt poured out letters from the oilskin bag onto the table, searching for any bearing the familiar hand. Though she said nothing, I knew she feared that Lucy had perished in childbirth, that there had been an accident, that they had been lost at sea. And then, when the long-awaited correspondence did arrive, it was a terse formal communiqué from Captain Grey, apprising Aunt of the birth at sea and death in Adelaide of their only child, Baby George. From Lucy, there had come not a word until, unexpectedly, she had sent two letters, both of which I had by heart.

To Aunt she wrote:

South Australia 1844

My Dearest Mama,

Such news! My husband has been appointed Governor of New Zealand, the youngest Governor yet appointed by the Colonial Office. It is a young country and his orders are that he must endeavour to rescue it from the bankruptcy into which it has fallen, to mediate between the Maori tribes and the European settlers, to regulate land sales and to restore order to the lawless Northern settlement of Kororareka where the rebel chief, John Heke, has been engaged in skirmishes against the Crown. He has, on several occasions, cut down the British flagpole . . . and, in his last skirmish, he murdered six of our gallant soldiers . . . But Captain Grey is confident that, with God's help, he is equal to the task ahead of him. I hope you will agree that it is a signal honour.

We leave very soon . . .

My letter was brief and desperate:

My dearest, dearest Fanny,

The most dreadful, dismal news imaginable. We are to leave Adelaide within the month. George has been posted to that frightful cannibal country, New Zealand . . . I beg you, Dearest Sister, to come to me . . .

And now, at last, we were to be reunited. Would she be greatly changed? Would we slip back again into our old sisterly relationship or be distanced from each other? While she had travelled so far, I had remained fixed at Albany, ignorant of the ways of the world outside Western Australia. Perhaps she would find me tediously narrow-minded. But could she be so much altered? She was, after all, only twenty-two years old . . . I pictured Lucy as I had last seen her, waving from the rail of the ship, her bonnet flung back, her dark ringlets blowing as she tossed kisses to us . . . Had *I* changed greatly since that time? Would *she* recognise *me*?

I was diverted from these thoughts by the arrival on deck of a number of other passengers, all eager to be among the first to catch sight of Auckland. Already it was possible to discern mountain-tops protruding from the long white cloud that obscured the coastline, and several hours later we passed into an enormous harbour scattered with small islands, one of which was crowned with three tall peaks. Far off, to the left of our ship, was a distant range of hazy blue-grey mountains, but ahead of us the land rose directly from the water's edge to a high plateau riven with deep gullies, atop and on the sides of which was laid out the settlement of Auckland, larger and more populated than I had anticipated. The horizon above the town was dominated by a windmill, its sails dipping in salute as we approached, and on a lower slope stood a church with a tall English spire. Beyond this were several perfectly conical hills, seemingly fortified with wooden ramparts made of stakes.

'Those are former Maori war settlements,' said Lieutenant Cowan, appearing suddenly beside me. He saw my involuntary look of alarm. 'I assure you we're in no danger. Here in Auckland, the natives are entirely subdued.'

'By our gallant British forces?'

'No, by Hongi Hika, one of the Northern chiefs. About twenty-five years ago, Mr Kendall, the missionary, took him to England, where he acquired great quantities of muskets. When they returned, Hongi armed his kinsmen and set about destroying his Southern enemies.'

'But surely, if the chief was with a missionary . . .?'

'The missionaries have long been the greatest gun-runners here . . . and, if the Governor is to be believed, land-grabbers, too.'

'Is there still much fighting in the rest of New Zealand?'

'There's still trouble in the south of the island, but since the signing of the Treaty, I believe the worst of it is over.'

'The Treaty?'

'It's a document, drawn up by Captain Hobson, in which the Maori chiefs swear their allegiance to the Queen.' He paused. 'The Maoris are an extraordinary race. They have no equal in bloodthirsty warfare, but in their battles they abide by a code of conduct which wouldn't disgrace an English gentleman. Since the arrival of the missionaries, they never fight on Sundays, and if one tribe is not ready to deploy themselves in a battle, the other side refuses to engage against them.'

'That sounds most honourable.'

'Yes. And they greatly revere the dead. After the battle of Puketutu, at Heke's pa . . .'

'My sister has written of Heke . . .'

'A murdering renegade who gives no quarter in battle and is greatly feared by our men for his ferocity. Yet, after our troops had been defeated, he invited the missionaries to perform burial services over our dead, and guaranteed their safety himself.' He glanced at me. 'I hope I'm not alarming you, Miss Thompson?'

'Not at all. I prefer to have some knowledge of my new home.'

He had the soldier's military bearing and unconsciously straightened his back. 'Ah, where was I? Yes, the terrain here is very difficult. Our soldiers are unused to fighting under such conditions and many are raw recruits. The chiefs retreat into their strongholds in the bush and we're powerless to pursue them. And we're woefully ill-equipped. But doubtless you'll hear all this from the Governor himself.'

We had drawn closer to land and were contained entirely within the shelter of the great harbour. The sunshine was tempered by a cool breeze and I reminded myself that it was November and still springtime. I could hear the whirring of the windmill's sails quite distinctly now, and also discern a wide area of flattened ground, apparently a road, ending in a long jetty beside a flour mill. I tried to make out which building might be Government House but the number of flags flying on the hillsides made it impossible to distinguish. At the far end of the jetty, on a narrow strip of shore, a crowd had gathered to meet us.

'Miss Thompson,' said Lieutenant Cowan, 'I have no wish appear too forward but . . . at some later date, I have a meeting with the Governor and I wondered . . . would you, perhaps, consider . . . allow me to present my compliments to you at that time? I should very much like to have the chance to converse with you again.'

I attempted to conceal my surprise. 'Why, yes. I shall be very pleased to renew acquaintance with you.'

'Thank you. But look . . . There, I'll wager, is your sister.'

I followed his pointing finger. While the rest of the welcoming group waited on shore behind a restraining rope, a solitary figure had broached the barrier and, bonnet flying, was racing along the jetty towards our vessel.

Lucy flung herself upon me, half-exclaiming, half-weeping. In her exuberance and eagerness to embrace me, she seemed not one jot altered from her former self.

'Fanny! My dearest, dearest Fanny. Oh, you can't imagine how much I've longed for your arrival. I told myself a thousand times a day that you'd change your mind and return Home with Mama, that you wouldn't be able to bear the thought of that frightful sea crossing, that—'

'Oh, Lucy, what a goose you are! Here I am, as you see, so all your fears were groundless.'

She wound her arm through mine. 'Imagine, after so long, you look just the same as ever. But your lovely hair is all out of sight under your bonnet. Take it off and shake out your ringlets for me, Fanny, then I'll know for certain it's you.'

'Not here, Lucy! We're in a public place. And hush a little. People are beginning to stare at us.'

It was true. Lucy, I could see, had been recognised by most of the citizens gathered there, and she and I had become the focus of much unwanted interest. Unwanted, that is, by me but not, I saw, by Lucy, who nodded and smiled in various directions in what I felt to be an unnecessarily queenly manner.

'This is such a small society,' she whispered. 'Stultifying in the extreme. I do hope you won't be too bored here, Fanny. It really is the dullest place on earth. You must promise me you won't take the next boat out.'

'Well, Albany is scarcely the liveliest of societies.' I looked up at the hillsides. 'Which one is Government House?'

'Ah, the House,' she said. 'I must warn you, it's so very uncomfortable and bleak. It cost upwards of ten thousand pounds, so one might expect it to be an imposing residence, with pillars or perhaps even a portico, but it's the most draughty dwelling you can possibly conceive of.'

'Better than being aboard ship. We were tossed about so much on the crossing it will be a pleasure just to ride in a trap again.'

'Oh, Fanny,' said Lucy, 'I'm afraid I have only the cart, for which I apologise profusely, but the noble Governor must needs take the horse and trap on his visit to the Maori chiefs on the North Shore of Auckland. We have no carriage, you know. My husband considers it a wicked extravagance. Only Colonel Wynyard has a carriage here. Can you imagine it — one carriage in the whole of Auckland? And that's always being bogged in the dreadful mud. You can't believe how much it rains here.'

'I've no objection at all to a cart. It's a great deal more agreeable than walking with one's baggage. But I'm sorry not to be meeting your husband when we arrive. Will he be away for long?'

'I have no notion. Possibly he'll return within the week . . . often, you know, he goes about the country for days on end and I'm generally the last to know his whereabouts.'

'Surely he doesn't traverse the country in a trap?'

'No, but even on his visits to nearby chiefs, he's frequently away for several days. Everything to do with the Maoris takes up a great deal of time. Their speeches are interminable. My husband has learnt to speak their language passably well, but he refuses to allow one of the natives to instruct me.'

As we made our way to the cart, I observed that though Lucy still had her beautiful black curls and milky skin, she had developed lines of discontent about her mouth.

She pulled me closer to her. 'Come, Fanny dearest, I'll call Ingrams to take your trunks and then we'll be off. I still can't believe that at last you're here. I keep thinking I'm in a dream and when I wake you'll be gone.'

While Lucy went to summon the servant, I gazed around me. The sea in the harbour sparkled blue and lapped the sand in low placid waves. On the ridge of the hill above stood a long fortified wall of solid masonry, punctuated by rectangular apertures I recognised as gun loops. Ahead lay the road I had observed from the ship, cut into the side of a steep hill and lined on either side with wooden buildings that appeared to be shops or stores. On the shore, dogs sniffed unchecked at boxes and packages, and a number of bullock drays were drawn up, presumably for hire. Ours was not the only vessel in the harbour. I counted twenty-three of varying sizes and shapes before Lucy returned with a lean, weather-beaten young man pushing a hand-cart.

'We'll take your reticule, of course,' she said, 'and your hatbox, too, I think. And perhaps your writing case. Ingrams will remove the trunks and the other boxes to the bullock dray.'

We climbed into the cart, Lucy taking the reins and geeing-up the tiny pony. 'You see that long sloping street?' She indicated with her whip the road I had just noted. 'That's Queen Street, named for her Gracious Majesty, and it's quite the most distinguished and elegant arcade in the entire town. It's hard to believe, I know. It's been built beside a little stream which floods whenever it rains so that the street regularly becomes a swamp of sewage. And the settlers here are, in the main, from such a very vulgar caste of people that, if you're obliged to visit the lower end of Queen Street, you must on no account stand anywhere near the gutters or the sides.'

'Why not?'

'Because when a "lady" at the top of the street feels the call of Nature, she responds to it by simply placing herself over the gutter and relieving herself there. For this reason, in Queen Street, the gentlemen always stand above the ladies so that they can pretend they have observed nothing.'

'Lucy! You're making up such a story to tease me.'

'I assure you it's absolutely the case, as you'll notice for yourself before too long.'

We set off. 'Ah, Fanny,' she said, beaming at me, 'you can't imagine how happy I am to have you with me at last. It's just like the old days when we were children. The two of us against the world!'

LYME REGIS, 1832

At Back Beach, the Spittles towering behind me, I watched the waves dwindle to a grey scum and sink through the sandy pores of the shore. I imagined myself a shell, a scuttling crab, shaped entirely by the sea, and shivered as I thought how the ocean's wistful sighing echoed Mama's as she sat looking down from her window at Lyme Bay.

Beside our house stood a great mulberry tree, monarch of the garden. Every spring it burst into pink blossom, and in late summer bore such an abundance of black fruits that our manservant, Joseph, was obliged to fashion supports for its branches. Sprouting from its gnarled trunk, these branches rose skywards, then flung themselves down again to form a canopy of leaves dense enough to provide a hiding place. Slipping within, my child self watched, unobserved, the doings of the house. Cocooned like a silkworm, I executed there the magic rituals I concocted to ward off the Evil Eye, the attentions of witches — and the fever. In saucers pilfered from the pantry, I stirred my potions with twigs torn from my sanctuary. Onto a mixture of assorted berries and flower-heads arranged on earth brought in my handkerchief from the churchyard, I squeezed milky ragwort juice, then added ingredients the more powerful since all but one had been stolen — a pinch of salt, another of sugar, a dab of best butter and a smear of honey, a little ash from the grate, a few fish scales, several hairs from Mama's brush and, most potent of all, several drops of my own blood. For this, I had been forced to puncture my skin with a needle lifted secretly from Martha's work-basket. Some of the resulting paste I spread on a knot in the tree's trunk, the handle to a hidden door that needed only the invocation of magic to one day reveal itself. The rest I deposited in tiny daubs and dollops about the house, taking particular care to place them where Mama might pass. I shadowed her with a wordless devotion, half-guarding her, half-protecting myself.

As she gazed out at Lyme Bay, I knew it was not the sea she saw but William, lying in the churchyard of St Michael the Archangel. She and I went often to his small grave, where I liked to trace with my finger the inscription on his tombstone:

William Ernest Thompson.
Beloved Son of Ernest and Charlotte Thompson
of this Parish.
Born ye 3rd March 1830.
Called Home Nov 16th 1831.

When we buried William, Papa was far away on his ship. The snowdrops and crocuses came and went, and primroses sprang from the ground in their place. The parson's sheep, grazing among the tombstones, nibbled at the fresh green grass, and I stood beside Mama, staring at the hard grey stone, while the rain fell softly on William. It was almost a year now since we had sponged and cooled him, trying to calm the terrifying convulsions of his body as he screamed and writhed, his eyes fixed on some invisible apparition. And then the crisis of heat and horror passed, and he lay limp in Mama's arms, the fever — and the life — gone from him. Sorrow curled itself around our house, filling every corner, tainting our food and drink, infecting the air we breathed, turning Mama into an ethereal stranger.

Whenever I tried to conjure Papa, only the faceless figure of a black-clad man came to me. Yet of William I had a clear recollection, his sweet baby scent, his fat infant hands clutching at my hair, his laughter as I chased him across the garden. When I thought of this, I ached for him to come back to us and for things to be as before.

Mama sat again at her window, her forehead against the glass. I saw she had been weeping, and attempted to console her.

'Oh, Mama,' I ventured. 'I should so much like to see William again.'

She started. Her face clouded and I feared I had made matters worse, not better. 'How long have you been standing there, child?' she said. 'Come and sit beside me.'

I averted my eyes from her mourning ring, fashioned from one of William's ringlets. Dry and lifeless, it resembled nothing more than horsehair, a mockery of his soft blond curls.

'I must be grateful,' she said, 'that at least the Lord has spared me my daughter.'

I sought for some way to turn her thoughts from William. 'Tell me about when we came to Lyme, Mama,' I said.

'Ah, we were living in Portsmouth. Such a terrible place. Every day, the dregs of human jetsam were flung from the ships to scrabble on the shore.' She brightened a little. 'But when you were just a ten-month infant, Papa's ship captured a Spanish vessel, and we were able to remove to this house in Lyme.'

Such accustomed talk, anchored in our old life, began to allay my feelings of unease. 'Shall I open the window, Mama?'

'Yes. Tell me what you can see on the Cobb.'

I flicked the window latch, breathing in the smell of the ocean, its salty tang thick with seaweed and gulls' cries. 'Another ship is leaving.'

Mama sighed. 'All these comings and goings put me in mind of Papa. Here we sit, safe and secure, while he serves His Majesty on the High Seas.'

In my head I conjured the High Seas, far beyond Lyme Bay, their great waves heaving and tossing the vessels of the King's Navy skywards like carts ascending a mountainside, up and up to the summit. Of what lay at the summit of the High Seas I had no idea, but I saw Papa's stately vessel, swaying a little above the water in the manner of a carriage on a rutted road. Tall at the prow, Papa stood gazing out for sight of a Spanish or Frenchie flag, the waves respectfully parting for his ship and the English fleet behind him.

'Tonight, in your prayers, you must ask God to bless your dearest Papa and bring him safely home to us.'

'Yes, Mama. I pray so every night.'

'And what is it that you ask of our Heavenly Father, Fanny?'

'Please, God,' I repeated, in the words Mama had earlier provided for me, 'make me a good and worthy child, bless my dearest mama, and guard the soul of my brother until we meet again in Heaven, may it please God.' I hesitated a moment. 'Watch over my beloved papa, Heavenly Father, speed his ship across the waves, spare him from the grapeshot, the cannon, the blood of battle, and the devils of France and Spain. And, if it is Thy will, bring him safely back home to us. Amen.'

I saw my prayers unroll like magic threads, ensnaring Papa and reeling him back to Lyme. With each prayer, I tried to recall his face, some lost scent of him, the sound of his voice but, in truth, I could remember nothing whatsoever to bring him to mind.

Mama put her arms around me. 'Ah, my good girl,' she said, and kissed me. 'I see you hold the image of your beloved papa close to your heart.'

AUCKLAND, 1845

Lucy and I spent my first few days in Auckland sitting together, recollecting old times. I had brought letters for her from Aunt and our brothers, and an embroidered cushion cover made by Gussie. We laughed and cried, endlessly recalled memories of our childhood, and delighted in being together again. I considered whether I should mention either Uncle or her lost infant son but decided, for the moment, it would be unwise. Though in many respects she was her old self, there was an edge to her, an agitation that I had never before observed and which troubled me. And whereas when I had last seen her in Albany she had been unable to keep herself from praising Captain Grey's accomplishments in almost every conversation, now she seemed reluctant even to mention his name.

'Have you heard yet from the Governor?' I asked as casually as I could when we were sitting together in the drawing room after dinner one evening.

'Not a word. Though that is scarcely unusual.' She put her arm around me. 'Oh, but there *is* some news I must tell you. I almost forgot. The Colonial Office has appointed a Lieutenant-Governor for the southern part of New Zealand.'

'Surely your husband . . .?'

She ignored me. 'Well, you will never guess who's been appointed. Mr Eyre!'

'The same Mr Eyre . . .'

'. . . who visited us years ago in Albany and tried to make love to Gussie. Yes, he's in Wellington now. He arrived only a few weeks ago—' She broke off at sounds from outside. 'Why, this must be my husband, home at last.' Biting at her bottom lip, she patted her hair and stood up, arranging her skirts.

Much as I remembered him, Governor Grey strode into the drawing room, bowed to us both and held out a hand to me. 'Miss Fanny, welcome. What a great pleasure to see you again after so long.'

Lucy took her husband's arm. 'Fanny and I have been reminiscing. Do you recall how—'

He shook off her hand. 'I'm too tired to wish to evoke old times, Eliza. I shall bid you both an immediate goodnight.'

'But, George, you haven't yet eaten.'

'I assure you, I have no appetite. There's great unrest again in the south of the island and I must return there very soon. I have weightier things on my mind than the pleasures of the table.'

I woke to the sound of a quarrel. As Lucy had said, the walls of Government House were no better than paper so I was able to distinguish, more clearly than I wished, every word of what passed between them.

'You do nothing to elevate my position, Eliza. A wife should be a helpmeet to her husband, but you're so young and silly — even the chiefs call you a mere child.'

I heard the remembered note of defiance in Lucy's voice. 'I see you place the opinions of cannibal savages above those of your wife.'

'It is not a wife's duty to have opinions.'

'But I would so much like to come with you. I could show Fanny something of the countryside. We could search out plant and flower species for my collection.'

'I am engaged in attempting to subdue Te Rau-paraha and Te Rangi-hae-ata, and I must urgently speak with Octavius Hadfield in Wellington. I'm far too busy with official duties to allow you time to dally along the way for bushes and branches.'

'But we shouldn't delay you, I promise, and Fanny could see in what esteem the chiefs hold you. After all, many of the chiefs take their senior wives on visits with them. We've entertained them here at Government House.'

'Really, Eliza, with every word you utter you display your ignorance of the workings of the world. Do you not realise we're at war? Men are falling every day in the service of Queen and Country, the tribes are engaged constantly in internecine strife, and yet you feel your own selfish needs must be considered above all of these.'

'But when you're away from me, I'm so uneasy until your return. And if I were to ride with you sometimes, we could share the burden of your duties.'

'Nonsense. You have Miss Fanny with you now and it's the lot of women to tend the home fires. I don't hear Mrs Selwyn complaining when the Bishop must be abroad.'

'Sarah Selwyn travels often with her husband.' She paused. 'And . . . and she has her children to occupy her while I—'

The Governor's tone was curt. 'My dear Aunt Julia has no children but she has devoted herself to good works and literary matters. You should follow her example.'

How sad, I thought, that in a mere six years their relations with each other have dwindled to this.

'I find it strange to hear the Governor calling you Eliza.'

'Only my husband and those people who have known us since we left England do so. Even George's family didn't address me that way at first. I dislike Eliza intensely.'

'But then why does he . . .?'

'About a year after we arrived in England, while we were staying at his stepfather's house at Bodiam, an express messenger arrived from Lord John Russell offering my husband the governorship of South Australia. He went straight up to London, resigned his commission and accepted. And when he returned, he told me he considered Lucy too frivolous a name for a colonial administrator's wife.'

I spoke before I could stop myself. 'How ridiculous. Why did you not say so?'

'I was dismayed, I confess, but I felt . . . I believed that if it was his wish, I should agree. But, even now, I sometimes find myself turning about to see whom he is addressing.'

Lucy and I sat together before the fire, listening to the howling of the wind.

'I detest the way the slightest noise resounds through this dreadful wooden building,' she said. 'When we first landed, I hadn't a single friend or acquaintance here. After six days we settled into this gloomy house and a day later, merely one week after our arrival, the Governor left me to ride north to the Bay of Islands and I had no idea when he might return. I lay in bed, feverish, with perfect strangers round me, listening to the horrible haunting sighings and creakings. I can't tell you how much I longed to be back with you all in Albany.'

'That was not a very happy beginning,' I said cautiously. 'And it has never been like you to be ill.'

'It started when we were in Adelaide. I seem to have become a very nervous person.'

I considered speaking of her infant but held back.

'But, you know,' she went on, 'I'm getting quite callous about my husband's leaving me. And now I have you, Fanny dearest, I'm sure to be my old self again very soon.'

'But I don't understand,' I ventured again. 'In Albany you were the healthiest of all of us. You never suffered a day's illness. Do you remember how you and Uncle used to walk up the slopes of Mount Clarence and leave the rest of us far behind?'

To my consternation, tears began to form in her eyes. 'Ah, those were such happy days,' she said. 'I used to think that once I was married I should be just like Mama . . . I believe she was in love with dearest Papa until the day he died.'

LYME REGIS, 1832

My bedroom, opposite Mama's, looked out to the garden, not the sweep of Lyme Bay. Martha occupied a room on the top floor with Mama's maid, Agnes. Joseph slept in the cellar and Ellen had a window-bed behind the shutters in the kitchen. Since William had died, it had become my habit when I could not sleep to steal out of bed and sit on the floor outside Mama's door, leaning against the jamb. On the nights I heard her weeping, I remained on guard at her door until I fell asleep and woke, from discomfort or cold, in time to creep back into my bed before Ellen should come to rouse and dress me.

It was Ellen's task to accompany me to and from the school gates, carrying my lunch pail. Mr England's Academy being the only such establishment in Lyme, and the parish requiring that we be educated, there was a mix of children to match the population of the town, some of us sent in tidy pinafores and buckled shoes, others ragged and barefoot, even in winter. The schoolroom, too, had its own ranks and hierarchies; already I knew very well that some of the others came from what Mama called 'those squalid tenements'.

'Ye've to come along wi' I now,' said Ellen as she collected me from school one bitter afternoon in February. Taking my hand, she sped down Church Road, forcing me to scurry to keep up with her. 'Come on, Miss Fanny. Us must hurry.' She jerked at my hand as we headed down the hill towards the butter market at Monmouth Street, then, suddenly, she turned off towards the George.

'Are we going to the Inn?'

'Nay. Us has other things to do.'

I was disappointed. Occasionally, Martha and I walked to the stables behind the George to watch the farriers replacing worn shoes on the travellers' horses and the stable-boys tossing hay. As we hurried past, the heavy stench of rotten manure wafted out.

Ellen wrinkled her nose. 'I niver could marry wi' a stable boy. Allus stinking of muck and filth.'

'But where are we bound, Ellen?'

'Curiosity killed they cat.'

We crossed the top end of Coombe Street, its tall buildings crowding the mean, narrow alleyways. These must be the tenements. I pressed even closer to Ellen, sniffing the warm thick air about us.

'What's that strange smell?'

'Be aye they Maltings. Be there them brews they beer.'

We slipped into a lane and skirted the side of the mill where a channel of water ran beside us. Opposite, three or four cottages abutted the path, and in one of them a woman was sweeping the yard with a besom.

'Take care,' said Ellen. 'Look away now. That one be a witch. Lyme be full of witches. Does ye know how to keep they away?'

'No,' I mumbled, my eyes averted from the witch.

'Ye takes a morsel of bacon and fixes it inside of they chimney, just away from they fire. Witches canna niver abide the smell of bacon.'

At the thought of witches descending inside our chimney, I shuddered. 'I think we should go home now.'

'Her be going indoors and us be nearly there.'

'Nearly where?'

'Why, Jericho.'

'But Jericho is in the Bible.'

'Nay this one. 'Tis by they Old Mill where they Lym make a deep pool. 'Tis where they Baptists dunks they fallen women.'

'Fallen women?'

'Aye, they women of no fortune and wild ways down by they harbour. They Baptists brings them to they lodging-house at Jericho. For shelter and food, they women agree them be baptised.'

'But aren't they baptised already?'

'Them has turned to sin. So they Baptists says them must be reborn.'

'To be reborn is not so bad,' I said, thinking of William.

'Nay, be very bad. They Baptists does push them, one then other, deep into they mill-pool there.'

'But if they can't swim . . .?'

'Aye, well, two of they Baptists stands by they bank a-holding of boathooks to fish they women out.'

We had reached the Old Mill, and I looked down warily into the deep, dark pool beside it.

'Now,' said Ellen, 'sit ye down on they bank. I sees a friend sudden over there.'

From a doorway of one of the tall crammed houses nearby a young man had emerged. He came sauntering towards us.

'Is he one of the Baptists?'

'Oh, aye. A real preacher, he.'

I studied the young man for evidence of a boathook and was relieved to see he carried nothing at all in either hand.

'Ye stay here while I do speak wi' he.'

I peered at the pool, surreptitiously watching Ellen and the Baptist from the sides of my eyes. He placed an arm about her waist and she did not recoil but seemed to like it, for she leaned her head briefly against his shoulder. Then I saw him raise a hand and stroke her hair. She tossed her head, and I heard her laugh and begin to talk to him in tones so low I could not catch what she said. To relieve my boredom, I took up some small stones and began casting them into the pool. Then it occurred to me to lie on my front and launch a leaf onto the water. I had just sent my craft on its way and was intently charting its progress when I was seized by Ellen and hauled to my feet.

'What be ye at, Miss Fanny? Look at ye pinafore, all earth and filth. What be I to say to Martha?' She made an attempt to brush me down. 'Now, Missy, if ye be they good girl and says ye fell in they churchyard . . .'

'But I . . .'

Ellen winked at me. 'Ye be there to see ye brother's marker. Ye trips and falls. Ye pinafore be dirtied. If ye be minded and says so, on us way home I be minded to show ye they Cat Woman. But ye must say niver a word of it to a living soul.'

I nodded. Now that I was standing again, I saw that we were being observed by people gathered at the tenement doorways and in small knots and clusters in the alleys.

'There are some people looking at us.'

'Oh, aye.' And she waved and nodded to them. 'Be nowt to fear.'

I was surprised Ellen should know such rough and ragged folk, but said nothing as she picked up her basket and we set off.

'The Baptist is watching us.'

'Aye, well . . .' said Ellen, and flashed a smile in his direction.

Hurrying back past the mill, we again entered the upper reach of Coombe Street and its close-packed houses. The lower end, with its lacemakers' shops, was familiar to me, but this seemed entirely different, almost sinister, and I looked about nervously. I gripped Ellen's hand as we turned in at a narrow passageway leading to a small poor square which, unlike the main streets nearby, was deserted.

'So,' she said, stopping and laying down the basket, 'ye wants to see they Cat Woman?'

I thought of my friend Harriet's kitten, its soft paws kneading at our hands as we played with it. 'Does she have many cats? And kittens?'

Ellen did not reply. Instead she said, 'Ye be sure to tell Martha ye fell?'

I nodded.

'Ye be they good girl. Stand ye there by they doorway. And nay a word from ye.' She lowered her voice. 'Look. See ye there?'

She pointed to a low arch opposite where I made out the crouching figure of an old woman. As I stared at her, she lifted her head, sniffed the air like a dog, then uttered a loud yowl, followed by a distinct meow.

'She is calling her cat,' I whispered. 'It must be lost.'

Ellen shook her head.

The woman shuffled forward into the little courtyard. She was a bulky old dame, her clothes torn and tattered, her feet falling out of broken, scuffed slippers which flapped as she walked.

'Watch ye,' warned Ellen.

Motioning me to stay where I was, she left our hiding place and crept up behind the old woman. 'Good day to thee, Mither,' she bellowed suddenly.

The old woman swung around. I expected her to aim a blow at Ellen but, instead, she stared blankly at her and meowed.

'Aye, be misty today,' said Ellen, as if the dame had answered her.

'Meow.'

'Think thee it will mebbee rain?'

'Meow, meow, meow.'

As she crossed the yard, she arched her back, hissed at Ellen and meowed again. It was clear that she could not or did not speak. Then, from a doorway, a little girl appeared. Catching the dame's hand, she pulled her inside, still meowing furiously.

'Ye sees why them calls her they Cat Woman.'

'But why is she like that?'

'Folks round these parts says it begun on they day them hanged her son.'

AUCKLAND, 1846

The Governor having returned from business in the North the evening before, we had retired to bed later than usual. Early in the morning, I awoke with a start to the sound of continuous low moaning, followed by a series of wails. Somewhere in the house, women were sobbing, and I thought I distinguished Lucy's voice. I dressed quickly and ran to her room. It was empty. Following the sound, I made my way to the drawing room and peered around the half-open door.

Surrounded by a group of Maoris, all of whom were weeping, Lucy and the Governor stood in silent misery as the natives with increasing tremors of their heads and hands began to lament and cry ever more loudly until they were all howling in the most desolate manner imaginable, tears pouring down their tattooed faces. Even Lucy and her husband had tears in their eyes.

I stood transfixed, imagining what disaster must have brought them to this state. My heart began to pound. Had they news that we were about to be attacked — perhaps eaten alive?

Then, to my amazement, they all suddenly dried their tears and, smiling, pressed noses, in turn, with the Governor and Lucy who also shed their expressions of misery and returned the joyful greetings of their visitors.

'Ah, Fanny,' said Lucy, catching sight of me, 'come and be introduced to the Arawa chiefs. They've come all the way from Rotorua. It's been such a long time since we've seen them.'

'But why was everyone weeping so piteously? I thought that some terrible slaughter must have occurred . . .'

Lucy shook her head. 'No, no. That is the Maori custom. Whenever a native has been away for a long period, on his return, all his tribe gathers round him and laments just as you saw. It's to show the depth of their suffering at being deprived of his company. Then, when that formality is over, they're free to express their feelings of joy at having him back among them again.'

'But you and the Governor are not from the Arawa tribe. Nor any other . . .'

'It's a mark of respect to my husband. And because I'm his wife, they include me in such ceremonial government occasions.' She lowered her voice, 'So you see why he requires a wife. To help him carry out his official duties.'

'Ah, Miss Fanny,' said the Governor, stepping out onto the veranda where I was reading. 'I'm pleased to see you're making use of my library.'

'I'm grateful to have access to such an extensive collection of books.'

'I wonder if I might have a word with you in confidence?'

'Certainly.' I rose and accompanied him into his study.

He motioned me to be seated.

'I hope I am not speaking out of turn but . . . you may have noticed that my wife . . . your sister . . . doesn't enjoy the best of health here. Since our arrival, she has had a number of *crises des nerfs*. I wonder if you might encourage her to ride more. Her physician is convinced that fresh air is stimulating to her constitution.'

'I will be happy to do everything possible to persuade her.' I paused and looked about me at the shelves of books. 'She has told me that you speak the Maori language fluently.'

'Yes, and I have often urged her to take up studying it, but she lacks the interest . . .'

This is strange, I thought, when Lucy herself has told me quite the opposite.

'She has always had a facility for languages,' I said. 'I might try to convince her to begin.'

'You're most thoughtful, but I fear Eliza's nerves won't permit close study. It is outdoor exercise that she requires.'

I made to leave.

'Thank you, Miss Fanny,' he said. He picked up a paper from his desk. 'But before you go back to your book, I have something here that I think may be of interest to you. It's a most original letter from Broughton, one of the Northern chiefs.'

'He has a very English-sounding name.'

'That's his adopted Pakeha name. The Maoris frequently take the names of Europeans they hold in high esteem; many girls have been named Wikitoria after Her Majesty. And the chief at Waikanae, Te Rangitake, has taken the name of William King, which he has translated into Maori as Wiremu Kingi, the name by which he is now always known.'

'I see.'

'I believe you will be touched by Broughton Tutukaka's letter.'

I sat down again.

'As the chief speaks no English,' said the Governor, 'it's written in Maori and he's asked me to translate it for him before I send it to the Queen. Let me read it to you first in its original language.' He cleared his throat, then began to read, and though I did not understand a word of what he uttered, the sound was rolling and very pleasing.

I said as much.

'You're right,' he said. 'Oratory is the skill the Maoris value most highly and their language has a sonorous beauty. The chiefs all speak fluently and, the better to make their points, they often employ metaphors and humour. Their speeches are extremely lengthy, but, no matter how long he speaks, no one is ever interrupted and no offensive language or insults are permitted among them. I've often thought that the Maoris in their assemblies could teach many lessons in courtesy to our colonial parliamentarians.' He turned back to the letter. 'And now for the translation.

'*Your Majesty the Queen.*

Farewell in your country in London. This is the message for you. Show love to the Maoris of New Zealand. This is the word — "Charity is the greatest of these three". May God bless us & keep us for ever & ever. God's love lasts for ever; man cannot erase it. These are all my words to you. And it is signed, *Broughton Te Manu Tutukaka.*'

'It's a very heartfelt message,' I said, 'but why is he writing to the Queen?'

'He considers her a chief equal in rank to himself and it's the Maori custom for great chiefs to exchange greetings. He's honouring Her Majesty.'

'And will you send it to the Queen?'

'I must. I have promised to do so.'

LYME REGIS, 1832

Wishing more than anything for Mama to return to her old ways and for us to be happy again, I concocted spells for Papa's safe return. One morning, as I sat in my cave of blossom whispering an incantation to bring him home, I heard Ellen calling me.

'Ye're to go a-visiting with ye mither,' she said as I slipped from the tree to the kitchen. 'Ye're to wear ye Sunday best.'

My heart leapt. This was the first times in many, many months that Mama had paid a call. 'But where are we going?'

'Thinks ye *I* ha' the knowing of it?'

'We are going to Cobb House,' said Mama, coming into the kitchen, 'to see Captain Spencer and his lady. He's an old naval acquaintance of your papa and they have nine children, so you will have no shortage of playfellows.'

Nine children! I tried to imagine such a quantity in one family, and failed. But to be going out again with Mama . . .

'Hold ye still, Miss,' said Ellen. 'How be I to dress ye ringlets?'

Lyme was all steeps and slopes, its streets and lanes slanting past the church on one side, the Customs House and the George Inn on the other, everything angled down towards the Cobb and the sea. A marble dropped in Upper Lyme would wend its way, faster and faster, down through the town, and across Marine Parade till it bounced over the rocks and splashed into the waiting water. Sometimes, I rolled the tiny rounded pebbles from the cliffs and watched as they sped off back to the shingle shore.

Our house stood high above the church of St Michael and All Angels and overlooked the remains of the Cobb, Lyme's great encircling harbour wall. I skipped beside Mama as we set off down

Church Road, past the Guildhall with its little tower, towards the Drill Hall and the gun-cliffs, and the butter market and the fish market, both closed on a Sunday. I hoped that Mama might stop at the confectioner's shop with its dazzling jars of butterscotch, stripy bull's-eyes, acid drops and raspberry balls, sticks of rock and, best of all, the rows of sugar mice sitting under their great glass dome, but she turned towards the Assembly Rooms and down onto the Cobb. I held Mama's hand as we promenaded along Marine Parade amongst Lyme's throng of fashionable citizens and visitors, stopping to look at the bathing machines and the street hawkers, the Punch and Judy stall, and the dozen other attractions that crowded the upper and lower reaches.

'Now, Fanny,' she said, 'when you meet Captain Spencer you must promise me you will on no account stare at his forehead.'

'His forehead?'

'Yes. The poor Captain suffered a horrid accident aboard ship. His forehead was hit by the ricochet of a cannon and he was terribly injured. Papa says it's quite miraculous he escaped with his life. His poor powder monkey was blown to . . . Ah, here we are. We've arrived.'

Set above three steps, on a little rise facing eastwards towards Charmouth, Cobb House looked directly out to Lyme Bay and the sweep of the ruined sea wall. To one side was a conservatory and beyond that a field in which grazed a number of sheep. We were admitted by a maid into a small elegant room where Mrs Spencer rose to greet us, surrounded by what seemed to me a very considerable number of boys. Unused to a brood of children, I shrank a little as I followed Mama, but she pushed me forward.

'This is Fanny,' she said.

'What a pretty little thing you are, Fanny,' said Mrs Spencer. 'Such beautiful fair hair.'

As I dropped my curtsey, two girls with black curls burst into the room.

'Now, my dear, here are Augusta and Lucy. This is Fanny, girls.' Mrs Spencer patted my head. 'They will take you to see the lamb they're rearing.'

I followed reluctantly. The older girl, Augusta, walked sedately ahead along the corridor while Lucy danced beside me, staring quizzically at my dress and every aspect of my person. We passed outside into an orchard where a lamb came bleating towards us, nuzzling and worrying at the girls' skirts.

'Stop it, Blanche,' said Lucy.

'Will she bite?'

'Of course not. She has no teeth yet.'

'Put your finger in her mouth,' said Augusta, 'and feel how she sucks on it.'

Tentatively, I held out a finger which Blanche seized between her hard little gums. With my free hand, I patted her woolly head and smelt her reassuring mix of wool and heat. 'I wish I had such a pretty lamb.'

'If you have a field for it, I'm sure Papa would give you one.'

'We have only a garden,' I said.

'Then she would eat all your flowers,' said Augusta, 'and I daresay your mama would be cross.'

I stood, tongue-tied.

'How old are you, Fanny?'

'Seven.'

'I'm just nine and Gussie is ten and a half.'

I mustered my meagre resources. 'I was born in 1824,' I said. 'On the twenty-third of November, the very night the Great Storm shattered the Cobb.' I did not add that my birth had not taken place in Lyme.

'Then you must be lucky,' said Lucy. 'I'm lucky, too, because I'm a seventh child. How many brothers and sisters do you have?'

Unwilling to speak of William, I shook my head. 'None.'

'Only one of you!' said Lucy. 'Why, that's no family at all. There are nine of us living and two in the churchyards in Portsmouth and Malta.'

'Where are all the others?

'Mary Ann is calling on a friend, and you saw the little boys in the drawing room,' said Augusta. 'Our eldest brothers, Hugh and Edward, are at the boatyard with Papa.'

'And when you meet Papa,' said Lucy, 'you must mark the great wound on his forehead. He was hit by a boatswain's oar in a jolly boat.'

'But I thought,' I said, unguardedly, 'he was injured by an exploding cannon.'

Augusta laughed. 'He loves to embroider the story to make it more daring, but it is certain it was an oar. We had it from Mama, didn't we, Liza-Lou?'

I felt a passing relief for the shattered powder monkey of Mama's story. Then, 'Why do you call her Liza-Lou?' I asked.

'Her real name is Eliza Lucy. But she's Papa's favourite and he has shortened it to Liza-Lou.'

'But why do you not like the name Eliza?'

'It sounds so harsh. Like an elderly great-aunt.'

For some time we stood in awkward silence.

'I daresay, if you're an only child,' said Lucy, 'you must be very spoilt and petted.'

'Lucy!'

I was stung. 'I'm not spoilt,' I said.

'Stop it at once, Lucy, or I shall tell Mama.'

'Well, you seem very timid. I suppose you're never disobedient.'

Augusta took my arm. 'Take no notice of her, Fanny. She's jealous because you're wearing such a pretty frock.'

I thought of my magic spells with their pilfered ingredients. 'I *am* disobedient. Sometimes.'

Lucy looked at me challengingly. 'Then come with me and scrump strawberries.'

'You know we're entirely forbidden to touch the strawberry beds, Lucy. If Papa finds out, you'll get a whipping.'

'Oh, pouf,' said Lucy. 'Of course he won't find out.'

'I'm not coming with you.'

'Well then, you can keep cave. Come on, Fanny.'

I was torn. By nature law-abiding, I admired boldness in others and Lucy seemed to me the epitome of daring. 'I . . .'

'You are *not* to take Fanny on a stealing expedition.'

'Nonsense, Gussie. Fanny is longing to come.' She turned to me. 'Aren't you?'

'I . . . I . . .'

'There. You see.' And, grabbing my hand, Lucy towed me to the far end of the orchard where several lines of green hummocks were studded with fat red berries.

'Quick. Pick some. These are the ripest.'

Feeling keenly the disgrace of being apprehended but even more afraid of Lucy's scorn, I crouched down, plucked a single strawberry and crammed it hastily into my mouth.

'Be sure not to spill any juice on your frock or we'll be discovered.'

I found my tongue. 'Perhaps . . . perhaps your sister will . . .'

'No, Gussie never tells tales. Hurry. Take just a few more before someone sees us.'

We wiped the traces of juice from our hands onto the grass, then made our guilty way past the conservatory and back towards Gussie, waiting at the end of the path.

'Now I see you're not a milksop,' said Lucy, 'shall we be best friends?'

I was flattered by this. I had friends at school but none as audacious as Lucy. 'Yes, I—'

'Then, to seal our friendship, we must make a solemn promise to be friends forever and, after that, we must cross our hearts and spit.'

'*Spit*? Here?'

'Yes, before we reach Gussie.' She stopped and drew herself up. 'Fanny,' she intoned, 'I give you my solemn promise to be your best friend forever. Now, you must say it.'

I was awed by the gravity of the occasion. 'I give you my solemn promise to be your best friend forever,' I whispered.

'And cross your heart, so, then, spit.'

She crossed her heart and, like a tobacco-chewing sailor, blew a line of spittle onto a row of poppies.

I looked round anxiously, summoned up saliva into my mouth and aimed it at Lucy's feet. Instead, it hit a low pane of the conservatory, where it trembled for a minute before sliding down the glass.

'Well, it will do,' said Lucy. 'And, after all, it's the crossing your heart that counts. Look, here's Gussie.'

'If Mama finds out you took Fanny stealing, Lucy, she'll be exceedingly vexed,' said Gussie. 'It's very wicked of you.'

'It's all right,' I said, eager to please my new best friend. 'This is not the first time I've stolen something.'

Lucy looked impressed. 'Have you been caught?'

'No.'

'I have. And whipped.'

This greatly elevated Lucy in my eyes, and I gazed at her admiringly, seeking for a way to further my own newly acquired status. 'Yes,' I said, 'I've stolen many times and' — I beckoned Lucy and Gussie closer — 'I have seen' — I lowered my voice — '*a real witch.*'

'What! Here in *Lyme*?' Lucy clutched my arm.

I nodded. 'Lyme is full of witches.'

Gussie's eyes were fixed on me. 'But where was she?'

'In Jericho.'

Lucy's reaction was entirely gratifying. 'You've been to *Jericho*, Fanny? But . . . it's by the tenements . . .'

'You surely didn't go alone?' said Gussie.

'No, I went with Ellen, our kitchen maid.'

'How brave you are. Weren't you afraid?'

I looked directly at Lucy and shook my head. 'No,' I said, 'because I had morsels of bacon in my pocket, and witches can never abide the smell of bacon.'

This account of my daring was abruptly cut short as a small boy ran up to us. 'You're to come at once, girls,' he said importantly. 'Papa wants to see you in his study.'

In seconds, my feelings of bravado evaporated and I saw that even Lucy looked uneasy. 'Do you think he saw us at the strawberry beds?' she muttered.

We shuffled indoors and crept nervously into a small, map-lined room filled almost entirely by a large desk.

'This is Fanny, Papa,' said Gussie.

Fixing my eyes on the floor, I dropped a curtsey.

'Well, now,' said the Captain, 'you are a pretty miss. And as fair as my good girls are dark. Let me see if you have your mama's blue eyes.' And, placing his hand under my chin, he turned my face up towards his. I sucked in my cheeks and resolved not to recoil. Half of his forehead was of ordinary skin, weathered like that of all sailors, but the other half seemed to be made of a livid shiny substance, resembling most an uncooked piece of meat. Below this, no eyebrow grew to match the other; in its stead, a promontory of twisted scarring jutted above what I saw, with relief, was a perfectly normal eye, matching its mate. Briefly, he locked his eyes with mine. Then he released me. 'Run along now, girls,' he said. 'Fanny's mama is waiting for her in the drawing room.'

The sun still shone as we walked home along the Cobb. The Punch and Judy show played on in its striped booth. As Mama and I stopped to watch, the crocodile's jaws suddenly emerged and Dog Toby, sitting in his ruff at the side of the stage, began barking to warn his master. We laughed with the rest of the crowd as Mr Punch beat the crocodile with his slapstick, and its long green mouth snapped closer and closer to him. Mama noticed the bottler making his way through the throng.

'We must go now,' she said. 'I have no small coins for him.'

And just as she spoke, the crocodile seized Mr Punch, pulling him off the stage, and poor Dog Toby's mournful howls followed us all along the Cobb.

AUCKLAND, 1846

Most mornings, just before dawn, I was awoken by an outpouring of birdsong. Accustomed to the harsh, shriller cries of the native birds in Albany, I found this melodious chorus entirely delightful. It began with the dulcet single note of a bell, then was joined by more and more chiming calls. As I lay listening, these ceased and gave way to a medley of other birdsong. On several occasions I had tiptoed to the window to try to observe the originators but had seen only the inquisitive little fantails darting through the trees, swinging upside-down to pick insects from the trunks. I was accustomed to their friendly presence in the garden and their noisy *cheet, cheet, cheet* as they shadowed us in the branches above our heads.

The gardens immediately around Government House had been planted with English roses which flowered abundantly, their scent drifting agreeably about us as we sat every fine morning on the veranda. Further away were stands of native flax and a number of tall cabbage trees, some with trunks more than twenty feet tall, and all with long, narrow leaves up to three feet long sprouting from their tops. Beyond the cultivated area of the garden lay an expanse of 'bush', the evergreen trees and plants that made up the greater part of New Zealand's vegetation. Even such a small area as that at Government House was dense and dark and seemingly impenetrable. Below the canopy of the trees, mosses underlay the large spreading ferns, and creeping vines twisted through and round, the whole giving the impression of an abundance of all shades of green, with here and there the flash of a white flower.

'But,' said Lucy, observing me as I tried to sketch my surroundings, 'it's almost impossible to capture how sinister it looks, especially after rain. There are all manner of rats and lizards and spiders hiding in there. So don't on any account decide to explore it, will you?'

'What I'd really like to see are the birds that sing so beautifully in the mornings.'

'Those are bellbirds and tuis. There are some here, but to see them properly we should visit the Domain. We can go on an outing there this afternoon. It affords a most beautiful view of Auckland and the harbour.'

We set out in the cart, the sky bright blue above us, the wind soft and mild. All traces of the previous day's torrential rain had entirely vanished. The rough track led up the side of a long hill to a high point above the town. After about twenty minutes, Lucy stopped the cart and we stepped out. 'I hope you've brought your sketch book,' she said. 'We can look for native birds and you'll find all sorts of new and different plants here as well. I often— Why, whatever's the matter?'

Without thinking, I had clutched violently at her arm.

'What is it? What's happened?' she asked.

A short distance away from us stood two men. At first glance, in their frockcoats, they appeared to be nothing other than ordinary gentlemen strolling together on the track. But at the sound of Lucy's voice, the taller one had turned towards us, revealing a hideous purple countenance disfigured by deeply carved lines, and displaying below the jacket a short skirt, apparently composed of strips of linen and reaching only to his naked knees and tattooed lower legs. He was unshod, his large splayed feet resting bare on the ground. As he looked at us, my hands flew to cover my face.

'No!' I cried out. I felt myself sway, grow faint and slip to the ground. I heard again my mother's ghostly voice in Rio. '*Take care, my darling girl, take care.*'

I came to myself on the chaise in the drawing room, Lucy dabbing at my forehead with a moistened handkerchief. 'You're safe home now,' she said, 'but you gave me such a fright.'

I struggled to recall where I was and what had happened. 'I don't remember . . .'

'Why, as we stood in the Domain, you suddenly cried out and caught at my arm, then you fell down in a swoon, and if it hadn't been for Te Toa and his friend who were standing nearby, I don't know what I should have done. They lifted you and settled you in the cart, then Te Toa accompanied us here on foot while his friend went for the physician.'

'The physician?'

'Yes, he's already been and examined you. He says you need rest and light nourishment.'

I was silent for a time, then I said, 'Who was that man? The one . . . so strangely attired?'

'Why, that was Te Toa. He's one of the chiefs of the Northern region, friendly towards the settlers and the government. He supports the Treaty.' She smiled at me. 'Now, I have a surprise for you. We're to hold a dinner. In your honour. And it's the Governor himself who suggested it; it's a mark of his esteem for you. In general, you know, he considers it an extravagance to entertain. There, what do you think of that?'

Still confused, I tried to rally myself and match her evident pleasure.

'We'll ask just those people whose society I'm sure you'll enjoy,' she continued. 'The Selwyns, Sir William and Lady Martin, Captain and Mrs Rough — he's the harbourmaster here, a tiny little man who always wears white kid gloves. And Colonel Wynyard and his wife, General Pitt and his eldest daughter, and' — she wagged an admonishing finger at me — 'Lieutenant Cowan . . . who's told my husband that you met on the boat. The Governor says he's most desirous of seeing you again.' She laughed. 'You're so secretive, Fanny. I hope he's handsome.'

For some time, absorbed in arrangements for the dinner in my honour, Lucy seemed much happier.

'I'm quite disappointed,' I said. 'You've often mentioned Mr Heke and even pledged me an audience with him but I've not yet met him. Surely he must be invited to this grand dinner?'

'I think not! And I'm not sure he'll do as a husband for you, Fanny.

I fear he would insist on tattooing your lips and, besides, I discovered he already has a wife.'

'Have you met her?'

'Yes. After the battle at Rua-peka-peka, when Heke and Kawiti were taken prisoner, my husband ordered they be treated well and properly fed, but Ingrams was indisposed and no other servant was available so I went myself to the barracks with food and other necessaries for them. And Heke's wife, Harata, the daughter of the chief, Hongi Hika, arrived there shortly afterwards and demanded an audience with my husband.'

'And were *her* lips tattooed?'

'Yes. And her chin. It's the mark of all Maori chieftainesses. But I shouldn't like you to have to fight her. She was beautiful but extremely belligerent.'

The day of the dinner was fine, with a cloudless blue sky.

'Such luck,' said Lucy. 'We can promenade on the veranda before dinner. Oh, I'm so delighted my husband proposed this celebration. We are only fourteen but just think what fun we'll have.'

By five o'clock, all was ready. The Governor, in his dress uniform, joined us on the veranda.

'You ladies look most elegant,' he said. 'And here comes our first guest, perfectly on time.'

Lieutenant Cowan strode towards us and bowed. 'Governor, Mrs Grey.' He bent over my hand. 'And Miss Thompson. What a great pleasure to meet you once more. How are you enjoying New Zealand?'

'Very much, but I've been so occupied with seeing my sister again I'm just becoming acquainted with Auckland. I hope to see more of the country later.'

'It's a singular place. Very wild and beautiful. Quite unlike anything at Home.'

I studied him as he spoke. Slightly over medium height, he presented a pleasing aspect, his eyes hazel and intelligent, his brown side-whiskers curling at either side of a rugged, genial face. Though his general comportment was that of a man used to commanding, he lacked the Governor's authoritarian manner.

'May I escort you into dinner?' he asked.

'Certainly.'

A tall dark-haired lady approached us, smiling at me warmly. 'I'm Sarah Selwyn,' she said. 'Eliza has spoken often of you, Miss Thompson. I'm so pleased to make your acquaintance. Now, you must meet my husband.'

Bishop Selwyn was an austere man, an impression reinforced by his clerical garb. He inclined his head towards me and said how much he was looking forward to seeing me in his congregation on the following Sunday. 'The Governor and his lady are stalwarts of our church,' he said, 'and when representatives of Her Majesty are seen at services, it becomes quite the thing for folk who wish to be fashionable. And they're most generous, too, in their support of our Mission work. They personally pay for the upkeep of a number of our Maori scholars, and the Governor has even been gracious enough to preach to the natives in their own tongue.'

I feared he might have gone on for longer, but I was rescued by Lucy. 'And here are General and Miss Pitt,' she cried, 'and Mr and Mrs Rough, and the Wynyards. There now, Fanny, all of fashionable Auckland society has assembled for you.'

Lieutenant Cowan appeared at my side again. 'You can see,' he said, 'that most of the guests are young. The majority of the settler population here is under the age of forty, which is why it's such a lively place. Even the rather sombre bishop is the youngest ever appointed. And that man there, engaged in conversation with the Governor, is Sir William Martin — only thirty-nine years old but already appointed Chief Justice. And here is his wife.' He bowed. 'Lady Martin.'

'I'm hoping,' said Lady Martin, 'that before too long you might call on me, Miss Thompson. I should like to show you my garden.'

'Ah, beware, Miss Thompson,' warned her husband, joining us with an expression of mock-seriousness. 'My wife is a regular Tartar when it comes to her garden. You won't escape our boundaries without an entire tour of her parade-ground. All the flowers and bushes will be drawn up for your inspection, the trees will be at attention and—'

'Stop it,' cried his wife, 'or you'll put her off entirely.'

There seemed such an agreeable accord between them, a shared good humour and amity, that I found myself eagerly accepting her invitation.

Lieutenant Cowan offered his arm to lead me into dinner. 'And I am hoping,' he said quietly, 'that before too long, you'll allow *me* to call on you again, Miss Thompson.'

Occupied with Lucy in decorating the drawing room and the dining room with boughs and branches for the evening's celebration, I had had no occasion to witness any of the preparations in the kitchen, so I was greatly surprised by the munificence of the dinner.

'Good gracious!' cried Lady Martin as we stood gazing at the spread before us. 'You've exceeded yourself, Mrs Grey.'

The long table, set with candles for whose bases Lucy and I had fashioned small floral garlands, now sported at one end a huge ham, surrounded by bowls of various Indian chutneys, a jar of gentleman's relish and a dish of English mustard, and at the other, a loin of veal beside which sat serving dishes of vegetables.

'Including the native kumara!' observed Mrs Selwyn.

'A particular favourite of mine,' said Mr Rough. 'And roast potatoes. What a feast indeed.'

Between the ham and the veal quivered the most astonishing quartet — a chaud-froid of fish and three different meat aspic jellies.

'Bravo!' called Lieutenant Cowan, and we all clapped in appreciation.

Lucy stood modestly but the flush in her cheeks betrayed her pleasure.

'And now,' said the Governor, pulling out a chair for her, 'come, my dear, let us be seated and attempt to do justice to such a magnificent repast.'

After dinner, the ladies withdrew to the drawing room while the gentlemen went to smoke on the veranda. We were chatting agreeably together when General Pitt appeared in the doorway.

'I've been sent as an emissary, ladies,' he said. 'We gentlemen request the pleasure of a little musical entertainment. It seems Lieutenant Cowan is a passable tenor and the Governor and I will cover the baritone parts, if you, Mrs Rough, can be prevailed upon to supply the piano accompaniment and you other ladies will offer soprano and contralto.'

'But the piano is so dreadfully out of tune,' said Lucy.

'All pianos in New Zealand are out of tune,' said the general. 'It's the weather. There is a fortune to be made here for an experienced accordeur. For now, we shall just have to tune our voices to the instrument we have.'

Pressed by Lucy, I agreed to sing a duet with Lieutenant Cowan of 'Home, Sweet Home'. Miss Pitt offered a ballad, 'Sleeping, I Dreamed of Love', then Mrs Wynyard, Lucy and I were persuaded to lead everyone in 'Auld Lang Syne'.

'And finally,' said Lieutenant Cowan, 'with your permission, Governor, I ask leave to dedicate this next piece to the ladies present.' And, having conferred in a whisper with Mrs Rough, he sang an affecting rendition of 'Believe Me If All Those Endearing Young Charms'.

'What an entirely splendid evening,' said Lucy when, finally, we waved goodnight to the last of the guests. 'I hope you enjoyed yourself, Fanny.'

'I don't recall ever having had a happier time.'

The Governor placed an arm around Lucy's waist and drew her slightly towards him. 'A great success, my dear. Indeed, I might even call it a triumph.'

LYME REGIS, 1833

In winter, as the mulberry's foliage fell, I was forced to crouch in the innermost recesses of my hiding place to try to conceal myself. The biting cold of February made the mixing of my potions almost impossible but I had devised several spoken spells which, to ensure their efficacy, had to be chanted in a whisper inside my magic cavern. One in particular I favoured:

Baby and I,
Were baked in a pie,
The pastry was terrible hot.
We had nothing to pay
To the baker that day,
And so we crept out of the pot.

Recited under my breath, within the tracery of frost-covered branches, it flew away in misty puffs, each one a shield against uncertainty and danger.

I was unleashing my charm after church one Sunday when Joseph passed, his arms laden with logs. From the kitchen doorway, Martha called to him. 'Stir thyself, now. Master comes home tomorrow.'

I craned as far forward as I dared, the icy ground stinging through my boots. I longed to go indoors to the warmth of the fire, but I could not risk revealing myself until I had heard more.

'Master? Home? Th'art sure?'

'Was Mistress told me.'

Joseph sighed. 'I canna white the front steps in such weather. 'Tis too cold.'

'Tha must. Master is particular, like all them naval men. Set thee to now or there be trouble tomorrow, 'tis certain. And lay the path here with cinders.'

Joseph disappeared, grumbling.

I slipped out of the tree and shuddered my way inside. The front steps to be whitened! Usually we entered the house through the side gate and the garden path that led to the kitchen and the back parlour. The front door, set above two steps that gave onto the cobbled footpath, was reserved for guests and special occasions.

Ellen took off my boots and I warmed my feet at the kitchen grate.

'Ye're to go up to ye mither directly,' she said, as she buttoned on my indoor shoes.

Mama sat before the drawing-room fire, holding a letter. As I entered, she rose and clasped me in her arms. 'Fanny, dearest, the most wonderful news. Papa is coming home! He has already left on the stage from Portsmouth. No school for you tomorrow. We must spend the day preparing ourselves.'

We woke next morning to snow. I longed to play outside in the soft white powder but was forbidden to stir from the house. After breakfast, Ellen dressed me in a clean shift, my lace pantaloons and two calico petticoats, then my best woollen frock, stockings and buckled kid shoes. Taking a bowl of water, she damped my ringlets, curled them about her fingers, and tied my head in a cloth till they should dry. I was obliged to eat my midday meal at the kitchen table, covered in a large sheet to guard against possible spillage. And afterwards I sat beside the back-parlour fire and dressed and re-dressed my doll, Marie, in her French finery. In every room, log fires roared, and from the kitchen came the smell of meat roasting on the grate. Though the snow muffled sounds, at every hushed noise from the street I started and peered anxiously towards the window. Papa's return was, after all, almost entirely of my doing. Though Mama had said that Heaven had regarded my nightly prayers with favour, I knew very well it was only my magical incantations that had brought him safely home to us.

It was mid-afternoon before Mama sent for me. She sat in her customary chair in the drawing room, but looked so unlike my real mama I stopped in the doorway and did not dare venture in. Her face had been powdered white, with red circles on either cheek, and her hair was caught up on her head from whence it fell in ringlets to match my own. On one cheek was a small black dot I had never seen before, and her blue silk gown, open above its lacing, displayed her powdered chest. Huge leg-of-mutton sleeves covered her arms and, as she stood up to embrace me, I noticed the small bulge of the bustle under the back of her gown. I knew she wished me to tell her how pretty she looked, but so great was my discomfiture at the change in her, I could not find the proper words.

'Why, Mama, you look . . . you look . . .'

'Come here, Fanny, and let me see you. Yes. You will do very well.'

There was a muffled clattering on the cobbles below the window. Mama caught my hand. 'It's Papa. I'm certain of it. He's here.'

Minutes later, a tall man strode into the room. I eyed him without recognition but it was surely Papa, for Mama ran immediately to him and clasped her arms about his neck. In return, he put his arms around her and drew her to him. Embarrassed by this display, I gazed into the flames of the fire till they should disentangle from each other and notice me where I sat.

For some time I remained forgotten until Mama, breaking from his embrace, cried, 'Fanny! Come here, child, and kiss your dearest papa.'

As I approached the strange man, I was aware of a familiar odour of tobacco mixed with the sharpness of earth, of . . . grass . . . of what exactly? I turned a little away from the strength of his smell as he bent down and grazed my cheek with rough lips.

'See how she has grown,' said Mama.

'Indeed she has.'

'And now, Ernest,' said Mama, 'you must be hungry, and Martha has prepared a roast for our supper. I thought tonight we should all dine together.'

'With the child?'

'Why, yes.'

'I'm not in favour of children dining with their elders but, if it is your wish, Charlotte, for tonight only she may dine with us and we shall give thanks together for my safe return.'

'Amen to that,' said Mama.

I did not like my papa. I did not like his heavy smell, his booming voice, the way he commanded all of Mama's time. Why had I so foolishly prayed to Heaven to send him back to us? Now, at every opportunity, I pressed myself into the mulberry tree, hissing magic spells and mixing noxious potions for his departure.

And Papa did not like me. 'You indulge her, Charlotte,' I heard him say to Mama as I stood with my ear pressed to the drawing-room door.

'You must be patient, Ernest. She's not yet used to you.'

'She should have a governess.'

'I don't wish to have any governess living in the house with us. They can be so very interfering. And Fanny is learning well in her dame's classes.'

'Perhaps she should be sent away to school.'

I slipped off to my bedroom where Ellen, not Mama, put me to bed and heard my prayers. It was late when I was woken by the noise of a door shutting. I knew it would be Papa. Although he occupied a bedroom of his own on the other side of Mama's, it seemed that on most nights he preferred to sleep in her room. I felt the unfairness of this keenly. If I, her beloved child, was not permitted to sleep in her bed, why should Papa be granted such a privilege?

Now, as strange noises emanated from her room, I became alarmed. Suppose Papa was being unkind to her, speaking to her as curtly as he did to me? I climbed out of bed and, cold in the night air, took up my sentinel's position against her door jamb.

I must have fallen asleep, for I was woken by a blow on my back, and tumbled to the floor as Mama's door opened.

'What the *devil* . . .?' shouted a voice.

Fully awake, I stared in fright at the dim outline of two large legs and a figure towering over me.

'What is it?' came Mama's voice. 'Wait, I'm lighting a candle.'

'It's that blasted child.' His voice rose to a roar. 'What is she doing here, spying on us?'

In the flicker of the candle, I saw the coarse hair that covered his legs, and was engulfed by a rank odour from under his nightshirt. Peering up beneath it, I discerned some kind of abominable mass hanging at the top of his thighs. He seized me roughly and hauled me upright. 'In the morning, girl, I shall whip you soundly.'

Mama rushed to us and pulled me to her. 'Leave her, Ernest, I beg you.'

Shuddering from fright and cold, I began to weep.

'Of course your own papa won't whip you. He merely spoke in fright after you caused him to stumble.'

'Indeed I did not. She must learn her place. I am her father. She must obey me.'

Glaring at Papa, Mama enclosed me in her arms. 'I remind you, Ernest, you are not on the quarter-deck now.'

From the stairs at the end of the corridor, Martha appeared in her shift, her hair hanging in a plait.

'Take the child and put her to bed,' ordered Papa.

'Go back to your room, Martha,' said Mama. 'I shall put Fanny to bed myself.'

I do not know what may have passed between them, but it was Mama, not Ellen, who woke me in the morning and who sat with me as Ellen dressed me. 'We are to forget all about last night's events,' she said, 'but you must promise me, Fanny, that you will not leave your bed so again.'

I ate my breakfast and midday meal with only Ellen for company. 'They mistress be a-walking with they master,' she said, 'and I be sent by Martha for they joint for they dinner tonight. Ye be they good girl now and play quiet indoors with ye doll. And keep ye pinafore clean.' She looked at me intently. 'No call to be upsetting they master.'

Bored with my own society, I wandered upstairs and slipped into Mama's room, where I fingered her china ornaments and tried out her hairbrush before laying my head against her pillow to catch the scent of her. It occurred to me then to peep quickly into Papa's room. His door stood ajar. I pushed it open and stepped inside. His large bed was covered by a plain white counterpane with none of the pretty embroidered butterflies and flowers that decorated Mama's. Against one wall stood his iron trunk, against another a plain deal chair over which was draped his nightshirt. Though there was no sign of his pipe, the air was tinged with tobacco smoke. Disappointed at the ordinariness of his room, I was turning to leave when I saw upon the window-sill an elegant brass spyglass. I had seen pictures of such an object but had never encountered a real one. I went over to the window. Feeling the weight of the metal, I brought the glass slowly to my right eye, screwed up my left as I had seen in my picture book, then looked at the distant Cobb.

For a moment, all I saw was a blur, then I began to discern the faces of men, women and horses, even dogs, all brought so close they might have been inhabiting our garden. Opening the window further, I trained the glass towards St Michael's churchyard. Sheep and gravestones sprang towards me.

I was watching the grazing sheep when there came a shout from behind me. I jumped back from the window and, in doing so, dropped the spyglass. As I bent to retrieve it, Papa seized my wrist.

'Leave it be!' he bellowed. 'How *dare* you enter my room and help yourself to my possessions?'

I tried to speak, to explain that I had merely been trying out the glass, not stealing it, but fright held me speechless and I stood mute, shaking, his grip on my wrist so tight that I feared he might snap it.

'You, Miss,' he cried, 'have been petted and indulged by your mama. It's time you learnt the ways of the world.'

'I—'

He shook me. 'Be quiet. Do you hear me?'

In a quandary now as to whether to be silent or answer him, I nodded.

'You have been permitted too much liberty and—'

'*Ernest*.' Mama stood, flushed, in the doorway.

I tried to pull away from Papa and run to her, but he jerked me back. 'Your mama cannot intercede for you this time.' He turned to her. 'I've caught the child in the very act of stealing.'

Mama looked at him in astonishment. 'Stealing . . . what?'

Papa brandished the spyglass he had retrieved from the floor. 'My glass. My most treasured—'

Mama's voice was very quiet. 'But why would Fanny need to steal a spyglass, my dear? It is hardly the normal accoutrement of an eight-year-old girl.'

With relief, I found I could speak again. 'I didn't steal it, Mama. I wanted only . . . to look through it . . . to see . . .'

Papa glared at me.

'I'm sure that's so, Ernest. Fanny was merely curious. Your glass is novel to her.'

'She has no business in my room at all. Does she not know the limitations of her place in this household?'

'I'm sure she does. I think perhaps a child's natural instinct overcame her. But you're right, my dear. She shouldn't have entered your room without permission. That was very wrong of you, Fanny. You must apologise to your dear papa.'

He was not my dear papa but I did not say so. 'I'm sorry, Papa.'

'There, Ernest, she has said she regrets what she did, so perhaps you may release your hold on her wrist. She is, after all, too small to inflict damage on such a strongly built man as yourself.'

She said this very mildly, but Papa at once dropped my wrist and strode downstairs.

AUCKLAND, 1846

Since the success of the party, both Lucy and her husband had appeared in better humour. Then, she and I came in to breakfast one morning to discover the Governor sitting grimly in his chair, clutching a letter.

'Why, George, whatever is the matter?' asked Lucy.

He laid aside the sheet of paper. 'The most shocking intelligence. Reverend FitzRoy is dead.' He paused. 'And by his own hand.'

Lucy took up the letter. '*You may not yet have received the sad tidings . . . my painful duty to inform you . . .* Oh, how very dreadful . . . *that he slit his throat with his shaving blade . . .* But how frightful for his poor wife and children.' She turned to me. 'Reverend FitzRoy was the cousin of the last Governor here. Not a very likeable character, I'm afraid.'

The Governor set his mouth in a disapproving line. 'You are speaking disrespectfully of the dead, Eliza. It does not befit your position.'

'I am speaking no more than the truth. Of course I'm grieved at this news, and especially at the manner of Reverend FitzRoy's death, but everyone here knows he caused nothing but trouble with the missionaries in the North. He was singularly gloomy, Fanny, and very dogmatic and fixed in his views. He and Governor FitzRoy held that every word of the Bible was the literal truth. People say that's why they fell out with Mr Darwin.'

I saw how the more she spoke, the more her husband's anger increased, but she seemed impervious to this.

'Madness must run in the FitzRoy family, I think, Fanny. Their uncle, Lord Castlereagh, took his own life, and in exactly the same manner, slitting his throat with his shav—'

Her husband slammed his fist on the table. 'Leave this room at once, Mrs Grey. You're allowing your foolish tongue to run away with you.'

'I will *not* leave this room. Not at all. The entire world knows the truth of what I'm saying. It was Lord Castlereagh's valet who found him. It was in all of the newspapers of the time. Fanny, can you imagine such a fearful sight?'

'No!' I said. 'And I've no wish to. Hush, Lucy, I beg you. Leave the dead in peace.'

'I can't help but think,' said wilful Lucy, 'how very odd it is that a man devoted to religion and the Word of God should commit the sin of self-slaughter.'

The Governor rose. He bowed to me. 'Your sentiments do you credit, Miss Fanny. Perhaps you could instil some of your gentility of manner into my wife. Her comments are extremely unbecoming to a lady.' And he left us.

Lucy's cheeks were flushed, but she held her composure. 'You see how pompous, how—'

'I see how very silly you are to antagonise him so. Couldn't you see his temper rising?'

'It's better than complete indifference.'

'He'd just received terrible news of his friend. He was certain to be a little—'

'His *friend*,' she cried. 'Theodosius FitzRoy was never his friend. My husband despised him. He often complained that FitzRoy was in an unholy alliance with his cousin, Captain FitzRoy. And he was the weakest, most ineffectual Governor, who fervently embraced the Holy Book but allowed grog-shops and houses of ill-repute to flourish unchecked in Kororareka. And now my husband pretends sorrow at the Reverend's passing. He's nothing but a hypocrite.'

'Lucy! Stop it. If poor Uncle could hear you speaking like this, he'd be grieved beyond measure. It's entirely possible and natural to feel sorrow at the death of any other fellow creature, no matter what views one held of him in life.'

The mention of Uncle seemed to calm her a little.

'You must apologise,' I said. 'Go to your husband and say . . . say . . .

your senses were disturbed at such distressing intelligence.'

'Then I'll be just as great a hypocrite as he is.'

'It's not hypocrisy, it's common sense. What will you profit from your husband's being in such ill-humour with you?'

She considered a moment. 'Well,' she said sulkily, 'I will do it, just for your sake.' She paused. 'But you know, Fanny, you're grown so very *parochial*.'

Lady Martin's house, at some distance from Auckland town, sat on a sloping hillside, looking towards the harbour. Lucy being engaged elsewhere, I was driven alone by Ingrams to pay my promised visit. I had not noticed at the dinner at Government House that Lady Martin suffered from some condition which made walking extremely difficult for her. She came now to greet me, leaning heavily on two sticks.

'Look there,' she said. 'In the bay below.'

'Maoris in canoes,' I said, a little alarmed. 'Are they friendly?'

'Entirely friendly and well disposed to us. Do you see that man with the flax kits? In those he has kumara and fish fresh from the sea, and by and by he'll bring them up to sell to my servants. I watch the natives every morning. They set out in their canoes with the sunrise and lay nets in the harbour. See, there's another one coming around the point, laden with vegetables. The Maoris cultivate abundant vegetable gardens on their lands on the North Shore opposite us.' She pointed across the harbour. 'The ground there is particularly fertile.'

'Are you afraid of them?'

'Not at all.'

'In Albany, we heard the most alarming accounts of their warlike habits.'

'And I daresay they were true,' said Lady Martin. 'In some parts of New Zealand, relations between the two races are not at all harmonious and there have been violent disputes over land. But here, in Auckland, we've had little trouble.'

'I was told that a Captain Wakefield and some of his men were murdered in cold blood by the Maoris ... after they had surrendered.'

'That was at Wairau and it was a most dreadful affair. But to the natives, surrender is an unknown act. Poor Captain Wakefield had no idea of this and, more importantly, Te Rau-paraha's— Have you heard of Te Rau-paraha?'

'The Governor calls him the Napoleon of the South.'

'His daughter, Rongo, the wife of his nephew, Te Rangi-hae-ata, was accidentally killed in the crossfire and it's the Maori way to have utu, or revenge, for any killing. That's why Captain Wakefield and his men were slaughtered.'

'The Governor says there are uprisings in the south. He intends go there soon to restore order. I hope he'll be safe.'

'Don't trouble yourself on that account. The Maoris will never harm him because of his great mana.'

'Mana?'

'It's a native word meaning high status or rank. All their chiefs and tohungas, their priests, have mana, and since the Governor is the representative of the Queen, he's regarded as our European paramount chief.'

'I confess I'm in awe of their appearance. The lines carved into their faces lend them such a ferocious air.'

'Some of them are extremely confrontational, but a great deal of their fighting takes place among themselves, you know. And things are much quieter now than they were. Not so long ago, while my husband went to take the thermal waters, I stayed with Mrs Watson, the wife of an old missionary, near Tauranga, and she told me of her life at the Mission there twenty years ago, when they were the only Europeans in the place. Two of the local tribes were engaged in a skirmish, and the battle raged around and about the Watsons' house.

'She was very nervous, she said, but the chiefs assured her husband they wouldn't be harmed provided they stayed inside. Unfortunately, her husband decided that, as a missionary, he couldn't merely stand and watch as one group slaughtered the other, so out he went to remonstrate with the natives and plead for them to turn to peace.'

'Was he killed?'

'No, no, he was quite unharmed. But the chiefs were very much angered at his intervention so, to teach him a lesson, both tribes joined forces and ransacked the Watsons' house, then, their looting and pillage over, they resumed battle with each other. Mrs Watson said she was most put out to observe one of the Maoris running about outside their house, mother-naked and clutching his tomahawk, with her best black bonnet tied on his head.'

I laughed.

'It was returned to her in due course — along with most of their other goods — but by then it smelt so highly of the fish oil that some of the Maoris use to dress their hair, she could never wear it again.'

I began increasingly to warm to Lady Martin and her frank, open manner.

'Do you never find life here a little . . . narrow . . . compared with England?' I asked.

'Why, sometimes, but in general I have a great deal more freedom here than ever I should have in an English shire. And I meet people from so many different backgrounds, none of whose society I'd be permitted at Home. Then there's my dear husband. He and I are very well suited and agree on most topics. And, of course, I have my garden.'

'Lu— Mrs Grey is not as happy as you are.'

Lady Martin considered for a moment, then she said, 'I've been in two minds as to whether I should speak to you. I've observed that you and Mrs Grey are very close. When she spoke of your arrival, she was as happy as I've ever seen her, and from that I assumed you were dear to each other.' She paused. 'She is sorely in need of a friend.'

I was torn. While I had no wish to speak of Lucy behind her back, I had become increasingly concerned for her. I did not feel Lady Martin to be either judgemental or a gossip; her concern seemed genuine.

'The Governor isn't perhaps the easiest of husbands,' I ventured.

'I should certainly say not.' She spoke so vigorously, I was startled. 'He has many excellent qualities and he's devoted to his studies of Maori lore and legends, but he's known throughout the colony as a man who nurses a grudge and pursues his opponents with undue ferocity. My husband says that the Governor is not satisfied merely to defeat his enemies but wishes to break them utterly. That's not the fabric from which an understanding husband is cut.'

Her candour, while it surprised me, made me decide to confide in her. 'At a gathering at the Mission after church last Sunday I met a Miss Cockcraft who was very . . . outspoken in what I can only describe as her . . . condemnation of Mrs Grey.'

'Ah, Emily Cockcraft. A notorious young Auckland gossip. She's in no way to be relied upon.'

I was relieved by this. 'I formed a similar impression.'

'You may trust,' said Lady Martin, 'that I shall at no time breathe a word of our conversation elsewhere. You may have complete faith in my confidentiality. I wish only to assist Mrs Grey.'

'As do I. Please speak as freely as you wish.'

'The Greys are not liked by many in Auckland,' said Lady Martin, 'partly because they succeeded the FitzRoys, and although Governor FitzRoy was very fixed in his opinions, he was agreeable and entertaining enough in company, and his wife loved society. She gave many very jolly dinners and balls, which, of course, made her popular with the settlers. With so few other events to look forward to, balls and parties are much desired here. And the children were delightful and accomplished. They were altogether a devoted family. My husband always said that provided one stayed away from the topics of religion and the Maori land sales, one could pass a most stimulating evening with FitzRoy. Then, too, the FitzRoys delighted so much in each other's company. He was most attentive and full of praise for her, and she for him likewise, whereas Governor Grey often speaks to his lady in tones that scarcely suggest the most tender of feelings. Sometimes he resembles an army commander giving orders to a subordinate. We all know woman is man's supposed inferior, but in this day and age no sensible man believes that in his heart.'

'You think not?'

'I'm certain of it. In a new country like this, where men and women must work together to accomplish even the simplest of tasks, ideas of the feebleness of our sex become difficult to sustain. But I'm not so sure the Governor subscribes to such a viewpoint.'

'I fear not.'

'It's been noted by many people how often he leaves his wife alone, and it's the talk here — for you know how folk love to gossip and make much of little — that he's charming but cold and that he forbids her even such simple pleasures as dancing. There's not enough gaiety or society in Government House.'

'You're right.'

'Now, mindful of these circumstances, I've called on Mrs Grey many times and sought to suggest outings, visits and other similar pastimes in order to supply her with some agreeable form of society but' — she hesitated — 'it's a little difficult to speak of. In the normal course of things I shouldn't presume to appear to criticise her . . .'

'Pray continue, I beg you. I shan't reveal to her one word of our conversation.'

'I've observed her closely since she has been in New Zealand. She's a clever woman, I believe, not in the least empty-headed.'

'You judge her correctly. She has many aptitudes. In South Australia, she set herself to learning the Arabic language with great success.'

'I'm restricted in my ability to walk but, knowing of her interest in flora, I suggested rides together to inspect the Domain. The New Zealand plant life is fascinating and she might gainfully be employed in cataloguing it for publication.'

'Has she told you that when she was first married and in London, she had her researches into Western Australian flora published in a catalogue of plants?'

'She has never breathed a word of it.' Lady Martin set down her teacup. 'I suggested, too, that she might assist us in the little hospital my husband and I have set up here, and I advanced the idea of visits to the native settlements, not merely because they're worthy of notice but because she might usefully acquire knowledge in those areas where her husband is presently so occupied.'

'You've been most thoughtful.'

'But it was all in vain. For, in truth, I've been met not merely with indifference but by what one must call a sort of arrogant aloofness.'

'I have seen it, though never in relation to myself. To me, she's always loving and affectionate.'

Lady Martin took up the teapot which the maid had replenished. 'I believe her to be very lonely and unhappy,' she continued, 'but her demeanour and all her actions serve only to render her more so. She's what my husband would call "her own worst enemy". This is a very small and inward-looking society. One is thrust up constantly against one's neighbours and it is essential — or so I consider it — that one should endeavour to forge common bonds with at least a certain number of them.'

'Which she refuses to do?'

'It seems so. And this has caused her to offend a great many people, not only here in Auckland but in Wellington where she was much criticised, particularly by the detestable Mrs Godley, for failing to leave her cards.'

'She has always scorned such niceties.'

'I feel exactly as she does but, in a place like New Zealand, and if she wishes her husband's advancement and popularity, she must cut her coat according to her cloth. And the Governor has difficulties enough. He's been something of a success in managing affairs with some of the natives, but he has grave troubles brewing with the settlers. From the outset, he's been much concerned with the situation of the Maoris and the land sales. My own husband, and I tell you this in the strictest confidence, Miss Thompson, considers that the New Zealand Company has acted most improperly, even illegally.'

'In what way?'

'In their sales of land to which there was no title.'

'You mean they didn't own it?'

'Not an acre. But this didn't prevent them from selling to unwary buyers in England who arrived to find that either their land didn't exist or that they had no legal claim to it. There are many people, particularly in Wellington, who've spent all their capital on what they believed to be large holdings, and then used up the last of their savings on passages for themselves and their families, only to land in New Zealand and find themselves ruined.'

'Can nothing be done for them?'

'Very little. Some have even been forced to work as labourers, housing their families in tents, while the Company directors have made fine profits for themselves.'

'I have heard nothing of this before, but it seems quite shocking.'

'It is entirely immoral. And, as I said, illegal. But I must ask you again to mention nothing of what I have said to either your host or hostess.'

'I assure you I will utter not a word of it.' I hesitated. Then I said, 'There's another . . . matter on which I would greatly value your opinion. But it's a very delicate one.'

'If I can advise or assist you, I shall.'

'Miss Cockcraft, when she spoke to me at the Mission, hinted at some . . . scandal connected with Lucy. It was to do with the Governor's former private secretary. She seemed to think I was aware of it, but the ignorance I professed to her was entirely genuine.'

Lady Martin sighed. 'From all I understand, it was a very trivial matter, or would have been had the Governor not overreacted so.'

'But surely . . .?'

'No, no. Nothing of *that* nature was ever imputed. The Governor's private secretary was a Mr Cooper, who had been on his staff in Adelaide. Mr Cooper was young, dashing and — more pertinently, I believe — lively in temperament. On several occasions when the Governor was absent, he and Mrs Grey rode together, but always in public places such as the Domain or the shoreline. Perhaps they were thoughtless but I'm sure they did no more than enjoy each other's company in the most innocent of ways. As I said, I think she is lonely and neglected, and Mr Cooper stimulated her interests.

'At any rate, for a time, she became most animated, organised a ball at Government House and paid for the restoration of a native's canoe to settle a dispute over its ownership. The people here began to warm to her. Then, or so my husband had it from a colleague, her husband returned early from the Waikato and found his wife with Mr Cooper in the middle of the day, sitting on the veranda, chatting together, unchaperoned.'

I laughed. 'Good Heavens! Government House is so poorly constructed that every conversation in any room can be heard from any other place. I should scarcely have thought they would choose the *veranda* if they wished to have a tryst.'

'I'm sure you're right. Mrs FitzRoy complained often about the lack of comfort and privacy in that house. But the Governor, who was no doubt tired and strained from travelling, exploded in rage, threatened to horsewhip Cooper and dismissed him on the spot.'

'But on what grounds?'

'Supposed misconduct and insubordination. It was an over-reaction of the grossest kind. Poor Cooper came to my husband, protesting his innocence and desirous of his intervention with the Governor.'

'And . . .?'

'My husband tried to soothe matters but, even he — and his rank as Chief Justice is almost equal to that of the Governor — was met with hostility and indifference. So Mr Cooper was forced to leave and, as you may only too well imagine, tongues here began wagging, especially as Mrs Grey appeared wan and unhappy.'

'The Governor is a very strange man,' I said. 'It's as if he desires a wife, yet he is not prepared in any way to set himself to be kind and gentle towards her, or to allow her those little pleasures that might soften her feelings towards him.'

'He's a hard man. There's no doubt he has a formidable intellect, but his lady has a great interest in learning and could be much more of a helpmeet to him if he would only permit it. She reads most extensively.'

'I know she longs to travel with her husband. I have heard her pleading with him on several occasions to take her with him.'

'He refuses?'

'Yes. And so she becomes ever more estranged from him. She has sought to learn the Maori language so that she might help him with his collection of native legends but that, too, he refuses to countenance.'

Lady Martin shook her head. 'It's no wonder she's miserable. And with no children to occupy her . . .'

'And little chance of—' I stopped.

'Perhaps you might interest her in good works with the education of the native children in the Mission school?'

'Most certainly I will but . . .' I pondered for some moments. 'There's something else I should like to confide in you. I dare not write to her sisters or to my dear aunt, since it would trouble them greatly and they're too far removed from here to be of any use to her in the matter.'

'I give you my word again that I shan't reveal the content of this conversation to anyone, not even to my husband.'

'I've been disturbed . . . worried . . . by a certain . . . recklessness

Lucy has developed in her character. It's as if . . . as if she desires to . . . goad her husband by the wildness of her views. She can't seem to curb herself when it would be more prudent to do so.'

LYME REGIS, 1833

'I thought you would *never* arrive, Fanny,' cried Lucy, as Ellen dropped me at the door of Cobb House.

'She's been peering from the window every five minutes since breakfast time,' said Gussie. 'Papa says on Judgement Day she'll be urging haste on the Archangel Michael.'

'Well, you're here now,' said Lucy. 'So let's go off together and find something to do. Come along, Gussie.'

On my visits to Cobb House, I had begun covertly to observe the Spencer girls and their papa. He was affectionate to all three of them, but Lucy he particularly favoured. How, being so pert, did she manage to please him so greatly? Gussie, and sometimes Mary Ann, he patted kindly on the head, but Lucy he seized in extravagant bear hugs, flipping her ringlets with his large hands and teasing her when she tossed her head at him. What would my own papa do if I were to conduct myself so? I did not think it prudent to attempt to find out, and spent my time keeping out his way.

'Today,' said Lucy, 'we are going to the boat-builders to show you the lifeboat Papa is designing. It's to be unsinkable.'

Though I had passed them often, I had never before entered the boat-builders' premises. As I followed Lucy and Gussie, I stared at the great spars of wood, the caulking vats, and the men clattering hammers, clinking chains, shouting and calling as they hauled and heaved. The sweet smell of wood mixed with choking fumes of tar from the outside yard.

'Over here,' called Lucy, leading us out of a doorway to an area fronting the sea.

Thigh-deep in the water, Captain Spencer and several other men bent over an upturned boat with large cylinders of copper strapped to its either side.

'Papa!' called Lucy.

He looked up in annoyance. 'What the *deuce* are you girls doing here?'

Lucy seemed unmoved by his scowl. 'We wish to see the new lifeboat.'

'You have no business in the boatyard unaccompanied.'

'I am not unaccompanied. Gussie and Fanny are with me.'

The Captain's face turned red. The other men stood silent, watching as he strode out of the water towards us. I trembled, and saw that Gussie, too, was apprehensive. She pulled at Lucy's arm. 'We're sorry, Papa,' she said. 'We will go home directly.'

'We will *not* go home,' said Lucy. 'I promised Fanny she might see your invention.'

His breeches dripping, Captain Spencer marched over the shingle and glowered at Lucy. 'You are wilful, Miss!' he bellowed.

'Indeed, I am not. I wished only—'

'Be quiet!' he roared. 'And you are defiant, Miss. Do you hear me?'

Lucy remained uncowed. 'I do,' she said. 'And why can we not complete our simple errand? Because my cruel papa doesn't think we should walk the little distance to the boatshed unescorted. Pah!'

I waited for her papa to strike her. They locked eyes, he red-faced and furious, she composed and cool. Suddenly, Captain Spencer threw back his head and let out a great roar of laughter. 'You minx, Liza-Lou,' he said. 'You have the true Spencer spirit.'

She smiled up at him. 'So now may we show Fanny the cleverness of my dear papa?'

How had she done it? How had she turned his anger to amusement and admiration? I thought of my papa's fury when he had caught me with the spyglass, and wished with all my heart that he might be like Captain Spencer — or that he would leave us and go back to his ship, and that Mama and I could return to our old life together. I longed to speak of this to Lucy but I dared not. What kind of unnatural child does not love her own papa?

Sheathed in the spring leaves of my tree, I muttered and mixed my spells and potions, seeking a charm strong enough to weaken Papa and send him back to the High Seas. But he remained untouched, even by the power of crushed sheep droppings from the churchyard scrambled together with spittle and blood. As hale as ever, he strode about taking up so much of Mama's time that it was Ellen who now heard me reading from my primer.

'Be I has nay they knowing of they letters like ye does, Miss Fanny, but I has aye an ear for they pretty phrase,' she said one evening as she listened amiably to my laborious deciphering of *Cobwebs to Catch Flies*.

I put down my book. 'Ellen?'

'Aye?'

'Ellen, you remember the witch? By the canal . . .'

'Oh, aye. She with they besom?'

I nodded.

'What have put ye in mind of she?'

I hesitated. 'I want . . . I . . . there's a . . . a boy at my school who . . . who is cruel to me. He doesn't like me . . .'

'Ye should tell they dame. Be her must see to he, not ye.'

'But I can't tell her. He . . . he'll find out. Ellen, do you know that witch?'

Ellen was offended. 'I has niver had truck in aye me life wi' any witch and niver shall!'

'Then, do you know a spell . . . or magic . . . to . . . to send him . . . that boy . . . away?'

She thought for a moment. 'Be old spell me grandam have used to frighten off they gypsies. Ye might try that one, mebbee.'

'But does it work?'

'Me grandam had niver in all of she life they tinkers near they door.'

'Will you tell it to me?'

Ellen looked around. 'Nay here. Be Martha may hear and then be trouble. Tomorrow, mebbee, in they woodshed.'

'But Joseph . . .'

'Be Joseph's afternoon off.'

The woodshed was dark and full of scuttling spiders. I hung back from the door.

'Quick, now,' said Ellen. 'Inside, afore Martha see us.'

The small side window was so cobwebbed it emitted only a filtered shaft of dim light. Ellen stood me before it in the centre of the space not occupied by logs. I thought I heard a rat scuffle.

'Perhaps we shouldn't . . .'

She shook her head and took from her pocket a small cloth bag. 'Stand ye very still now and nay speak a word.'

From the bag she drew a fistful of dried bay leaves, which she crumpled and sprinkled around me in a circle. Their pungent odour was a relief from the dank sour smell of the shed. Then she took from her pocket another bag, this one full of ashes, and carefully scattered them on top of the bay leaves. 'Listen careful now. Speak nay a word out loud, but in ye head ye says three times they name of they boy be cruel to ye.'

For a moment I was confused. I had forgotten my lie of yesterday. She mistook my confusion for fear. 'Be nowt to be affrighted of. Ye be safe in they circle. Now, close ye eyes while I chants they spell.'

Passing slowly around the outside of the circle of bay and ashes, she began to recite in a singsong voice:

They divil take they wicked soul,
And bring they cruelty down,
They divil take, thee, wicked one,
And fling thee from they town.

Papa, I said silently to myself, Papa, Papa.

Ellen turned and paced solemnly in the other direction around the circle.

And all they evil, dreadful things,
That thee has done to I,
Comes back to thee a thousand-fold
And bring thee aye to die.

'No!' I cried. 'No, Ellen, not to die. I do not wish Pa— that boy to die. Just . . . to go away from Lyme.'

Ellen was cross. 'Be bad luck to break they spell. Hush ye, now. Be not finished.'

'But not to die, Ellen. Please!'

'A spell be a spell. They words be they words. Be nay for ye or I to change. Think powerful in they head, then, for they going away of they boy, not they dying.'

I watched Papa, fearing to see him develop a tremor, a pallor, some indication of his imminent death, but he continued to be his usual self. Guilt stole my appetite, weighing on me so heavily I could no longer take pleasure in any of my former pastimes. Once, Mama would have quickly noted such a change in me, but she, herself, was unwell. She had a strange whiteness in her complexion, and on several occasions I heard her calling for Martha to bring her a basin, into which she would then be violently sick.

And then it came to me. I understood what was wrong with Mama. I had interrupted Ellen as she recited her spell, and it had fallen not upon Papa but Mama . . .

I crept about the house, praying to God to forgive me, promising even to sacrifice Marie if it would restore Mama to health. But Mama kept now to her bed, her door closed against me. I crawled inside my tree, frantically stirred flower petals, sugar lumps, honey and any other sweet and fragrant ingredients into a healing paste, then stole inside to smear it on the floorboards and about the door by Mama's room, taking care that none of the servants or Papa should catch me.

Mama did not recover.

'Mistress be no stronger today,' said Martha to Joseph, 'so Master be dining at the Rooms again tonight. Be weeks now since she be out of her bed.'

Eating my bread and milk at the kitchen table, I listened dejectedly.

'Where be ye doll?' asked Ellen, as she put me to bed.

I had left Marie as a sacrifice, laid out in her best French frock on a slab of wood inside my tree. I thought of rats gnawing at her beautiful face and her delicate arms . . . how cold she must be, how lonely without me . . . Unable to sleep, I quit my bed, determined to pray by Mama's door. But what if Papa should find me there? And had I not promised Mama I would never again take up a vigil outside her room? I shut the door and knelt at my own door jamb, opposite hers. 'I am sorry, God,' I wept. 'Please, I beg You, restore Mama. Let me be ill, not her. I will . . . I will even throw Marie off Church Cliffs if You will give Mama back to me again.'

Tears flowed down my cheeks; I shivered in the night chill. And then . . . I must have fallen asleep, for I woke at the sound of heavy footsteps. Scrambling to my feet in panic, I tried to gain the safety of my bed before Papa should see me. But my legs were numb, and I stumbled and fell again to the floor, sobbing from a mixture of misery and fear as he loomed over me. The strange thick smell of the Maltings engulfed me, whisking me back to the canal by the mill and the sight of Ellen's witch. I trembled and shuddered.

'Why, what's all this?' said a voice. 'What has happened, child?'

I felt myself lifted up.

'It wasn't Mama's door,' I cried. 'I promised only her door, not my own.'

'Ssh, ssh,' said Papa, 'or you'll wake poor Mama and that would never do. Come now, we'll go downstairs to the fire and warm you a little.'

I quivered against him. 'And then you will whip me?'

Momentarily, my papa looked shamefaced, then he said, 'Of course I shan't whip you if you've done no wrong.'

'But I have done wrong. Very wrong. It's all my doing that Mama is dying and—'

'Your mama is not dying. Not a bit of it.'

'Then why is she all the time in bed?'

'Why, she is merely . . . a little indisposed . . .'

Desperate with misery, I laid my head against his jacket and wept. 'And now I have sacrificed Marie and the rats are eating her.'

'Sacrificed Marie?'

'My doll, my beautiful French doll.'

'And why would the rats be eating her?'

'I promised God that if He would restore Mama, I would sacrifice

Marie. She's alone in the garden . . . and she has never been away from me before.'

'Dear me,' said my papa, 'what a very sorry and complicated state of affairs. Now, where is this unfortunate Marie?'

I cried harder. 'Under the mulberry tree.'

'Wait there,' said Papa, placing me in a chair by the fire. He strode to the door and disappeared into the garden, returning in minutes carrying Marie, damp but unharmed.

He handed her to me.

I shook my head. 'I promised God . . .'

'I don't think God has any need of Marie and, if He had wanted her as a sacrifice, He would surely have sent the rats to seize her by now. I'm quite sure He wishes you to take her and look after her kindly.'

'And Mama?'

'Tomorrow, you may go in and see your mama. But you must promise to be good and quiet and not disturb her. She has need of rest just now.'

I sat slowly absorbing warmth from the fire. 'Papa?'

'What is it?'

'It's Ellen who hears my primer now, and she doesn't know her letters so . . . my dame is vexed with my reading.'

'That will never do. Sleep now, and tomorrow we will see what we can manage.'

AUCKLAND, 1846

I stared out of the window. 'How long will this rain continue?'

'It's impossible to say. Sometimes it lasts for an hour and at other times for days.'

'I much prefer to be indoors until it clears.'

'So do I.' Lucy put her arm through mine and squeezed it. 'I'll ring for tea and then let's sit cosily in here and talk about Albany again. Do you remember when we arrived there?'

'Very well.'

'I thought it would be exactly like Lyme but there was no town—'

'Not even a village—'

'—no streets, no carriages—'

'—no carts or horses, no trippers—'

'—no Assembly Rooms and—'

'—no Cobb!' we cried together, laughing.

Lucy looked serious for a moment. 'I often think of poor Mama, you know. All of us and so few servants and that horrid little cottage, and she was only two months away from her last confinement.'

'And yet I can't recall having once heard her complain.'

'Nor I.'

We sat in silence before the fire.

'Mama wrote to me, you know,' said Lucy suddenly.

I looked at her, puzzled.

'After . . . after my little Georgie . . .'

I said nothing.

'She said, she wrote, that she knew . . . she could understand how I felt. Because she had lost her own first-born. In Malta. He was ten months old, she said, and when Papa was posted from Valetta she could scarcely bring herself to go and leave her infant behind, alone, in foreign soil.'

She was weeping now. I sat still, uncertain of what best to do.

'Oh, Fanny, you can't believe what a beautiful child he was. I so much wish you could have seen him. He had the prettiest black curls and dark eyes, just like my own. And the most excellent disposition. He smiled and cooed at everything. His papa was much admiring of him and had plans for his fine boy to become a soldier in the family tradition. And I loved him to distraction. When he . . . when I lost him . . . I thought I should die myself of grief.'

I moved to her and placed my arm about her shoulders. 'I know nothing can replace a lost child, but, Lucy, there will be others. Look at your dear mama.'

She hid her face in her hands. 'I think not. Ever since we were in Adelaide, my husband has become so . . . distant. He scorns me, Fanny. And now he never . . . comes to my bed. It is as if . . . as if . . . he despises me. He speaks to me in such an unkind manner. You have heard him yourself.'

I sought for the best way to comfort her. 'If he is so heavily occupied with pressing matters, it's no wonder he's sometimes a little curt. I've noticed that the old wound in his hip seems to be troubling him.'

'That's the climate here, the damp. But you've seen how he alternates between dark moods and over-violent exertion.'

'I daresay he has a great deal of official business to attend to and it weighs heavily on him.'

She laughed harshly. 'At this very moment he's away again, cruising about I know not where. I begin to think he is growing very fond of going around as a bachelor. When we first arrived here, he passed ten weeks out of the first nineteen away from home and I had not a notion of where he might be.'

She had ceased weeping.

'I think it is simply the cares of state,' I ventured. 'I've noticed he seems absorbed in his duties here,'

'Oh no, Fanny. That is not it at all.' Her tears began to flow again.

'Then what is it?'

'I must tell someone,' she sobbed, 'and I dare not say a word even to Sarah or Lady Martin.'

'You may trust me. I am your sister.'

She struggled to compose herself again. 'I can hardly bring myself to utter it, but the truth is that . . . that . . . my husband blames *me* for my infant's death. There! I've said it.'

'Surely not!'

'He has charged me with it repeatedly since my poor darling was buried. He's told me countless times that I was a neglectful mother.'

'I am certain you've misunderstood him.'

She looked at me sadly. 'I only wish that were so.'

'But surely Baby Georgie had a nursemaid?'

'Yes, and she loved him as a mother. Almost as much as I did. But my husband's mind is made up against me, and nothing can turn him from his belief that it is I who caused my own infant's death.'

'This is quite the most wicked accusation I've ever heard, Lucy. You know very well it's untrue.'

'Indeed I do. It is not *I* who brought about Baby's demise. It is my husband.'

'Lucy! What are you saying?'

She gazed at me, her eyes unnaturally bright. 'That is no more than the truth before God. It is my husband who weakened my little boy's constitution by insisting I must be confined at sea.'

I stared at her, aghast.

'Yes,' she went on, and I saw she had become almost feverish, 'I was in great hopes that my husband would delay our departure from England for Adelaide, but Lord Russell stressed the urgency of his immediate departure. So George's dear mama urged me to remain with them at Bodiam for my confinement and follow with my new darling when I had regained my strength. But my selfish husband was adamant I must accompany him. I dread sea voyages and I had the greatest trepidation about what was to come . . . but he must have his way.

'I was dangerously ill, but it pleased God to spare my life, which at one stage was quite despaired of, and on February sixteenth, a week short of Rio, my little Georgie was safely delivered at sea. For the remainder of the voyage I was almost insensible of my surroundings.'

'I—'

She was speaking very quickly; she seemed almost unaware of my presence. 'When we arrived, we were installed in Government

House, which was a very grand residence, certainly the most splendid in Adelaide. The original Government House, we were told, was a horrid little mud dwelling with a thatched roof, called by the locals Government Hut. But although this was a newly completed house, it was a huge, imposing stone building, cold and echoing, with loneliness in every corridor. I was so entirely wretched and I detested Adelaide. I begged my husband to allow me to return to you all at Albany for a visit with Baby, but he refused. He said my duty lay with him. So, you see, it is his own cruelty to me that—'

'Stop this! Can you not see that in your mutual grief each of you is blaming the other for an event which emanated solely from the Will of God? Neither of you is responsible for the death of your infant. If you go on like this, you'll destroy each other.'

She laid her head against my shoulder. 'You're the only person to whom I've confided this. I dared not speak of it to any other.'

'Then listen to me carefully. You must try to show just a modicum of tenderness towards your husband.'

'Why should—'

'Because it will be to your own benefit. And his. Nothing can bring back your lost child, but it behoves you ill to live in mutual hatred of each other. What good can come of that?'

For a long time she was silent. I thought she was considering my words. Then she said, 'Do you remember, Fanny, that strange old fortune-teller we saw so long ago with Papa, and how she said I should return to Rio? Perhaps she truly did have the second sight.'

For several days after our conversation, despite her husband's return, Lucy kept to her bed. But when she finally reappeared she seemed more like her former self.

'I was thinking,' she said, 'of when we were children in Lyme. Do you remember how we slipped away together to the lacemakers' and you showed me the far end of Coombe Street where you said a witch lived?'

I laughed. 'And how I stole bacon from our cool room to stow in our pockets to protect us? I had to hack it from the hock, and the knife was so blunt I was terrified someone would suspect me. And poor Ellen thought she would be accused of stealing, so she told Joseph she had startled a rat gnawing at it.'

'I love to recall those happy days,' she said. 'I believed my childhood was endless. It never occurred to me to think of myself as an adult.' She smiled. 'Do you remember Blanche, our little lamb? You were so afraid she would bite you. And Gussie and I— Oh!' She broke off abruptly. 'But here is my husband.' She moved towards him and laid a tentative hand upon his forearm. 'You seem in better spirits, George.'

He did not reciprocate with a tender touch, but neither did he withdraw his arm.

'I am feeling in improved health,' he said. 'But I will allow myself a few days' more rest here before I return south. I intend to meet with Mr Hadfield as soon as I arrive in Wellington.'

Lucy saw my look of enquiry. 'Mr Hadfield is a missionary stationed at Otaki and at Waikanae, about thirty miles from Wellington. He's an exceptional man. He speaks fluent Maori and has the trust of all the tribes, yet he lives inside the pas there in the most primitive circumstances imaginable.'

'He is the one man in all New Zealand,' said the Governor, 'who entirely understands native affairs. But he's been gravely ill and has had to go to Wellington for treatment. I hope he will have recovered enough to receive me. I'm in urgent need of his counsel.' He patted Lucy's hand. 'I shall send him your good wishes.'

She smiled at him. 'Yes, please, my dear. We are all very fond of Mr Hadfield.'

I felt the very slightest twinge of hope. Perhaps she had heeded my words. Perhaps speaking of her agony at the loss of her child had finally afforded her some relief.

LYME REGIS, 1834

I was sitting at the desk in the drawing room, attempting to capture Mama's profile in my sketch book when Papa returned from the Assembly Rooms in high spirits. 'I have the most agreeable intelligence,' he said, as he strode in to join us.

'And what is that?' Mama put down her needlework.

'Captain Spencer has had a knighthood conferred on him. The Order of the Guelph, in the gift of the King himself. I shall send my congratulations immediately.'

'Please to add mine, Ernest. And to Mrs — Lady — Spencer.'

'I wonder if this honour will change Spencer's mind,' said Papa, sitting down beside Mama on the sofa. 'He says he's considering emigrating. With the cost of living as it is, he has no means of setting up his sons and procuring successful marriages for his girls.'

Emigrating! How would I bear it if Lucy were to leave Lyme? I worked away with my charcoal, secretly listening intently to Papa's every word.

'There is always the Navy,' said Mama.

'The second son is enrolled in Dartmouth already, but Spencer is finding the expense too great. And the four youngest boys will want feeding and educating for some time yet.'

'But emigration seems a very drastic remedy.'

'I doubt he will decide to go, but he says land is cheap in Western Australia. There are government grants to be had and the conditions are excellent for wheat and sheep. He would take stock with him. Or so he says.'

'On such a long journey? Surely not?'

'What chance would he have to buy animals there? The natives are nomads who grub a living from the desert. Their only meat is lizards and serpents.'

I spoke before I could stop myself. 'Lucy would never eat a lizard. Or a serpent. She would rather starve'

'I was joking, you silly goosey.' Papa stood up and came over to the desk. 'Why, this is a very tolerable likeness of Mama.' He smiled at me. 'Will you let me have it as a keepsake?'

It was autumn now, too cold for donkey rides on the sands, too late to watch the bathing woman submerging her victims from the horse-drawn machines on Marine Parade.

'Come along,' said Papa. 'Ask Ellen to put on your bonnet and cape. We'll walk to the Cobb and look at the ships.'

I walked beside him a little warily, anxious not to incur his displeasure, but as we approached Cockmoil Square I heard a familiar sound and, without thinking, clutched his arm and cried out, 'The organ-grinder. He's back. Please, Papa, may we listen? Please?'

Balanced on his peg-leg, the organ-grinder leaned against the barrel-organ and turned its iron handle. As the music flowed out, his monkey, strung upon a chain, danced on the barrel in time to the tunes. He wore a tiny soldier's jacket and a cap with a jaunty feather and, when the music stopped, he jumped from his perch, snatched up a tin cup and ran, begging, among the crowd. Stopping beside me, he lifted his sad wrinkled face and held forth his cup, entreating me. I, in turn looked beseechingly at Papa, who hesitated, then handed me a ha'penny. I placed it in the monkey's small leathery palm. He lifted it, bit it and dropped it in his cup.

'Thank the pretty little lady, Jacko,' called the organ-grinder. 'Hold out your arm, Miss.'

As I stretched my arm forward, Jacko jumped from the ground and stood upon it, examining me with two shrewd black eyes set in the mask of his face. I wished for nothing more than that he could be mine, that I could carry him home and set him free from his chain to dance upon my window-sill. As I stared at him longingly, he put his head on one side and held out his cup again.

'Here's a farthing for you, then,' said Papa, but Jacko, to the delight of the crowd, took it, examined it and, shaking his head, handed it back to Papa.

'He desires another ha'penny,' I said.

'I see you are a connoisseur, Jacko,' said Papa, and he pulled out another coin. Again the monkey seized it, bit it and dropped it with a clatter in his cup. Then he swung down from my arm, bowed solemnly to us and scampered back to the organ.

'Oh, Papa,' I said, 'I should love a monkey of my own.'

'I own Jacko is a most engaging fellow, but monkeys never make pets. They carry fleas and lice and all manner of diseases and . . . just think what Mama would say if he were to perform his natural functions in the kitchen or the drawing room.'

Though I was astonished to hear my own papa speak so, this thought made me laugh considerably and he smiled back at me. For a moment, I leaned a little against him and inhaled the smell of him. His sharp, smoky tang no longer disturbed me.

The leaves were falling fast from my mulberry tree. Coming home from school, I felt a winter chill in the air and when I entered the drawing room I saw that Martha had stoked up the fire. Before its blaze sat Papa, drawing sombrely on his pipe.

'I have heavy news, Fanny,' he said. 'I had hopes of being at home a little longer with you and Mama, but this morning I received orders from the Admiralty. The *Monarch* has been refitted and I must join her at Portsmouth in five days.'

'But why must *you* captain her?'

'If I failed to re-join my ship, I should be in great trouble with the Navy. And where would I find the money to feed us all?' He pulled me onto his knee. 'I have something important to ask of you, Fanny. While I'm away, I want you to take very good care of your mama. Will you do that?'

I nodded.

'Will you be a kind and thoughtful girl, and if Mama should be . . . tired, perhaps . . . or in need of help, will you do everything in your power to assist her?'

'Yes, but there is Agnes . . . and Martha and . . .'

'They are servants. I'm charging you with a much greater duty than that of a servant. I need you to watch over your dear mama and see to all those little comforts that may make her life easy.'

'I promise,' I said. 'I give you my solemn word.' And, as I crossed my heart and spat into the fire, I saw Papa's lips twitch.

I thought of how Papa and I had walked along the Cobb, of my hand in his as we stopped to watch the Morris men in Cockmoil Square, the sugar mice I had chosen when he took me to the confectioner's.

'I miss Papa,' I said as I sat at Mama's feet by the fire.

She stroked my hair. 'I know,' she said. 'But it makes me so glad that you and Papa love each other.' She paused. 'I have something to tell you, Fanny. Some news I think will cheer you. Quite soon, you are to have a new brother or sister. There. What do you think of that?'

I was astonished. 'Is it true? Are you sure, Mama?'

She laughed. 'Quite certain.'

'But when?'

'In just a few weeks.'

'Then I must go at once with Ellen to visit Lucy and tell her.'

'Not tonight. It's far too late. But I promise you we will call on the Spencers tomorrow.'

'How exciting,' said Lucy. 'And so much better than a lamb. We can take it in turns to hold him and carry him about the garden.'

'Perhaps it will be a sister.'

'No,' said Lucy. 'It will be a brother. I always know about these things. I'm a seventh child so I have the second sight.'

As we rattled home in Sir Richard's carriage amidst the comforting smell of leather and beeswax, I leaned against Mama, and sank drowsily into her soft, plump warmth. She put her arm about me. 'I'm pleased you and the Spencer girls are so happy in one another's company. Lady Spencer says she is especially gratified that you and Lucy have become such particular friends.'

'We're best friends,' I said.

'Today,' said Mama, 'she asked me if you might wish to share their governess's lessons with them.'

'But my school . . .'

'It will not be until springtime. What do you think of the idea?'

'I should like it very much.'

'Well, we shall have to write and lay it before Papa, but he is certain to approve.'

I was roused from sleep by a low groaning, then screams. For a few moments I remained locked in my dream, then I realised the noise came from Mama's room. I leapt from my bed. Her door stood ajar and I gasped as I caught the hum of whispering voices and recognised the bulky shapes of the doctor and Martha at her bedside.

Dr Judd swung around. 'Hush, Fanny. Don't trouble yourself about Mama. She is better now, but she is sleeping and we mustn't wake her. She needs rest and quiet.' He smiled at me. 'And I have very happy news for you. You have a little sister.'

'A *sister*! But where is she? Where did she come from?'

'From the Lord. About ten minutes ago. Is that not a wonderful surprise?'

'Can I . . . can I see her?'

'Only for a moment. She is resting too. For such a tiny mite she has caused us all the greatest fuss and upheaval. Now, tiptoe over here and peep at her.'

I expected some smooth and rounded pink-cheeked beauty, like my beloved Marie, but when the doctor turned down the sheet beside Mama I saw only the wizened head of a tortoise.

'Ah,' said Martha, 'so beautiful.'

'But . . . she's yellow,' I said. 'Like the Chinamen at the Cobb.'

'Saints preserve us,' hissed Martha. 'What are you saying, child?'

'She's arrived a little early,' said Dr Judd, 'which is why she's so yellow. But that will fade and soon she'll be as fair as you are, Fanny.'

'And she's all . . . gnarled . . . like an old woman,' I said through sudden tears.

'She's in need of a little fattening up, that's all. Before you know it, she'll be plump and perfect. Martha, poor Fanny is quite overcome. Can you see to her?'

'Aye,' said Martha. 'Come downstairs now, Missy. Let's warm you and set you something to eat.'

She placed me in a chair by the grate, poked at the fire to make it flare, and threw new logs upon it, then handed me a bowl of bread and milk.

'Stay here now,' she said, and vanished upstairs.

By the slate-grey ashes of the long-dead fire, I awoke to the iron cold of dawn. Peering through the curtains of Ellen's window-bed, I saw it was empty. Upstairs, the door of Mama's room was still ajar, but her fire had been stoked and Martha dozed in a chair beside it. I crawled into my own bed and fell asleep.

It was late in the morning when Ellen woke me. 'Ye've a new sister,' were her first words as she unhooked the shutters to let in the shadowy December daylight.

'I know,' I said, 'and Mama is ill.'

'Nay, she be tired, be all. Quick now. Put on ye new shift and petticoats. Martha has set I to all manner of tasks. Ye must have ye hair left for today. I has nay time for owt.'

With no one about to chide me, I took from the pantry a piece of loaf and a morsel of cheese, wandered out into the garden and slipped between the ribs of my tree. I had no mind at all for the chanting of spells or the mixing of potions, and sat numbly under its bare canopy, its leaves a rotting carpet beneath my feet. Presently, I heard the sound of a carriage halting, followed by a knocking at our front door. I made my way inside, where Martha was admitting Lady Spencer, elegantly shawled and bonneted. I smoothed down my rumpled pinafore and dropped a curtsey. She kissed my forehead.

'I hear you have a new sister, Fanny. Does she resemble you?'

'No, Ma'am,' I said, 'or, at least, I hope not, for she's exceedingly ugly. Yellow and wrinkled as a walnut.'

'A fine way to speak of your own sister, you naughty minx,' said Martha crossly.

Lady Spencer placed an arm about my shoulders. 'I'm sure she is but speaking the truth, Martha. At least two of my own were quite horrid in appearance when first they were born. Crinkled and crushed as prunes. But, you know, Fanny, they've grown into very handsome boys.'

'And I have not seen Mama since my sister arrived.'

'Now that is why I am here, Fanny dear. Mama needs her rest and I should like very much to take you back with me to Cobb House, just for tonight and tomorrow, so that she won't fret and worry about you. Lucy is very desirous of your company. She wants to hear all about your new sister.'

'But Mama and the baby—'

'Martha and the other servants will look after them.'

'But—'

Lady Spencer drew me close to her. 'It is only for a little while.'

'But when will I see Mama again?'

'Why, the day after tomorrow. And you'll find her quite restored to herself by then.' She turned to Martha. 'I think perhaps Fanny might tiptoe in to kiss her dear mama goodbye.'

Stealing into Mama's room where she lay sleeping, I placed a kiss on her brow and gazed at my sister, her face still saffron yellow against the white of the sheet. I put out a tentative finger and stroked her sunken cheek. At once, twisting her face towards my finger, she opened her toothless mouth. Had I woken her? Would she begin to mewl and howl and waken Mama? Recalling Blanche, I hastily laid my knuckle against her gums. She nuzzled it weakly, then settled back to sleep.

'Goodbye, Mama,' I whispered, but there was no response.

On my return from the Spencers, I found Mama propped against her pillows, looking rosy and well, my sister beside her in a basket. 'Fanny, my darling,' she cried.

'I've come only to deliver Fanny back to you,' said Lady Spencer, 'and to bring you a mutton broth. Ah, here is the cause of all the fuss.' She gazed into the basket. 'Why, she's like a tiny doll. Her features are so delicate I'm sure she'll be another beauty.'

'You've been very kind,' said Mama.

'Pouf,' said Lady Spencer, 'it was a trifle only.'

'And now,' said Mama, when Lady Spencer had left us, 'you may hold your sister, Fanny.'

I thought of the shrunken tortoise head. 'Perhaps I should wait until she is bigger.'

'Nonsense,' said Mama. 'Come.'

The bundle Martha laid in my unwilling arms was so swaddled in shawls I could barely make out its face. I peeped quickly between the folds and saw with relief that it seemed paler.

'So, whom does she resemble?'

I hesitated. 'At first, I thought she looked like a Chinaman and very . . . wrinkled.'

Mama's smile reassured me.

'But now,' I went on, 'she seems only a little squashed . . .'

'I meant to ask whether she resembled Papa or me. Or you.'

'Not me,' I said hastily. 'At least, I—'

'I think she has a likeness to Papa, but we'll have to see. Now, as to her name . . . Nothing Frenchie, I think. A pretty English name. What do you say?'

The warmth of my sister's body began to seep into me; a tiny pulse beat in her temple. I stroked the fine down that covered her head. 'She's very small.'

'She will grow.'

'We might call her Harriet.'

'What other names do you favour?'

'Louisa is pretty.'

'Very pretty,' said Mama, 'and it suits her well. Shall we call her Louisa Ann, after Lady Spencer who has been so kind?'

'I like those names very much,' I said.

'Then it's settled. I shall write and tell Papa.'

'Please to tell Papa,' I said, 'that Louisa is a very *comfortable* baby, and that I promise to take care of her as he charged me to do with you, dearest Mama.'

For several days, all was well, so I was surprised on returning from school to find Dr Judd conferring with Martha in the kitchen.

'What has happened?' I asked, in panic.

'There is nothing at all to worry about,' said the doctor. 'Mama has developed a slight fever and I have come to see her only as a precaution.'

I ran upstairs to where Mama lay against her pillows. She beckoned me to her and I kissed her cheek.

'Are you ill, Mama?'

'Just a little tired.' Her voice was faint and I strained to hear her words. 'Now, Fanny, my own sweet girl, I have a very foolish whim. I shan't be easy in my mind until Baby Louisa is baptised, so Parson Hodges has agreed to perform the ceremony here this evening.'

I stared at her, then at my sister who lay pallid and almost motionless beside her.

Mama opened her half-closed eyelids and smiled at me. Her hand lifted, as if to pat my cheek, but fell back against the counterpane. 'Go downstairs now to Ellen, Fanny dear.'

I do not know what impulse woke me so early at dawn next day. No sound came from anywhere in the house, but I rose and, as if by instinct, went straight to Mama's room and opened the shutters. In the soft, pale light, I saw she lay as ashen as my sister. I bent towards her, expecting to be enveloped in her sweet, familiar scent, but recoiled from the repulsive smell of the fish market that seemed suddenly to engulf me. Panicked, I saw that beads of feverish sweat had formed on her forehead and, in an effort to cool her, I turned back her covers.

The lower part of her nightgown was stained purplish-red. As I watched, crimson trickles oozed down her lower legs and across her feet, seeping into the bedding beneath her. For a moment I stood aghast, then, stumbling into the corridor, I began to scream.

'Martha! Ellen! *Come at once*. Mama is lying in a bed of blood.'

Of the funeral I remember almost nothing. I recall that from somewhere were conjured for me a black mourning frock, petticoats and bonnet; that I stood, numb, by William's grave, staring at the bottomless space beside it as it received the coffin in which lay Mama with Baby Louisa in her arms. I know that it rained, for I remember thinking that I should never again, in all my life, see the sun shine. And, through it all, I was engulfed by the constant sad toll of the funeral bell.

I recall only snatches of the time following but, even now, I can bring to mind that bitter afternoon when I climbed the small incline in St Michael's churchyard and, surrounded by tombstones, sat on William's grave beside the grassless rectangle where Mama and Louisa lay. I gazed up at the weathercock on the church tower, and I recollect still how the grey sky above it was reflected in the water of Lyme Bay below.

It was Ellen who told me I was to live with 'they grand family at they Cobb'.

'Them be off to Australia and them is to take ye wi' they. They master have agreed.'

I stared at her, uncomprehending.

'Ye is to stay here till they Christmas Eve. Then ye is to go to they Spencers and all ye on to Charmouth and after, I knows nay where. But, come they April or May, ye and they leaves for Australia.'

I felt the wetness of tears on my cheeks.

'Ye must nay cry now. They Spencers be very good folk. And it be sure ye will come back some day.'

My tree stood skeleton-stark in the garden. Agnes had left us for another situation, Joseph was about the business of the house, and Martha and Ellen were packing my trunks. Very soon, Lady Spencer would come in the carriage to fetch me. I crept into the garden and stood, frozen with misery and cold, gazing at it in farewell. Then, seized by a sudden frenzy, I rushed to my mulberry tree, tore from it twigs and branches, and, with bloodied fingers, ripped and twisted at Mama's holly bush. Weeping, I fled out of the gate into Church Street. My boots rang out on the frosty cobbles, hammers on a blacksmith's anvil; white trails of my breath pursued me as I ran. And in St Michael's churchyard, swept by bleak winter winds, I heaped the drab grey tombstone and the scarred earth beside it with my magic twigs and red and green holly boughs, a Christmas offering to Mama and William and Baby Louisa for whom now all seasons were as one.

II

AOTEAROA

Consider the significance of the beginning — every beginning — how the seed sprouts forth to become the adult plant. Who is it who nurtures the kauri seed to flourish into the giant of the forest? Tane-Mahuta, guardian of the trees? His brother, vengeful Tawhiri, god of the winds and storms, who blows the seed to its home and waters it with his rainstorms? Or their brother, Rongo, who, for the sake of his mother, Papatuanuku, nourishes it as it grows, then gives it to his youngest brother, Tu, who fashions from it the canoes in which he sends the tribes to war one against another? How can we know who determines the beginning . . . or the end? How far off may the seed fall yet still grow to fulfil its destiny? Now, I am only a phantom swirling in the sea fog but, then, I was of the seed of the mighty chief, Te Rau-paraha.

THE HIGH SEAS, 1835

The cracks in our cabin walls became portals through which our ship released a nocturnal army. At the onset of darkness, drawn by the sour reek of vomit, waving their feelers, clacking their varnished wings, hundreds of cockroaches crawled out to plague us. In vain did we stuff every aperture with paper, stop any gaps with strips of cloth, even wedge buttons sideways into the larger openings. Still they squeezed out from the tiniest crevices. And if we crushed them, a horrible stench rose from the carcasses and thousands of tiny eggs were released to hatch into yet more tormentors.

The *Buffalo* rose up on giant swells and slammed down their breaking sides, struggling against the sea's attempts to swamp and claim us. When I opened my eyes, I saw Lucy in the opposite bunk, Mary Ann and Gussie in their berths above. Perhaps I was dreaming? But when I closed my eyes, then opened them again, the Spencer girls were still there with me.

I could not collect my thoughts. Disoriented by the endless pitching of the sea, I fancied I had died and gone to Hell.

'Mama,' I heard someone call.

'Hush, Fanny,' said a soothing voice.

'Mama!' I cried, raising my head.

A damp cloth wiped the tears from my face. I caught the pleasant drift of lavender but, aching for the sweet familiar smell of my own mama, I burst out into gasping sobs. 'Please, Ma'am, I want to go home. To Lyme.'

For three weeks now we had been at sea, and still Gussie and I were struggling against sea-sickness.

'Fanny,' said Lucy, sitting on my berth, 'Mama wishes to see you.'

I staggered behind her to Lady Spencer's cabin.

'Now, my dear,' she said, 'I have something to say to you. Sir Richard and I have grown very fond of you and, as you've become part of our family, we should like you to call us Uncle and Aunt.'

'If she's one of the family, why shouldn't she call you Mama and Papa?'

'Because, Lucy, she has a papa of her own. What do you think of that idea, Fanny?'

'I . . . It's very kind, Ma'am.'

She patted my hand. 'It's very kind . . . Aunt.'

Tears started in my eyes and I fought to keep them back.

'My papa . . . Perhaps he thinks I am dead, too.'

'My dear child, he thinks no such thing. Sir Richard has written to him. As soon as his ship docks at Portsmouth, your papa will seek a ship bound for Western Australia and join us at Albany.'

'Are you certain . . . Aunt?'

'As I sit here. Your papa will come to you.'

'And take me back to Lyme?'

'We will decide all that when he comes.'

Like Noah's Ark, our ship floated alone on a vast empty ocean stretching endlessly to the horizon. Having found our sea-legs, Lucy and I roamed unchecked about the ship, taking care to avoid the hatches at the stern, from which rose the stench and shrieks of the transport women manacled in the hold.

'Let's go to the mid-decks,' said Lucy.

'But we're forbidden to—'

'Pouf. Who's to know where we are?'

As we slipped down the stairway, a pungent land odour wafted from below and a vision of Ellen rose unexpectedly before me.

'Why, it smells . . . exactly like the stables at the George Inn.'

As we descended further, we heard clucking and odd scraping noises.

'Hens!' I cried. 'And look . . .'

There, in pens and crates, were two sheepdogs, a quantity of fowls, a number of goats and ewes, and a ram that glowered wickedly from a separate cage.

'Those are *our* animals,' said Lucy. 'And that's Papa's stallion, Thunder. But how thin and wretched he is. We must find Hugh at once.'

Hugh, Lucy's eldest brother, was taken aback by our indignation.

'Why are the animals confined so?' demanded Lucy. 'It's most terribly cruel.'

'How could we allow them to stray about the ship?' said Hugh. 'They'd be overboard in a moment. And there's nothing cruel about it at all. The sheep and goats and fowls are quite content in their quarters, the cows are led about the decks on halters twice a week and the dogs are walked by the crew every morning.'

'And Thunder?'

'Yes, it is hard for him. He's taken three or four times a week to walk in a halter, but he's in such terror of his surroundings we can scarcely persuade him to move at all. We have hopes of exercising him in Rio.'

RIO DE JANEIRO, 1835

Rio holds no charms for me. I remember the strangeness of the looming, oddly shaped mountains and the dark green forests as we approached, the gradual discerning of the people clustering at the quayside. We left the *Buffalo* and were lodged for five days with the Resident, Mr Tully, in an imposing house with white columns, but the ship remained with us. As we lay in our beds, or walked about the large garden, suddenly the ground would seem to heave beneath us like a great wave.

'Only five days on land,' said Lucy. 'I would rather stay here forever than have to return to that smelly ship.'

'Nonsense,' said Uncle. 'Shipboard life is capital. Now, my good girls, this is our second day here and you are quite rested, so I propose to take you the three of you on an excursion into Rio town. It will be a chance to test my command of the Portuguese language.'

'I didn't know you spoke the native language, Papa.'

'Yes, indeed, Augusta. I have put ashore here many times when I was captaining my ship. And I first came to Rio as a midshipman.'

Lucy laughed. 'I can't imagine my dear papa as a middy.'

Uncle Spencer ruffled her hair. 'Come along now. Fetch your bonnets and we shall be off.'

So, while Aunt rested in the shade, gossiping with Mrs Tully, and the younger boys played among the brightly coloured flowers, we four set off together. The flamboyance of the vegetation, the heat and the proliferation of dark-skinned people chattering in a language I could not understand made our surroundings feel like a mirage. Strangely garbed men passed in mule-trains, women balanced baskets of unknown fruits on their heads, ragged children grubbed in the dust.

A woman in a tattered purple gown darted towards us, her skin and hair soot-black. 'Fortuna, fortuna,' she cried, clutching at Gussie's hand.

Uncle snapped something at her, and she spat on the ground and flounced off. 'She's harmless enough,' he said. 'A rogue, certainly, but I doubt she's a thief.'

'What did she want, Papa?'

'Money, of course, Liza-Lou. For telling your fortunes. It's a speciality of the natives in this part of the world. They claim to have the second sight.'

Lucy seized her father's arm. 'Oh, Papa, please, please. I long to have my fortune told.'

'It's nothing but stuff and nonsense. *You will be rich, you will marry a handsome man, have a fine horse and carriage* . . . All that babble, that's what they will tell you. And for that, you must part with a silver coin.'

'But, Papa, dearest Papa, I wish so much to hear my fortune.'

I knew that, of all his children, it was Lucy who could coax Uncle from the angry rages which sometimes overtook him, often for no more reason than a fly's alighting on his arm. These were provoked, so Gussie had told me, by the livid flattened scar on his forehead which, from time to time, pressed upon the humours of his temperament. It was always Lucy whom Aunt sent with cooling cloths and brandy to bring him to himself again. Wheedling and teasing, she could calm him in minutes.

There, in Rio, he looked at her pleading face and shook his head, but Gussie and I knew she would have her way. 'Well,' he said finally, 'if you're so set upon it, Liza-Lou, I suppose I must accede.' He paused. 'But . . . we won't take the services of one of these street peddlers.' And he led us off into a side alley, from thence into another, and on through a maze of narrow passageways until we came to a low dwelling set apart from a huddle of poor huts. Made of mud, with open holes for doors and windows, it could scarcely claim to be a house, though a few red- and yellow-flowered bushes sprouted in the dusty yard before it.

'Wait for me,' said Uncle, leaving us by the broken fence. He stepped into the yard, stood by the entrance and called out in a foreign tongue.

A young girl appeared, black-eyed, dark-haired, her worn frock filthy, her feet bare. '*O que você quer?*'

He spoke to her. She shrugged and vanished. It was very hot by now and the dust had made me thirsty; I could feel the sun beating on my head through my bonnet. The girl reappeared and beckoned us into the hovel.

It took several minutes for my eyes to adjust to the darkness. We walked on earth floors into an empty room and from thence into another in which I gradually distinguished two chairs and several rough boxes set as seats. On the walls hung masks carved like grotesques in a carnival. From further inside the dwelling, the girl led out a very old woman. As she shuffled towards us, I realised she was blind, her pupils glazed with white film. She lifted her head a little and seemed to sniff the air. I thought of Ellen and the cat woman. My heart began to thud. I longed to escape.

Uncle stepped forward, spoke to her in that strange tongue, extracted from his waistcoat some silver coins and laid them in her open palm. She ran a careful finger round the rim of each, and bit them all in turn, before secreting them in a pocket in her skirt. I had a sudden recollection of the organ-grinder's monkey in Lyme and a sharp pain seized my chest.

'She says she will tell your fortunes, one by one, starting with Gussie,' said Uncle.

Lucy frowned. 'But how will we know what she says?'

'Because, Goosey, I shall decipher it for you. You will see that she talks in riddles, like the Sphinx. But it's said in Rio that she has the true second sight. I'm told it's sometimes given to the blind.'

The old woman sat in one of the chairs, and the girl, indicating that Uncle should take the other and we girls the boxes, set a little stool before the old woman's chair.

'Come, Augusta. You first.'

'I'm not sure I wish to know my fortune, Papa.'

'It's merely entertainment. Step forward.'

Tentatively, Gussie sat upon the stool and held out her hand. The fortune-teller took it, raised it and, as Gussie flinched a little, traced a finger over her palm. She spoke.

'She says, "You have a good heart",' said Uncle, 'which we all know is true. "You will marry for love. You will travel long and far, and you will have many children. In your old age you will be content."'

Gussie's hand was released.

'There,' he said, 'that was a splendid fortune indeed.'

Lucy was fairly dancing towards the stool.

'Yes, yes,' he said. 'Now it's your turn, Liza-Lou.'

Lifting Lucy's hand, the fortune-teller bent over it as if she were not blind at all and could see it clearly. A long silence fell. Then,

'She says, "You lack patience,"' said Uncle.

At this, we all laughed, even Lucy.

'"... which will be the cause of much trouble in your life if you do not seek to master it."'

'Oh dear,' said Lucy, 'this is surely a homily, not a fortune.'

The old woman raised her head and seemed to stare into Lucy's face. '"You will rise high and you will sink low. You will reign like a queen and slink like a cur. You will marry but not for love. You will travel the world but come home. When crowds greet you and praise you, remember the fickleness of fortune. You will be pious ..."'

We were unable to smother our amusement.

'"... and you will do good works. For much of your life, dark men will surround you. The man who will wed you will be elevated but base, the man who will claim you will be noble of heart but far away."' She dropped Lucy's hand abruptly. Then she spoke again, very loudly. '"You will have a long life,"' Uncle translated. A pause. 'And she says, "One day you will come again to Rio."'

The woman sank back in her chair, muttering.

By this time, I was entirely uneasy. I trembled as Uncle motioned me to the stool. The room felt suddenly darker, the carved faces on the walls seemed to grimace at me. I shrank back. 'I ... I should prefer not to ...'

He rose and propelled me gently towards the old woman who stretched out a shrivelled hand and clasped my own so that I was forced to sit, in dread, upon the fateful seat. Despite the heat in the room, her touch was cool and papery, and she seemed almost to caress my palm. Without warning, she lifted my hand to her lips. I sat frozen, unable to move, as she spoke in her sing-song voice.

'She says, "Poor child, you have suffered much and must suffer more but your entire life will not be one of suffering."' She released my hand. '"From the sea will come your greatest sorrow and your greatest happiness. You will not be brought high but neither will you sink low. You will have your time of sorrow and pain but, when you least expect it, God will reward you and show you a miracle. And you, too, will return to Rio."'

I supposed this to be the end, but she spoke again. '"Little sister, listen to your own heart and not to the words of others. Beware the serpent in your friend's house."'

I stared at her, confused. The film across her eyes seemed to glitter. '"Do not step on him for another's sake or the Worm will bruise your heel . . . and hers. In the face of loss of honour, guard your own."'

She let my hand fall and I sat, unable to move, seized by a terrible dread. She leaned towards me, muttering.

'She says,' said Uncle, '"Do not be afraid. There is nothing to fear."'

And from her skirts she drew out a tiny manikin, waxy-pink and clad in a skirt and bonnet. She motioned me to take it; I shook my head. The room seemed silent, empty of everyone but us two. I breathed faster. The walls shrank and pressed in upon me. Again she held out the manikin; again I resisted. She held it to her cheek, whispering to it and, as she did so, its face swelled so that it resembled one of the gargoyles on the walls. It eyes stared at me, its lips parted, and from its ghastly mouth I heard Mama's voice: *Take care, my darling girl, take care.*

I remember nothing more. Lucy told me later that I screamed and fell insensible from the stool, striking my head on the floor, and that Uncle carried me from that evil room, calling my name and saying over and over, 'What a fool I've been.'

Dazed, I came to myself propped against the broken palings of the dusty yard with its monstrous bright flowers. I recall that we stopped at a coffee shop where someone brought me a sharp cordial tasting of bitter oranges which Uncle urged me to swallow as a restorative. I passed the remainder of the journey back to the Tullys' house like one in a nightmare who cannot escape into the daylight of reality. When, at last, we came to the peaceful garden, I sank into Aunt's arms, hot and tearful.

'Why, Fanny, what is it? And you're covered in dust.'

'No cause for alarm,' said Uncle, quickly and too heartily. 'She took a tumble in the street and now she's a little over-heated. A trifle overwrought.'

By which I understood that our visit to the fortune-teller must remain a secret from Aunt.

Lucy did not quiz or tease me. Instead, she paid me little attentions and made me laugh greatly at her impersonations of Mrs Tully scolding her servants. She was as clever a mimic as ever I saw in my life.

ALBANY, WESTERN AUSTRALIA, 1835

For several days, a ridge of land smudged the horizon and a great cheer rose from the entire ship's complement when the Captain of the *Buffalo* announced that we should soon arrive in King George's Sound and then at Princess Royal Harbour. 'King George', 'Princess Royal'. Such familiar, comforting names. I felt a rush of expectancy as our ship passed through a narrow inlet and entered a large sheltered body of water which, to my eye, very much resembled the expanse and form of Lyme Bay. We strained to see the town or any evidence of habitation, but the land seemed almost deserted. No jetty extended from the shore; the only buildings were a few makeshift dwellings and what seemed to be a small army barracks. A sparse knot of people had gathered to watch our arrival. Echoing my mounting dismay, Hugh said, 'But where is the town?'

'And where are the houses?' demanded Lucy. 'I can see nothing but those ugly huts.'

'Calm yourself, Liza-Lou,' said Uncle. 'The town and its houses are not visible from here.'

'But how are we to get ashore, sir?' asked Hugh.

'Hush,' said Aunt. 'At least we are here at last and I, for one, will be heartily pleased to be off this ship, however far away the town may be.'

'I think the bay is a little like Lyme,' I ventured.

'Nonsense, Fanny,' snapped Lucy. 'It doesn't resemble Lyme in the least. Where are the shops and the Rooms? There's not even a church that I can see. I believe it has no civilisation at all.' She turned to her papa. 'How *can* you have brought us to such a horrid place?' she demanded, and burst into hysterical weeping.

I saw the pulse in Uncle's injured temple begin to throb.

'We are all tired after such a long voyage,' said Aunt. 'Take your sister below, Hugh, until she's a little more composed.'

'I shall never be composed in my life again, and the moment I'm of age I shall return to Lyme.'

'Look,' said Gussie, craning out over the rail, 'the sand is white, like marble.'

'An excellent sign,' said Uncle. 'Capital.'

The *Buffalo* dropped anchor and two jolly boats rowed out to take us and our possessions to a number of carts drawn into the shallower water. 'We'll be temporarily housed in Albany-town,' said Aunt, 'but Papa has already purchased Sir James Stirling's house at Strawberry Hill, only a mile or so away. Such a pretty name.'

'I wager there'll be no strawberries and no dwelling either.'

'Lucy, I'm becoming exceedingly vexed with your constant complaining.'

'Stop it at once, Lucy,' said Gussie. 'Can't you see that Mama is tired? In her condition, she shouldn't be upset.'

I felt a stab of fear and pulled Gussie aside. 'What is the condition Aunt is in?'

'Why, Fanny, has no one told you? We're soon to have another brother or sister.'

Panic seized me. Before I could stop myself, I heard my own voice saying, 'Will she die?'

'Of course not. Whatever gave you such an idea?' Then, comprehending, she put her arm about me. 'Mama has borne eleven children already and you see she's quite alive and well.' She blotted my tears with her handkerchief. 'Just think, Fanny, how wonderful it will be to have a dear little baby brother or sister.'

I recollected Louisa's yellow face. 'Or perhaps . . . the baby will die.'

'I think it very unlikely. Let us wipe your eyes again. There, that's better. Now, let's think of some names for this new little baby.'

'If it's a boy,' I said, 'and if I could choose, I should call him William.'

We were handed down from the *Buffalo*, rowed to the carts and arrived at the shore with our lower parts wet and dripping. Sprawled to dry on the glittering white sand, we watched as load after load of our possessions was brought from the ship. Trunks of clothing were dumped next to furniture, books, huge sacks of flour, rice and sugar wrapped in oiled cloth, kitchen and farm implements, plants, bushes, even several large fruit trees. Finally, the livestock was disembarked, the goats and sheep bleating, the chickens and ducks squawking and quacking, the cows lowing desperately. The ram butted at the sides of his prison with determined ferocity and I prayed the slats would hold.

Despite this cacophony, Lucy fell asleep on the sand. I dozed beside her while the older Spencer children talked.

'Whatever are those?' asked Mary Ann, as assorted wooden rectangles were propped beside the ram's cage.

'Frames for windows and doors,' said Edward, panting as he started out again for the jolly boat. 'And there are doors and glass to go in them, and tiles and slates and—'

'And even the carriage,' put in Hugh, sitting down for a moment beside Mary Ann, 'though that, thank goodness, won't arrive till the *Captain Stirling* puts in and it'll be of no use at all here. There are no roads anywhere.'

'There are certain to be better roads over the ridge at Albanytown,' said Mary Ann.

Hugh looked discomforted. 'There's something I must tell you.' He paused. 'There *is* no other town here, only those mean dwellings we saw from the *Buffalo*.'

'*What*? That rough little settlement is surely not Albany?'

'I'm afraid it is.'

'But . . . there must be some mistake. Papa has brought us here for our betterment. You've heard him say so many times in Lyme.'

'Whatever he may have said in Lyme, I'm as sure as I'm sitting here that this is all Albany consists of. There are only twenty-seven inhabitants, just nine meagre houses, a barracks and a miserable little gaol. When Captain Sadler went to seek provisions for the *Buffalo*, he found the people so improvident he could get nothing but water. It seems they were in hopes of our ship being able to supply *them*.'

'But what are we to do? Where will we sleep?'

'Mama is to be housed with the garrison commander's wife, but for tonight and I suppose for some time,' said Hugh, 'the rest of us are to sleep in tents pitched near the barracks.'

'In *tents*?'

'Papa has borrowed them from the garrison commander.'

Our tents stood together a little further down the beach from the soldiers' quarters, and we were permitted to make use of the barracks' foul-smelling earth closet. We were obliged to crawl into the tents through a flap of material. 'Look at our beds,' said Lucy. 'Merely coverlets laid on sand. I shan't be able to sleep a wink.'

'Nor I,' I said, loyally.

We woke in the morning to dazzling sunlight and the buffeting of the tent in the wind. As we struggled outside, Uncle, Hugh and Edward appeared, mounted on a horse and two mules also borrowed from the garrison commander. Poor Thunder, too weak to be ridden, had been temporarily quartered in the garrison stables.

'We rode out early to Strawberry Hill to examine the premises,' said Uncle.

'It's a very pretty name,' said Gussie, carefully. 'Is it a . . . pretty house?'

Uncle said nothing, but Hugh answered for him. 'It is no house whatever,' he said. 'Just a small wattle and daub cottage, ramshackle and sagging in every direction, with two small shacks nearby in similar condition. The servants and the men from the *Buffalo* will help us shore up the main dwelling immediately and then we'll see to the others.'

'So it's very fortunate,' said Uncle, 'that I had the foresight to bring timber and roofing from Lyme.'

'But very *un*fortunate,' said Lucy, 'that you didn't have the foresight to ascertain the condition of our new home.'

I had only once before seen Uncle in one of his worst rages. Now he snatched up his riding-whip and advanced towards Lucy, shouting incoherently, the damaged half of his forehead glowing scarlet. Hugh and Gussie rushed to either side of him, clutching his arms in an attempt to restrain him.

To my astonishment, Lucy remained where she stood, staring boldly at him. 'Go ahead,' she said. 'Whip me. I've spoken nothing but the truth. If the truth is an offence, then punish me. I'm suffering enough already. What is a little more pain to me?'

Gussie knelt on the sand and clasped her arms around her father's knees. 'I beg you, Papa, leave Lucy alone. What will poor Mama say if she knows you've whipped her? *Please*, Papa.'

'Get up, Gussie,' said Lucy. 'If my father wishes to flog me like a common Jack Tar, so be it.'

She held her father's gaze.

Uncle faltered, stopped and threw down the crop. 'Hugh, Edward,' he shouted, 'we must begin work at once. I've no time to waste on an impudent girl. Come.' And he sprang onto his borrowed horse.

Lucy bent down and picked up his whip. 'You will need this, I think.'

Snatching it, Uncle brandished it at her, but in a half-hearted manner, then he circled his horse and the three of them rode away.

Gussie sighed. 'Stop it, Lucy, or we'll be in even worse straits. For the rest of today, I implore you to stay out of Papa's way.'

It was five days before we children saw our new home. We set off on foot in procession along the dusty track from Albany and after an hour arrived at Strawberry Hill. On a plateau beside a river, halfway up the slope of a squat outcrop, sat a low four-room cottage with a steep roof of thatch.

'It's so *small*,' whispered Gussie.

We peered through the windows at the cramped rooms; there was no elegant drawing room, no parlour. Attached to the back wall was a tiny scullery and beside it a rudimentary outdoor kitchen, open entirely to the elements. Pitched by the back door, a large tent served as a dining-room, incongruously housing Aunt's walnut table and chairs, and her handsome sideboard. Since one room had to be used to store Uncle's building materials, only three rooms were left for our habitation. The biggest, at the back, was Aunt's; one front room would hold us four girls, two to a bed, the other the younger boys. A small hut, at some distance from the cottage, was the women servants' quarters and a larger cabin housed the men.

'The house is simply a hovel,' said Lucy. 'How *could* Papa be so cruel to us? Our lovely house in Lyme . . .'

Gussie began to weep. 'It's quite the most dreadful place I ever saw.'

I, too, started to cry, though more for the loss of my own home than the condition of the one I was about to inhabit, but Lucy was too angry for tears. 'I shall never, never forgive Papa. I don't believe he cares for any of us.'

'I keep believing I'm in a nightmare,' sobbed Gussie, 'and that when I wake up I'll find myself back in dear Cobb House. What will poor Mama say when she sees our new home?'

While Aunt had been lodging in Albany-town, none of us had seen her. We were all feeling the lack of her calm presence.

'Mama will be here soon,' Hugh said, 'and, as there's nowhere else for us to live, we must make do with this. Come, Gussie and Fanny, dry your tears. For Mama's sake, we must all put on brave faces.'

Uncle galloped up on his borrowed horse. 'The servants are to line up in the usual way,' he ordered. 'Is there water in her ladyship's room?'

I glanced at Aunt's maid, Helen. Her grey hair was dishevelled, and her usually immaculate gown was crumpled and stained. Lucy had told me that Helen was a widow, rescued from poverty by Aunt, and so devoted to her mistress that she, like some of the other servants, had chosen to accompany us to Albany. She seemed drawn and exhausted but she gave a deep curtsey. 'Yes, Sir Richard.'

'You children will stand over there to greet your mama.' He glared briefly at Lucy. 'I trust you find your new home congenial enough, Liza-Lou?'

Hugh nudged her.

'It will serve,' said Lucy frostily.

'Hugh and Edward are to stand here with me to hand down the chaise. Now, form a semi-circle to each side of the door, family to the right, servants to the left. Stand tall, stand tall.' A general inspecting his troops, Uncle rode along the assembled half-circle. 'Robert, you are fidgeting. Be still.'

'He's not used to this heat, Papa.'

'Thank you, Mary Ann, but I shall be the judge of his conduct, not you.'

Now we could hear the rattle of the cart wheels, the laboured breathing of the mule and the slow plodding of its hooves over the stones.

'At-ten-tion!' bellowed Uncle as the cart finally came into view.

It contained only a small chaise, the legs of which had been lashed to the shafts with ropes to secure it. Over it had been erected a parasol which swayed at a giddy angle with each movement of the cart but afforded at least a modicum of shade. Half-sitting, half-reclining on the chaise was Aunt, looking hot and extremely stout. We watched silently as, from her half-prone position, she surveyed her new home. Uncle rode forward and dismounted, Hugh and Edward fell in behind him, and we all waited to hear what she would say.

'Why, Richard,' she said, 'how charming it is. See, Lady Stirling has planted roses by the door.'

Uncle seemed to expand. 'It's a little . . . smaller than we're accustomed to,' he said, his humble tone quite different from the one he used to us children or the servants.

'I daresay when we're properly settled it can be enlarged.'

'That has been my intention from the outset.'

Aunt smiled at us lined up for her inspection. 'My children already look so healthy. And here are all our loyal servants . . . why it's almost like home. Now, Richard, I feel I am ready to descend from this cart.'

Each day the sun dazzled in the sky until it sank in a blazing disc of orange and scarlet. Long creeping shadows stole briefly about us, then a thick black fog descended, stranding us in a haunted darkness, prey to witches and prowling evil spirits. A cacophony of night noises began, and unknown shapes flitted and bounded through the gloom. On our third night at Strawberry Hill, we saw, moving noiselessly across the area behind the cabins, an army of strange ghostly figures. They stood upright on huge haunched back legs, two small arms dangling before their chests.

'Aborigines,' said Aunt.

'No,' said Uncle. 'Kangaroos.'

Lucy and I stared at them as they hopped nearer. Their rabbit-shaped heads had small furry ears, and several of them sported pouches on their stomachs from which protruded tiny heads. Uncle advanced towards them, swinging the storm lantern, and they sped away at the pace of horses.

In the daytime, flocks of black cockatoos streamed from the trees, malevolent familiars screeching and cawing as they swept down towards the dining tent in the hope of securing any carelessly dropped morsels of food. Huge scaly lizards basked on rocks, flicking out their tongues to display their brightly coloured throats; poisonous red-back spiders scuttled from under fallen logs. Most frightening of all were the serpents that slid noiselessly everywhere, the deadly tiger snakes, instantly recognisable by their yellow and black stripes, and the dull brown dugites, often up to six feet long, whose tiny heads were capable of inflicting mortal bites.

'But do you know,' said Lucy, 'even though their venom is deadly, the Aboriginal children catch them and carry them about on sticks? Hugh has seen them. And then they hold them over the fire and cook them and eat them. When we go back Home, it's certain no one in Lyme will ever believe *that*.'

Our bedroom was so cramped that all four of us girls could scarcely fit into it together except to sleep. Curled in one of the narrow beds, Lucy and I listened miserably to the wind that seemed to howl perpetually around the house.

'But that's not the wind.' She sat up, almost tipping me to the floor. 'Those are *voices*.'

We crowded the window, peering from behind the thin curtains into the moonlight. At first, we could see nothing.

'Look,' I whispered. '*Men*.'

'Quite unclothed,' hissed Lucy.

'And black,' moaned Gussie. 'Cannibals.' And she fell, praying, to her knees.

From one of the tents came a familiar voice. 'What the *deuce* are you fellows up to?'

In his nightshirt, Hugh behind him, Uncle stood brandishing a shotgun. The naked black men, moving closer, opened their hands in a gesture seeming to signify that they were not armed.

'Off with you,' ordered Uncle.

In response, one of them indicated the side of the tent and laid himself down against it. He was instantly followed by his fellows.

'I believe they wish to sleep here, sir,' we heard Hugh say.

'Then we shall have to let them. I've no wish to start a skirmish, especially as Stirling says the local Aborigines are disposed to be friendly.'

'What if they murder us all in our beds?' asked Gussie.

'You heard Papa say they wish to be friendly.'

'Thus far, Mary Ann,' said Lucy, 'Papa has not been at all reliable. We must be vigilant throughout the night. Fanny and I will take the first watch, then you and Gussie can stay *en garde*.'

Uncle and Hugh retreated into their tent. Cramped and wretched, pressed hard against Lucy, I stared out of the tiny window, alert for the slightest sign of movement from the dark shapes apparently sleeping beside it.

'What if they should suddenly rise up and overcome us?' I whispered.

'We must scream our loudest to alert Papa.'

It occurred to me that by then it would be too late for Uncle and Hugh to save us, but I said nothing and remained gazing at the inert forms, almost indistinguishable now against the shadow of the tent. After an interminable time, Lucy roused Gussie and Mary Ann, and we two squashed ourselves into our narrow bed as they stood guard at the window.

Despite my certainty that I would never sleep, I was shaken awake by Mary Ann.

'They've gone. But we didn't see or hear anything.'

'You fell asleep,' said Lucy, indignantly.

'No, not at all, did we, Gussie?'

Gussie shook her head. 'One moment they were sleeping by the tent, then, without a single sound, they'd vanished.'

We stumbled sleepily outdoors and assembled as usual for family prayers. The day's reading was from The Beatitudes, and Uncle had reached the words, *Blessed are the meek* . . . when there was a commotion from behind the male servants' cabin, and a large company of men, women and children marched towards us, all quite naked save for pieces of skin or bark hung before the men's privy parts. We sat paralysed, staring at them. They were tall, their skins glistened shiny black, and their hair stood out in woolly curls around their heads.

'Lord, preserve us!' cried Helen.

Clutching a wooden spear, their leader guided his companions behind our rows of chairs where they seated themselves on the ground and proceeded to give the impression of listening intently to Uncle's words.

'I shall continue,' said Uncle, 'and you will all make no sign that anything is unusual or amiss. The Lord, as we know, moves in mysterious ways.'

We recited the Our Father in unison, the natives making unintelligible mumbling sounds in accompaniment. Uncle pronounced the blessing, then, 'These are Aborigines,' he said, 'from the local Minang tribe. Sir James Stirling says we have no need to fear them. You will treat them with all respect and kindness; they are God's creatures as much as we are.'

It was impossible not to stare at the Aborigines. Their height, their strange colour and most of all their brazen nakedness fascinated us, and the little Spencer boys were too young to conceal their interest. Robert ran forward to touch one of the children, who pulled away and clutched at a woman nearby. She patted Robert's shoulder and I watched to see if the blackness of her hand would leave a mark on his skin.

'They have come for food, I believe,' said Uncle to Aunt. 'It was Stirling's habit to provide them with flour and suet from the government stores.'

'But why?'

'They are under the protection of the British Crown and if we wish to bring them to an understanding of the benefits of civilisation — and to purchase their land — it's our duty to provide for them.'

'Are they warlike?' said Aunt.

'Very, if they wish to fight. But they have no quarrel with us, only with other tribes who trespass on their territory.'

'Do they have guns?'

'They have no need of guns. They fashion their own weapons of wood and bone. Now, Gussie, my good girl, run to Helen and ask her to provide you with a little quantity of suet and flour.'

The reception of these offerings showed Uncle was correct in his surmise. Squatting on the ground, the Aborigines commenced a parley in dumb show.

'In return for rations,' said Uncle, 'they seem to be agreeing to provide day labour for the clearing of the land, which will be very welcome.'

But the unexpected arrival of the entire tribe was not.

'They've set up camp just beyond the men's cabin,' said Aunt in dismay.

'I'm afraid, as the Resident, I'm obliged to feed them and provide for them.'

'I should mind less,' said Aunt, 'if only the women and children would cover themselves.'

AUCKLAND, 1846

Lady Martin and Mrs Selwyn came to tea.

'I must tell you, Miss Thompson,' said Lady Martin, 'how kind and charitable your sister and the Governor have been to us at our little hospital at Taurarua. We don't know what we should have done without their generosity.'

Lucy looked pleased.

'We had an epidemic of fever,' continued Lady Martin, 'with so many patients that we were quite overrun, but the Governor and his lady here sent a servant out the two miles to us every day with wine and brandy, sugar, broth and all manner of delicacies, and on some days the Governor himself rode out to make the deliveries and to see to our welfare.'

'Lady Martin and her husband set up the hospital four years ago,' said Lucy, 'when they saw that there was no provision at all for the natives if they fell ill.'

'Our first building was very primitive — just two rough huts and a tent made of blankets — but we raised money from charitable friends in England and had a three-roomed building constructed from native timber and flax panels but with two English windows and a door.'

'They were so very diligent,' said Mrs Selwyn. 'They built raised platforms for beds and on these they put mattresses of freshly cut fern so that, after each patient, they could be replaced with new. There hasn't been a single case of hospital fever.'

'And now, with the subscriptions we've raised — and here again your sister and her husband have been extremely generous to us — we're able to employ a proper nurse, an excellent woman, more skilled than any doctor. When next you call on me, I'll take you on a visit, if that would please you.'

'Very much.'

'And you'll doubtless find Sarah and her boys with us. They'll be staying at our house while the Bishop is away.'

'He's away *again*?' said Lucy

Mrs Selwyn nodded. 'Alas, yes.'

'Don't you find it very hard to be left so often?' I asked.

'Exceedingly, but what can I do? It's in the nature of his calling. I tell myself he's on God's business so I've no right to be so selfish and wish him here. And I have my boys. And my own work with the Maoris.'

'She sees to the running of the Bishop's Mission school and the Bible classes for the converts,' said Lady Martin. 'The Maoris are devoted to her. They call her Mata Pihopa, Mother Bishop, and they follow her constantly.'

'I should like to do some good works with the Maoris myself,' said Lucy, 'but my husband tells me the chiefs say I'm only a child.'

To my surprise, this remark caused both Lady Martin and Mrs Selwyn to laugh loudly.

'That's exactly what the chiefs said about me when I first arrived,' said Mrs Selwyn, 'and I'm more than ten years older than you. And they said the same about you, didn't they, Lady Martin?'

'Yes, indeed. I felt quite flattered to be thought a girl again. And, you know, when my husband showed the chiefs a likeness of the Queen, they shook their heads and said, "Too young to be a great chief. Merely a girl." But you must ask dear Sarah to recount to you some of her early experiences at Waimate. She and the Bishop were once surrounded in their house by a war party led by John Heke.'

'Good Heavens! How horrifying.'

'We were only newly arrived in New Zealand, so I was quite terrified and seized Willie to try to hide him. But whatever the situation, the Bishop is always an oasis of calm. "Compose yourself, Sarah," he said. "We are under God's protection."'

'But why were they attacking you?'

'One of our Maori boys at the Mission had unwittingly shot some wild ducks at a place that had been designated tapu. That's their word for sacred, you know, and they fear the gods' anger if such a tapu is violated. So a fighting party came to our house and began performing one of their war dances in the garden, demanding retribution. And my dear George Augustus, to my horror, went out to them, armed only with a Bible, while I cowered wretchedly inside with Willie, barely able to watch lest I should see them fall on him with their tomahawks.'

'And . . .'

'John Heke advanced upon my husband with a spear, but George Augustus stood calm and unmoving and then, barely two feet away, Heke suddenly stopped and threw the spear into the ground. My husband asked him the cause of the disturbance and, when he was apprised of it, invited Heke and the elders into our house to discuss the matter. They were all in an extremely angry mood and much agitated from their war dancing, but they sat on chairs while the rest of the party gathered outside, peering in at our windows. The sight of all those crowding tattooed faces made me suddenly long for my parents' tranquil home in Wimbledon . . .' She sighed. 'So George Augustus set me to making a large quantity of stirabout — with plenty of sugar — which I presented in the only large receptacle to hand, Willie's baby bath, while he apologised for the offence and asked whether they would like restitution under Maori or Christian law. After a consultation with his friends, Heke said, "Christian law", so George Augustus read to them, in Maori, Zacchaeus's direction that anything taken should be restored four-fold, and said he would pay four times the value of each of the ducks. As you may imagine, they found this wholly satisfactory, so, having received their payment, they fell upon the stirabout, then took very affectionate leave of us, pressing noses with us and professing their everlasting friendship. So, I can truthfully say that I have rubbed noses with John Heke.'

'The same Maori who cut down the British flagpole?'

'Yes, but this was before he started the war in the North.'

'So, you see, life here is never dull,' said Lady Martin.

'Sarah Selwyn is calling on us again this afternoon and she's bringing her two delightful little boys, Willie and Johnny. I'm sure you'll love them just as much as I do.'

Mrs Selwyn, even paler than I remembered, the loose drapery

of her gown barely concealing her condition, sat unhappily on the veranda, watching as Lucy led the children to a large chest filled with toys and games.

'Eliza is so very kind,' she said. 'She dotes on children and my two can scarcely wait to visit.'

'How old are they?' I asked but, to my consternation, she burst into tears.

Lucy came running to her. 'Why, Sarah, what's the matter?'

'I . . . it's nothing. A nervous headache. But it's not that which . . . Oh, Eliza' — and here she began sobbing again — 'George Augustus says that Willie must go Home to school. How will I part with him? He's only six years old.'

'But why must he be sent away?' I asked. 'Are there no schools here?'

'There's our Mission school, of course, but . . . my husband feels it would be preferable for Willie to be sent to his family at Home to be prepared for Eton.'

'Can't he be persuaded to leave it a little longer? Perhaps until Willie is eight or nine?'

'Oh, Eliza, I've begged him, pleaded with him, but his mind is made up. It's entirely selfishness on my part. I know it will be such an advantage for Willie, but the journey . . . it's so long. So far. And he'll be quite alone, my poor baby.'

'When will he leave?'

'When the *Dido* next puts in at Auckland.'

'The Bishop is entirely selfish,' declared Lucy, after Mrs Selwyn and her children had left us.

'It does seem such a long voyage for—'

'He is quite unconcerned for her welfare. Do you know, on their voyage out from Home, when their vessel reached Sydney he left Sarah with Willie, who was just a baby, and embarked alone on a brig for New Zealand?'

'Perhaps he intended to prepare the way for her.'

'Not at all. Ten days after he landed in the Bay of Islands, he set off on his first visitation tour, and when she and Willie arrived, she had no idea at all where he might be. It was six months before she saw him again.'

'Six months!'

'Yes, he had covered more than two thousand miles of terrain, at least a third of it on foot, and was so gaunt and worn she scarcely recognised him when he returned. If it hadn't been for Lady Martin, she would have been utterly distraught. And destitute. But she never complains.'

'She appears quite devoted to the Bishop.'

'And to her boys. They are all she has to comfort her while he's away. And now . . .'

We had been discussing Mrs Selwyn's plight for several days when Lady Martin paid us an unexpected call.

'I've come on a particularly difficult undertaking,' she said, not at all her usual cheerful self.

Lucy looked alarmed. 'I hope it's not an outbreak at the hosp—'

'No, it concerns the Selwyns. The *Dido* has arrived at the Bay of Islands and is expected here within a few days.' She turned to me. 'The Bishop is determined that Willie should be sent Home for his education.'

'I know,' I said, 'but Mrs Selwyn was so greatly upset at the idea, I thought perhaps he might change his mind.'

She shook her head. 'Never. When George Augustus's mind is made up, he's obdurate. It's certain that Willie will leave with the *Dido* and then, poor, poor Sarah . . . We must do our utmost to ensure she's not left alone here with only Johnny for company.'

'But the Bishop . . .'

'He's setting off for the South Island very soon. She'll be quite desperate at the loss of them both.'

'Surely he'll wait until she's confined,' said Lucy. 'It's only a matter of a month at most.'

'I have the greatest respect for the Bishop's honesty and his upholding of Christian principles, but I fear he doesn't always look to the necessity to practise compassion in his domestic affairs. We're happy to have Sarah and Johnny to stay with us at Taurarua, but in a month my husband has to go to New Plymouth on government business and I'm to accompany him.'

'Then she must come here to us.'

'Good. That's what I was hoping you would suggest. Sarah says she's so occupied by the prospect of losing Willie she can take no pleasure in this coming infant. She confided to me that she had actually prayed for the *Dido* to be lost before it reached Auckland. She was shocked at her own callousness.'

'I'm not shocked,' I said.

'Nor I,' said Lucy. 'But, of course, even if that were to happen, the Bishop would simply find another vessel to convey Willie.'

Willie Selwyn had the natural excitement of any child at the prospect of a new experience, more particularly since he was too young to understand how permanent would be their parting. His mother could barely speak of it, while his father assured him constantly what an adventure it was going to be.

On the appointed hour of the *Dido*'s sailing, at the request of the Selwyns, the Governor, Lucy and I accompanied the family to the jetty.

'For Willie's sake, I mustn't weep,' said his mother, but her hands shook and her face was set.

The child's trunk had been taken on board the night before and he clutched a model ship given him by the Martins who had farewelled him a day earlier. The ship's chaplain, who had agreed to take him under his charge, stood with us at the quayside as we said our farewells.

'And now, Willie,' said the chaplain, a little too heartily, 'you promised to beat me at Ducks and Drakes, so we must get aboard and start our game.' He turned to Mrs Selwyn. 'I'll take Willie directly to my cabin. I think it would be the kindest way . . .'

Unable to speak, she nodded her assent.

'You'll be quite the man when we see you again,' said the Bishop, shaking hands with Willie. Mrs Selwyn made a choking sound, reached forward and clasped the child to her, kissing him repeatedly. 'You must say goodbye to Johnny now,' said his father. 'And you're to recite your catechism and say your prayers every day like a good Christian boy.' He laid his hand on Willie's head. 'God keep you, my son.'

I recall how very small Willie seemed as, his hand clutching the chaplain's, he skipped along the jetty away from us.

We stood silently watching as the ship made sail and moved out into the harbour. I saw that Lucy was weeping.

Suddenly, Johnny began to scream. '*Dido,* bring Willie back! *Dido,* come back!'

The Governor bent down and scooped him up. 'Now, Johnny,' he said, 'hush for a moment and we'll see what I have in my pocket.'

And, as Johnny gave another wail, he drew out his compass and moved it so that the needle swung about. Within several minutes, the little boy's attention had been diverted.

No one spoke as we walked back to Government House to take tea, then Mrs Selwyn said in a lifeless voice, 'I simply cannot bear it.'

Her husband placed an arm about her shoulders. 'You must be strong. Willie is under the Lord's protection and, very soon, you'll have a new infant to occupy you.'

'I don't want a new infant,' she said. 'I want Willie.'

I never saw the child again, and it would be seven years before his parents were reunited with him in England.

Lucy and I had settled down to chat by the fire after supper when the Martins' servant was admitted, bearing a message. Lucy read it, handed it to me, then began to weep.

> *As you know, the Bishop left for Melanesia yesterday and Sarah and Johnny are here with us in Taurarua. I regret to have to inform you that Sarah has been delivered of her infant early. It was a little boy but he was stillborn. She is in a very low state and the doctor fears for her life, too. Can I send Johnny to you while we attempt to nurse her back to health?*

Johnny's presence in the house instantly lifted our spirits. Lucy devised little pastimes and entertainments for him, sang to him and endlessly occupied herself with him. We took him in the trap to the Domain, played hide-and-seek in the Government House gardens, read to him and told him stories. For the month he stayed with us, I heard not one argument between Lucy and her husband, and the house seemed to have a new purpose. The Governor even acquired a pony, and he and Lucy took the child riding almost every morning. Then came the news we had all been secretly dreading.

'Tomorrow, Sarah will come to take Johnny home,' said Lucy. 'The time has passed so quickly. It's selfish, I know, but if only he could have been with us just a little longer . . .'

Sarah Selwyn, paler and more drawn than ever, was overjoyed to be reunited with her child. Clasping Johnny to her, she showered him with kisses. 'I've missed him so much,' she said.

'He's been nothing but a pleasure,' said Lucy, and I saw how near she was to tears.

The Governor ruffled the child's hair affectionately. 'Now, Johnny,' he said, 'you're to be a good boy and to take the greatest care of your mama.'

Johnny leaned his face against his mother's shoulder.

'Here's your little lamb,' said Lucy. 'You mustn't leave him behind. Think how lonely he would be without you. And you must come back and see us very soon.'

As we waved them farewell, Lucy stood plucking at the fabric of her skirt, tears now coursing down her face.

The Governor put a gentle arm around her shoulders. 'Come, Eliza,' he said, 'I've arranged for the horses to be saddled up, and you and I shall go for a ride together along the sands.'

And as he led her away, I thought of how, with his swinging compass, he had so deftly distracted Johnny from the pain of parting, and how it had taken the loss of the Selwyns' little boy to turn him towards his wife again. They are in desperate want of a child, I thought.

ALBANY, 1835

Despite the kindness of the Spencers and my closeness to Lucy, I continued to long for Papa's arrival. In these strange, inhospitable surroundings, so unlike Lyme, I dreamt of the day he would come to carry me back to our comfortable, familiar house and our garden with its towering mulberry tree. One morning, not long after our arrival at Strawberry Hill, I slipped away from Lucy, climbed the slope behind the cottage and stood craning for a sight of a ship bringing a letter from Papa, perhaps even carrying him aboard. Though in its form the great sweep of water below me resembled Lyme Bay, the southerly breeze was not a soft Dorset wind but carried a chill cold that cut against the sun. Here it was the north wind that brought the mild weather. No familiar smell of bladder-wrack and salt drifted up to me; I breathed in only dust and desolation. To find me, Papa would have to traverse the whole world. But, I told myself, has not Aunt *promised* he will come?

'Fanny!'

I looked up to see Lucy scrambling up the hill towards me. 'Where have you been? I've been looking for you everywhere.' She flung herself down on the rough ground. 'I loathe this place. I long to go home again.'

'I know,' I said. 'There's no school—'

'And no society but our own—'

'And no Cockmoil Square and—'

'Oh, Fanny, do you remember the Christmas market by the fountain?'

By now we were both in tears, but then I was seized with a sudden idea.

'You know my papa is coming to take me home with him?'

'I heard Mama say so.'

'Well, why don't we take you back with us? We three could live in our house in Lyme. Just think, we'd be together all the time . . .'

'We could go to the Cobb—'

'And the Rooms—'

Lucy flung her arms around me and hugged me. 'Oh, yes, Fanny. Please, *please*. Take me home with you. Do you swear it?'

'I swear it.'

'But for the moment, until your papa comes, it would be better to keep it our secret. We mustn't breathe a word of it to anyone.'

'The *Captain Stirling* has arrived in King George's Sound,' said Uncle, 'and she's brought mail from Home.'

We sat waiting around the dining table, Aunt, now enormously stout, on a wide padded stool at its foot. From the large oilskin mailbag, Uncle pulled out the packages of envelopes and read aloud the names of the recipients. At last, he held one out to me. 'For you, Fanny.'

'From Papa!' I cried, looking at the familiar script. I seized the paper-knife, slit the envelope and unfolded the letter inside.

My Dearest Child,

I think that my own little girl will receive this on board the Buffalo or perhaps even in Australia, should the mails be slow. Lady Spencer has told me of your courage and tender care of your dearest mama and sister which is no less than I would expect of my own good daughter. Until we can be together again, she and Sir Richard have graciously offered you a home, an offer which, since there is no other relative to whom I can entrust your care, I have gratefully accepted. I know that in their charge you will receive the kindest and most loving attention and that your demeanour and conduct will always reflect the Christian virtues instilled in you by your dearest, lamented mama.

I have but to complete this tour of duty then I shall return to Lyme, deal with my effects and be bound for Albany where I shall be reunited with my darling child within a four or five month.

Be good and helpful to Lady Spencer and mindful of her great benevolence towards you. She tells me her girls already love you as a sister. I charge you now with the duty of your nightly prayers to that great Heavenly Father who guards and guides us all. Remember, dearest child, that you are my most treasured earthly possession and know that I pray for you daily as I most sincerely believe you do for Mama and your brother and sister, and for me.

May God protect and guide you always,
Your own most loving,
Papa.

So engrossed was I that it was some time before I sensed the change in the atmosphere about me. While the little boys chattered in their usual fashion, Aunt, holding a black-edged letter, dabbed at her eyes, and Uncle looked grave and solemn. I glanced at Lucy.

'Mama has had sorrowful news,' she whispered. 'Her dear aunt has died.'

'I am feeling very tired,' said Aunt, 'so I shall bid you all goodnight and take supper in my room.'

As soon as I could, I drew Lucy aside. 'Papa will be here within a four or five month.'

She flung her arms about me. 'Oh, Fanny! I'm so happy. I can stand any amount of misery here if I know I'm to return home to Lyme.'

My letter secure beneath my pillow, I fell into a deep sleep and woke feeling more contented than I had for many months.

'Mama is asking for you, Fanny,' said Gussie, next morning.

I knocked on Aunt's door and tiptoed in. She lay on her bed, her feet elevated on an embroidered cushion.

'Come and kiss me, Fanny, and sit here beside me. Now, dear child, although I wish it otherwise, I must speak with you on a sad and serious topic.'

'If I have offended, Aunt, I'm sure I'm very sorry.'

'You have not offended at all. You're a good, obedient child.'

I was relieved at this. 'My papa, in his letter, charges me to be so.'

She looked grave. 'It is of your dear papa that I wish to speak.' She hesitated. 'You saw last night I . . . that is . . . Uncle . . . and I received a letter which bore most distressing tidings?'

I nodded. 'I'm sorry that your aunt . . .'

'Fanny, my dear, I must tell you the . . . the subject of this saddest of news. This letter is from the Admiralty. It informs us—' She stopped for a moment. 'It regrets to inform us . . . that your dearest, dearest papa has been lost in the Bay of Biscay.' She placed her arm about my shoulders. 'I'm so very, very sorry, Fanny.'

'But, Aunt,' I said, 'that cannot be. Here is Papa's letter. He says he is coming to Albany. He arrives within a four or five month.'

'Fanny,' she said gently, 'show me your letter. What date does it bear?'

'The twentieth of July. So he cannot . . .'

She held out the black-edged letter. 'And here, you see, is the date on this letter. The eighth of August. Fanny, dearest girl, I am more sorry than I can express . . . Look, here is the Admiralty stamp. I'm afraid it is quite certain that your brave papa perished with all hands on the *Monarch*. She was holed on a rock and sank very quickly.'

I was quite unable to comprehend what Aunt was telling me. 'But where is Papa now?'

'Why . . . where . . . where he would most desire to be, where all sailors wish to lie. In the bosom of the ocean.'

I recalled how Papa and I, walking on the beach at Lyme, once saw a ghastly, bloated thing floating off the breakwater.

'Is it a log, Papa?' I asked.

And Papa had said gravely, 'Somehow, my child, I think it is not.' And then, as we drew closer and could see the skirt ballooning about the swollen legs, he said sharply, 'Turn away, Fanny. At once.'

'But Fanny dear,' said Aunt, 'you know Papa's soul is with God, in Heaven.'

'Then he has gone to join Mama and William and Baby Louisa,' I cried. 'And they have left me behind.'

I became an automaton. Unable to respond to any overtures of kindness, I ate as one in a stupor and did exactly as I was bidden. One afternoon I was going through the motions of my daily tasks when Lucy came to find me. 'Mama is at her time,' she said.

I looked at her blankly and carried on with my sewing.

'Come,' she said. 'Put that aside. You and I must to take the little boys for a walk and when we return it will all be over and our new brother or sister will be here.'

Summoned to Aunt's room, I entered slowly, my head down, my shoulders bowed.

'Sit here, Fanny,' said Aunt, 'and hold your new brother.'

I looked up in astonishment. '*I*?'

'Gussie has told me that you favour the name William, and Uncle and I are agreed it is a fine choice. He is to be William Albany and, as you have named him, you must be the first to meet him.'

I sat by the bed and let Helen lower William into my arms. Gazing at his crescent fingernails and the slight curves of his tiny eyebrows, I put my finger against his hand and he seized it in his fist.

'You see,' said Aunt. 'He loves you already.'

AUCKLAND, 1847

With Johnny's departure, relations between Lucy and her husband again became strained. She withdrew to her room for long periods and showed no interest in my suggested expeditions or even in riding with me. I had hoped that when the Governor left for the south she might recover her spirits a little but, despite all my attempts to coax her from her low humour, she remained confined to her bed. I was on the point of seeking advice from Lady Martin when the Governor returned unexpectedly.

He limped into the drawing room where I was sitting alone with my needlework. 'Ah, Miss Fanny. I thought perhaps Eliza was . . .'

I sought for an excuse. 'She's retired to bed early. She was feeling rather fatigued.'

'Or she may be developing another *crise des nerfs*. May I join you for a moment?'

'Certainly. Would you like me to ring for late supper?'

'No, thank you. I've taken a little medication but, at the present moment, I have no stomach for any kind of nourishment.'

I saw that he looked exhausted, his face pallid and drained. He continued to stare at the fire for some time, then he said, almost inaudibly, 'I have just returned from Wellington.'

I nodded.

'The state of affairs there is most troubling.'

A silence.

'I have no wish to alarm you by discussing such matters.'

'I'm not easily alarmed,' I said. 'I should be interested to hear of the situation in the south.'

I saw his hand pressing hard against his upper thigh, a gesture Lucy had told me meant his old hip wound was troubling him.

'May I ask, Miss Fanny,' he said suddenly, 'whether you've ever suffered from nervous affliction?'

'No, never.'

'Mrs Selwyn, too, has such attacks. I believe the climate here may in some way contribute to their onset . . . And yet Lady Martin, for all her other infirmities, seems untroubled by them . . .'

'You mentioned that there were difficulties in Wellington.'

The Governor sighed. 'The Colonial Secretary has drawn up and sent me the most ridiculous constitution imaginable. The country is to be divided into two provinces, New Ulster in the north, New Munster in the south, each with its own lieutenant-governor, and I am to be Governor-in-Chief.'

'Surely that would ease your burdens a little?'

'No, it would merely increase them. Only those literate in English will be permitted to vote. And, since the Maoris greatly outnumber the settlers, here in the North about four and a half thousand settlers would be placed in jurisdiction over more than a hundred thousand disenfranchised natives. It is a recipe for war.'

'But I understood the natives' rights are enshrined in the Treaty.'

The Governor snorted. 'I've received another letter from the Colonial Secretary in which he writes that I'm to uphold the Treaty of Waitangi — except at those times when I may be forced to ignore it!'

Even in the low lamplight, I could see that the tip of his nose had begun to redden, a sign, as I had observed before, of mounting anger.

'And, to add to these burdens, there's been another vile murder, this time at Whanganui. When Eliza hears of it, it may precipitate a further deterioration in her health.'

'Need she hear of it?'

'Within a few days it will be in all of the newspapers and spoken of everywhere. It was a particularly bloodthirsty attack on a woman and her children.'

'But I thought the natives never attack the defenceless, that they scorn such cowardly acts?'

'In general, you are correct. But this was not in any way a usual occurrence. And now the settlers are demanding more troops to protect them and we simply don't have the numbers needed for such permanent garrisons. The entire south is in uproar over this latest outrage.'

'What provoked such an attack?'

The Governor was quiet for a time, and seemed almost to have forgotten my presence. I reached forward and laid another log on the dying fire.

'It arose from a misunderstanding,' he said at last. 'A soldier at the Whanganui garrison was cleaning his rifle, accidentally discharged it and wounded his Maori servant. The injury was minor and the servant shrugged it off as a trifle, but someone from his tribe carried word of it upriver and a party of his kinsmen set out for the settlement to exact revenge. Then, on their way into the township, they came across an out-settler, a Mr Gilfillan, and his eldest son, at work on their farm.'

'They attacked them?'

'Yes, wounding Gilfillan very severely in the neck with a tomahawk. But the Gilfillans managed to get the edge of the attackers and raced furiously to their homestead, rushed inside and barricaded the doors and windows.'

'And?'

'The doors began to give under the furious onslaughts of the natives. Mrs Gilfillan, who knew of the Maori code of honour, urged her husband and son to escape through a side door leading to the stable and ride into the town for help while she remained inside with her other five children. She was certain, poor woman, that the natives would not harm them, defenceless as they were.'

'But . . .?'

'She was grievously mistaken. Had it been a raiding party under the command of a chief, she would undoubtedly have been spared. The chiefs' honour is of paramount importance to them. But this was a ragged group of disaffected Maoris, and by the time they had broken down the door I'm in no doubt their passions had increased to frenzy.' He paused. 'The poor woman and three of her children were hacked to pieces, and another child left for dead who, by the grace of God, has now recovered.' He seemed almost at the point of tears. 'One was only an infant.' He covered his eyes with his hand; his voice was so low I could barely hear him. 'After everything the Bishop has done to promote Christian virtues . . . It's too horrible. There's no doubt it was utu, a revenge killing. When the soldier accidentally shot his servant, the bullet grazed the native's face just below the cheekbone. On their arrival at the Gilfillans' farm, the troops found that . . . a piece of Mrs Gilfillan's cheek had been eaten . . . raw . . .'

I stared at him, appalled, and he seemed to recollect himself. 'Miss Fanny, I apologise. I don't know what I was thinking of to have spoken to you so. It's quite unforgivable.'

I struggled to overcome my revulsion and speak.

'There's no need to seek my forgiveness, Governor. I'm naturally very shocked by what you've told me, but I'm in no way about to dissolve into the vapours because of it. What I most wish to know is whether it will be possible to find the perpetrators?'

'They've already been apprehended. A group of Maoris, friendly to the government and horrified at the baseness of their fellows, gave chase to the murderers and seized them. Four of them have already been hanged.'

We were both silent. Then the Governor said, 'We're expecting reinforcements from Sydney and England. The 58th Regiment is to return here very soon.'

'I'm sure that will heighten morale.'

'Perhaps, if you would be kind enough . . . if you feel it possible . . . to tell a rather gentler version of this frightful story to Eliza, it might mitigate its effects on her.'

'Of course. I'll do so tomorrow. But for now, I'll bid you goodnight, Governor. I feel sure you must be in need of rest.'

I was almost out of the room when he called me back. 'Miss Fanny?'

'Yes?'

'I . . . Your company here is most welcome. I hope you'll feel able to remain with us for a long time. You're a very . . . soothing presence in the household.'

ALBANY, 1837

As Government Resident, Uncle presided over the little local court in Albany. Among the natives and the few Europeans, feuds arose from disputes about land or the shortage of daily necessities, while drunken whalers and sealers regularly fought over women. Each day, a garrison soldier toiled up to Strawberry Hill to report the goings-on in the settlement so that Uncle could write his dispatches for the Colonial Office in London. His official duties discharged, he then joined the older boys and the menservants in clearing large tracts of land for pasture. They were at this work when Lieutenant Stewart arrived to apprise Uncle of the arrival of the *Alligator* and of news that put Uncle in high spirits.

'The Captain of the *Alligator* requests the pleasure of the company of Sir Richard and Lady Spencer, the Misses Mary Ann and Augusta, and Mr Hugh and Mr Edward Spencer to dine aboard the vessel tomorrow evening.'

'Splendid,' said Uncle, and began at once to make preparations. 'We must see to my uniform and decorations. And our means of transport. It is the greatest pity the terrain here doesn't permit the use of the carriage.'

The carriage, which had arrived long ago, was useless on the rocky ground and languished in a large tent some distance from the cottage. The Minang were in the greatest awe of it and refused even to approach the tent, rendering vain all Uncle's efforts to persuade them to assist in creating a flat carriage track.

'We must show that we have not lost sight of true English standards. If we but had the use of the carriage it would afford me the dignity of my station here . . .'

'Your station does not reside in such trappings,' said Aunt soothingly. 'See, Gussie has brought your cross and we shall have Helen polish your medals tomorrow.'

'And my cocked hat? Are the lace and feathers in good repair?'

'Papa?'

'What is it, Liza-Lou?'

'Fanny and I would like to go with you.'

'Quite impossible,' said Aunt. 'You have not been invited.'

'I'm sure if the Captain knew of our existence, he'd most willingly include us.'

'You are not going and that is the end of it,' said Aunt.

'I shall ride Thunder,' said Uncle. 'Perhaps, my dear, Helen might decorate his bridle with a ribbon or two? Hugh, you and Edward will direct the servants in harnessing the mules to the stock cart and setting up chairs in it for your mama and the girls.'

Lucy and I watched as the menservants carried out our three best armchairs.

'No, no,' cried Uncle, appearing suddenly beside us, 'not the blue chair. Look, it has a tear in the armrest. We can't possibly use that — unless, perhaps, Helen can mend it in time.'

'Helen and the other servants are already fully occupied with the outfitting of the girls and the preparation of your lace,' said Aunt, drawn outside by the commotion. 'I doubt any of them will have time.'

'Have we no better furniture? I'm the Resident here. We can't descend to the *Alligator* like peasants in tatters.'

The rest of us watched the procession set off. At its head, on Thunder, rode Uncle, resplendent in his naval uniform and his cross and ribbon of the Order of the Guelph. The sun glinted on his medals, and with every trotting movement the feathers in his cocked hat dipped and fluttered.

'Like a rooster's,' whispered Lucy.

Next came the cart. Aunt sat in the armchair, facing backwards towards us, while on the upright chairs opposite perched Mary Ann and Gussie, fetching in their muslins and shawls and best bonnets. Over the cart swung a canopy constructed from unpicked oilskin mailbags, and above Aunt's head, hoisted on a pole, fluttered the

Union Jack. Hugh and Edward, each wearing one of Uncle's old naval jackets, their mounts tightly reined in, brought up the rear. This curious convoy made its way slowly down the sloping track towards Albany, and we waved and cheered until it vanished from sight. It was almost an hour before we heard the boom of the *Alligator*'s guns announcing their arrival.

'But,' said Lucy, 'now I see what a nonsense has been created of such a small thing, I wouldn't give a pin's fee to dine aboard the *Alligator*.'

Mary Ann and Gussie had acquired suitors, Mr Arthur Trimmer and Captain Egerton-Warburton, whom they had met at the dinner aboard the *Alligator*. Within a month, both young men has asked Uncle's leave to call on us and, by the end of their visits, Mr Trimmer had sought permission to marry Mary Ann and Captain Egerton-Warburton had asked for Gussie's hand, and each proposal had been accepted.

'So now,' said Lucy, 'they'll spend all their lives on isolated farms at the Swan River and never have a chance to return to Lyme.'

'And what sort of lives would they lead in Lyme if they were to return?' I asked. 'Governesses? Ladies' companions? Mr Trimmer and Captain Egerton-Warburton have prospects. Mary Ann and Gussie are in love with them. And our sisters have such agreeable natures they will be happy anywhere.'

'Well, at least we are to be bridesmaids and have a double wedding party. That will be fine fun.'

'Yes, indeed it will,' I said, but try as I might I could not shake off my feelings of sorrow and abandonment. The Spencers were as kind and loving to me as any blood relations, yet I continued to ache for my own lost family, for our familiar house, for Lyme. Despite the excitement of wedding preparations, I became assailed by nameless fears, slept fitfully and dreamt constantly of the visit to the fortune-teller in Rio. My night visions were peopled with grinning devilish faces and evil murmurings, the ragged remnants of which clouded my waking, gradually dispersing as the day progressed but returning when I lay down to sleep. So occupied was the rest of the household in wedding preparations that my increasing withdrawal from the daily activities went unnoticed. Only Lucy, woken by my night-time tossings and feverish mutterings, quizzed me as to what was wrong.

'Last night, you kicked me almost black and blue, then you cried out that we were in mortal danger and must sail off from Rio at once.'

'I . . . I'm sorry,' I said.

'Well, it's of no real matter. But if you kick again tonight, I shall wake you immediately.' She paused. 'It's strange you should talk of Rio. Do you remember that old woman in the hovel where Papa took us?'

My chest tightened.

'I could recall almost nothing after, except that I should reign like a queen, but Gussie has the most prodigious memory. Long ago, she writ down nearly every word of it and I believe she has it almost pat.'

'I . . .'

'Though not quite all. None of us knew what the old crone whispered to you at the end, before you . . . before we left. Papa said he could hear nothing of what she said.'

The tightness in my chest subsided a little, but I woke next morning with a pain around my heart, a dull ache of misery that clutched at me and drove me out of doors to seek some respite from it. The wind blew remorselessly; huge strips of bark hung forlornly from the trunks of the eucalyptus trees; and, as I gazed around at the utter emptiness of the landscape, I ached again for Lyme with its crowded streets, its clustered houses, its jostle of people, for Mama, Papa . . . Suddenly, there appeared in front of me the great mulberry tree from our garden, its canopy of branches offering me familiar shelter. I ran towards it. It dissolved like a phantom. I stared about me in disbelief; was I mad? This is a warning, I thought wildly. Since my arrival in Albany, I have not chanted a single word of my magical incantations, never concocted one of my secret spells. This is a punishment for my dereliction of duty. The pain growing in my chest is an intimation of my death. The need for a place to hide overwhelmed me, and I looked about for somewhere — anywhere — I might safely and secretly recite aloud a protective rhyme, an invocation . . .

Ahead of me loomed the tent in which the carriage was now housed, the tent that was almost never visited, that the Minang refused even to approach. Oblivious to the sound of scuttling rodent feet, I pushed my way through the heavy folds of its entrance and, not thinking what I did, clambered into the carriage and sank onto its dusty buttoned seat. At once I was enveloped by a familiar smell from long ago, a musty mix of leather and beeswax, exactly like the scents I had breathed in with Mama when . . . My heart raced . . . It was indeed the same smell; this was the very same carriage. Here, on this seat, Mama and I had sat together, in Lyme, and she had told me I was to have lessons with the Spencer girls. I tried to recollect her face, to bring her back to me, to remember her eyes, her hair, her voice . . . But I could not. She was entirely gone from me. All that remained was this carriage waft of polish and harness.

Something tight and hard in my chest broke, and I began to weep. Great sobs tore from my throat, tears poured across my face, my whole body racked and heaved. I wept for Mama, for William and Baby Louisa, for Papa, for my lost home in Lyme. I cried until I had no more tears, then exhaustion overcame me and I lay down on the grimy seat and fell asleep.

I awoke feeling lighter than I had done for many months. My face was swollen and hot but the pain in my chest had gone entirely. I sat up and lowered my feet onto the iron step of the carriage. As I moved, I heard hissing. Coiled on the ground by the tent flap was a tiger snake.

I stood, transfixed, on the step. Beneath its jutting brow ridges, the snake's dark eyes held mine. I could not break my gaze and dared not move or call out. Its evil forked tongue flicked in and out of its mouth. Uncoiling itself, it slithered nearer, and a narrow slit of light from the tent flap shone briefly on the dark scales of its flat, blunt head. I watched, helpless, as it raised itself up a little, its tongue still darting at me. Its neck flattened as its mouth opened, revealing a hideous pink cavern with fangs on either side. I could not utter a sound but I knew that, even were I to scream, no one would hear me. Not a soul knew where I was. The snake swayed a little. It will make a sudden strike, I thought, then I will feel the poison of its venom slowly filling my body. And then, said another voice in my head, you will be reunited with Mama and Papa in Heaven . . . But what of Lucy, of dear Aunt and Uncle, of Baby William? said my other self. 'I am not ready to die,' I said aloud. 'Not yet.' Life seemed suddenly very dear to me. I desired nothing more than to skip from the prison of the tent to the house, to whisper secrets with Lucy, to see William smiling at me . . .

The snake hissed more loudly. I stood on the step, attempting in my terror to invoke some form of miraculous incantation. Then, I heard again in my head the words of Ellen's grandam's spell:

They divil take they wicked soul,
And bring they cruelty down,
They divil take, thee, wicked one . . .

There was a scurrying beneath the carriage and a rat darted towards the tent flap. In an instant, the snake swung its gaze from me, launched itself at the creature, seized it in its jaws and, slithering between the tent folds, bore it away.

I stood watching it, shaking uncontrollably but still unable to run. It was some minutes before I reclaimed my senses, stepped down tentatively from the carriage and, stamping my feet heavily on the ground, raced from the tent back to the house. Never had the air tasted cleaner, the sun seemed brighter, or my surroundings more desirable. Happiness swept over me as I burst into the house and embraced dear, startled Aunt.

'Why, Fanny,' she said, 'where have you been? Lucy has been looking for you everywhere. You girls are to be fitted for your bridesmaids' dresses.'

'What news from Perth and the Swan River?' asked Uncle.

Governor Hutt, who had come from Perth for our sisters'

weddings, sighed. 'The usual troubles. It's obvious the Colonial Office has no idea of our situation here . . . which reminds me, I've just had a Captain Grey call on me with a note of introduction from the Colonial Secretary. He wants to mount an expedition to explore north-west of the Swan River. He's convinced an inland waterway system exists in the interior.'

'Like other fools before him. Surely you're not prepared to support such an idiotic venture?'

'How can I refuse? And I'm not asked to fund the enterprise, merely to provide a schooner and as much information as I can. Besides, Grey is exceedingly well connected. He's a protégé of Archbishop Whately.'

'Ah,' said Uncle, 'connections. The cornerstones of every man's fortune.'

Engrossed in the journals and newspapers Governor Hutt had brought from Perth, Gussie and I were exclaiming over the London fashions when Lucy burst in on us.

'*Mama*,' she cried, 'I can't believe you didn't tell us before! Papa says you— How *could* you? How *could* Papa?'

'I have no idea what you're talking about,' said Aunt. 'Sit down and compose yourself.'

Lucy threw herself onto a chair.

'Now,' said Aunt, 'please to tell me in a civilised manner what's brought about such a childish tantrum.'

'I was . . . I went for a walk with Papa,' began Lucy, then, to our astonishment, broke into a storm of weeping.

Aunt rose in alarm. 'Has something happened to Papa?'

'No, no.'

'Then you're a cruel and foolish girl to frighten me so. Now, what is causing all this to-do?'

Her face flushed, her hands plucking at her skirts, Lucy struggled to contain herself. She took a deep breath and, choking on her words, finally managed to speak. 'Papa has sold Cobb House.'

Gussie was aghast. '*Sold* it? Why?'

'Because,' said Aunt, 'we have no need of a house on the other side of the world and the money from the sale of Cobb House will provide a great many of the things we require here.'

'So we're never going back?'

'No, Lucy, and I don't ever recall any mention of our returning to Cobb House.'

Lucy gave way to a fury of weeping.

I had never before seen Aunt so angry. 'Go immediately to your room,' she said, 'and remain there till you've regained your proper temper.'

Lucy did not appear at table that evening. At bedtime, I knocked before entering our room.

'Who is it?' Her voice was muffled.

'Fanny.'

As she opened the door, I saw her face was puffy and her eyes were red, but whether her tears were of rage, sorrow or contrition I had no idea. I said nothing as I slipped from my clothes and climbed into bed in my shift.

'It's too bad. It's quite the most wicked thing for Papa to do.'

'I don't think you should speak so.'

'It's all very well for you, Fanny. You still have your own beautiful house in Lyme.'

I found this exceedingly cruel. 'How can you say that? I have no house in Lyme. Or anywhere.'

'You do. It's let by an agent at present, but I heard Mama and Papa discussing it. When you're of age, it will be yours to do with as you like. Whereas I . . .'

I was astounded by this intelligence which Lucy clearly believed to be true. 'Poor Aunt,' I said, 'has been crying.'

She ignored this. 'It's been a most terrible day. When Papa and I set out on our walk we climbed up to the lookout. And Papa said' — her voice broke — '"I want you to mind what I say very well, Liza-Lou. It's only to you that I intend to commit this confidence. It would simply distress your poor mama. Do you see this place where I'm now standing? When the time comes, it's here that I wish to be buried." I was alarmed to hear him speak so. I told him that I loved him too much ever to let him leave us.

'And then Papa said, "Now you must promise me, Liza-Lou, that when I die, you will ensure that I am buried here. This is the place I have chosen. Do you give me your word?" So I gave my promise, though I heartily wished our conversation over. And then he said he had a second wish.'

'Which was?'

'That English sailors should be ordered to cut a flagpole from native timber and erect it over his grave, and the White Ensign must fly from it so that — and these were his actual words, Fanny — "I may lie below the flag under which I have so often fought."'

'You promised?'

'Yes, but then I asked him why he wouldn't want to be buried in Lyme after our return there. And he told me that Cobb House had been sold. I . . . I can't remember exactly what I did. I know I ran back to the house. I—'

'I think you should sleep now and tomorrow you must go to Aunt and tell her you're sorry. But you must *on no account* tell her a single word of what passed between you and Uncle.'

'I'll do it for her sake, and yours, Fanny, but you must know I'm not at all sorry for what I said.'

'You're just like Uncle,' I said. 'Mulish and always right. No wonder he loves you the best of all of us.'

And I saw that, in some strange way, this comforted her.

III

ALBANY, 1839

'Now, I must tell you all of a case which will come before me tomorrow,' said Uncle, as we sat at supper. 'Last Friday, Lieutenant Stewart apprehended an Aboriginal woman for stealing a chemise from a washing line in Albany. He wishes me to impose a strict sentence on her to set an example to the Aborigines, but I'm inclined to be lenient with her. We've spent so long urging the Minang to cover themselves that . . .'

Suddenly, his face contorted in a spasm, his limbs began to twitch and jerk uncontrollably, and foam frothed from his mouth. For some minutes, he struggled against the paroxysm, then the seizure abated and he fell forward, lifeless, across the table. So swift and unexpected was it, for some moments we could only stare in hopeless terror.

Uncle was buried at the place he had chosen. We gathered in the winter cold for the service which, since Albany had no clergyman and there was no vessel in the harbour carrying a ship's chaplain, was read by Mr Steele, the deputy district magistrate.

'But when the flagstaff is erected,' said Aunt, 'we shall hold another service, led by an ordained clergyman.'

Though Lieutenant Stewart daily sent a working party of convicts and guards from Albany-town to work on the farm, the house was pervaded by a feeling of emptiness; a great reservoir of energy and bustle had vanished, leaving us rudderless and drifting. Lucy did not weep as Gussie and I did, but withdrew into silence. She no longer complained about the dullness of our lives or argued her opinions with the rest of us but, ignoring my attempts to comfort her, went off for hours by herself. Sent by Aunt one day to search for her, I found her standing beside Uncle's grave.

'You should come back to the house. Aunt is worried about you.'

'I must stay here, near Papa.'

I hesitated. 'You know that Governor Hutt arrives very soon from Perth with . . . with Uncle's replacement?'

'I can't bear to think of anyone in Papa's place.'

'Governor Hutt will choose someone skilled and capable.'

'I shall detest anyone who isn't my dearest, dearest papa.'

Governor Hutt took Aunt's hand in his. 'My dear Lady Spencer, may I offer you my sincerest condolences.'

'Thank you, Governor.'

I took in the Governor's companion, whose military bearing made him seem taller than his six feet. His curly dark brown hair was smoothed down so that only at the sides did it escape into little quarter-ringlets. He sported discreet side-whiskers, and his dark grey eyes were set deep below a high and noble brow. Coupled with a long, straight nose and determined chin, these features at first lent his face a handsome aspect, but closer inspection revealed something of petulance to his mouth. Overall, the combination contrived to produce the effect of effeminacy, and I surmised that in his early years he had been indulged and petted.

'Ma'am,' said Governor Hutt, 'this is a most painful duty but I must perform it. Until we hear from London, I am obliged to appoint an Acting Resident Magistrate here in Albany. I believe most sincerely that your husband would have approved of my choice. May I present to you, Lady Spencer, Captain George Grey?'

Captain Grey moved into one of the larger cabins on our property. Aunt found his presence congenial and he was most courteous and attentive to her. It did not take long for him to win her affections and those of the youngest Spencer boys, William, who was already four, Richard seven, and Robert and Joseph, ten and eleven.

'I have younger half-brothers,' he explained, 'of whom I'm very fond.'

'Was your mother widowed?' asked Aunt.

'In the Peninsular War, at Badajoz. But when I was five years old, she married my stepfather, the Reverend Sir John Thomas. He was a widower with three daughters and a son, so I have a sister, three step-sisters and a step-brother all older than I, and, from their union, I have four half-sisters and two half-brothers. I miss them all excessively.'

'Good gracious,' said Aunt. 'I've lost count already.'

'It comes to twelve in all, Ma'am. Eight girls and four boys.'

'Why, that's exactly the number of my own family. But they are all the progeny of my late husband, and two, who died as infants, lie far off in churchyards in Malta and Portsmouth.'

'It is a great sorrow to lose children in infancy.'

'Ah, yes. I often wonder, had they lived, what manner of grown men they might be.'

It was the first time since Uncle's death that I had heard Aunt engage so long in conversation and, in gratitude, I determined to overcome my initial mistrust of Captain Grey.

That Sunday, as we sat down to our usual morning service, there was a clamour in the yard. It was the Minang, returned from one of their frequent walkabouts. The men swarmed into the house and sat about on the drawing-room floor and the adjacent hallway, while the women and children clustered beneath the windows. Captain Grey, prayer book in hand, gazed at the scene in astonishment.

'Is this a daily occurrence, Ma'am?'

'They are come to hear the service, Captain.'

The Aborigines regarded Captain Grey with interest and gave every appearance of following his words intently. Then, to our amazement, having finished with the Our Father, the Captain commenced to speak to them in their own tongue.

'Fanny!'

'I'm here in the garden, Aunt. With Robert. We've just collected the vegetables for dinner.'

'Thank goodness. Lucy is in the drawing room quarrelling

violently with Captain Grey. Listen.'

From the window floated Lucy's voice, her words indistinguishable but her tone excited and argumentative.

'Go in at once, Fanny, and deflect her.'

'She's surely not alone with him?'

'No, no. Richard and William are there, but you know how headstrong she is.'

I pushed open the drawing-room door and entered. Occupied with lead soldiers, Richard and William were taking little notice of anything around them.

The Captain rose and bowed.

Lucy took my arm. 'As you see, Fanny, the Captain and I are engaged in a most spirited argument.'

'Not too spirited, I trust.'

'We've been speaking of the mutiny on HMS *Bounty*, Miss Fanny.'

'And Captain Grey asserts that, no matter what the provocation, the mutineers were in all respects at fault, whereas I say—'

'The laws of the Navy are unequivocal. The mutineers were nothing more than pirates.'

'No, no, Captain. Poor Mr Heywood cannot be deemed a pirate. And Captain Bligh was a most brutal master. Didn't Papa himself say so, Fanny?'

I nodded.

'If standards and codes of conduct were not strictly enforced, the Navy would be entirely enfeebled, and then who would protect our High Seas?'

'It is not a question of enforcement but of justice. The law should never be enforced against innocent men.'

I determined to change the subject to something less contentious. 'I see you will never concur,' I said, 'so you must agree to differ. I wonder, Captain Grey, if Lucy has shown you her botanic specimens and drawings?'

'The Captain has no wish to bother himself with my modest scratchings.'

'You're in error, Miss Lucy. I should very much like to see them.'

'For all his air of self-satisfaction,' said Lucy, 'I must own the Captain has certain merits.'

'Which are . . .?'

'He believes poor people should be given grants of land. He says that as long as Irish landlords are absent and the church does nothing to ameliorate the situation there, the insurrections will continue.'

I squinted at the tree I was sketching. 'Oh, I have my perspective all wrong . . . Is Captain Grey a Whig, then?'

'He says the Whig reforms have done nothing to assist the Irish peasantry, but I suppose him more a Whig than a Tory.'

'Like Uncle.'

'Ah yes. If only Papa were here to interrogate the Captain, they would have many a fine argument, you can be sure.'

There, I disagreed strongly with Lucy, but I forbore to say so.

The late September native wild flowers were blooming in abundance as we struck out on the slopes of nearby Mount Clarence for a picnic organised by Aunt and Captain Grey.

'I notice you're limping, Captain,' said Aunt. 'Have you injured yourself?'

'No, Ma'am. It's an old injury I sustained when I was on my expedition to seek for inland waterways north of Perth. I was speared in the thigh by a native. Several Aborigines had been stalking us for some days, and one of our party very foolishly fired in their direction, so they retaliated.'

'But surely the wound should have healed by now?'

'The Aborigines anoint their weapons with poisonous substances. It's not simply the lesion itself but the toxin which prevents it from healing.'

'And now,' said Lucy, joining us, 'I'm off to search for new specimens for my album.'

'But I'm a collector of plants myself. If I may be permitted to accompany you . . .' Captain Grey turned to Aunt. 'Will you allow me to escort Miss Lucy, Ma'am?'

'Certainly, but you must take Fanny with you, if she's willing.'

We three set off together, but I soon fell a little behind their steady pace. At one point, I lost sight of them completely, and when I caught them up, the Captain was kneeling close beside Lucy, assisting her in the digging up of a plant. As she rose, he placed a solicitous hand below her elbow to help her to her feet. I had never before known Lucy in need of help to rise, nor seen her blush. Their sparring seemed to have abated and he listened attentively as she pointed out the features and habits of various specimens.

'Your knowledge is exceptional, Miss Lucy,' he said, 'and equalled only by your powers of observation and meticulous record-keeping. I should like to send some drawings of what you've collected to my friend, Mr Robert Brown, at the British Museum. He's a noted horticulturist and I'm sure they'd interest him greatly.'

'I can't imagine for one moment—'

'If you permit, I'll enclose a covering letter.'

Nothing the Captain might have offered could have gratified Lucy more. I saw at once, as I am sure he did, that not merely her attention but her affections were engaged. They walked on, talking animatedly. We descended Mount Clarence, the Captain laden with Lucy's plant specimens, she with her sketch book and I trailing behind, my head full of speculation.

That evening, Lucy took me aside. 'Oh, Fanny, Captain Grey is so intelligent.'

'Yes.'

'And so heroic. He has such courage and high principles.'

'Perhaps . . .'

'Well, don't you at least think him handsome?'

'I'm sure he is.'

'But you don't like him?'

'Not at all. I mean . . . I . . . like him well enough. Of course I do.'

'Well, I have something important to tell you. Come over here beside me. Now,' she took my hand, 'you'll never guess . . .' She paused. 'The Captain has asked me to marry him, Fanny.'

'*Marry* him?'

'Yes, and I've accepted him. I'm sixteen, I'm of age, and I'm sure we'll have Mama's blessing. And you shall be my bridesmaid.'

'But . . . this is so sudden. Are you in love with him?'

'I greatly respect his bravery and his intellect and judgement. I shall look to him for guidance and the furtherance of my own studies.'

As I kissed her, I felt a sense of unease. She did not bear the same bloom of happiness that had transformed Mary Ann and Gussie at their engagements. 'If this is what you truly desire, Lucy,' I said, 'I'm very glad for you. When is the ceremony to be?'

'On the second of November.'

'But that's less than five weeks away.'

'George sees no advantage in delaying. There's a ship due in the last week of October so we can have the services of an ordained clergyman. Now, Fanny, you must smile and rejoice with me. This is news to cheer us all. And once we're married, I'll set about finding a suitor for *you*.'

'I'm not yet fifteen, Lucy. I've no wish to marry.'

'Be careful. You don't want to end up an old maid marooned here in Albany forever.'

Lucy's wedding was a much simpler affair than the festivities we had had for Mary Ann and Gussie. With barely five weeks in which to organise the celebration, it was clear that neither Mary Ann nor Gussie and their husbands would be able to travel in time from the Swan River, so I was to be the only female attendant. Hugh gave away the bride and Edward served as the groom's best man, while Robert, Richard and William were somewhat reluctant page-boys. Aunt cried much at the ceremony but I believe they were tears of remembrance of her own happy marriage.

Since Captain Grey could not put aside his official duties, the newlyweds did not take a honeymoon but remained with us at Strawberry Hill. The Captain removed from his cabin and he and Lucy took over the larger bedroom that had been shared by Mary Ann and Gussie. I had expected that Lucy's new status might create an awkwardness between us, but as she was still living with us, and her husband was so was fully occupied, we passed our days together much as before. Apart from discharging his duties as Resident, Captain

Grey was engaged in finishing a work begun in Perth, his *Vocabulary of the Dialects Spoken by the Aborigine Races of South Australia*. Lucy was openly admiring of his scholarship and continually shushed the little boys so they did not disturb him at his writing. And when he was free, they spent their time in collecting plants for Lucy's new enterprise, an album of drawings and descriptions intended for Mr Brown at the British Museum.

We had been living in this manner for only a few months when Lucy came running into the drawing room one afternoon, waving a letter. 'It's from the Colonial Office in London. You'll never believe it! George has been recalled to *England*. We're to sail in early March.'

'But that's barely a month off,' said Aunt, in dismay. 'Am I to lose you so soon?'

'Oh, Mama, dearest Mama, it won't be forever. George will be given another posting and he's certain it will be in South Africa, or perhaps even here in Australia.'

'South Africa is very far off and even New South Wales is scarcely close to us.'

'But we shall be in England. *Home.* You must rejoice for me, I beg you. I'm to meet George's dear family and see all the places he's described to me.' She flung her arms about Aunt's neck. 'Dearest Mama, say you're pleased for me.'

'Of course I am,' said Aunt quietly. 'But I shall rejoice even more to see you back again.'

'And you, my darling Fanny, say you are pleased for me, too.'

'I am . . . but I'll miss you so much.'

'I promise I'll write to you, all of you, every day that I'm away.'

We laughed at this extravagant vow.

'No, I *swear* I shall.'

AUCKLAND, 1847

'Do you know, Fanny, in all the time we were in England, I never returned to Lyme. I longed to, and my husband promised we would, but he was appointed so suddenly to the governorship in Adelaide we had almost no time to do any of the things we had planned. We spent most of our time in Bodiam with George's family, or in London with his dear Aunt Julia.'

'You said in your letters that you liked his family very much.'

'Exceedingly so, and my particular favourites were Aunt Julia and George's younger half-brother, Godfrey Thomas. He was most amusing and organised such agreeable entertainments for all the family. We often went riding and had the greatest fun together. Oh, Fanny, you would so love London! We saw all the sights and we had such a gay time. Aunt Julia is a very well-educated lady but she has no children, so she devotes herself to good works and literary matters. George is greatly attached to her and I was disposed to like her very much.'

'And your mother-in-law?'

'Lady Thomas was also exceedingly kind to me and took me about often with her at Bodiam. Coming from Australia, I was quite a curiosity, but it was strange to me to see what erroneous notions many people held about life there. At one soirée, a lady asked me how many times we had had to fend off the natives with our spears, and another how often we were forced to eat snake and kangaroo.'

I laughed. 'Did you tell them about the Minang?'

'No. I thought better of it. But Godfrey was so inspired by George's accounts that he decided to visit Australia himself. He came to us at Adelaide before we left.'

'I don't recall . . .'

'No. I fear I was a dreadful correspondent at that time. But as soon as he arrived he seemed to dispel the gloom of Government House. I was charged with getting a suitable mount for him, and he and I made a number of expeditions together on horseback which afforded us both great pleasure. The very day after his arrival, we took our horses through the swampland to the beach where we enjoyed a gallop along the wet sand, though my horse, Selim, was uneasy with the surf curling about his feet and shied several times. Then Godfrey persuaded George that the three of us should ride in the countryside out of Adelaide and camp overnight in tents in the bush. I was reminded of our very first days in Albany. Do you remember, Fanny, how we were obliged to sleep in tents on the beach?'

'Very well.'

'And Godfrey organised parties and a ball at Government House, and George who, as you know, can be so very parsimonious, was quite convinced of the necessity for a little light entertainment.'

I observed how the more she spoke of her brother-in-law, the more animated she became.

'Godfrey said we should consider ourselves truly fortunate to be involved in the "Great Adventure" of living in an infant colony. He believes that, in a settlement such as Adelaide, where one is thrown into the society of those whom one would never naturally meet at Home, a man of merit discovers his true nature. And when I expressed concern that my husband was so overworked, Godfrey assured me that it has ever been in George's nature to be diligent and meticulous, and it is these qualities which render him so statesmanlike.'

'In that, I am sure he's quite right.'

'But you can't believe how much easier in manner my husband became with Godfrey present. George was determined to find some government position for him, and when his secretary left for Home, he decided that there was no better candidate to replace him than his brother, so we enjoyed Godfrey's society until we left for New Zealand. I miss him exceedingly.'

'It's a pity he couldn't accompany you here.'

'There was no post for him. George inherited his predecessor's secretary, a Mr Cooper.'

Recalling Lady Martin's conversation, I kept my voice carefully neutral. 'And was he also . . . lively?'

She sighed. 'He was every bit as entertaining and full of fun as Godfrey but . . . my husband was . . . obliged to let him go.' She turned the thin gold ring I had noticed before on the little finger of her right hand. 'Before Mr Cooper left, he gave me this.'

'A *ring*? Lucy, what were you thinking of to have accepted it? Surely your husband doesn't know?'

'Oh, Fanny, you are wearing your parochial face again. Of course my husband doesn't know. And it was not any sort of promise or love token . . .'

'Are you sure?'

'Quite certain. It was a mark of friendship, he said. It belonged to his sister who died young.'

'Then *of course* it was a token. Lucy, I beg you, be careful. Your husband is a jealous man, and if he became aware that another man was paying court to you he would have every right to—'

'Mr Cooper was *not* paying court to me. All we did was to ride out together and take pleasure in each other's society. It was certainly not criminal conversation, if that is what you mean. It was no more than the sort of entertainment I enjoyed with Godfrey.'

'But Mr Godfrey is your brother-in-law. Surely you can see the difference?'

For a moment, Lucy looked sulky. 'If my husband were more inclined to wish for my society—'

'Stop!' I said. 'And think about how your actions might have brought you into real danger. It would be utter foolishness to cross the Governor.'

'Well,' she said, 'it's always possible that Godfrey may join us here now George is in want of a secretary. Godfrey's so thoughtful, you know. After we left Adelaide, he did his best to reclaim our old Aboriginal servant, Nancy.'

'Nancy?'

'Yes, we took her from the Mission, though she was a far from ideal servant. But when we left, she threw aside her English clothes and lived like a savage, wrapped in a tattered blanket by the Torrens River near the old City Bridge. Godfrey said she was the picture of misery but all his efforts proved hopeless. So you see how kind he is.'

'Yes,' I said, my thoughts in turmoil.

In the February heat, when Lucy and I were alone together in the garden, I had fallen into the habit of dispensing with my stockings and shoes, the better to enjoy the feel of the grass under my feet.

'Fanny, you are becoming like a native, walking about barefoot.'

'Yes, indeed,' I said, wriggling my toes, freed from their usual confinement. 'Very soon, I shall adopt a flax skirt and have my chin tattooed.'

Lucy pointed a mock-admonishing finger at me. 'That settles it! I am quite determined now on finding you a husband.'

'You may spare yourself the trouble,' I said, 'I have no wish to marry *anyone*.'

'But why not? Sooner or later all women must marry.'

'Not necessarily. At the moment, I can see no possible advantage in marrying. I'm an independent woman with an income of my own. If I were to take a husband, my property and income would immediately become his to do with as he wished and I'd have no more control over my own life than that which he permitted me.'

'True. But if you were to fall in love?'

'Then I might change my mind. But, for now, I'm quite content as I am.' I stretched out my legs on the grass. 'And you still haven't given me my audience with John Heke, you know.'

'I thought we were agreed he is already spoken for. Lieutenant Cowan, on the other hand . . .'

'I am certainly not in love with the Lieutenant. Or anyone else.'

'But don't you sometimes long for romance?'

I considered this. I was not entirely sure what was meant by romance. Courtship? Passion? The delight in another's company? I remembered Mary Ann and Gussie and their animation in the company of their suitors. Now they were both mothers, settled at the Swan River, and had seemed on their rare visits to Albany to be quite contented with their lot. But when I recalled Lucy as she had been before and after her marriage, I felt no desire to emulate her. As far as I could judge, romance was a fleeting state, maybe even one of delusion, designed to bring about conjugal union and propagate the species.

'I'm not sure I believe in romance,' I said.

Lucy groaned. 'Oh Fanny, what *am* I to do with you? If you go on like this, you will die an old maid.'

I reflected on this conversation as I lay later that night in my bed, the heat-swollen timbers of Government House creaking and rasping around me as they shrank again in the cooler night air. I thought of myself within the Spencer family, of how, though they had treated me entirely as their own, I had felt always an observer — a watcher, not a participant. But, I told myself, this had been my habit long before. I recalled myself within the embrace of my mulberry tree, eavesdropping on Martha and Joseph, spying on Ellen or Papa, studying Mama zealously for indications of her mood . . . And if the family mirrors the wider world, even a colony such as Auckland is but a greater reflection of the web of kinship within that first microcosm. Is this, perhaps, the reason I am so reluctant to give up my independence, I wondered, why to marry is of no interest to me?

ALBANY, 1845

'Fanny, my dear,' said Aunt, 'I have something I must show you.'

I laid aside the sampler I was embroidering, followed her to her bedroom and waited while she rummaged in a drawer. Gazing at her pretty Empire-style dressing table, I recalled the rough box with its muslin curtain which had served for her toilette when first we arrived at Strawberry Hill.

'Sit down here,' said Aunt, indicating her footstool. 'I wish to speak to you of important matters.'

I sat, a trifle apprehensively.

'Perhaps I should have waited until you're a little older,' said Aunt, 'but I feel I should not leave this matter any longer.'

She held out a long envelope, sealed with red wax.

'This is for you, Fanny. But as your dear father apprised me of them, I know its contents. It contains a copy of his Will and the deeds to the house in Lyme. The house is let now but in November, when you attain your majority, it will be yours to do with it as you wish. You have a sizeable income, Fanny, all held in trust for you by your papa's solicitor in Lyme. He's a good, honest man and, when the time comes, you may have confidence in his advice.'

I stared, bewildered.

'And here,' continued Aunt, 'I have something for you which I very much hope will please you. You're a good, loving girl and, as you know, we all regard you as one of our own, but your dearest mother loved you very much and it's fitting you should have some keepsake and memento of her. When you are twenty-one, her jewellery and effects will come to you. In the meantime, this is for you to remember her by.'

She passed me a small package.

I opened it and drew out a brooch, a cameo I recognised instantly as a likeness of my mama.

'Look carefully, Fanny. You'll see it's fashioned from a lock of hair. And, do you see, interwoven with that darker blonde lock are tiny strands of paler hair?'

'Yes.'

'They're from your own hair, child. After your mama had left us, I clipped a lock from her head and a ringlet from your own and had them shaped into this piece of mourning jewellery so that you might have your mama with you always.'

Tears fell on my cheeks.

'I have not given it to you before,' said Aunt, 'because I felt it might only excite more grief. But now I believe the time is right for you to have it. I know you will cherish it for your dear mama's sake.'

'For a wonder,' said Aunt, 'we have two ships in the harbour at the same time, so here' — and she indicated a large oiled sack beside the table — 'is another consignment of mail.' She looked at me. 'I think you must have a secret admirer, Fanny. There's a large box addressed to you.'

'There I must disappoint you,' I said. 'It's from London and I ordered it myself.'

'Gracious,' said Aunt, 'what *have* you been up to?'

I cannot remember when I have ever felt quite such pleasure as on opening that box, which I did first alone in my room, after begging Richard and Robert to carry it there for me. Having ascertained that the contents were exactly what I had commissioned, I was then obliged to ask them to transfer it to the drawing room where, after supper, I announced a surprise.

Lifting the lid from the wooden box, I drew out a long cardboard package bearing the name of the fashionable milliner I had gleaned from the London newspapers.

'This is for you, Aunt,' I said, passing it to her. 'A present.'

'But . . .' She looked at the name printed on the lid. 'Surely not for *me*? Are you certain?'

Opening it, she lifted up the layers of paper and gasped when she saw revealed beneath them a most fashionable bonnet of purple silk decorated with black and rose-pink trimmings. 'Why, Fanny, I . . . It's much too fine. And how beautiful.' She stroked the silk with her finger.

'And, there, beside it, are matching kid gloves.'

'Fanny, my dear, I cannot possibly accept such a splendid gift. I can't begin to think how much it must have cost you.' She took up the bonnet and examined it. 'Just look at the workmanship and the exquisite stitching.'

'You must try it on,' I said.

She shook her head.

'Indeed you must, Mama,' said Robert. 'You mustn't injure Fanny's feelings when she has gone to such trouble for you.'

'And *you* mustn't injure my feelings either, 'I said, 'by refusing to accept this.' And I handed Robert another package.

I felt William's gaze upon me. 'Alas, William,' I said, teasing him, as I peered into the box, 'I fear there is nothing at all here for you.'

William was now almost eleven years old and, along with his brothers, was constantly in some scrape or other. Aunt spoke often of her worries about them running wild, and her concern for their education. Since Uncle's death, she had petitioned the Admiralty constantly for his naval pension to be awarded to her but, in almost six years, had never yet received a response. Without funds, she could not consider even hiring a tutor for the boys.

'It's all right, Fanny,' said William, plainly disappointed. 'I was not in expectation of a—'

'Wait!' I cried, inspecting the contents again. 'I believe . . . yes, here it is. *This* is for you. And there's another here for Richard.'

William undid the wrapping. 'A magnifying glass. And with slides. See, Mama. Oh, Fanny, it's magnificent.'

'I have a fine pocket knife,' said Robert.

'And I a fishing rod.'

'But what of yourself?' said Aunt. 'Here we are, all with our splendid gifts and you have nothing.'

'I have a bonnet, too,' I said, 'and a beautiful new frock but the box is a very large one and by no means empty yet. We are *all* to have new clothes, and there are shoes for you and me, and boots for all my brothers. Then, so that we may have a celebration, there's a whole tinned ham, some potted meats, relishes, a tinned Dundee cake, tins of pineapple, strawberry jam and sugared plums, preserved ginger, Madeira wine and—'

'Stop, stop!' cried Robert, 'it's too much. I'm already hungry at the thought of it. Come, we must all kiss Fanny and thank her.'

Aunt drew me aside. 'Fanny, it is so very, very good of you but I'm horrified at the thought of the cost of such extravagant gifts.'

'You're disappointed with your bonnet?'

'Why, it is quite the most beautiful thing I've ever owned, but I do not wish you to spend such enormous sums on us.'

'I would like you to sit down, Aunt. I must talk to you.'

She looked at me in surprise but did as I asked.

'I am rich, Aunt. Not immensely so, but I am very comfortably off and I have no need of such a large sum of money for myself. It gives me the greatest pleasure to be able to indulge you all a little. Only consider how very good you and Uncle have been to me. It's gratifying to be in a position to repay just a fraction of your kindness.'

'Fanny, I won't hear any talk of *repayment*. You have been a joy and pleasure to us, the dearest of daughters. That is quite repayment enough.'

'I am sorry to defy your wishes, Aunt, but I fear I must.'

'Why, Fanny, you are sounding now like Lucy!'

'I have written to my solicitor in Lyme instructing him to give notice to my tenants.'

'You are returning to Lyme?'

'No, Aunt, *you* are going there, with Robert and Richard and William. I have taken the very great liberty of procuring four ship's passages for you all and of depositing a sum of money for your use in Lyme for your living expenses and the boys' education. And while you are there, you may petition the Admiralty directly for your pension.'

'Fanny, I . . . I cannot possibly . . .'

'It is done, Aunt.'

For a moment, Aunt covered her face with her hands. 'Ah,' she whispered, 'Lyme, dear, dear Lyme . . .' She looked up at me. 'I simply don't know what to say to such generosity, Fanny. And you? Are you coming with us?'

I shook my head. 'No,' I said. '*I* am going to New Zealand. To Lucy.'

IV

AOTEAROA

Tihe mauri ora.
Tihe mauri ora.
Tihe mauri ora.

Listen to my words. I was there. I know the truth of what took place. Listen to my story. Listen to my breath. Listen to my confession.

My name is Makareta, but long ago, in the beginning, I was called Hine-moana, the Girl from the Ocean. I was born on Kapiti Island. Men call it an island but, in truth, it is a lone grey mountain rising sharply from the water, brooding alone at the edge of Tai-o-Rehua, the Tasman Sea. Now, I am only a phantom swirling in the sea fog; then, I was of the tribe of the mighty rangatira, Te Rau-paraha.

Te Rau-paraha, the warrior, the eagle, the wily serpent. It was said that he ate the eyes and the sexual parts of the fighters whom he captured, the better to enhance his spirit. It was true. My mother, herself, saw it. He drove off the white settlers and burnt their dwellings, defied the English Government and their powerful Queen. His war canoes penetrated to the farthest reaches of the Southern Island, to the northernmost point of the North. Thousands fled before him. He was a living god; his mana was supreme. Every other tribe lived in terror of him. And so did we, his own people.

Once I was Makareta; now I am a wraith. I did not heed my mother's warnings of the danger of makutu, witchcraft. I boasted that I, too, could cast powerful spells. And that very witchcraft rose up against me and consumed me, so that now my bones lie far from my homeland and I am less than nothing. In my lifetime, I believed I, too, would follow the Broad Path of Tane, treading it across the sea to Hawai'iki. But, when the time came, when the poison of the Serpent caught and burnt me, the way remained barred to me forever. I could not follow my ancestors.

Turned away, I have become a kikokiko, a ghost soul, weeping as I haunt the world I once inhabited. I am the wind in the chimney, the rattle at the window pane, the creak of the stair . . .

Though I move among them, the living cannot see me. Yearning to be again as they are, I peer in at their windows, I stand behind them, blowing a chill wind at their necks, I enter their dreams while they sleep. This is my eternal punishment. I did wrong, I know, but what else could I have done? What power does a woman have, no matter that she is of noble parentage?

I remember nothing at all of my father, though his chiefly blood flows in me. The first man I can recall in our life was not a Maori but a white man.

'Put away prejudice,' said my mother, Kahe. 'A good man is a good man whatever the misfortune of the colour of his skin. And a woman and her children are safe only under the protection of a good man.'

My father was Te Rau-paraha's nephew. His favourite. The son of his treasured older sister, he was beloved even more than the chief's own son, and second only to the chief's son-in-law, brutal Te Rangi-hae-ata. But, as our great leader's mana grew, said my mother, so he became a tyrant, unpredictable in his temper, capricious in his whims, murdering for the sport of it, insatiable in his appetites for women, war and blood. Our tribe lived in impregnable isolation, surrounded on all sides by the sea. Who could invade our stronghold? Where might his dissenters flee? On all sides, mighty Te Rau-paraha commanded the ocean.

But, in time, my father and his friends grew weary of the battles of Te Rau-paraha and Te Rangi-hae-ata, of the endless forays and skirmishes, the alliances forged and broken. Our crops were neglected, our fishing boats idle. In defiance of the laws of the sea-god, Tangaroa, the bodies of the conquered were flung into the deep waters, the circling sharks drawn by the scent of yet more blood.

Then came the day when Te Rau-paraha's tohunga, on reading the omens, refused to disclose their message, saying that he dare not for his life speak them aloud.

When he heard this, the great chief became enraged and attempted to violate the sanctity of the priestly rites, advancing upon his tohunga with his greenstone mere and swearing to kill him for his disobedience. Then my father and his friends, in their own turn, broke the holy laws of tapu by laying hands upon the sacred body of Te Rau-paraha and restraining their leader.

Prevailed upon by Te Rangi-hae-ata, on his father-in-law's behalf, to deliver the message of the gods, the tohunga, in greatest fear and distress, revealed that, at the time of a future fourth full moon, the great chief would be captured and his mana broken.

Incensed, Te Rau-paraha ordered the slaying of his own tohunga, an act against all the laws of Heaven. It was Te Rangi-hae-ata who carried out this vile, unnatural murder before the gathered tribe, cutting off first the tongue and then the privy parts of the priest before despatching him with a merciful blow to the side of his head.

'And now,' said Te Rau-paraha, 'throw his body to the dogs, and when they have had their fill, scatter his remains from the highest cliff-top.'

Much disturbed by the offences of his uncle and the predictions of the tohunga, my father took counsel with his friends, all of them alarmed in great measure by what had taken place. It was agreed among them that they should band together and, by force of arms, overthrow Te Rau-paraha. My father would seek an audience with his uncle and, at a pre-arranged signal, the others would burst in, armed, and together they would kill him. In this way, saved from the ignominy of surrender or defeat, Te Rau-paraha might be permitted to die with his mana preserved.

An hour before the meeting, with darkness already shrouding the sky, a woman appeared by the door of our whare. 'You are betrayed,' she told my father. 'Your uncle is apprised of your plans by a traitor among you. Te Rau-paraha is sending scouts to capture you. He has vowed to wipe out the stain of your treachery from his family. He already holds your mother prisoner and he swears that, before he puts you to death, you will be forced to watch him roast your children and have his warriors dishonour your wife in the presence of the entire tribe. I must flee for my own safety. His rage is uncontrollable. If he should discover I have come to warn you, he will surely kill *me*.'

My mother sank to the ground. 'He would not do this. You are his favourite.'

My father raised her up. 'He will be merciless. It is his way. I have seen him on our war parties. It is too late for me, but you must flee now with our children. Save yourselves and them. Take my fishing canoe and paddle to the mainland. Hurry.'

The woman, still hovering at the door, spoke again. 'On your uncle's orders, your fishing canoe has been holed and destroyed.'

'He has desecrated my *canoe*?'

'Yes. And all our other canoes he had taken away and hidden so no escape is possible for you.'

'You must come with us,' said my mother to my father.

'I cannot. It is enough that you save our children and yourself.'

'Then I will climb the mountain, Tutere-moana, and hide there.'

'If you go to the mountain-top, he will hunt you down and discover you. Go to the sea. Cast yourself on the mercy of Tangaroa and swim to the sanctuary of the Mission at Otaki.'

'*Swim*, Husband? But the mainland is so far distant.'

'It is your only chance. Take these kete. There will be rope on the shore. Quickly! They will be here for me at any moment.'

He took flax cloth, tore it, and with the strips bound my mouth and that of my brother. I was fifteen months old, my brother three years, and we fought as he gagged us.

'Now, Kahe, Wife-of-my-Heart, you must be strong. You cannot reach the shore before they come. Conceal yourselves in the latrine pit at the edge of the pa and wait there until they have taken me. Hurry, I beg you.'

'I will *never* descend into the latrine pit. It is noa, filthy. I should be dishonoured forever.'

'You prefer that other dishonour? I think not. And it is because the pit is noa that I demand you hide there. That is the one place they will never look for you. They will not wish to defile themselves; they will believe you have fled to the mountain-top.'

For a moment they embraced, then, lifting us both, my mother took the kete, crept to the edge of the pa and concealed us in the stinking pit. Minutes later, she heard shouting, and the orange light of flaming torches illuminated our whare. For the last time she saw my father, standing proudly by the doorway to meet his betrayers, as befitted a chief's son. She heard his voice, raised so that she might catch his final words. 'You have no need to bind me. I shall walk to my fate of my own free will.'

Another voice. 'Where is your wife, Kahe Te Rau-o-te-rangi? Where are your children?'

'They are under the protection of the gods.'

'We have orders to set fire to your whare. And all of your possessions. Is your family within?'

'I do not choose to answer you.'

Mired in the unbearable stench of the pit, my mother caught a glimpse of a moving flame which blazed up to light the sky. Forcing herself not to cough in the acrid smoke, she sank lower, pulling us down with her as we fought and struggled against our bindings.

When the fire had died down and my father had been dragged away, she crept weeping to the shore, half-hauling me inside the kete, clutching my frantic brother in her arms. There, she hastily gathered pieces of wood from the ruined canoe and lashed them with rope into a small raft on which she tied my brother. Placing me in the kete, she strapped it high on her back, my head raised above her own, then, praying to Tangaroa to preserve us, she slid into the water. The tide was with her, ingoing to the mainland, a sign of the sea-god's favour. Waist-deep in water, she secured the raft loosely to her front, freeing her arms. Then she began to swim.

Noise travels across the sea. The increasing swell of drums beat as if in her own head; she thought she discerned within it the thunderous tones of Te Rau-paraha, and willed herself not to think of my father and his fate. Suddenly, the drums ceased and from the Kapiti mountainside behind us floated screams, followed by a silence, then a collective sigh that made her shudder. She did not know then that the wailing she heard was the sorrowful massed voice of the tribe, forced to watch as Te Rau-paraha massacred his sister in front of her son. The smell of fire drifted over the sea and, mingled with the bitter tang of burning tawa and kanuka, came the unmistakable odour of roasting flesh.

Defeated by what she knew must be its hideous source, her strength already spent, my mother ceased to swim. Exhausted from struggling against his bonds, my brother had fallen asleep but I, high on the prow of my mother canoe, reached down and, clutching in my hands locks of her drenched hair, hauled on them in the manner of reins. The pain of this shook her from her stupor, and she began again to move her arms and legs, propelling us slowly, slowly through the water.

And then appeared an omen, a further sign from Tangaroa. The waves, which had been rippling about us, became deeper and more powerful, lifting us on each new crest, bearing us closer and closer to the mainland shore.

In his rush cottage, not far from that seashore, Mr Octavius Hadfield, the Christian missionary, friend of the Maori, knowledgeable of their ways, had heard the drums on Kapiti, had caught the drift of burning flesh and, full of unease, had gone to the water's edge to try to observe the better what might be the cause of such disturbance. As the morning light rose from the horizon, he saw, to his sorrow, three bodies washed up on the sand. The largest lay sprawled lifeless, a dead infant strapped to its back, the third, another child, rested motionless on a makeshift raft. In horror, the missionary saw that the children had their lower faces bound, and reached down to untie the infant's tiny mouth. At this, it gave a feeble, angry cry, and he saw that it lived. Running to the other child, he unbound him and saw that he, too, was alive. What of the woman, who must surely be their mother? Turning her body, he saw infinitesimal movements of her chest.

By now, the night's commotion from Kapiti had drawn curious others. Summoned by Mr Hadfield, they carried the half-drowned trio back to his hut at the Mission station.

And in this manner, and by the grace of the sea-god, my mother, my brother and I were saved from the wrath of Te Rau-paraha.

AUCKLAND, 1847

'The mistress has been looking for you, Ma'am,' said Johnson. She peered at me from under a furrowed brow, heightening her general air of gloom and disapproval.

'Where is she now?'

Johnson shrugged. 'I really couldn't say, Ma'am. Possibly in the garden.' And she flapped away into the house in her ill-fitting shoes.

'Why do you keep such a bad-tempered servant?' I had asked Lucy shortly after my arrival.

'We've little choice. We constantly have to reprimand Johnson, but getting servants anywhere in New Zealand is almost impossible. If she decided to give notice, it would be very difficult to find a replacement for her.'

'She's quite horrid to poor Ingrams.'

'She's quite horrid to everyone. Servants in New Zealand have no concept of their place.'

Lucy waved to me from the grove of native flax bushes at the far end of the garden. 'Here you are at last, Fanny. I've been searching for you everywhere. I have the most wonderful news. Godfrey is coming here!' She ran up and seized my arm. 'We'll all have such fun together. I told you how he loves parties and dancing. I've missed him dreadfully since we left Adelaide.' She checked herself. 'Oh, Fanny, you must think me so ungrateful when I have *you* here. But my husband dotes on his brother, which will be good for us all. Godfrey always knows how to coax the Governor from a bad humour. You'll see it at once.'

'When will he arrive?'

'Very soon, but the mails are so slow, I've only just heard. I must set about to have his room made ready.'

Mr Godfrey Thomas was, indeed, a refreshing addition to Government House. As unlike the Governor in looks as it was possible to imagine, he similarly differed entirely from his brother in temperament, being almost unfailingly cheerful and disposed to find everything about his new surroundings agreeable. To me, Mr Godfrey was courteous and attentive, frequently making me laugh with his impersonations of Johnson in disapproving mood. It was clear that he was easy in the company of ladies.

Shortly after his arrival, he persuaded the Governor to agree to hold a ball. 'A little gaiety and dancing will do no harm,' he said, 'and, after all, the officers of the 58th are in sore need of some light relief.'

To my surprise, the Governor agreed. 'I daresay, if you and the ladies are prepared to organise it, there's no reason why not. But it will have to wait until I have settled affairs in the south.'

'Of course. And, George, why shouldn't Eliza and her sister travel with us to Wellington next month? It would provide some interest and distraction for Eliza, and Miss Thompson could see something of the rest of the country.'

'Well, I suppose that may be possible, too.'

But the day before we were due to sail to Wellington aboard the government brig, I developed a fever and pains in my chest.

'I shan't consider going now,' declared Lucy. 'I must stay here with you, Fanny, and nurse you back to health.'

'It's merely a chill,' I said. 'In two or three days I'll be quite well again. You are not to stay behind on my account. The servants can see to my needs, and I can send to Lady Martin or Mrs Selwyn if I need extra assistance.'

Eventually, she was induced to leave with her husband and brother-in-law and for the following two days I took to my bed, rising on the third day restored to health again. The weather being fine, I sent a message by Ingrams to Lady Martin, accepting her invitation to tea that afternoon.

On my return I was set down at the gates of Government House by the Martins' groom. It had begun to rain a little and, as I made my way to the veranda, I saw that a black stallion was grazing in the horse paddock. Wearing her usual grim expression, Johnson opened the door to me almost immediately; I had the notion she had been standing there waiting for my return.

'Ma'am,' she said, 'I must beg you to come directly to the reception room. There is a . . . gen . . . a man . . . a person . . . insisting he won't leave until he's seen His Excellency.'

'Have you told him the Governor isn't at home?'

'Several times, Ma'am, but to no purpose. He refuses to go. And, excepting yourself, there's no one but the servants here.'

'Then I daresay I must see to him.'

In the reception room, a fire burned in the grate but the gas lamps had not yet been lit. Beyond the windows, the rain had begun to fall with its usual Auckland ferocity, darkening the room so completely that I did not at first discern the man standing beside the Governor's bookcases. He turned towards me and, with a shock, I saw that he was a native, with a heavily tattooed face. He smiled, showing a flash of white within the purple of his skin, and instinctively I stepped back.

'Kia ora,' he said, then, seeing my incomprehension, 'it is our "Good day". You must excuse me. Te Kawana Kerei speaks to me usually in Maori.'

'Te Kawana Kerei?'

'Governor Grey.'

'The Governor is not at home. He and his lady sailed for Wellington three days ago.'

'It is most important I speak with him. I have urgent matters that cannot wait. When will he return?'

'Not for some time.'

I discreetly studied the man before me. Tall and strongly built, he wore the usual native flax kilt, his legs and feet bare beneath it, and, above it, an Englishman's shirt, jacket and waistcoat, without necktie or cravat. I was accustomed by now to the sight of such bizarre combinations of clothing among the natives.

'I don't believe we have met,' I said. 'I'm Miss Thompson, Mrs Grey's sister.'

'I know it,' he said. 'Because it was I who carried you here from the Domain when you became ill.'

'Then I'm pleased to have the chance to thank you in person. It was most kind.'

He bowed again, and the jade ornament encircling his neck swung forward and briefly caught the low firelight. Carved in the form of a manikin, its twisted arms and legs encircled its body; the huge iridescent eyes in its angled head sought mine, seeming to stare at me pitilessly. I stepped back, recollecting just such a remorseless gaze but unable to fathom . . . then . . .

'Rio,' I said aloud.

Puzzled, the man looked directly at me, so that I was uncomfortably aware of the twists and swirls of the whorls incised into his face. I willed myself not to show my nervousness at being alone with him. 'I . . . I'll ring for tea. Please to sit down.'

Within the savage mutilation of his face, his eyes, I saw, were kind. 'I believe it is you who should sit down, Miss Thompson.' And he drew up a chair for me before the fire and another opposite for himself.

'I'm sorry that the Governor isn't here,' I said, 'but I'm quite powerless to help you, and I must tell you . . . please not to be offended but . . . it isn't quite proper that I should . . . that you and I should . . . that we are alone together unchaperoned.'

He laughed. 'Ah, you Pakeha, with your respectability and your correctness. Tell me, do you think it is proper to steal? It is in the Bible, is it not, *Thou shalt not steal*?'

I nodded.

'And, *Thou shalt not covet thy neighbour's house, thou shalt not covet thy neighbour's wife, nor his manservant, nor his maidservant, nor his ox, nor his ass, nor any thing that is thy neighbour's*?'

In my astonishment, I forgot myself. 'You have studied the Bible?'

'Most certainly. I often attend the church at Waimate where Te Pihopa, the Bishop, preaches. I am very well acquainted with the Bible. It is true, is it not, as Pihopa Selwyn says, that we must keep the Ten Commandments?'

'Yes, it is true.'

'So tell me then, Miss Thompson, why has that great chief, Mata Wikitoria, allowed the Pakeha to come here and covet our land?' He drew a paper from his jacket. 'Here I have a letter for Te Kawana that I must without delay deliver to him. Once again the New Zealand Company seeks to take our lands in the North and on the West Coast. I wish to tell Te Kawana we will fight with all our strength to prevent this.'

I shrank a little.

'Do not be afraid, Miss Thompson. We will not fight *you*.'

A terrible thought occurred to me. I breathed in deeply. 'Are you . . . is your name . . . John Heke?'

He laughed again. 'I? Hone Heke? That is a most excellent joke, Miss Thompson. It is possible that at this moment Heke is planning once again to cut down the British flagpole at Kororareka, though I think not. But that is not a concern of mine.' He narrowed his eyes a little, and the carvings on his face reassembled themselves into a ferocious scowl. 'Now, if you were Maori and not Pakeha, I should not have been so entertained. To be mistaken for Heke by a Maori would be a deadly insult, but as you know nothing of Maori affairs I have chosen to be amused.'

'If I've offended . . .'

'I will tell you. Heke is a little chief who has discovered a clever way to insult the British and increase his own reputation but, while he is in combat with flagpoles, behind his back more and more British are creeping in at the south and west of our land and snatching for themselves what they can.'

'But some of the land has been legally bought.'

'A little, true, but who has sold it? A Maori who says it is his land and that he may sell it in return for a few blankets and a musket? No single man owns our land. It belongs to the tribe, so only the tribe may agree to sell it. And the tribes do not wish to sell their lands. Only rarely, such as to the missionaries, and by common consent, will we do this.'

Suddenly, the grandfather clock chimed. It was only six o'clock, but it was now completely dark in the reception room.

'I'm very sorry,' I said, 'but in what manner do you think the Governor can help you?'

'I have brought this letter I have written to Mata Wikitoria. It is in Maori, for the greater honour and respect to her, but I am sure Te Kawana will translate it and send it to her in both English and Maori. I do not believe your Queen understands our language.'

'I think not.'

'But if she is a great and good ruler, as Te Kawana and Pihopa tell us, and if she believes in the justice of the Bible, she will help us.'

I did not know what to say, how to answer him. 'I'll ring for tea now,' I said, 'and ask Johnson to light the lamps. As soon as the Governor comes home, I shall tell him you wish to speak with him urgently. When will you return?'

'I will not return,' he said simply, 'because I am not going. I will remain here until he comes back.'

'*Here*? At Government House?'

'I have stayed here many times before, and with Te Kawana FitzRoy also.'

'But I . . . we are alone . . . I . . .'

He looked at me keenly. 'Miss Thompson, you need not be afraid of me. I am a paramount chief. We rangatira do not dishonour the houses of our hosts. We are not savages. You are safe. I shall not eat you.' He smiled, this time showing perfect white teeth. 'Not tonight.'

I rose next morning unsure whether the events of the night before had been some kind of hallucination. From my window, I saw the black stallion still cropping grass in the horse paddock.

I took breakfast in my room and, as soon as I might, paid an uninvited call on Lady Martin.

'There's a native chief at present at Government House. He seems to have taken up residence and says he'll leave only after he's seen the Governor.'

'Is he uncommonly tall?'

'Yes.'

'With a fine black stallion?'

'At present in the horse paddock.'

'Then it's certain to be Te Toa. He's from the North, near Waimate. Has he told you what it is he wants?'

'He says it's a dispute about land that only the Governor can resolve.'

'Is he troubling you in any way?'

'Not at all, though he speaks very good English and seems surprisingly deft in his arguments.'

Lady Martin smiled. 'Then there's no doubt it's Te Toa. My husband says that were he to study the law, he'd make a splendid advocate at the English bar. He learnt our language from Governor FitzRoy and he is almost completely fluent in it. They were great friends and spent a lot of time together in the North. So, you see how truly I spoke when I told you that the Maoris are a most interesting race?'

'Is it true they are still cannibals?'

'Many of them, but we're slowly turning them towards Christianity and leading them to a better life. I'm sure you won't be shocked if I tell you that the chiefs and some high-born men generally have several wives.'

'I believe it was the same with our local Aborigines in Albany.'

'I daresay it's their way. And the Maori young people, too, are much more lax in their morals than we might wish. But many have begun to adopt some of our habits and customs. As the Bishop says, we can but pray for the rest to follow, though I fear the temptation of the native girls has been a little too much for a number of our young English settlers. Several of them now quite openly co-habit with Maori women.'

'And don't marry them?'

'Sometimes they marry. Which is, perhaps, a preferable state of affairs.'

'And if an English woman were to marry a native?'

Lady Martin shuddered. 'Now, *that* does not bear thinking about.'

Since Te Toa was now in residence, it seemed polite that we should dine together. Uncertain of what food a native might eat, I ordered cutlets, and sat down at table determined to mask my awkwardness.

Te Toa sat opposite me and I was relieved to see that he held his knife and fork in the manner of a civilised Englishman.

'The weather remains bad,' he said, indicating the still-falling rain, 'though it is good for our kumara crops. Last year, it was so dry we had a very poor yield.'

'I'm sorry to hear that.'

There was a silence.

'I fear Te Kawana will be delayed. I am told there are storms along the coast. So I shall be here for a little longer, Miss Thompson. Perhaps, if the weather improves, you would come with me to ride in the Domain.'

I did not wish to offend him but I could not possibly accept such an offer. 'I . . . I . . .'

'Ah,' he said, 'I see perhaps you do not consider it *proper*?'

Embarrassed, I nodded.

'You are very concerned with what is proper, Miss Thompson.'

'Naturally.'

'But what is this "proper"?'

'Why, standards of good behaviour . . . conduct becoming . . . the honourable values upheld by Englishmen throughout the Empire.'

'But not by savages?'

I flushed. 'I'm sorry. I had no wish to affront you.'

'Often I am angered, sometimes puzzled, by Englishmen and their doings, but I am never affronted. Now, Miss Thompson, since we must spend time in each other's company, I shall tell you a story and we will look together at these honourable values of Englishmen throughout their British Empire. You permit me this?'

'Pray continue.'

'You know that in the North of New Zealand there has been a war between the tribes and the British?'

'I have heard so.'

'At two of the battles my people were victorious, but in the third, the British soldiers defeated the Maori. Now, British soldiers may be considered very *proper* men, do you not agree?'

'I . . . I imagine so.'

'Of course they are proper. They belong to the army of Mata Wikitoria, the great paramount chief in England.'

'Yes.'

'And Te Kawana is a brave soldier of the army, sent by Mata Wikitoria to Aotearoa . . . New Zealand. And we know that Te Kawana is a very proper man and a noble commander.'

My head began to swim. I nodded again.

'When we Maori go to fight in battle, each man must obey the orders of his chief and observe the rules of warfare. Now, in this battle I tell you of, the defeated men of the tribe were, naturally, taken prisoner, so that the women and children were left defenceless. If this combat had been fought between tribe and tribe, they would have been taken as slaves or for ransom, but this the British soldiers did not do. Instead, those men entered the huts, and even the sacred meeting house, where they found the women huddled together, and there they violated every one of them, young and old, then left them, dishonoured forever. Is this "proper" English behaviour, Miss Thompson?'

I did not meet his eye.

He laid down his knife and fork. 'So tell me,' he said, his voice suddenly harsh, 'who is the *savage* here?'

For the next two days, I did not see Te Toa. The rain became ferocious; hailstones hammered on the iron roof and, through the deluge, I discerned that the stallion no longer pawed in the paddock. Since it was too wet to contemplate going out, I remained confined until, on the third day, in the fashion of Auckland weather, the sun burst forth and within hours the sky was cloudless. The ground had turned to mud; the trees and bushes swelled and quivered in the warmth like birds shaking themselves after a water bath. As I stepped out onto the veranda, I saw that the black horse had returned and, minutes later, Te Toa appeared beside me.

'I am sorry,' he said, 'for my conversation of the other evening. It was not correct that I should suffer you to hear my complaints. Te Kawana knows already the feelings of the chiefs on the matter. It is not your affair.'

'Nevertheless, I was very shocked to hear of it.'

'That is gracious of you, Miss Thompson. If you have forgiven me, perhaps you will ride with me to the Domain?'

I was about to explain again that it would be unseemly for me to ride unchaperoned when I recalled Lady Martin's comments about Te Toa, and the chief's own remarks.

'Why, that is a very kind offer. It's such a beautiful morning and I've been obliged to keep to the house for so long, a ride would be very welcome.'

'I believe you will enjoy it. And a little beyond the Domain is a deserted Maori settlement which it may interest you to see.'

'Thank you. I should like that very much.' And as I said it, I realised it was true.

AOTEAROA

Since the day Mr Hadfield brought us from the shore, we had lived in a raupo hut beside his own house, in the very centre of the pa, safe only because of his great mana. All the tribes on the coast were eager to have a missionary of their own; they wished to learn the Pakeha reading and writing, and Te Rangitake, son of the mighty chief Te Rereta-whanga-whanga, at Waikanae, was proud that he had persuaded Mr Hadfield to live among his people. These Ngatiawa Maori were no friends of Te Rau-paraha, nor of his cousin, Te Whatanui, the Ngati-rau-kawa rangatira at Otaki, and because we had been persecuted by Te Rau-paraha and taken in by Mr Hadfield, they accepted us. Mr Hadfield was also the missionary at Otaki where he sometimes dwelt in a little tent in the pa. Te Whatanui was bound by ties of blood to Te Rau-paraha, he would do nothing to anger his missionary, so we were protected as long as Mr Hadfield remained there.

But as I grew older, my mother, Kahe, became increasingly uneasy. 'Even here, we cannot be sure we are safe,' she said.

'Why not?' I asked. 'Who is it we have to fear?'

'Te Rau-paraha. Sooner or later he will seek vengeance for your father's betrayal, so I am not safe, your brother Hone is not safe, and you are the least safe of all.'

'I! What have *I* done to the great chief?'

'You have dishonoured him twice. First, because you are your father's daughter. And second because, at your birth, you were promised to the grandson of his ally, the great Ngapuhi rangatira, Tamati Waka Nene. That would have been indeed a powerful union. But now . . .'

'I have never even seen Te Rau-paraha,' I cried. 'I am only a young girl. Surely he will not seek to avenge himself on *me*?'

'Be certain,' said my mother, 'that, in time, Te Rau-paraha will try to take his revenge. He will have utu on us all.'

Fearing that to preserve Te Rau-paraha's honour, I might be snatched from the shore by a raiding party, she begged from Mr Hadfield a dead cockerel. This she sewed inside a flax kete before carrying it to the edge of the Christian burial grounds where, with great lamentations, she dug out a small grave and there laid the body, wailing to all, 'I have lost my only daughter.' During my funeral rites, I played happily with my brother inside the little hut lent to us by Mr Hadfield, as noble a man as any Maori warrior.

Over the cockerel's grave, my mother asked Mr Hadfield to erect a small cross and write upon it the Christian name he had given me when he baptised us all, Rahira, for Rachel of the Pakeha Bible.

My mother, Kahe, said that when she first inhabited Mr Hadfield's small rush house she could not comprehend that the same white sink, raised on a stand, was for the washing of everything — the vegetables, the clothing, the body . . . How noa is the Pakeha, she thought, that he washes himself and his food in the same receptacle. And Mr Hadfield is a missionary . . .

'At all times you must be humble and helpful to Mr Hadfield,' she said. 'As you know, our safety depends on the grace of his kindness and the shelter of the cloak of his mana.'

'But I am dead now,' I said.

'Wait,' said my mother. 'Only wait.' And she spoke very quietly to Mr Hadfield, who spoke to Te Rangitake at Waikanae so that, under his protection, I was able to come alive again, the cockerel in the little grave forgotten in the universal joy at my reappearance.

'Surely a Christian miracle,' said my mother. 'Your God is generous.'

And, to celebrate my rebirth, she gave me a new name, Makareta.

'Do nothing to draw attention to yourself, Makareta,' she told me. 'Always remember we are protected only within the halo of Mr Hadfield's Christian goodness.'

'People will see me,' I said. 'Someone will tell the great rangatira on Kapiti that I am alive.'

'They will not dare to speak of you,' said my mother, 'because Mr Hadfield has spoken with Te Rangitake who has prohibited any mention of your name. Who would dare to incur the wrath of a chief by speaking of what is forbidden? Now, Mr Hadfield has again become sick. Go to him and tell him that you will feed his hens until he has recovered.'

I went out behind the hut to the large wire run with its whare where the chickens slept at night. 'A Maori-built hen run,' said my mother, often, 'so it is entirely rat-proof.' And, indeed, no rat had ever penetrated that stronghold.

As I entered, the hens came rushing towards me in a great flock. How many? I tried to count, but in the whirr and flurry of wings, the clutching and squawking, scratching and pecking, and the oncoming battalion of white and brown and scarlet legs, I could only guess. Perhaps a hundred. I took up the large tin container from which Mr Hadfield strewed the corn, dipped it into the sack, filled it and flung the grains as far from my bare feet as I could.

'Beware!' I warned the advancing army. 'I am dead. I am a kikokiko.'

For a long time Mr Hadfield lived in a small tent in the very centre of the pa at Waikanae.

'How uncomfortable,' said my mother. 'Cold at night and too hot in the day.'

Although the tribe had now built him a house, he kept the tent set up in his little garden. We frequently poked our heads inside it to see what new things Mr Hadfield might recently have acquired.

'Blankets,' said Hone. 'Bricks for the chimney of the house he is building at Otaki, and books, many, many books. Mr Hadfield is a learned man.'

Waikanae was a very large pa; the outer palisades were a Pakeha mile around and stretched to the sand-hills and the bush behind us, with the Tararua Ranges beyond. In the gardens outside the stockade grew apple trees, wheat, barley and oats, and grass for the goats and horses. Although he was content in his little Waikanae whare and had moved his possessions into this home, Mr Hadfield was building a second house at Otaki, one and a half hours away on horseback, where he had his other Mission.

'And why is he building another whare there?' asked my mother. 'Because Te Rau-paraha is jealous and angry. He, too, wants a missionary. He has complained to Mr Hadfield that he spends too much time at Waikanae, and the tribes at Kapiti and Otaki have been overlooked. If Mr Hadfield does not do as he wants, he threatens to mount an attack on Waikanae.'

'What did Mr Hadfield say to him?' asked Hone.

'Nothing,' said my mother. 'When Te Rau-paraha had left, Mr Hadfield said he was quite disgusted by him but, because of the chief's great influence, he must continue to humour him and be civil to him. And, yesterday Te Rau-paraha came here to our school in Waikanae and sat with a slate on his knee, demanding to be taught how to read and write. And afterwards, he ordered Mr Hadfield to sit with him, alone in Mr Hadfield's whare, so they might speak of building a church at Otaki.'

'That is not so bad,' said Hone.

'You think not?' said my mother. 'Mr Hadfield alone with that serpent. Do you know that once, when he was fleeing his enemies, he threw into the sea any of his slaves who could not assist in paddling so that he could lighten and speed his canoe?'

But later that day she said to us, 'In both Te Rau-paraha and Mr Hadfield you see the power of great mana. The chief's mana comes from his whakapapa, his lineage, but Mr Hadfield's lies in his goodness and humility, and the way he conducts himself. You should learn from watching him how it is possible in this life to gain mana simply from being true to your own beliefs.'

'Christian beliefs?' asked Hone.

'Of course not,' said our mother. 'What have Christian beliefs to do with it? It is not his Christianity which gives Mr Hadfield his mana. It is his own integrity.'

Hone pulled me away. 'I think it takes too much effort to be so good. Come and watch the canoes bringing in the fishing nets.'

On Saturday night, Mr Hadfield appeared unexpectedly at the doorway of our hut.

'I have come on an errand of some urgency, Kahe,' he said. 'I must tell you that, tomorrow, Te Rau-paraha will attend Sunday worship here at Waikanae. I think it may be prudent to ensure that all of you keep close in the hut or go to Otaki until he departs.'

'But Harawira,' my mother said, politely using Mr Hadfield's Maori name, 'does this mean Te Rau-paraha is now, suddenly, a convert?'

'Not at all. He remains as Heathen as ever, but he wishes to attend the service so that he can enjoy the meal afterwards. He is particularly partial to an English breakfast.'

Mr Hadfield came again to our whare. 'Kahe, I have cheering news. When Te Rau-paraha came to our service, here at Waikanae—'

My mother's eyes narrowed. 'I saw him.'

'—he was so impressed by the beauty of our church that he vowed to build an even finer one in the pa at Otaki, using totara trees from his own lands.'

'I heard,' said my mother, 'that he intended to send a raiding party to advance on the Pakeha settlement in the Hutt Valley.'

'That's true,' said Mr Hadfield, 'but I have managed to dissuade him from such a course.' He paused. 'Te Rau-paraha is a man of extraordinary contradictions.'

'Indeed,' said my mother. 'And therefore not to be trusted. Remember, Harawira, the shark does not feed on kumara.'

AUCKLAND, 1847

At the summit, Te Toa reined in his stallion. 'I know you have visited already the Domain, Miss Thompson, but do you know its history?'

'No, not at all.' I gazed across the bay at the three peaks of Rangitoto Island that dominated the skyline. 'Mrs Grey and I come here mainly to look at the panorama and the plants.'

'You know that it is very large?'

'Yes, and much of it seems extremely inaccessible. Such dense vegetation will take a long time to clear and replant.'

We rode on again, the damp smell of green bush undercut with the sharp tang of kanuka rising around us.

'You have seen before much harakeke,' he said, 'but there, do you see, are manuka and nikau. And the great green stars in the gullies below us are the tops of the ponga ferns. Over here are your English oaks and cherry trees, but I do not think they will defeat our Maori plants.' He stopped his horse. 'Now, Miss Thompson, I shall show you the crater.'

'What crater?'

'You are riding now along the edge of it.' He gestured inland. 'Pukekawa, the Hill of Bitter Tears. It was here that my own ancestors of Ngapuhi fought Ngati Whatua. All around us are volcanoes, but this was the mightiest.'

'Will they erupt?'

He shrugged. 'I think not, but that is in the hands of the gods. Pukekawa is spent from an eruption long ago, but the others . . . Who knows? Not so many years ago, Ngati Whatua sold this ancestral land to the Pakeha to make a great park for the town. Come, I will show you.'

We veered off the track and onto an unseen pathway. The fronds of the great native ferns brushed me as we passed.

'Look,' said Te Toa, 'that is the floor of the crater. In that swamp are eels, good for eating.'

I peered at the dark water in the pit below us.

'And on the other side, over there, Ngati Whatua once had fine kumara fields. But then they sold their land, so it is gone forever. And now, as I promised, we will go to the little settlement.'

We pushed on, the vegetation restricting our horses to a walking pace, until Te Toa suddenly stopped his stallion and sprang from its back. Stretching out his hand, he took my reins and I dismounted. He tethered the horses and, after a brief hesitation, I followed him into the dense, seemingly impenetrable greenery, bending below the ponga fronds he held up for me, uneasy, but pulled forward by the strange call of something I had neither invited nor understood. Was this how Lucy had felt in her youth at Albany, I wondered — curious and unafraid of the unknown? I did not know then, and I do not know now, why I followed Te Toa with such blind confidence.

We had passed quite some way into the depths of the bush when it suddenly opened out onto a clearing in the middle of which was a huddle of small, ramshackle native dwellings in a rough semi-circle. A few sticks protruded from the ground and a cooking pot lay on its side before one of the low doorways.

'Where are we?'

'It is an abandoned slave settlement.'

'*Slaves*?'

'Of course. In the past, all the tribes had slaves. Even today . . .'

'When Mrs Grey and I lived in Australia we had a cook, a Dutchman from the garrison settlement, who had a native wife. "My lubra", he called her, and he treated her exactly as a slave, poor woman. She had a number of half-caste children, and every morning he made his wife and children search the cooking area and the fireplace for snakes and poisonous lizards before he lit the fire. Then they spent the day carrying logs and water for him. He regularly beat her, and his children, if they didn't obey his orders quickly enough. Slavery debases human nature.'

'That is true but it is also in man's nature to seek power over others. And there are no longer slaves in this place. It was abandoned long ago.'

'And the slaves?'

'Killed, eaten . . . perhaps freed, but I do not think so.'

The bush around us that had seemed so peaceful now took on a more sinister aspect. Who or what might be concealed within it?

He saw my discomfort. 'There is no reason to be afraid. No harm will come to you. Be brave and follow me, and we shall look inside the huts. And behind, there are the remains of small kumara gardens . . .'

I thought again of Lucy. I shall not be *parochial*, I told myself.

To still my fears I forced the conversation to more mundane matters.

'I've never seen it rain so often and as heavily as in New Zealand, and these houses offer very little protection. How do you keep yourselves and your possessions dry?'

'If we are out in wet weather, we wear waterproof cloaks. We chiefs have several for different occasions, all fashioned from rare bird feathers, and very beautiful. Our possessions we keep in our whare in the pa, stored in carved boxes suspended from the rafters.' He guided me towards the centre of the circle of huts. 'You are not at all seeing a true pa here. When you come to visit my pa at Waimate, you will see that our present-day dwellings are much finer — made of reeds and harakeke — and that the doors and windows are very small to keep out the weather.'

When you come to visit my pa at Waimate . . . Had Lucy already told him that we might pay a visit to the Selwyns' Mission there?

For more than an hour, Te Toa and I explored the ruins, examining the walls and roofs of roughly woven flax, stooping through low doorways into the meagre interiors. We saw only one piece of carving, a post driven into the ground beside the largest of the huts and hacked into the shape of a crude figure.

'It is not at all an accomplished piece of carving,' said Te Toa, squatting to examine it.

Embarrassed, I turned away.

He stood up again and moved towards me. 'Ah,' he said. 'It is a man and he is unclothed. Is this what concerns you?'

I felt a blush staining my entire face and neck.

'But he is no different in form from any other man. So why does this shame you?'

'It . . . it . . . I am unmarried.'

'Married, unmarried, what is the difference? Surely you Pakeha know men from women? Even our smallest Maori child is aware of that. From the instant of birth, one is either a man or a woman and one's entire life is shaped accordingly. Is that not true?'

'It . . . it's not something of which we may speak openly.'

Te Toa shook his head. 'I do not understand you Pakeha. So many things I cannot comprehend at all. Here are your men who take our women to them and make free with them, yet their own women they prefer to keep ignorant of the most important of human desires. So their women are stiff and formal, they do not move easily in their bodies. Perhaps they do not even know their own needs. Look at poor Mata Kawana . . .'

'I don't think we should continue this conversation. It's not at all proper.'

'Ah, once again, this proper!'

'I have tried to explain . . . it's a question of good behaviour. It's what should be done. Or, sometimes, what should not. It's what keeps society . . . what holds society together . . .' I struggled for a moment. 'It is right conduct.'

'And who decides what is right conduct?'

'I . . . God, I suppose. And Her Majesty. It is why England is a great and good country that leads the world.'

'Do you remember that I asked you whether it was proper for Pakeha to take our lands?'

'Yes.'

'Now I ask you, as a Christian lady, just as I am a Christian Maori . . . sometimes . . . whether the Lord God thinks it is proper for us to work on the Sabbath.'

'No. Or so the church teaches us.'

'Indeed so. And yet, when my people were fighting the British at the Bats' Nest, Rua-peka-peka, and we stopped for the Sabbath, the British did not observe Sunday worship and ambushed us at prayer. Is that proper?'

'No! It is not.'

'So you see, Miss Thompson, as I said before, "proper" is very often a matter of what is expedient. And now, I think I have embarrassed you enough and we should go back.'

The Wellington travellers returned the next day. Te Toa stood on the veranda and greeted them as if he, not the Governor, were master of the house.

'Te Kawana Kerei,' he said, bowing, 'I must tell you I have been here many days awaiting your return, and Miss Thompson has been to me a most excellent hostess. She has instructed me in important matters of British society and customs. Is that not so, Miss Thompson?'

Unable to discern from his expression whether or not he mocked me, I nodded.

'Ah, Fanny,' cried Lucy, embracing me, 'we've had the gayest time. Godfrey and I went riding in the hills and we met a friend of his who crossed over from Adelaide with him.'

'Petre,' said Mr Godfrey. 'He's lodging in Wellington with a Mr Domett, one of George's officials there.'

'Domett is an excellent man,' said the Governor. 'I'm so convinced of his abilities I've appointed him Colonial Secretary here.'

'I liked Domett very much and I'm most taken with Wellington,' said Mr Godfrey, 'though its society is not one bit as jolly as here in Auckland.'

'Even horrid Charlotte Godley was charmed by Godfrey. And her little Arthur remembered me, Fanny. He ran to me at once. He's the most darling child.'

'And George has passed valuable time with Mr Hadfield,' said Mr Godfrey. 'He spoke most informatively about native affairs in the south.'

'So the only thing wanting for our complete happiness,' said Lucy, 'was you, Fanny dearest. You seem quite well again. I do hope you haven't been bored all alone here.'

AOTEAROA

Hone and I went down to the Waikanae shore. On the sands were others from the tribe, collecting seaweed and shellfish, rolling nets, beaching fishing canoes. They hung back from us and waved but did not speak. We dug in the smaller sand-hills, not for food but for the pleasure of creating a cave under the crab grass. After some time, I became suddenly aware of a repetitive sound, something familiar yet not quite known.

Hone clutched at me. 'Makareta, turn around! But slowly, carefully.'

I moved warily in a half-circle and saw, to my horror, a number of waka moving steadily across the ocean towards Waikanae — from Kapiti Island.

'Waka taua?' I whispered.

Hone shook his head. 'No, they are too few. There are only seven, perhaps eight, of them. And they are not large enough for war canoes. But they are certainly not fishing canoes. Look at the leader.'

At the head of the flotilla rode a canoe with a most intricately carved prow, and in it stood a slight figure staring ahead or, so it seemed, directly at us.

I was transfixed with fear. 'It must be Te Rau-paraha.'

'A raiding party. Mr Hadfield is in Wellington and the chief may have seized his advantage.'

'But what shall we do?'

'I doubt Te Rau-paraha has identified us, and we cannot be seen to run or we will reveal ourselves. Let us turn very calmly and walk up from the sands back to the pa. We should be there before they land.'

As we turned, the steady harmony of the raised and lowered oars, dipping in and out of the water, became clearer and clearer, and now we could hear the song of the paddlers as they advanced.

Full of foreboding, we walked as much in our usual fashion as we could and gained the slightly raised ground. There, still in full view of the waka, we did not dare to move any faster. The distance from the shore to the pa seemed to have trebled, so it was with a sense of deliverance that we saw our mother striding towards us.

'Come at once,' she said. 'That is Te Rau-paraha's raiding canoe. We must hide.'

'But, Mata, where can we go?'

'We will conceal ourselves in Mr Hadfield's hen whare.'

'But . . . the stench . . . the birds . . .'

'It is better than death,' said our mother, 'and in my lifetime, I have endured worse.'

The hens fussed and squawked around us as we crossed the yard and pressed ourselves into the tiny whare where, at night, they slept together on roosts. The rank, acrid reek of their droppings entirely filled our noses and we were so cramped we were unable to move. As if there had been some unspoken signal, the everyday noises of the pa had ceased now and everyone seemed to have melted away. All was still. Even the fleas were no longer jumping. Only the voices of the strangers carried to us in our hiding place.

We applied our eyes to the crack at the top of the doorway where, unseen, we were afforded a clear view of all who might go by. It was some time before anyone passed. I prayed desperately to the Maori gods, to Mr Hadfield's Te Ariki, to the spirit of my unknown father, to protect us, to ensure that no one would stop and examine our hiding place, to save us from the demon, Te Rau-paraha.

Though the bare feet of the warriors made no sound on the earth, we caught the rattle of their flax kilts. Then, a group of figures flashed past the hen house, heads bent, topknots bobbing, as they stole about the hushed pa. We could not tell whether the other inhabitants had hidden or fled, but we knew very well that Te Rau-paraha sought only us. He would not risk an attack on the powerful Te Rereta-whanga-whanga and Te Rangitake.

My mother nudged me as, through the crack, we spied a solitary figure walking towards us. I studied his face with its heavy moko, the sloping forehead above the sharp hooked nose and jutting top lip. But most arresting were his eyes, small, deep-sunken and almost obscured by hooded, wrinkled eyelids. As I peered at him, unseen, he seemed to look back at me, raising those lids to reveal a pair of cold, penetrating eyes. I shuddered, knowing instantly why my mother did not trust him and why she had so often quoted to us what others said of him: 'Ko te uri o Kapu manawa witi.' 'No one can know his thoughts, whether they are for good or evil.'

We heard other noises, distant voices murmuring greetings, the bustle of the life of the pa slowly resuming. The feathery dust of the hen whare was almost choking me, and I was terrified I might sneeze. It was stifling hot and my limbs were numb from standing crushed in that tiny space, but I dared not move. Voices drifted from outside and now we could hear quite clearly that the Kapiti men were questioning the Waikanae people.

'No,' we heard frequently. 'Not today, at least.' And another voice, 'Never.'

I felt my mother stiffen. They are talking about *me*, I thought. They are saying they have never seen me. And I prayed that no one would mention my return from the world of the spirits.

Many times, the searchers passed the hen whare but without troubling to examine it. The hens had long ago resumed their scratching and squabbling in the yard. Finally, a long, long time later, we caught the sound of fading voices, then of paddles, and under cover of the night, we crept from our hiding-place to our hut.

'But,' said our mother, 'Mr Hadfield is often sick now. I must think of a way to protect us so that we are safe even in his absence.'

'Surely no one would dare to oppose Mr Hadfield's wishes?' said Hone.

'When Mr Hadfield is not here, no one will dare to defy the will of Te Rau-paraha. And if he were to snatch us, you may be sure no one would have seen or heard anything. On Mr Hadfield's return, he would be told we had left of our own free will and, even if he knew it to be a lie, what could he do then? It would be too late. The magic and power of the Maori is far greater than that of the Pakeha.'

'But what of the power of Jesus, Te Ariki?' asked Hone. 'Mr Hadfield says Te Ariki made the earth and all things in it.'

Our mother shrugged. 'Mr Hadfield is an honourable man but, here, he is in error. As every sorcerer and every tohunga knows, it is the Maori gods who created the universe. But in this world in which we are obliged to live, we must remember that while we honour the gods, the laws of the Pakeha are also powerful.'

'Since I cannot take a Maori husband of my own rank,' said our mother, Kahe, 'I have decided to marry a Pakeha. Then we three shall be protected by not only the Christian church but also by the laws of the great Pakeha Queen.'

'But who is this Pakeha husband?' asked Hone.

Our mother looked triumphant. 'It is Mr Nicoll, the inn-keeper at Otaki. He is a good man and he has asked me many times to marry him. Before, I would not consent, but now, with Mr Hadfield so often sick and away in Wellington, I must accept him.'

Mr Hadfield was delighted. 'It has been my fervent wish to see the two races united. And Mr Nicoll is a devout Christian and an honourable man. You have chosen well, Kahe.'

My mother's marriage took place in the church at Waikanae and, for a short while afterwards, we moved to Mr Nicoll's inn at Otaki. But there, on Te Rau-paraha's cousin's mainland territory, my mother once more grew uneasy. When Mr Nicoll was away on business in Wellington, we were again without a protector. So, since there were only ten Pakeha miles between Otaki and Waikanae, we moved back to our old reed house next door to Mr Hadfield's at the Waikanae pa, and every day Mr Nicoll rode to Otaki to the inn. But because Mr Nicoll did not like the noise and dirt of life at the pa, we spent time also in Otaki when we knew that Te Rau-paraha was not in residence. I had no recollection of my true Maori father and, as Mr Nicoll was kind and affectionate to Hone and to me, we lived happily together in this fashion for some time.

AUCKLAND, 1847

Several days after the Greys and Mr Godfrey had returned, I sought out the Governor. 'I wonder if I may have a word with you, in private.'

'Why, certainly, Miss Fanny. Come into my study.' He looked momentarily anxious. 'I hope Eliza is not unwell again. She seemed in better health in Wellington.'

'No, it's not that at all.' I sat on the chair he indicated. 'I have been with you now for a considerable time,' I said, 'and while I've greatly appreciated your hospitality, I—'

He rose. 'I beg you, do not say you are about to leave us. The change you've brought about in my wife's spirits has been noted by us all.'

'I'm not in the least desirous of leaving but, Governor, if I am to stay on here, I must ask that you permit me to . . . how can I put this . . . contribute to my own keep.'

'I assure you, in your attentions to Eliza you have more than recompensed us.'

'You are very kind but I must insist. I have substantial means of my own, and were I to take on an establishment here in Auckland I should be obliged to meet the expenses of the running of a household.' I looked directly at him. 'I am most serious about this, sir. If you do not agree, I shall be forced to leave you.'

'I should be deeply embarrassed by such an arrangement. You have already been more than generous to my mother-in-law and her younger children. I understand it was you who made it possible for them to return to Lyme and for the boys to be educated.'

'Whatever I may have done for dear Aunt and my brothers should be regarded as the smallest recognition of the immense debt I owe them. Sir Richard and Lady Spencer took me in when I was orphaned, and I have ever been treated exactly as one of their own. I can think of no greater generosity than that. But it is in no way relevant to my situation here. I have drawn a draft on my bank, Governor, and I implore you now to allow me my pride and to accept it.'

I laid the envelope on his desk. He was silent for some time.

'Well,' he said, finally, 'I see that you are set on your course and we would be much poorer for the loss of your company. So, with the greatest of reluctance, I shall accept. I thank you.'

'There is one other matter . . .'

'And that is?'

'Miss Pitt intends to sell her mount, Tsarina.'

'A very fine horse.'

'Yes, indeed. And I would very much like to purchase her. Would you permit me to house her here in your stables? I should be entirely responsible for her upkeep.'

'With the greatest of pleasure.'

'Thank you, Governor.'

As I rose to leave, he held out his hand to me. 'You are an admirable lady, Miss Fanny, and your influence on Eliza has been immeasurable.'

'Kia ora, my friend, Miss Thompson.'

'Why, Te Toa. This is a surprise. I thought you had completed your urgent business with the Governor.'

'Alas, no, Te Kawana refuses to become involved in this matter. I have returned to ask him to reconsider, but he says it is a local disputation and not of interest to the government. I am most disappointed by his decision.'

'I'm sorry . . .'

'It concerns part of the land of my grandmother's tribe which is now the subject of a great dispute. A group of Pakeha claim they have bought this land from three Maori who sold it in exchange for muskets and ammunition, but the tribal elders say the land was never sold. So, since Te Kawana will not assist me, I am now on my way to consult Sir William Martin about the matter.' He dismounted. 'I have plenty of time. Shall we take tea, Miss Fanny?'

I noted the familiar use of my name and said quickly, 'I'll ask Johnson to prepare it for us. I regret that neither the Governor nor his lady is at home.'

'I know this. That is why I have come. I wished to speak to you alone.'

'To *me*? Why?'

'I wish to inform you of important matters that perhaps you should know.'

'I must tell you that I'm not able to help you. I have no influence with the Governor.'

'I am not asking for your help, and I think no one has influence over Te Kawana, except his brother, Mr Thomas.'

'I have no sway over Mr Thomas either, I assure you.'

'I think you should listen to what I wish to tell you.'

I thought what an incongruous sight we must present, a muslin-clad Englishwoman in her bonnet pouring tea from a china pot for a tattooed native dressed in a motley of English and Maori garments.

Te Toa sipped delicately from his cup. 'I am fond of the English tea, Miss Fanny.' He paused. 'And now, here is what you should know. Te Kawana has many enemies, more among Pakeha even than Maori. He has been most persecuting to many, and they will not forgive him for this. Do you know that he has written to the Missionary Society of the Church and to the government in England to complain of Mr Williams, the missionary?'

'I am sure that is not so.'

'It is very so. In his letters, he accuses Mr Williams of stealing land from the Maori to enrich his own situation, so the Church has instructed Mr Williams to give up all his property. Which he does not wish to do. And, in truth, much of that land was given freely to him by Ngapuhi in the Far North. And Pihopa Selwyn, who believes all that Te Kawana tells him, supports these government actions and has told Mr Williams and the other missionaries to obey. Now, if the lands were given back to us Maori, that is one thing, but those lands, says Te Kawana, must be returned to the Crown — that is, to the Pakeha government.' He looked at me quizzically. 'Is this "proper", Miss Fanny?'

'If what you say is true, it's not at all just.'

'I am always a rangatira, and very often a Christian. I do not speak falsely.'

'Then I apologise, but I find it hard to comprehend what you tell me.'

'Mr Williams will never release those lands, so now Te Kawana will do his best to destroy him.'

'But why?'

'Te Kawana does not want opposition to his power among the settlers or Maori, and Mr Williams has great influence with the tribes in the North.'

'I see.'

'And in Wellington, or so I am told by the mighty Waka Nene who has his ear placed to those cracks in the earth along which news travels, the settlers do not like Te Kawana. They wish to govern themselves and they do not like Mr Eyre, the little Pakeha chief Te Kawana has set in place to rule for him. And Te Kawana keeps Mr Eyre impoverished so he cannot mutiny, forcing him to dwell in a miserable whare with holes in the roof and almost no furniture. So, daily, Mr Eyre, too, becomes more rebellious.'

'But Mr Eyre is the Governor's lieutenant in Wellington.'

'They are not friends, the Ngati Toa chiefs say, because in the beginning Mr Eyre did not send his government dispatches first to Te Kawana but directly to the officers of Mata Wikitoria in England. And in some of these dispatches he made great criticism of Te Kawana. But Mr Eyre also does not make the settlers love him. He walks about Wellington wearing his silver and gold uniform with his foolish feathered hat.'

'That does seem imprudent. But I have no knowledge at all of these things and nor, I am certain, has Mrs Grey.'

'And now Te Kawana has more problems to come between the Waikato tribes and the settlers in Taranaki. Te Rangitake, Wiremu Kingi, the great Ngatiawa chief, has left his lands at Waikanae . . .'

'Where is Waikanae?'

'It is a very large pa at the river mouth opposite Kapiti Island, about three or four hours' ride from Wellington. Mr Hadfield has one of his Mission stations there and he says he fears there will be war. Kingi has taken more than six hundred of his people to Taranaki where Pakeha settlers are squatting on his tribe's most fertile land. Kingi's people intend to re-inhabit their land and plant crops there.

They have horses and cattle and muskets—'

'Muskets!'

'Of course. The settlers have muskets. Why should not Maori have them, too?'

'I—'

'Already there is violence there. Some of the settlers have persuaded our people to sell them land secretly, so now Kingi has said he will personally kill any Maori found guilty of doing so.'

'Have you told the Governor of all this?'

'Of course not. He will not listen even to Waka Nene. Why should he pay attention to me?'

'I'm dismayed by what you tell me.'

'I see I have frightened you. There will be no war here in Auckland. And I did not wish to upset you, merely to ask whether you know of someone who has influence over Te Kawana.'

'As you said, only his brother.'

'His brother will not be long here in Auckland. He wishes to be in Wellington with his old friend, Mr Petre, and his new friend, Mr Domett.'

'I wonder,' I said, 'if perhaps, Sir William Martin . . .'

'He is a good man. Upright and noble. But Te Kawana does not heed even his advice. And now, I think we have spoken enough of these matters. The teapot is empty and you are tired.'

'I am not so much tired as anxious.'

'I am sorry for this, but you understand why I have decided to speak to you freely?'

'I think so.' I paused, then I said, 'Tell me truthfully, Te Toa, do you like the Governor?'

'It is a question not of like or dislike. It is a matter of trust or distrust.'

'Then, do you trust him?'

'I do not trust *any* of Mata Wikitoria's emissaries. Captain Wakefield from the New Zealand Company was a hawk that swooped down and snatched our young ones out of the nest. Now we have Te Kawana Kerei, a rat chewing at the bottom of the nest to undermine it so our little ones fall out. But I like *you*, Miss Fanny. You have an honourable character. And a most charming face. I wish to invite you to come again to ride with me.'

AOTEAROA

'Throughout our lives,' said my mother, 'Death walks beside us. Beware of makutu, witchcraft. Never break tapu. Do not allow one hair of your head, the smallest shred of your clothing, to fall into the hands of your enemies. And when you walk on the sands, tread below the waterline so that the waves will wash away your footprints before your foes can step into them and steal your spirit.'

I stared at her.

'The power of the tohunga is greater than all other forces. Only he can command the spirits and foretell the future. For this reason he is tapu and it is forbidden to lay hands upon any part of his person. Even when he has been fed with a long stick, because of his sacredness, that stick becomes tapu also and must be thrown into the fire to be consumed. If he comes near you, you must cast down your eyes until he passes. It is most dangerous to catch the eye of a tohunga.

'And remember,' she continued, 'that *blood* is the most powerful force of all. Even a single bead of blood can bring Death to the living.'

I was very young; as yet, I could barely speak.

But, 'Hear me, my children,' ordered my mother.

And my infant self drank in her words like her milk.

Since I knew nothing of the Pakeha way of life in the settlements, my own life seemed to me entirely satisfactory. Three times a week, the stage-coach between Wellington and Foxton thundered along the sandy beach, stopping at my stepfather's inn at Otaki before making the ferry trip across the river. Hone and I went often to watch it pass, waving at the passengers and the coach driver who, when he saw us, would sometimes sound a blast on his long brass horn. On Sundays, we attended service at the church in the pa at Waikanae, where Mr Hadfield, clad in white robes, mounted the pulpit and spoke to the five hundred or more Maori attending of Te Ariki, of the Holy Bible and the Ten Commandments. And, afterwards, some of us took English breakfast with Mr Hadfield. We ate eggs and sometimes pork, with slices of cooked bread spread with an orange sweet paste made especially for Mr Hadfield by his mother and sisters in far-off England where they lived with Kuini Wikitoria.

On one such Sunday morning, Hone came running to where my mother and stepfather and I were standing talking with other worshippers. 'Come at once,' he cried, 'and see. Mr Hadfield has with him another Pakeha with four eyes.'

I raced after him to where the two Pakeha sat outside the meeting house, and stared amazed at Mr Hadfield's companion. He had two ordinary eyes, exactly the same as ours, but blue, like the sky, and in front of them were two extra eyes, transparent and surrounded by black wire, reflecting the morning light.

Behind us gathered the great company of Mr Hadfield's parishioners, gazing in astonishment. Then I heard the voice of my stepfather. 'Why, it's Mr Henry Williams.' He advanced through the crowd, his right hand extended in a Pakeha greeting. 'You stayed at my inn at Otaki, sir, when you took the Treaty around New Zealand for the chiefs to sign.'

Mr Williams stepped forward and seized my stepfather's hand in his own. 'Mr Nicoll. How do you do? How very pleasant to see you again.' He looked at the crowd of onlookers. 'But tell me, Mr Nicoll, how does it come about that I am commanding such undivided attention?'

'It's your spectacles, sir. No one here has seen them before. They think you have four eyes.'

Mr Williams threw back his head and let out a bellow of laughter. 'Ah, of course. In the North, the Maori call me Te Kara Wha, Four Eyes.' He peeled the front eyes from his face and passed them to my stepfather. 'Here, let them look through these.'

There passed a most fascinating time while we took it in turn to see for ourselves how these extra eyes enlarged and distorted everything about us.

'A clever Pakeha invention,' said my mother, 'but of course we Maori have no need of them.'

Mr Hadfield was again sick. My mother sent me to his little house with a kete of kumara boiled with healing herbs.

'How kind, Makareta,' said Mr Hadfield, who was lying on a long chair in his sitting room.

'And I am to take care of your hens every day until you are better.'

'Now that takes a great weight from my mind. You will find the corn in the usual sack on the shelf in the hen house. And when you have finished, come and join me in a cup of English tea.'

After I had fed the hens and replenished the water gourds, I set about hunting for eggs, which I placed in a large woven basket, then made my way back to the cottage. As I entered the kitchen, I heard voices. Mr Hadfield had received a visitor.

Peeping into the sitting room, I saw it was another missionary, Mr Taylor. Unsure of the polite thing to do when two Pakeha were talking together, I did not interrupt their conversation but neither could I rudely creep away. Instead, I sat on the kitchen floor, out of sight, waiting till Mr Hadfield might realise that I was there.

'I should like to know, Octavius,' I heard Mr Taylor say, 'how you've managed to gain such influence with our Maori brothers.'

'As to that,' said Mr Hadfield, 'I must tell you it is a combination of diligence in learning their language and observing their customs, and a very great deal of luck. When first I came to Otaki, Te Matia, a chief second only in importance to Te Whatanui, was violently opposed to all missionaries and to me in particular and, when I held a service, he would attend and shout noisily during the sermon and the prayers. After one such interruption, I visited him in his gardens to remonstrate with him, but he ignored me, so I very thoughtlessly sat down on the ground, picked up a piece of kumara and bit into it. This, of course, was a serious breach of tapu, and he ran at me with his tomahawk and would have cut me down but for his daughter and the son of another chief who rushed up and placed themselves between me and Te Matia, their hands over my head, so that it was impossible for him to hit me without first striking them. Others then came forward to my aid and, after some time, his rage abated and he sat down near me.

'I attempted to explain that, as a foreigner who had not been long among them, I had not been aware that I was causing offence. But before I could finish my explanation, the chief's tohunga, Hereiwi, interrupted and pronounced a curse upon me. "You will either die," he shouted in Maori, "or be driven from Otaki by evil spirits."'

'So what did you do?'

'I told him his curse would neither affect my life nor influence my intentions but was much more likely to injure *him*. And then I left them and set off later that day for Waikanae.

'On my return, a few days later, I learnt that during the night, after our altercation in the kumara gardens, Hereiwi had died. Well, this produced a profound impression on his fellows, who attributed his death to his cursing me. I tried in vain to explain that I had heard from some Englishmen who knew Hereiwi that he had been suffering from a lung complaint and that his death had been caused by the rupture of a large blood vessel. They were not at all convinced, and resolved in future to allow me to disregard all of their tapu ceremonies and go where I liked. And after that, Te Matia and I were on friendly terms, or at least we lived together peacefully.'

I crept stealthily from Mr Hadfield's kitchen and ran home.

'How is Mr Hadfield today?' asked my mother.

'Better,' I lied.

But to myself I thought perhaps this illness was Mr Hadfield's punishment from the gods for breaking the sacred law of tapu. And when Mr Hadfield became so sick that he was taken to Wellington to the Pakeha tohunga there, I knew it was indeed a further sign of the gods' displeasure.

AUCKLAND, 1848

'I have called upon you again, Miss Fanny, as you observe. I wish to invite you and Mata Kawana on an honourable visit to my pa near Waimate. Pihopa and Mata Pihopa Selwyn will be at the Mission House then, so you may stay with them and visit me. You will ride from Auckland and camp in tents on the way. The countryside is more beautiful than you will find anywhere else in New Zealand. Do you like this proposal?'

'Very much, and I'm sure Mata Kawana will also. But I hope the Governor will allow us to go.'

'He has agreed already.'

'And will we be safe, two women alone?'

'You will not be alone. You will take the servant, Ingrams, and I will supply guides from my tribe. If you are under my protection, your safety is assured.'

'Then I'll speak to Mrs Grey. I'm certain she'll be delighted by the idea. She longs to travel more in the interior.'

'So, it is settled. Te Kawana will be from home and the time is propitious.'

'Propitious? How so?'

'I have consulted my tohunga, my priest, and he has cast the omens to determine this.'

'Are you saying he is able to see the future?'

'Of course, if the gods will it. The power of the tohunga is very great. Only he can call upon the gods and make them speak.'

I felt the strangeness that affected me whenever I was with Te Toa. For much of the time, in his manners and conversation, he seemed like an Englishman and then, unexpectedly, he would reveal the nature of the savage.

'Why would the tohunga ask the gods to speak?'

'I do not know. That is tapu, the sacred bond between the tohunga and the gods. One is not permitted to ask such things. But what is important is that the omens are favourable. And Te Kawana will be happy for you to see the Mission House of his friend, Pihopa Selwyn, especially when, as I told you, he hopes to weaken the power of Mr Williams and the missionaries in the North. I think, too, Te Kawana wishes to please me and his old ally, Waka Nene, in consenting to your visit.'

'Does Waka Nene also dislike Mr Williams?'

'By no means. Nene is too great a chief to engage in the petty squabbles of Pakeha, even those of Te Kawana.'

Still bemused by my conversation with Te Toa, I was interrupted by Lucy.

'Fanny, you must come and see this letter I've just received. I'm in two minds as to whether I should show it to my husband. Here, read it for yourself.'

'*Mata Te Kawana Rangatira*,' I read. I looked questioningly at Lucy.

'Mother Governor Chief. It's the polite form of Maori address to the Governor's lady. Do go on.'

You know I am a speaking man and not a writing man so I am asking Mr Williams, missionary, to write this letter from me to you, just as I want to say it. Mr Williams is a good man. He will put only my words and not his own.

Mata Te Kawana, now we Maori must live in Aotearoa beside the Pakeha. But some of the Pakeha steal our lands. I have told Te Kawana we will fight forever to keep this land which has been ours since the time of the first chiefs. But Te Kawana does not hear me. He favours only the Waikato tribes and has turned his face against us Ngapuhi. You have seen my nephew, John Heke. He has told me of your kindness to him when he was a prisoner of Mata Wikitoria. I have written to this Queen as one paramount chief to another. Perhaps she has not received my letter for she has sent me no reply, no messenger.

My son has been killed in this fighting, many of the Ngati

Wikitoria soldiers also. I say to you, Mata Te Kawana, we should stop this fighting. Ask Te Kawana to restore our stolen lands. We have given lands to the missionaries of Te Ariki; we have given lands to the Queen as a mark of honour. Do not take more from us. Let us cease this bloodshed. My nephew, John Heke, tells me you are the daughter of a paramount chief of the English Navy. And you are the wife of a paramount chief. Mata, I do plead with you, use your great mana. Ask Te Kawana to end this bloody slaughter. Everywhere is hatred and murder. Te Rau-paraha has many muskets. Soon he will come both north and south to kill us all. He is not to be trusted.

In the name of my ancestors and of Jesus Christ, Te Ariki, I ask you, Mata Te Kawana, to bring this, my message, before your honoured husband.

May the Gods preserve you and me and all of us, eh-Mata.

Hori Te Marama Kotuora.

I paused. 'There are strange markings here, and underneath Mr Williams has written in brackets, "*his moko mark*". What does he mean?'

'Because the chief can't read or write, he signs his name with his tattoo markings,' said Lucy. 'Just like a cross. Well, do you think I should show it to my husband?'

'It's a very sad, sincere message sent in good faith, so I suppose you must.' I thought of Te Toa's words. 'But I fear the Governor may accuse Mr Williams of putting words into the chief's mouth"

Lucy shook her head. 'Mr Williams is a missionary. I'm sure my husband wouldn't consider that for a minute.'

V

It came to the ears of Mr Hadfield that Te Rau-paraha and his allies were plotting together to attack the settlers near Wellington and seize Ngatiawa territory.

'My health is much improved,' said Mr Hadfield to my mother, 'and I have no fears for my own safety. Te Rau-paraha cannot harm you or your family while you are under my protection, so, for the moment, you are safe at Waikanae. But if he and Te Rangi-hae-ata and Te Mamaku attack the settlements at Wellington, the settlers will form vigilante groups, there will be war and no one will be safe. The government troops would have no chance of quelling such a revolt. I have sent a Maori messenger from Wellington to carry an urgent message to Te Kawana Kerei in Auckland, asking him to come south with all speed.'

'As things stand,' said my mother, 'nothing but your own mana, Harawira, can prevent war between Maori and Pakeha. But listen to me carefully. Thirteen years I have waited and, at last, it is my own turn to have utu. Believe me. I have vowed to the gods that, even if it is with my dying breath, I shall see Te Rau-paraha brought down.'

AUCKLAND, 1848

I tossed in my berth as the sea rolled about us. Dimly, I heard cannon boom, and was half-aware of their momentary flashes of fire lighting the night sky. Water began seeping into the cabin; with terrifying rapidity it rose to lap, then engulf, my bedding. A fish flapped against my face.

'It's too bad,' said a voice beside me. 'Entirely vexing. Wake up, Fanny! We're almost drowned here.'

As I struggled from my dream and sat up, a piece of the sodden fabric of our tent slapped my face and shoulder. Thunder cracked and a lightning flash briefly illuminated our surroundings.

'The storm's directly above us now,' said Lucy, 'but when it passes, this rain will become torrential.'

My bedding was sopping and another strike of lightning showed our boots and habits soaked and drenched where we had left them. 'This really is the most detestable climate,' said Lucy.

I shivered. 'How long do you think the storm will last?'

'Impossible to say, but as soon as it's light, we'll call the guides and ride on to the Selwyns at the Mission House. I'm sure it can't be more than an hour's ride. Two at most.'

The thought of riding in saturated clothing for even half an hour was unappealing but I said nothing, my thoughts having turned to more worrying possibilities. 'But where are *our* guides?' I poked my head from the tent but could see nothing.

'Halloo!' called Lucy. She looked at me nervously. 'They should be outside.'

The lightning flashed again, giving me a clear view of the deserted clearing around our tent, the empty beach just below us, and the forbidding stands of bush encircling us on three other sides. 'There's no sign of them,' I said. 'Nor of Ingrams.'

'He was to have slept near the guides.'

'Could he . . . could they have . . . kidnapped him, do you suppose?'

'I hardly think so.' But Lucy moved closer to me and we sat, trembling with cold.

'Well,' I said, trying to sound braver than I felt and to quell the recollection of Lady Martin's tale of the natives with their tomahawks, 'Te Toa assured me the Maoris here are friendly. So we have nothing at all to fear. But do you have any real idea of where we are, Lucy?'

'Only that we're somewhere between Government House and Waimate. Quite a long way from Auckland.'

I flung back the tent flap in hopes of scrutinising our surroundings again in the next illumination. The rain was abating a little and sheet lightning flared across the ocean. Thunder rumbled all round us, and I fancied I saw shapes moving in the bush. If the Maoris do return to capture us, I thought, we will at least have a chance of escape if we are in the open.

I began to pull on my soaked habit and forced my feet into my sodden boots. Tsarina and Blaze, tethered by the bush, were whinnying and fretting. 'We can't sit in this tent forever,' I said. 'We're so wet already the rain will make no difference. And the horses will be calmer if we are with them.'

'But which way shall we go?' said Lucy. 'We have no compass and there's no sun or even any light yet.'

'We could always ride along the beach.'

'Much too dangerous. Listen to those waves crashing. But I fancy we were following some kind of track yesterday.' She paused. 'Do you remember that poor woman in Whanganui? Massacred with her—'

'Stop it!' I cried. But I was, myself, conjuring up visions of sinister men creeping stealthily upon us. 'It seems,' I said, in as calm a voice as I could muster, 'that we must shift for ourselves and ride on alone. So, let's start at once.'

'What about the tent?'

'Ingrams can strike it if . . . when . . . he returns.'

'Can you see his mule?'

'It's gone.' I clutched Lucy's hand. 'Come. Let's hurry. We should set off at once.'

Soaked and bedraggled, we were fumbling with the horses' bridles when there came the sound of approaching hooves.

'Quickly,' hissed Lucy. 'Into the bush. Here.'

This was not at all easy. Pushing into the densely entwined undergrowth, we were drenched from the branches above and sluiced by the low-lying ferns and foliage. Water ran down my back beneath my clothing, squelched inside my boots, trickled across my forehead. Finally, we managed to force our way far enough into the bush to be concealed from our pursuers. Peering at the clearing through the tangle of branches, we huddled together, listening to the oncoming horses. Though the lightning had moved even further south, I became suddenly afraid that that even one burst of illumination might reveal our hiding-place, and I tried to press Lucy deeper within the tangle of vegetation.

Into the clearing galloped two horses followed by a shambling mule.

'Ingrams,' I whispered to Lucy. 'And our Maori guides.'

She grasped my arm. 'I think we should stay here until we are quite sure of their intentions.'

'Ma'am,' called Ingrams, dismounting and making his way to the empty tent. He turned to the guides and spread his hands. 'Gone,' he said.

Shaking his head, one of the guides jumped from his horse and went over to our mounts.

I pushed Lucy forward. 'We're here,' I cried, 'sheltering from the fury of the storm.'

At the sight of us, the guides attempted to apprise us in dumb show that they had ridden with Ingrams through the night to let the Bishop know of our impending arrival — or so we understood. Recalling my terror of massacring natives, kidnap and slaughter, I felt ashamed of my own cowardice. 'That was very kind of you,' I said.

'And how far off is the Mission House?' asked Lucy.

'No more than an hour or so, Ma'am. Perhaps a little longer. The ground is so sodden now it will make for a slower riding pace.'

We set off together. When at last we approached the Mission House, I was relieved to see that it was a stout wooden building, fronted with a wide veranda and surrounded by what appeared, through the rain, to be a small orchard. The Bishop, in ulster and shovel hat, strode through the downpour to meet us. Dismounting, I briefly took in my surroundings. Close at hand stood apple, pear and apricot trees . . . and then, suddenly, I felt my heart lurch and heard again Te Toa's words: *the omens are favourable.* At a distance from the other plantings, I discerned a small but sturdy mulberry tree.

'Ah,' said the Bishop, following my gaze, 'you are admiring our mulberry. We've allowed it space to flourish to its full magnificence. Are you familiar with the species?'

'Yes, indeed, my Lord. I spent all of my childhood years in the company of just such a tree, but one that was entirely fully grown.'

It was two days before Te Toa joined us.

'The Governor is making an overland expedition to New Plymouth, I hear,' said the Bishop, 'but I'm afraid he'll find the tribes there hostile.'

'I do not think,' said Te Toa, 'that Wiremu Kingi will allow any attack while Te Kawana is present, though it may be he is not permitted into the pa.'

'They would surely not refuse the *Governor* entry?' said the Bishop, in alarm.

'It is possible. We will have to see. Kingi is greatly angered at the theft of his lands, and it is my belief he will attack the settlers in Taranaki if they do not give up the land they have stolen.'

'But Kingi has always been a friend to the British Crown.'

'So he will expect Te Kawana's support against the settlers. But now, Pihopa, if I may be permitted to kidnap your ladies, the sun is shining and the conditions excellent for a gallop to my pa.'

Te Toa's pa sat at the top of a small incline, enclosed within several rectangles of fences, one behind another. The outermost fence was of sharp stakes set between large wooden posts, lashed together with supplejack and flax bindings. About a foot behind this fence was a second one, similarly constructed. This contained pits where warriors with muskets could conceal themselves behind the heaped earth and fern barricades while aiming their weapons through the inner fence at any advancing enemy.

As we followed Te Toa up the excavated pathway to the entrance, I stopped, the better to marvel at the gateway. So narrow that it permitted the passage of only one person at a time, it was topped by a monstrous carved figure, decorated with feathers and the iridescent native paua shell.

'You see,' said Te Toa, turning back towards me, 'how the position of the rifle pits at all times commands the entry to the gate? Now, if you were another chief, or Te Kawana, I should be obliged to welcome you with great ceremony, but you are here only to see for yourself a true Maori village.'

We passed beneath the huge carved figure and into the interior of the pa. It seemed to me like an alien country, containing not a single house of sawn wood, such as we had in Auckland. Each dwelling was of an oblong shape, with a central doorway so low it was impossible to enter without stooping, on either side of which was a meagre window. The ridgepole was topped by a sharply sloping roof covered with thatch and the walls consisted of wrapped bundles of flax reeds, tightly lashed together to keep out the elements. Clustered together in a loose semi-circle, the huts stood at some distance from a smaller dwelling perched on a tall wooden pole, and another, much larger, version of the small houses, decorated with intricately carved figures with shining paua-shell eyes.

'Is that your house?' I asked, thinking it fit for a chief's dwelling.

Te Toa shook his head. 'No, that is the whare runanga, our meeting house. In a moment, we will look at it, but here' — and he indicated a hut which, although a little larger than its fellows, was low and undistinguished — 'is my own whare.'

Fronted like the others by a thatched veranda, its only distinguishing feature was a large carving atop the central apex of the roof. I dared not look too closely at it lest it replicate the one at the slave dwellings.

'You must be seen to examine most carefully the reed panels at the entranceway,' whispered Lucy. 'They contain his lineage.'

I looked intently at the intricate black, red and white patterning, but saw no evidence of genealogy. 'These are very fine,' I said.

'Thank you,' said Te Toa. 'And now I will show you the beautiful carvings in the whare runanga.'

Groups of bare-breasted native women squatted on the ground, apparently ignoring us until, as we passed, several of them called out to us in their own language.

'They are greeting you,' said Te Toa. 'Haere mai . . . Come here . . . they are saying.'

He called out something in return, and the women laughed. I averted my eyes from their casual semi-nakedness and looked towards a clutch of young boys, entirely naked but at a distance from us, who were taking it in turns to swing from a rope attached to a pole.

'Our kumara gardens are over there,' said Te Toa, 'behind their swing. And they have another swing by the river where they take it in turns to launch themselves into the water. It is good for boys to be agile and fearless.'

'I'm very glad to have seen your pa. Thank you, Te Toa.'

'It was a great pleasure to me to escort you and Mata Kawana, Miss Fanny.'

And I saw Lucy frown slightly at the familiar use of my name.

Te Toa accompanied us on our return to the Selwyns' house. In some manner he contrived for a few moments to stand alone with me.

'That was a most interesting experience,' I said.

'I wish to tell you that you will see me again, Miss Fanny. And soon. My tohunga has read it in the omens.'

AOTEAROA

I had heard much of Te Kawana Kerei before I ever saw him. My mother said that, for a Pakeha, he had fine chiefly bearing. And, as a paramount chief of their Kuini Wikitoria, he had great mana. 'Since he arrived in Aotearoa,' said my mother, 'he has often sought advice from Mr Hadfield on Maori affairs. He has learned to speak our language and he has great affection for our people. This shows us that he is a good man. And he is coming tonight to this house to speak with Mr Hadfield again. I have asked to be present, but you children must take yourselves out of sight and hearing of this meeting.'

So Hone and I waited until they had exchanged their greetings, then stole under the small high window and pressed ourselves into the shadow of the wall. We heard the voice of the unseen Te Kawana speaking in our own language: 'Te Rau-paraha is too powerful among the chiefs and these murderous attacks cannot be allowed to continue. The time has come when I must humble him. I have no choice.'

'True,' said Mr Hadfield, 'but first you must catch him.'

'I know it,' said Te Kawana, 'but how am I to succeed? He is wily and well guarded.'

'We must think very carefully,' Mr Hadfield said. 'You will have only one such chance, Governor. If you fail, he will be forever on his guard against you.'

There was a long silence. Hone stirred beside me and I prodded him with my finger.

'If you look out from Peka-peka beach at Waikanae to his stronghold, Kapiti Island,' said Mr Hadfield, 'it appears deserted. Of the pa, the palisades, the kumara grounds, even the whaling station at its southernmost tip, there is not a trace. It is only when unwary voyagers land on its more hospitable eastern shore they discover, to their misfortune, that it is, indeed, the impregnable stronghold of the Napoleon of the South. You cannot take Te Rau-paraha on Kapiti.'

We heard our mother's voice. 'Harawira is right. And since you will never take him on Kapiti, you must outwit him and capture him by trickery and stealth. I know the workings of the mind of that butcher, and I have a plan whereby Te Kawana may entrap him.'

AUCKLAND, 1848

Two days after we returned from our visit to Waimate, a letter arrived from the Governor.

'He says that Mr Hadfield's health is much better, but the situation in Wellington is grave, so he must remain in the south for some time,' said Lucy.

'I'm relieved to hear that Mr Hadfield is well again,' said Lady Martin, who had called on us. 'There's no other man in New Zealand who better understands the Maoris and their ways. If anyone can avert war, he can. The natives are devoted to him. Even Te Rauparaha's nephew, Te Rangi-hae-ata, who's bitterly opposed to all Englishmen and is an even more ferocious warrior than his uncle, called on Mr Hadfield when he was convalescing at the St Hills' in Wellington last month.'

'If I were Mrs St Hill, I should have been very afraid at his presence in my house,' I said.

'She was terrified, but she said he stood quietly by the doorway, waiting for her husband to invite him inside. He's a most magnificent specimen of a man, over six and a half feet tall, with long black hair swept into the topknot and eyes like a hawk's. Mrs St Hill said he looked neither right nor left and did not greet either her or her husband but merely swept into the room where Mr Hadfield lay on his couch, and bent and pressed noses with him, speaking to him urgently in Maori. The St Hills don't speak the native tongue, but Mr Hadfield explained that Te Rangi-hae-ata had brought his tohunga with him to assist Mr Hadfield's recovery and asked if they would mind allowing the Maori priest to enter and perform his ceremonies.

'Mr St Hill was inclined to feel that he should remain to guard Mr Hadfield, but the missionary said he was quite confident of Te Rangi-hae-ata's good intentions. So the St Hills left the three of them alone and, although it is probably merely a coincidence, Mrs St Hill claims that the very next day Mr Hadfield's strength began to return. She says that, for another three days, Te Rangi-hae-ata and his tohunga, mounted on their horses, sat at a distance from the St Hills' homestead, keeping watch over Mr Hadfield's spirit . . . or so Mr Hadfield told them.'

'What an extraordinary story.' I said.

'Yes,' said Lady Martin. 'I told you the Maoris are an extraordinary race.'

In the Governor's absence, Lucy spent long periods of time closeted with Mr Godfrey over preparations for the ball. It had become her principal topic of conversation so, when she came running to find me in the garden, I assumed they had devised some new form of entertainment. She was quite breathless. 'Sit down, Fanny. The most *wonderful* news! You'll never guess.'

'You've thought of a novel amusement for the ball?'

'No, no. Much more exciting than that.' She took a breath and caught my hand. 'George has been honoured with a knighthood. He sent me word this very morning.'

'As you observe, Miss Fanny, I have come to see you.'

'Good morning, Te Toa. Are you well?'

'I am most well. I have come to ask you an important question, if you are happy to answer me.'

'I'll do my best. Would you like tea?'

'Thank you, no, but perhaps we may sit on that seat there, below the pohutukawa?'

We settled ourselves on the bench beneath the great spreading canopy.

'So, what is this important question?'

Te Toa seemed to be thinking. Finally, 'Is Te Kawana a son or nephew of Mata Wikitoria?' he asked.

'Neither. He has no kinship ties to her,'

'Then why has she given this honour to him?'

'Well, he has served his country and his Queen . . .'

'Are you sure of this? I am told that many of the dispatches that Te Kawana sends to London are not true.'

'If her Majesty didn't think the Governor was a worthy man, she wouldn't honour him.'

'Naturally. The question is not what Mata Wikitoria *thinks*. The question is whether Te Kawana is, *in fact*, a worthy man.'

I decided to change the subject. 'Since you are a paramount chief, will you attend the investiture?'

'It seems so. There is a government vessel reserved to bring all the Northern chiefs, and another to carry the chiefs from the south.'

'But if there will be chiefs from many regions attending, what if fighting should break out among them?'

Te Toa was deeply affronted. 'Miss Thompson, you have heard me speak often of our Maori ways. No chief would ever dishonour such a ceremony. We are not engaged to fight one another and we will not.' And he rose and strode away.

Without thinking, I ran after him and caught his arm.

'I'm sorry, Te Toa. I didn't mean to offend you. I was concerned not only for the Governor's safety but for yours.'

As I said it, I knew it to be true but, if I could have, I would have recalled my words instantly.

He stopped. 'Thank you for this concern but I am a warrior. I have no need of women to protect me.'

I stared at him. His face had taken on a sinister aspect.

No matter that he speaks so courteously, that he is deft and clever in his arguments, he remains a savage, I thought. And those who meddle with fire risk a burning.

AOTEAROA

We knew, my brother Hone and I, that something was about to happen. We could tell it from the suppressed anxiety of our mother, from the slightest agitation in the demeanour of Mr Hadfield.

At last came the day when my mother said, 'Tonight, before you go to sleep, you will stop your ears with plugs of flax. You will hear nothing and you will make no sound.'

'Why?' said Hone.

'Because,' said my mother, 'there will be nothing to hear. Do as you are bidden.'

So, as soon as she had left us, we pulled the flax from our ears and peered from the doorway of our hut. It was a silent night and there was no moon. In the distance we heard the faint splash of oars, but this was no new sound. Often, fishing canoes put out at night-time. Voices hummed lightly across the water, and almost instantly were stilled.

'There is a ship off Peka-peka,' whispered Hone. 'Look. You can just make out its shadowy shape on the horizon.'

As we stared and our eyes grew accustomed to the darkness, we saw that two smaller boats beside the vessel were making for the shore.

'Are they coming here, to Waikanae?'

Hone shook his head. 'No, they are moving further along the coast. Nearer to Otaki.'

'But that is Te Rau-paraha's cousin's mainland pa. What is happening?'

From Mr Hadfield's house, three figures slipped soundlessly into the night — Mr Hadfield, our stepfather and, 'Our mother!'

They made their way in the direction of the beach where we could see that the two small boats had now landed. From each disembarked a party of men.

'Soldiers!' murmured Hone. 'And they are armed. You can see the glint of their muskets in the starlight.'

Mr Hadfield, our mother and stepfather now joined the soldiers on the sands, and the party set off on foot along the beach towards Otaki. Not a sound gave away their presence. We knew there would be no scouts guarding the Otaki pa; none of the tribes on our coast was at war. Resolved to see what was happening, Hone and I followed them at a distance. It was more than three hours before we arrived at Otaki and, as we slipped along the shoreline, we noticed a small boat skirting the coast, shadowing the figures in front of us. Its oars were tied about with cloth so that they made no sound.

The group ahead of us left the beach and mounted the sand-hills. Just before the entrance to the pa, I saw my mother in conversation with a tall figure I took to be Te Kawana. She pointed to one of the huts and, at a signal from the man, the soldiers raised their muskets together and fired a volley of shots. Then, accompanied by a party of soldiers, he burst into the hut. There came the high-pitched sound of women wailing, and several minutes later the soldiers reappeared, one holding a lantern, three more leading a naked man covered in red ochre, and the rest holding captive two naked women.

'That is Te Rau-paraha,' whispered Hone. 'I recognise him from the hen house. And those must be his wives. He has been taken sleeping, and with *women*. What dishonour for a great chief not to be captured in battle with warriors.'

'We will have more than dishonour if our mother sees us,' I said. 'Quickly. We must run back before she returns.'

'Run?' said Hone. 'I am already so tired I can scarcely walk.' He grabbed my arm. 'But, look, they have Te Rau-paraha in the little boat now and they are rowing him out to the larger vessel. It is the government brig, *Calliope*.'

'While you were sleeping,' said our mother next morning, 'there was a great to-do in the night. Te Rau-paraha has been taken prisoner at Otaki by Te Kawana and the Pakeha forces. What humiliation for him. A great chief to be captured so, not on the battlefield but exposed naked in his bed. Terrible, indeed.' She smiled. But it was a smile of hatred. 'So, after thirteen years, the gods have favoured me. I have broken the power of Te Rau-paraha's mana and avenged my husband and the tohunga.'

'Mr Hadfield says we should not harbour thoughts of revenge,' said Hone, 'but that we should learn to turn the other cheek.'

'How curious,' said our mother. 'For is it not written in the Bible of Te Ariki: *An eye for an eye and a tooth for a tooth*?'

AUCKLAND, 1848

The Governor strode over to where I was sketching in the garden. I laid aside my crayon. 'Welcome back, Sir George. And my congratulations on such a great honour.'

'Thank you. But I shall not be styled so until after my investiture, of course.'

'Was your recent business in Wellington successful?'

'Entirely. I've arrested Te Rau-paraha on a charge of treason.'

'And imprisoned him?'

'No, no. I could never imprison him like a common criminal. That would be seen as an unacceptably shocking act by all Maoris, even his enemies. It would destroy his mana and enrage Ngati Toa. So he is now a "guest" of his old ally in the North, Tamati Waka Nene.'

'But surely, if he is an ally, he'll let the chief escape?'

'That is not at all the Maori way. Waka Nene has promised to contain Te Rau-paraha and it's certain he'll do so.'

'And Te Rau-paraha's nephew? Won't he seek revenge?'

'Not while his uncle remains with the great Waka Nene. So now we have a little more breathing space in the south.'

'And Mr Hadfield?'

'After Te Rau-paraha's capture, he was obliged to go back to Wellington for his health. He is recovering well but still in need of medical attention. He's a most astonishing man. I accompanied him to Wellington, and there he asked me if I would consider riding back to Otaki with a message for Nohorua, Te Rau-paraha's brother. He wished it to be carried by me since it required a Pakeha of the highest mana to deliver it.

'You will understand that I was a little uneasy about such a mission, most particularly since the entire tribe was aware that it was solely on my instructions, and in my presence, that their chief had been so ignominiously arrested.

'Mr Hadfield assured me I would not be harmed, but the nearer my horse drew to Otaki the more, I confess, my apprehension grew. It was a Sunday and I had been told I should find Nohorua at church at Mr Hadfield's Mission.

'I dismounted, was greeted a little curtly by one or two of the natives, and delivered my letter to Nohorua, then, as I had promised Mr Hadfield, I knelt down to pray with the congregation which was almost entirely Maori. And at no time did a single one of them threaten me or attempt utu for my kidnapping of their great leader. I went among them freely and left in peace.'

AOTEAROA

So Te Rau-paraha stayed many months in the North as a 'guest' of Ngapuhi, his former allies, and when the time was auspicious, Te Kawana returned him to Ngati Toa. I saw this return. I was fifteen years old.

Though the chief's mana had been broken, Te Kawana had no wish to humiliate him further, and on the shore at Otaki a gathering of more than five hundred people watched as the government brig carried the chief back to his ancestral lands. When Te Rau-paraha set foot upon the sands, we saw that he wore a splendid British naval uniform, a present from Te Kawana, and carried a magnificent sword, another of Te Kawana's gifts. As the tribe moaned and wailed and the men stamped a welcome, the chief Poho-tiraha stepped forward to greet him. Then Te Rau-paraha raised high his weapon and thrust it into the ground in front of Poho-tiraha, crying out, 'Take hold of this sword. I no longer wish for honour on earth but for honour in Heaven. We shall build a church upon this ground.'

But all of this, the rejoicing, the singing and the great feasting, I was permitted to watch only from the safety of the pa. My mother remembered still what had happened to my father. Even with his mana broken, she did not trust Te Rau-paraha.

Mr Hadfield, his health fully restored, returned to us at Waikanae And so we continued to live happily near the Mission, my mother, Mr Nicoll, Hone and I, until — and still I can scarcely bear to remember it — until the Pakeha fever swept through Wellington, Otaki, the Manawatu, the Whanganui, claiming within a month more than eighty lives. When I think of it, my heart twists with bitter grief. Among those struck down were both my mother and stepfather.

'Makareta, Hine-moana,' said my mother as she lay dying, her breath rasping harshly in her throat, 'sit here beside me and listen carefully to my words.'

I squatted next to her where she lay, flushed and fevered.

'Hear what I say. Look, now, at Tutere-moana, the mountain-top of Kapiti.'

I peered through the doorway of our hut.

'What do you see?'

'Only the head of the mountain thrusting into the sky.'

'And at its peak?'

'Nothing but the grey stones at the summit.'

My mother sighed. 'Then it is certain I am about to rejoin the spirits of my ancestors.'

I clutched her hand. 'You must not leave us!' I cried.

'If it is ordained, then my time on this earth is almost done. No one can defy the will of the gods. Attend to what I tell you. Around the brow of Tutere-moana, I see a wreath of cloud.'

'No!'

'Hush, and obey my wishes. This is the funeral wreath, the sign of impending death. No mortal can gainsay it. Now, when I have left you to join our ancestors, Mr Hadfield will wish to give me a Christian burial. Do not oppose him in this. He has been good to us; he will protect you. And what are a few Pakeha words spoken over the dead? They change nothing. And, afterwards, he will lay my bones in the graveyard of Te Ariki here at the Mission. Do not grieve that I am in such a place. The land here is the land of the Maori; my bones will lie safely in the earth of Aotearoa and my spirit will have returned to Hawai'iki. This is the only thing that is important. Accede to the desires of Mr Hadfield in all of this.'

Each night, by my mother's grave, I recited the karakia, the sacred songs and prayers she had taught me, and waited for her spirit to visit me, but she did not come.

'Ah, Makareta,' said Mr Hadfield, appearing beside me, 'I see you are reciting your Christian prayers. You must take comfort from knowing that your dear mother and stepfather are now safe in Heaven in the arms of Te Ariki.'

'Where is this Heaven?' I asked, and he pointed to the sky.

Though I did not say so to Mr Hadfield, I could make out no sign of anything but clouds. And had not my mother, herself, told me that when the time came her spirit would walk to Te Reinga, slide down the sacred pohutukawa into the sea, and pass along the Broad Path of Tane to Hawai'iki, the ancestral lands?

'Shall I pray with you, Makareta?' said Mr Hadfield.

I began to say no, but thought better of it. Suppose my mother was, after all, in the Heaven of Te Ariki? Would it not be wise for me to intercede with Him . . . as a precaution?

AUCKLAND, 1848

The day of the long-awaited ball dawned clear, but at midday, as it clouded over and rain threatened, Lucy became increasingly dismayed.

'It's no use fretting,' said Mr Godfrey. 'We can do nothing to control the weather.'

The veranda at Government House had been enclosed to afford a space for the guests to promenade, and the two reception rooms, which opened one into the other, provided a large space for the dancing. Supper was to be offered in a marquee on the lawn, where tables and benches had been set out to accommodate about two hundred people. Lucy and I had assisted the servants in creating garlands to be twined around the pillars of the marquee and the sides of the dancing rooms. Flags, greenery and ribbons decorated the poles of the veranda and the sides of the temporary bandstand erected in the garden.

'And I'm fervently hoping,' said Lucy, 'that the food will be sufficient.'

'Tomorrow,' said Mr Godfrey, 'you'll be sending the servants to Lady Martin's little hospital with the leftovers, mark my words.'

Lucy and I had just finished dressing when we heard a loud commotion, much shouting and laughter, and the heavy creaking of wheels. The band of the 58th had arrived, transported with their instruments in three bullock drays. We stepped out to greet them in our new gowns from Sydney, Lucy's an elegant shade of pale cream that set off her dark looks, and mine a glowing midnight blue.

'How fine you look, Fanny. Every unmarried man will be scrambling to inscribe his name on your dancing card.'

'I shall be the first,' said Mr Godfrey, appearing on the veranda.

'Please allow me to engage you for the opening dance. And, Eliza, can I mark your card for the second?'

'Here is our host,' I said. 'How splendid he looks in his dress uniform.'

The Governor bowed to us both.

'Two such beautiful ladies,' said Mr Godfrey. 'We're quite spoilt here, George.'

'Have the Maori chiefs accepted their invitations?' I whispered to Lucy.

'Of course. They'd be most upset to miss such a celebration.'

'Will they dance?'

'No. They watch our festivities and participate in the eating and drinking, but they eschew our way of dancing . . . Ah, here are our first arrivals.'

Sir William Martin, almost invisible within oilskins, strode out in front of two lines of natives bearing a litter.

'It's Lady Martin,' cried Lucy. 'She's been carried here in a potato kit strung on poles.'

'And with a large umbrella above me to deflect the rain,' called Lady Martin. 'It's a most comfortable form of transport. I can highly recommend it!'

The Maori bearers gently lowered the kit to the floor and helped her to extricate herself.

'I have my fan and gloves safely wrapped in another kit,' she said. 'They're so splendid for keeping things dry. But you have more guests arriving. You must leave me and see to them.'

Securely shrouded against the weather, Miss Pitt, wearing the general's jackboots, made her way along the muddy path towards us. Several gentlemen now appeared, pick-a-backed by Maoris who had offered their services for a fee.

'But,' said the Governor, more amused than I had ever yet seen him, 'the prize for ingenuity must surely go to Mr Outhwaite. He's pushing his wife in a wheelbarrow.'

'Lieutenant Cowan has arrived, Fanny,' said Lucy. 'He looks uncommonly handsome in his uniform.'

The Lieutenant stepped forward to greet his host and hostess, and bowed to me. 'I've been away with my regiment and I'm delighted to be back in Auckland. I hope I may claim you for at least one dance, Miss Thompson.'

Our attention was attracted by the arrival of a party of Maoris who rode up, wrapped in magnificent full-length feather cloaks. When they dismounted, I was astonished to see that beneath these they were, men and women alike, clad in immaculate English evening dress, the ladies' ball gowns being equal in style and splendour to those of any of the other ladies present.

A second group of Maoris on horseback came into view at almost the same moment as the band struck up. I saw they were in traditional native costume, their hair dressed with feathers, and that one of them was Te Toa.

Lady Martin turned to Lucy. 'I see Te Toa hasn't brought either of his wives.'

I froze.

His *wives*? 'He . . . he has more than one wife?' I ventured quietly.

Lady Martin nodded. 'Two. That's quite normal for the chiefs, though there's generally one particular favourite. The great Northern chief, Waka Nene, has three, but it's only the senior wife who accompanies her husband to events like this. Look, there's Waka Nene with his principal wife over there.'

I glanced to where she indicated, and saw an elderly Maori, his curly hair tinged with grey, his face very heavily tattooed, immaculate in white tie but with a long jade ornament in one ear.

'*That* is Waka Nene? He looks exactly like a benevolent uncle.'

'I assure you he's a most formidable adversary to his foes.'

The dancing now being about to commence, Mr Godfrey approached the sofa where Lady Martin and I sat.

'Away you go, my dear,' she said. 'I'm not able to dance but I love to watch, and my husband enjoys it greatly.'

I had not danced since my sisters' weddings at Albany, and the whirling and wheeling, the lively music, the colourful gowns and the scarlet and white uniforms of the 58th mingled in a heady mix of exhilaration. But beneath my enjoyment ran the thread of horror I had felt at Lady Martin's revelation. I shall put it entirely from my mind, I told myself. After all, what right have I to judge Te Toa's way of life?

As I sat, fanning myself, Lieutenant Cowan appeared, to remind me I had promised to accompany him to supper. 'I've stolen a glimpse,' he said, 'that cold collation will be very welcome after the heat in here.'

He offered me his arm and led me to the marquee, where he deposited me at a table and went off to fill our plates.

'Good evening, Miss Fanny. You look like a midnight sky.'

'Te Toa! I . . . I'm waiting for Lieutenant Cowan.'

'He is in a long line of other people also hungry for their food. He will be some time, so I have decided to come and speak with you. I would ask you to dance, Miss Fanny, but I do not know the Pakeha dancing and nor do I like it.'

He had removed his great cloak and was clad in a flax kilt, with a short feather cape flung across his shoulders, caught by two red tapes at the chest. His splayed feet were bare. I looked at him, then away. I could not think of anything to say to him. He is a *savage*, I thought, a native with two wives.

'You are a little cold to me, I think. For my rudeness last week, I apologise most sincerely. I have affronted you.'

I shook my head.

'You are not telling me the truth. Is it because I have not asked you to dance?'

'No, not that. I . . .'

'What is it? You must tell me.'

Tears had begun to start in my eyes. 'Please, Te Toa, I beg you, leave me now. I wish to enjoy the dancing, the festivities . . . Please go away.'

He bowed. 'Because you wish it, I will go. But, Miss Fanny, I will be back.'

'So much excitement,' said Lucy. 'First the ball and now the investiture. And only two weeks between. I've hardly had time to catch my breath. Come, Fanny, we must hurry and finish dressing. The general is sending his carriage for us and it will arrive at any moment.'

A pavilion had been set up. In front of it was a guard of honour of the 58th Regiment, impressive in their red and white; at its far end stood a dais covered in scarlet cloth, topped with a pedestal holding a crimson velvet throne trimmed with gold bullion lace. To the right was a chair of state for the Queen's Commissioner, to the left another for the Knight-Elect, with rows of seats behind them. Flags of all nations adorned the ceiling, and the ridgepoles were decorated with elaborate garlands of flowers and evergreen branches.

'Stop day-dreaming, Fanny,' said Lucy. 'Everyone else has taken their seats. It's time for us to go in.'

The ladies' procession party lined up, all of us clad in our best ball gowns although it was just after midday, and to loud applause Lucy led us into the pavilion. As wife of the Queen's Commissioner, Lady Martin followed her, leaning heavily on her sticks. Then came General Wynyard's lady, next Mrs Selwyn, and, after her, the wives of the Sheriff, the Colonial Secretary and the Surveyor-General. Feeling very self-conscious, I brought up the rear. We ascended the dais and took our seats behind the three seats of honour. It was close in the pavilion in the November heat, and we fanned ourselves discreetly as we waited until, at exactly one o'clock, the trumpeters of the 58th unleashed a fanfare to announce the start of the ceremony.

To the strains of 'God Save the Queen', the guard presented arms and the official procession moved forward, at its head, Sir William Martin, resplendent in scarlet and gold. Behind came the Deputy Sheriff and the Colonial Secretary in ceremonial dress, and after them marched Bishop Selwyn and other members of the clergy. They seated themselves on the platform as the procession continued with naval, military and staff officers, marching two by two. Lieutenant-Governor Eyre, Mr Domett and the Attorney-General brought up the rear, followed by Mr Percy, the King at Arms, holding aloft the Royal Commission on a crimson velvet cushion.

The band fell silent. Another fanfare heralded the entrance of the Honourable Constantine Dillon, bearing on a second scarlet velvet cushion the insignia of the Order of the Bath, and then a salvo of trumpets sounded for the arrival of the four Esquires of the Knight-Elect. I was astonished to see that flanking Mr Blackmore and Mr Thatcher were Waka Nene and another native. 'Te Puni,' whispered my neighbour, Mrs Wynyard. 'The Governor has chosen to honour two of the chiefs loyal to Her Majesty.' A long solo trumpet blast reverberated around us, the troops again presented arms, and a stiff, solitary figure in white dress uniform, over which was draped a magnificent crimson robe with trimmings of fur, slowly processed towards us.

'He must be sweltering,' hissed Mrs Wynyard.

I watched the Governor nod graciously here and there at faces he recognised in the throng, and saw, too, Lucy try in vain to catch his eye. The petulant expression which he so often wore at home was entirely absent. In this public arena, he was the epitome of regal grace and condescension. As he approached the throne, he made three reverences before ascending the first step where he remained while the Chief Justice read the commission. Then, he mounted the platform and stood before Sir William, who invested him with the insignia, thanked the Sheriff and invited us all to congratulate 'Her Majesty's new Knight Commander of the Order of the Bath, Sir George Grey'.

With much cheering, the assembled company stood and made its way towards the dais. Rising quickly from her seat, Lucy moved to her husband's side and reached up to kiss his cheek. He turned instantly away from her towards Waka Nene.

Most of the settler population of New Zealand seemed to be present, everyone parading in finery. I could not help but notice how the feathers in the cockades of the hats of the European men mirrored the white-banded black feathers fixed into the topknots of the high-ranking Maoris. In the line of well-wishers I saw Te Toa, who gave me no sign of recognition. I looked for anyone nearby who might be his wife, but he was in the company of a group of native men who were greeting an English clergyman and a youthful, rather sullen, Maori girl.

I turned to Lady Martin. 'Who is that man there, with the young native wife?'

'Gracious me! She's not his wife in any sense, I assure you. That's Mr Hadfield, the missionary, and a more upright man it would be hard to find. The girl lives in the pa at Otaki. Her mother died earlier this year in the fever epidemic. She's something of a heroine among her own people; as an infant she swam from Kapiti Island to the mainland. Or so the legend has it . . .'

I saw how, already, this honour had altered the new knight, seated majestically like a king on the scarlet throne. I watched the crowd of people congratulating him, fawning over his hand, and noted how some of them, having moved away, whispered obviously unkind remarks. The heat was intense, yet all continued to mill about inside the marquee, promenading and preening. I had recognised Mr Eyre at once from Te Toa's description of his uniform, and noticed how self-importantly he moved among the crowd, nodding regally to left and right.

Everything here, including the ceremony that had just taken place, seemed only to emphasise the valiant futility of employing such extravagant pomp and ceremony to try to replicate the standards of Home. One by one, the chiefs were now congratulating Sir George, yet there was a gravity in their demeanour and a restrained quality to their ceremonial dress that spoke more of sincerity than all the gold epaulettes and braided uniforms parading before us. What do the natives really think of this display? I wondered. The vulgarity in the 'splendour' of our Pakeha costumes, in the posturing and show, reminded me uncomfortably of Te Toa's talk of the Maori strictures on immodesty. Are the chiefs impressed by all this, or do they see it only as another puzzling European custom, like our dancing? Here we stand, I thought, stultified, imprisoned in yards of muslin, satin, bombazine, silk and serge.

Seized by the need to leave the stifling marquee, I sought an open tent flap and escaped to the shade of a nearby tree, gulping in breaths of cooler air.

A figure crossed the lawn towards me. 'Kia ora, Miss Fanny. I saw you leave the pavilion and I have followed you.'

'Good afternoon, Te Toa,' I said awkwardly. 'I hope you enjoyed the ceremony.'

'Yes, like all the chiefs, I was most interested by it. We are very honoured that Te Kawana chose Waka Nene and Te Puni as his escorts.'

'It was a very fine procession and the chiefs looked resplendent,' I said.

'Some of us had hoped that Mata Wikitoria herself might attend the ceremony.'

'New Zealand is very far off, and she has many demands on her time.'

'I am sure that is so, and Sir William's speech was most gracious and profound. All the chiefs feel great happiness for the Governor's success.'

There was a silence. I searched for something to say. 'The 58th look very colourful.'

'It is true they are very pretty in their red and white uniforms, but these they wear also in battle. I fear they do not understand the benefits of concealment. When they are fighting, it is very easy for our warriors to see them, even from great distances. This is a grave error in warfare.'

We stood uneasily for a moment. In the distance, I saw Lucy waving to me. 'Please excuse me,' I said. 'My sister wants me to join her.'

He nodded, and I walked away.

AOTEAROA

Because I was so cast down by the death of my mother, kind Mr Hadfield took me with him to Auckland for a ceremony of grand magnificence in which Te Kawana became a very paramount chief of Mata Wikitoria. And with him were two Maori rangatira — on his one side, Tamati Waka Nene, and on his other, Te Puni. Carrying their taiaha, as befitted great rangatira, they wore long ceremonial feather cloaks over their flax kilts, and their topknots were stuck with combs and precious huia feathers. From their earlobes hung large pieces of pounamu, and each chief had a jade hei-tiki tied about his neck. I knew better than to stare at the glittering eyes of those hei-tiki. Or at the chiefs or their moko. I watched them secretly from the sides of my eyes.

I gazed a little longer at Te Kawana. This was the first time I had properly seen him. Over his white soldier's clothing of the army of Kuini Wikitoria was a thick red cloak, so heavy he was obliged to walk like a stiff wooden carving. How stupid, I thought, for a soldier to wear white garments. And so tight against his body. How can he move in battle? As he went forward, his sword clanked loudly at his side and the plumage on his large white helmet fluttered. I have never seen such feathers here in Aotearoa. They must be from a bird of Mata Wikitoria.

There was much clapping and some cheering but no dancing and no singing. Even the speeches of the orators were short and did not roll sonorously from their mouths. This surprised me greatly, though I did not say so later to Mr Hadfield. As he walked in the procession, in his clergyman's suit with the white band at his throat like a tui's marking, he seemed to me more noble and dignified than any of the other Pakeha present.

I gazed around from the seat where Mr Hadfield had left me. The Maori wahine there were chieftainesses; all had moko kauae, and I could smell the sweet scent of the titoki oil they had used to dress their hair. Some of them wore patterned flax anklets and precious ancestral kiwi-feather cloaks. I felt their scornful eyes upon me, their disdain at my poor simple Pakeha dress. They do not know, I thought, that I am the equal of them all, that my mother was a high-born princess. I thought of how, so long ago, I had been promised to the grandson of Waka Nene, and I lowered my eyes down, down . . . then turned away to look at the Pakeha women.

Their dresses were very beautiful, it is true, but how could they walk about in such garments? At the waist, they were held in so rigidly I could not see how they could breathe freely, and beneath and around their armpits large damp patches stained the fabric of their clothing. I should like a dress of this coloured material, I told myself, but not fashioned into such a shape. My own garment was a Mission frock, plain and simple, designed, so said Mr Hadfield, for modesty and concealment, not adornment. 'Te Ariki,' said Mr Hadfield, often, 'wishes us to be humble and self-effacing.' But, as I looked about me at the Pakeha, I could not see that any of them, but for Mr Hadfield, displayed such humbleness. I turned towards the stage where Te Kawana and the others were seated, and watched as the people began to surge towards it. Two pretty Pakeha wahine stood smiling together near Te Kawana.

'The dark-haired lady,' said Mr Hadfield, appearing beside me, 'is Te Kawana's wife, and the other, the fair one, her sister.'

I stared at them. They are like day and night, I thought, light and shadow.

And, as I watched, I saw the dark one run forward and reach up to place her mouth against her husband's cheek. And I saw, too, how he did not bend towards her but turned away, towards Waka Nene.

He does not care for her, I thought. And the maggot of ambition hatched in me.

'Come, Makareta,' said Mr Hadfield, 'we must offer our congratulations to Te Kawana.'

Conscious of the poverty of my dress, I walked forward slowly beside him. We stopped at the foot of the red platform and I followed him as he stepped up to the throne on which sat Te Kawana. Mr Hadfield bowed and kissed his proffered hand. 'My warmest congratulations, Sir George.'

I said nothing but sank down into the curtsey my mother had long ago taught me. I went to rise but, before I could do so, Te Kawana stood and, taking my hand, drew me to my feet. I remained silent, my head politely lowered until, just as he released my hand, and only for a single moment, I looked full into his eyes, then away again. I felt my heart beat faster; my body seemed on fire. For the first time, I was swept by the blaze of passion. I looked at Te Kawana again and felt his gaze lock with mine. I had snared him in my net.

My head still bent, I walked from the platform behind Mr Hadfield, looking neither right nor left as he greeted his many assembled Maori and Pakeha friends. I wished to be invisible to the eye of the mighty Waka Nene. I did not want him to recognise in me the bride long ago promised to his grandson . . .

And I was afraid lest that good man, Mr Hadfield, had observed me and had understood the wicked workings of my heart. He said nothing, but three days later, when we returned to Otaki and he led the household at evening worship, he did not pray as usual but read to us from the Holy Bible of Te Ariki and, as he spoke, I felt his eyes burning into my stirring flesh.

Mr Hadfield's face was very solemn. 'We shall listen carefully to the Word of the Lord,' he said, 'then reflect upon our own sins.' And, in the voice of an orator, he began to read. '*And the Lord God caused a deep sleep to fall upon Adam and he slept: and he took one of his ribs, and closed up the flesh instead thereof; and the rib, which the Lord God had taken from man, made he a woman, and brought her unto the man. And Adam said, This is now bone of my bones, and flesh of my flesh: she shall be called Woman, because she was taken out of Man. Therefore shall a man leave his father and his mother, and shall cleave unto his wife: and they shall be one flesh. And they were both naked, the man and his wife, and were not ashamed.*

'Now the Serpent was more subtle than any beast of the field which the Lord God had made. And he said unto the woman, Yea, hath God said, ye shall not eat of every tree of the garden? And the woman said unto the Serpent, We may eat of the fruit of the trees of the garden: but of the fruit of the tree which is in the midst of the garden, God hath said, ye shall not eat of it, neither shall ye touch it, lest ye die. And the Serpent said unto the woman, ye shall not surely die.'

I stared at the earth floor beneath my feet and thought of Te Kawana and how he had raised me up. I could not lift my eyes to Mr Hadfield's but I knew that he peered into the hidden corners of my soul . . .

'*The Serpent beguiled me, and I did eat.*'

I did not dare to ask Mr Hadfield, so I questioned my brother, Hone. 'How might we recognise a serpent? We have no snakes here in Aotearoa. How could we know the form of such a creature?'

He looked at me, puzzled. 'Since there are none here, how should I know? But I believe they may be thick as rope, and scaly, and have pointed tails and toothless heads with evil, poisonous fangs. And that their eyes resemble the Devil's.'

Now, every night it seemed, Mr Hadfield returned to reading from the Book of Genesis at evening prayers. 'I hope you are heeding carefully the Word of God, Hone and Makareta,' he said, and we bent our heads, murmuring in assent. '*And when the woman saw that the tree was good for food, and that it was pleasant to the eyes, and a tree to be desired to make one wise,*' read Mr Hadfield, '*she took of the fruit thereof, and did eat, and gave also unto her husband with her; and he did eat. And the eyes of them both were opened, and they knew that they were naked; and they sewed fig leaves together, and made themselves aprons. And they heard the voice of the Lord God walking in the garden in the cool of the day: and Adam and his wife hid themselves from the presence of the Lord God amongst the trees of the garden.*'

And Mr Hadfield looked at me sorrowfully. But he said nothing.

AUCKLAND, 1848–49

'Your sister said I should find you on the veranda, Miss Thompson. May I join you?'

'Certainly.'

Lieutenant Cowan settled himself in a chair. 'I saw you at the investiture but only from a distance. Such a magnificent ceremony. I felt it embodied all the finest elements of Empire. It makes one realise one's great fortune in being born British.'

'I—'

'And the gracious way in which the Governor permitted the Maoris to participate underlines the importance of British colonisation in bringing civilisation to the disadvantaged native races.'

He spoke with such complete self-assurance I felt annoyance rising in me. 'Perhaps they are even more disadvantaged by those unscrupulous British colonists who illegally seize their lands.'

The Lieutenant looked at me in surprise. 'I . . . well, as to that, I'm sure they may look to the British rule of law for restitution.'

We were silent for a few moments, then he said, 'I confess I'm surprised, Miss Thompson. I had not formed the opinion that you were quite so . . . frank in your views.'

'I lay no claim to having views,' I said, 'but I am on the side of justice and honour.'

'I applaud your sentiments but we must remember that the Maoris, like all inferior native races, are savages at heart and in the greatest need of our wisdom and guidance. Perhaps we should turn our talk to lighter subjects. I understand from Lady Grey that Mr Thomas proposes a picnic tomorrow.'

'Yes. We intend to ride to the seashore, spread a cloth on the sands and, afterwards, have a gallop.'

'Lady Grey says Sir George is too occupied with his Polynesian researches to accompany you, but she suggested I might join your party. Would my presence be acceptable to you?'

'Certainly,' I said, though I knew now that, however agreeable he might be, on important issues the Lieutenant and I would never be in accord.

We picnicked under a pohutukawa. 'The New Zealand Christmas tree,' said Mr Godfrey. 'I hope you've catalogued it, Eliza.'

She shook her head.

'Well, you must begin work again on your plant studies. You're much too talented to neglect them.'

'I should like to see your drawings, Lady Grey,' said Lieutenant Cowan.

'I fear you'll be disappointed. Godfrey flatters me.'

'Not a bit,' said Mr Godfrey. 'Come, we'll pick some of the lower flowers and you may take them home, draw them and press them.'

'Perhaps you'd like a walk on the sands, Miss Thompson?' said the Lieutenant. 'I promised to collect some New Zealand shells and send them to my sister in Bath.'

'Thank you, but no,' I said. 'I'm content to stay here and enjoy watching you all.'

The Lieutenant set off to the shoreline, and Lucy and Mr Godfrey moved away to a larger tree in search of more pohutukawa flowers. From where I sat I could see them clearly and noted with unease that he had lain a hand about her shoulders and she had leaned her head against his chest. You're being foolish, I admonished myself. Lucy is his sister-in-law. It's only natural that they should show affection towards each other. And then I saw him place a hand tenderly on her head and twist one of her curls around his finger. She looked up at him. To my horror, I saw him pull her even closer and quickly kiss her.

'Lieutenant Cowan has begged leave from my husband to speak to you, Fanny.'

'It's kind of the Lieutenant, but I have nothing to say to him.'

'Fanny, I'm certain he means to propose to you, and Sir George believes he has excellent prospects.'

'I have entirely no wish to marry him.'

'But why not? He's handsome, gallant, and much admiring of you. He told my husband you were the finest specimen of womanhood he had ever met.'

I groaned.

'Then is it because you're tired of Auckland? That you don't want to marry him and be trapped here forever? But he'll be certain to be posted Home before too long, Sir George says.'

'It is not that at all. Auckland suits me exceedingly well. I've never been happier.'

Lucy clutched my arm. 'Then promise me, Fanny dearest, that you'll never leave me. Say you'll stay here forever. If I were to lose you or Godfrey, I . . . I don't know what I would do. I simply couldn't bear it.'

Escaping the progressing summer's heat in the stables, I had just rested my head against Tsarina's comforting flank when I heard whispers. It took me some moments to recognise the voices of Lucy . . . and Mr Godfrey. Some instinct made me decide not to reveal myself, and I moved away to press into the dark corner by the hay bales, sparing them any embarrassment at my unexpected presence.

My eyes growing accustomed to the gloom, I saw that they were standing very close together at the farther end of the stables. As I watched, I quite distinctly saw Mr Godfrey clasp Lucy to him and kiss her fervently, then saw her return his kiss with equal ardour. So what I had witnessed on the picnic had not been merely a foolish moment of indiscretion. She is in grave danger, I thought. If Sir George should discover their dalliance, it is *she* who will be blamed, not his brother.

I was greatly relieved when, several weeks later, Lucy sought me out with news that clearly delighted her.

'My husband has said you and I may travel with him to New

Plymouth. We leave shortly on the government brig. There! What do you think of that?'

'Will Mr Godfrey be travelling with us?'

'No, alas. He has business in Wellington.'

I thought quickly. 'I'm afraid,' I said, 'that I've promised to help Lady Martin at the hospital. I can't disappoint her.'

Lucy looked downcast. 'But I'm sure she'll understand.'

'No,' I said. 'I'll wait until the next voyage. You won't be away for long, and it will be good for the Governor to have your society to himself.'

They had barely been gone when I received a letter. It was evening before it was delivered so I took it with me to my bedroom.

New Plymouth
Feb. 10th, 1849

My Dearest Fanny

You will be surprised to hear from me so soon but the government brig which brought us here is carrying this letter back to Auckland. You have missed a most unpleasant adventure. Here in NP there is no harbour and at times a heavy surf, and the day we arrived it was very violent. We were lifted into the little boat and proceeded towards the shore. Just as we neared the surf we were assured it was 'all right', though I felt all was wrong, and the next minute we were in the surf, and in another, the boat filled and we were drenched. The boat capsized and fortunately remained on its side, for had we been thrown out, we should certainly have been drowned. As it was we escaped with the thorough wetting of ourselves and our baggage . . .

I put aside the letter and drifted off to sleep in the close February heat. I dreamed not of the ocean and shipwrecks but of the Minang, clutching their wooden spears, their naked bodies decorated with white clay and ochre, dancing about their crackling bonfire with shrieks and yells. So vivid was my dream that the smell of suffocating smoke and heat woke me. Still half-asleep, I realised that the odour of burning was not an illusion but a reality.

Flinging apart the shutters, I saw a great orange light in the night sky. Panicked, I stepped outside onto the veranda, where I saw that shafts of flame engulfed the western end of Government House. I raced into my room, snatched up the brooch of Mama's likeness, then seized from Lucy's bedroom a lock of Baby Georgie's hair and a keepsake of her papa, all of which I threw as far as I might from the veranda onto the lawn.

The servants, I thought suddenly, and began shouting, 'Fire! Fire!' From far off, I heard the constant tolling of a bell. Someone in the settlement had seen the conflagration; help must surely be on its way. Of Johnson, Ingrams or the stable lad, I could see no sign. Calling their names, I beat upon Johnson's door. She stumbled forth.

'Flee into the garden,' I cried. 'The house is ablaze.'

Ingrams now appeared, clad in his nightshirt.

'The stable lad?'

''E be wi' his brother at Barracks.'

'Then we must release the horses at once.'

The fire had taken hold of the entire western part of the house, and Johnson was already occupied in tossing chairs and small objects of furniture into the gardens.

'Stables be too near to blaze, Ma'am,' said Ingrams, panting at my elbow, his voice almost inaudible above the roar of the flames.

'But the horses—'

'Ma'am, they be lost.'

Throwing aside my shawl, clad only in my shift, I sped to the stables, the heat almost forcing me back as I approached. The fire had not caught hold of the building, but it could not be long before the dry wood was aflame. Within, the terrified horses crashed and stamped. Fumbling, my fingers numb, I managed to unbolt one of the stable doors. Lucy's horse, Blaze, came stampeding out, knocking me down in his desperation. I rolled to one side, just in time to avoid being trampled by my own Tsarina, Sir George's stallion, Nelson, Mr Godfrey's gelding, Wager, and the tiny pony, Midget. But as I scrambled to my feet, a shard of burning wood fell from the roof onto the straw; I felt a scorching pain in my shoulder, the sear of a flame at my back. And, as I screamed for help, I saw swirling towards me through the smoke the phantom of my nightmares, the demon figure from long ago in Rio.

I awoke I knew not where, my left shoulder and my feet burning and throbbing, and looked into the face of Te Toa.

'Government House is entirely destroyed,' he said.

For some minutes, I could not understand him.

'There was a fire,' he said, 'but now all is well.'

'The house, you say, is—'

'Ruined. But what is a house compared with the lives of people and horses?'

'I can't quite . . . my feet . . . my shoulder . . .'

'They have put leaves and healing herbs on your wounds.'

'Am I at Lady Martin's hospital?'

'No, I have brought you to Waimate, to the Mission House.'

Te Rau-paraha sickened and died. At his tangi were all the great chiefs who had been his allies. Te Mamaku and his tribe paddled their canoes from the west; from the North, in the government brig, came Waka Nene and Te Kawana; but Te Rangi-hae-ata, when he heard the doleful news of his uncle's demise, rode all night from the other side of the Hutt Valley, alone.

It was Mr Hadfield who gave the Christian burial to Te Rau-paraha. All those hundreds of Maori present sang worship to Te Ariki while, outside the church, Te Rangi-hae-ata sat on his chestnut stallion, gazing scornfully about him. When his uncle's body had been lowered into the grave in the churchyard, Te Rangi-hae-ata descended in silence from his mount and walked to the edge of the burial place. The other mourners, even Te Kawana and Mr Hadfield, shrank back from him. Tall, magnificent and ferocious, he stood by his uncle's resting-place and, taking from under his cloak a sharp shell, he slashed his chest till it bled, to show the agony of his grief. Then, amid a hushed stillness, he remounted his horse and rode away.

The three days of the tangi were over; the visiting tribes had departed. Hone and I returned to our hut and had settled to sleep when, in the dead of night, I heard horses' hooves approaching, then silence.

I shook Hone. 'Someone is out there.' For a moment, I thought it might even be Te Rau-paraha's spirit, come to claim me.

Hone roused himself from sleep and motioned me to follow him from our hut. We slipped between the other dwellings towards the churchyard.

'Look,' breathed Hone.

I froze in dread. By Te Rau-paraha's grave stood an immensely tall, topknotted figure, shadowy-dark but for his eyes, which glittered menacingly in the moonlight. I clutched Hone's arm and he covered my mouth with his hand to stifle my cry of terror. Beside the figure, two smaller forms, bearing spades, dug deep into the holy earth of Te Ariki. There was not a sound but, at a signal from one of the diggers, the tall man strode forward and, as we watched, lifted from the hole in the ground a Pakeha coffin and, with his greenstone axe, prised open the lid. Gently, reverently, he picked up what lay within and carried it tenderly in his arms back to his mount where he laid it across his horse's back and rode away. The two men in the graveyard replaced the disturbed earth, smoothed it over, then, like their master, melted into the night.

'Te Rangi-hae-ata,' I whispered.

Hone nodded. 'He has taken his uncle's body, and now he will wrap it in the chief's finest cloak and hide it for Maori burial in a cave where no one will ever discover it.'

I thought of my mother, Kahe, of how much I wished I, too, could carry her away for a Maori burial. But who would raise her body for me and where might I find such a cave?

AUCKLAND, 1849

'Fanny dearest, you're a heroine! All Auckland is talking about your bravery. And, though it's a terrible thing to say, I'm glad the old house burned down. It was always the most uncomfortable place imaginable and here we are in delightful new surroundings. Just look at that splendid view across the Grafton Gully.'

'But how long are we to remain here?'

'Why, as long as we need. Until a new Government House can be built. But I'm in no hurry for that. I like it very well here at Moleskin Hall. It's so much better appointed than the old Government House. Now, I'm obliged to take provisions to the hospital, so I've ordered a light lunch for you, and the physician says you're to take a little walk in the grounds, then rest. I shall see you later this afternoon.'

I was dozing beneath a tree in the sloping gardens when I became aware I had company.

'Te Toa!'

'Miss Fanny.'

'I must thank you for all you've done for me.'

'There are no marks of the burns on your shoulder and your feet?'

'They're quite healed. I didn't know leaves could soothe so.'

'It was not the leaves alone. At first, we applied a poultice of herbs to your shoulder, then bound the leaves about it.'

'We?'

'I did not myself touch you, but I watched the tohunga as he tended you.'

'But . . . but . . . my shift was cut from me. My . . . when I woke I had no clothing on my . . . upper parts.'

'Clothing would have prevented the healing.'

I said nothing, but Te Toa appeared to read my thoughts. 'Our women never cover their breasts. It is only at the Mission that they are obliged to be unnatural, and then only when Pihopa is present. And he and Mata were not at Waimate when I took you there.' He paused. 'Will you ride with me again?'

I looked away.

'But, first, you must tell me what has turned you against me?'

I was silent.

'Please. Miss Fanny.'

'It . . . I . . .'

'I am listening most carefully.'

'Te Toa, I know you are married.'

He laughed. 'We do not call it married but, yes, I have two wives.' He scrutinised my face and grew immediately serious. '*This* is what has made you so . . . unfriendly to me? But why? What have my wives to do with—?'

I began to weep.

'You like me, I think, Miss Fanny.'

'I do,' I said, through sobs. 'That is exactly the problem. You and I, we are not allowed to . . . We are always obliged to meet in secret. There's no other person to whom I can speak as freely as I do to you, and yet, were it to be known that—'

'You are right,' he said, 'and I have been very foolish not to have seen it.'

'You are not only . . . so different from me but you are *married*. And you have two wives. The church does not permit it.'

'In these matters, the opinion of the church is of no importance. It is our own customs that we follow. And, I assure you, for a chief of my rank, I am very modest in my needs. Many others of my station have three or four wives.'

'I know this, but . . . Are you in love with your wives?'

'Listen to me, Fanny. We chiefs do not marry for love. We are married for alliances, for land, to end warfare. Our wives are high-born, the daughters of chiefs; our fathers and uncles, our grandfathers, arrange such unions between us. I am an honourable man; I treat my wives and my children with respect and kindness, but this is not the same as love in the way that I believe you speak of it. And is it not the same for you Pakeha? Do you tell me that Te Kawana loves Mata? Or she, him? It is a useful alliance between them. And even Pihopa Selwyn loves his Mission and his Christian god, Te Ariki, more than he loves Mata Pihopa.'

'But one is *supposed* to love God more than any other.'

'So? Pihopa has made an alliance with Te Ariki in just the way that my grandfather made the alliances between me and my wives. It is right to be united for reasons of power and conquest. And for land. Even the church wishes to have our land for Te Ariki.'

'No, it is the New Zealand Company that wants land — and for themselves.'

'It is also the church. The land for the Missions, the land on which the churches are to be built. "Give them to us for Te Ariki," says Pihopa, says Mr Williams, says even Mr Hadfield.'

'But this is not to do with love.'

'No, indeed. It is to do with power and alliance. Just like my wives.'

'If you were a Pakeha, you would choose your wife for love.'

Te Toa looked at me and shook his head. 'Where are these Pakeha who have chosen a wife for love? Mr Eyre needs a wife to look after him and to provide children for him, Mr Godley wants a wife who will command him, Te Kawana has a wife because it is proper, like Pihopa and—'

'Sir William and Lady Martin married for love.'

'There, I think you are correct. But see how rare it is? If it is so with Pakeha, why not also with Maori?'

I sat in silence.

'And this — my wives — is why you have made a distance between us?'

I nodded.

'But now that you understand the nature of our alliances, may we again become friends?' He moved towards me, but then drew back. 'Fanny, I was at General Wynyard's when I saw the flames, when I understood that Government House was burning, and I could not stop myself from fleeing at once to find you. It was my greatest fear that you might have perished, that I might have lost you . . .' He paused. 'Perhaps you might call this love. How can I know? I am a paramount chief. I cannot confide these thoughts to other Maori. I should never speak so to any other woman. Only with you can I be so truthful.'

And I saw that he was right. It was as if the two most unlike people in the world had been flung together — a puppet show for dispassionate gods. And only to each other could we acknowledge the strange bond between us.

'And I, too, can never speak of it to my sister or any other, not even to Lady Martin. For all her compassion, she would not, could not, comprehend or condone such an alliance.'

'I know this. If you were the man and I the woman, there would be no difficulty. It is well known that many important Pakeha men take our women to live with them and appear quite openly with them in society. But, for us . . .'

'Then would it be . . . perhaps we should not meet again?'

'If you prefer it, then we will not. But I do not think you prefer it. Nor I. It is only by chance that you are here in Aotearoa, that you and I have met, but if the gods have seen fit to bring us together, should we oppose their design?'

'You can't imagine how much I wish to see you, Te Toa, how much I've missed your company.'

'And I. You enter my thoughts when I am engaged on other business. I hear your voice, I feel you in the air about me. I believe this may be the love of which you speak. So then, though I do not love my wives, Fanny, it is possible I may love you.'

'I . . .'

'And you?'

'Yes.'

'I knew this. I have always known it since we went together to the slave settlement. Do you remember?'

I nodded. 'Te Toa, there is something else which troubles me very greatly. But I can't speak of it, even to you. *Especially* to you . . .'

'I believe I know what this may be.'

'So, can you answer me?'

'If you want to have my answer, you must first have the courage to ask me your question.'

I tried to speak but could not. I fought with myself to frame the words but was unable to utter them.

'You cannot ask this question of me because you do not wish to hear my truthful reply. But, if you do not know the truth, like the matter of my wives, this business will stand always between us.'

'I know. But how can I say it?'

'I think you have no choice.'

I could not meet Te Toa's eye. I looked down, drew in my breath and forced myself to speak. 'I . . . Te Toa . . .?'

'Yes?'

Blood rushed into my face; tears started in my eyes; the words came in a sudden rush. 'Have you eaten *human flesh*?'

'Of course.'

'But you are so wise and kind. How *could* you commit that most terrible crime?'

'Because I do not consider it so. I think you have no understanding of such things. I do not eat the flesh of others every day. Sometimes, it is true, after battle, our defeated enemies are slain and roasted in our ovens. And there are stories of times of famine when raids were made to capture supplies of food but, usually, it is only the custom during battle. If I have defeated my opponent, I will slay him, and my tohunga will then offer prayers over his body and make a sacred fire. On this, he will place my enemy, open his chest and lift out the organs containing his wairua, his spirit, and in the slowly curling smoke the gods will reveal a message to my tohunga. "Carry on this battle", or "Allow the conquered to retire vanquished", they will tell him. And then, to obtain the power of my rival, I will consume his heart and his liver.'

I stared in utter horror. Te Toa gently touched my arm with his hand, the hand with which he had placed human flesh in his mouth. 'I am sorry,' he said. 'I can see how greatly this shocks you. But it is our custom. And, surely, it is not so very different from your Christianity?'

'It is entirely different! Christianity would *never* condone such a thing.'

'Fanny, you are wrong. In his church, every Sunday, and often on other days, Pihopa performs this very same action and he is not even engaged in battle.'

'What are you saying?'

'That perhaps it is *Pihopa* who exceeds himself. We Maori eat one another, but we would never commit the sin of eating our own gods.'

I looked at him in confusion.

'Is this not true? "The body and blood of Te Ariki," says Pihopa, and he holds up the liquid and the little disc.'

'But that is Holy Communion.'

'So it is with me when I am consuming my enemy's spirit.'

'The Bishop doesn't eat the *real* flesh of Christ. For the Communion, he uses bread and wine.'

'I know this, but it is exactly the same. Each time, does not Pihopa say so?'

'The Communion is only symbolic . . .'

'And it is symbolic also when one chief ritually eats his rival. Do you take the Holy Communion of Pihopa?'

'Yes.'

'And does he not tell you it is Te Ariki you are swallowing?'

'Yes, but Pihopa has not *slain* Te Ariki!'

'He tells us Te Ariki was killed by his own tribe. And, over and over again, he becomes holy food.' Te Toa sat down beside me. 'So, now, are we again friends as before? Think, Fanny. For all of the time you have known me, I have always had my wives, I have always done these things about which we are speaking. When you did not know this, you were my friend. Now I have been truthful to you — and you turn away. But I am exactly the same man.'

I tried to summon those principles that I believed myself to honour. I thought of Lucy, Aunt, my sisters, their distress should my conduct ever become known to them. For a moment, I seemed to step outside of myself and watch us, sitting together. I am in danger, I told myself. I should, I *must* leave now. At once. Instead, I heard my own voice saying, 'I am afraid, Te Toa.'

'Of me?'

'No, of what people may say.'

'Who are these people? I am well known to the Pakeha as a man of honour. Your own honour will not be compromised by riding with me. Do not Te Kawana and General Wynyard ride often with pretty young girls?'

'It's not you, I fear. It is . . . myself.'

Te Toa put his arms about me and held me to him. I made no resistance.

I rode alone to the Domain, tethered Tsarina and, as instructed by Te Toa, pushed through the undergrowth on foot to the deserted slave settlement. He strode towards me and I ran to him. 'I have left my own mount far away,' he said, in answer to my unspoken question. 'No one will disturb us or suspect we are here together.'

There was about Te Toa the dense, heavy tang of earth, overlaid with a pungency like that of some of the green plants we plucked. As I rested against his unclothed chest, I was enveloped by a heady, spicy odour that, in its unfamiliarity, both drew and deterred me. Nakedness seemed entirely natural to him.

'Te Toa,' I said, seeking by conversation to cover my own apprehension, 'how old are you?'

He looked puzzled. 'Why, the age I am now.'

'No, in what year were you born?'

'I was born at the third new moon after my father's conquest of Ngati Whatua.'

It was my turn to look bemused. 'On what day?'

'That day, itself.'

'But you must know how many years you've been alive.'

He shook his head. 'No, I have been a child, then a young boy, and now I am a man. That is how many years I have been alive.'

I was astounded. 'I was born in 1824,' I said, 'so I will be twenty-five years old in November.'

'This is very helpful Pakeha reckoning, I am sure, but for us Maori it is of no use at all. And now,' he said gently, reaching to caress my face, 'we should stop this talking. Come here, beside me.'

After some time, and his stroking of my arms and cheeks, I consented to part with everything but my shift and, though it was not cold, stood shivering before him. He placed his arms around me. 'When you asked if I loved my wives, I said I did not think I knew what you meant. Now I know that I have this most difficult feeling for you, so it is certain to me that I feel love for you.'

'Being in love is not supposed to be difficult . . .'

'Are you sure of this? It seems to me very difficult. I am thinking of you when I should not, I am telling myself every day I must not ride to see you. I must not betray by a single word or look what I feel for you. And all the time, I wish to be with you.'

'I know.'

'Fanny, you must tell me. Do you understand what happens between a man and a woman?'

'I . . . I . . . It's not something I can speak about, even to my sister . . .'

'You remember the carvings at my pa? In the wharenui?'

I said nothing.

'I know that you saw them. I saw you redden and look away. And then, a little later, I saw you look again, but quickly. You were ashamed.'

'I thought they were . . . that they should have been . . . somewhere more private.'

'But why? In the wharenui, everyone may see them. Every child grows up beside them, so no one is obliged to do as I am doing now, to put into words what must be done between the bodies of a man and a woman.'

I felt a sudden panic. 'I don't think I—'

He held me tighter. 'You are a grown woman. This should be natural for you. It is not something to be feared. Let me take off your shift.'

Trembling, I raised my arms.

'There,' he said. Tossing it to one side, he looked directly at my naked body. 'Ah, Fanny, you are most lovely.' He laid his forehead against mine and I felt the warmth of his breath on my face.

'Tihe mauri ora,' he said.

I looked at him, puzzled.

'The breath of life.'

He drew me towards him again, and gently placed his hands on my breasts. I flinched. 'Lie down,' he said, 'and I will show you what pleasant and most delightful feelings there can be between us.'

Gently, he began to stroke my breasts, then, suddenly, he leaned forward and placed his mouth to them, kissing and sucking me softly. I felt a throbbing, a strange rush of heat throughout my body.

'That is better,' said Te Toa. 'And now, you must do the same to me.'

'I . . .?'

'Of course.'

He lay back and I began, shyly, to trace the whorls and spirals of the tattoos on his upper arms and chest. 'Did it hurt?'

'My moko? Naturally.'

'Did you cry out?'

He shook his head. 'If I had cried out, my father and my ancestors would have been shamed, and I would not have been worthy to become a chief.' He took my hand and laid it against his chest. 'Do you see this? And here, on the other side, another matching it exactly?' He moved my hand upwards. And here, on my cheeks and above my eyebrows? Each of these tells a story. On me is written the whole story of our ancestors.' He drew me closer. 'And now, it is time for us to stop all this talking,' he said, and covered my lips with his own.

AOTEAROA

Once, long ago, my mother told us an ancient story. 'Listen, and heed,' she said. 'One day, I will be gone from you. When that day comes you must remember this story and the truth within it.'

Hone and I sat, silent.

'Who is the guardian of the Underworld?' said my mother. 'Great Hine-nui-te-po, she who rules the night, she who is the rosy colour of the sunset. Her body is a woman's but her hair is of bladder-wrack, her eyes of greenstone jade, and hidden in her mouth and her teke are the hideous obsidian fangs of a barracuda.

'When it was revealed to her that her husband, the god Tane, was also her father, she fled from the light of day into the Underworld to hide her shame in its darkness at the edge of the sky. And it was there the demi-god Maui, accompanied by his friends, the fantail bird and the robin, came to seek immortality for all mankind.

'Hine-nui-te-po lay sleeping, her immense thighs spread so that Maui could see the flash of the obsidian teeth in her secret parts. "If I crawl into her teke," he said, "pass through her body and come out again from her mouth, I will reverse the path of birth, and mankind will become immortal."

'But the fantail, amused to see Maui disappearing into the body of the goddess, laughed, and woke her. Then great Hine-nui-te-po clapped her thighs together, crushing the demi-god with the obsidian teeth of her teke. And so Maui became the first man to die and, because of this, all living beings are mortal and Hine-nui-te-po remains forever at the gateway to the dark Underworld through which all human souls must pass.'

I did not fully understand her words but, at the thought of entering the darkness of the Underworld, I shuddered uncontrollably.

My mother told me, also, of a sorceress she once knew. This was an old, old woman who lived away from the rest of her tribe. They were too afraid of her powers to dwell near her, but every day they left food and water for her at a safe distance. My mother said she could command the gods, that even Te Rau-paraha was in awe of her. Perhaps the sorceress has gone to the ancestors. But if she is living still and if I knew where to find her, I would go to her and ask her to read for me the omens of my future. For, with my mother gone, whom else might I ask?

AUCKLAND, 1850

Returning from a ride on the shore, Lucy and I found the Selwyns sitting on the veranda with the Governor.

'We've had such a bracing gallop,' cried Lucy. 'I only wish you'd been with us.'

'We're here with news of a fresh arrival in the colony,' said the Bishop. 'I've just received a letter from my old friend, Sir Frederick Colville. His sister, Maud, will land here very soon.'

'Is she travelling with her husband or . . .?'

'No, Eliza,' said Mrs Selwyn. 'She's unmarried.'

'Ah, then perhaps she's in hope of finding a husband in Auckland.'

'I doubt it,' said the Bishop. 'Maud is even older than I am and, as I understand, is entirely set against marriage.'

'I've met her only once,' said Mrs Selwyn. 'Long ago, at the home of my husband's parents. And I confess I found her a most daunting and very formidable lady.'

'Maud is rather . . . unusual,' said the Bishop. 'Very individual in her opinions. She holds strong views on the education of women — she's even written pamphlets on the subject. And she scandalised her family by working for some time in the slums of London with . . . er . . . fallen women.'

'As does dear Mr Gladstone,' said Mrs Selwyn.

Bishop Selwyn looked awkward. 'I wonder,' he said, 'if, as a great favour, you might consider allowing Maud to lodge here with you until she's settled. As you know, we're overrun at the Mission House in Kohimarama; we have scholars tucked into every corner.'

'Willingly,' said Lucy. 'When should we expect her?'

The Bishop looked even more uncomfortable. 'If it's not too great an inconvenience, perhaps I might escort her here the day after tomorrow?'

'Why, yes. It is a little short notice but I'm sure I can have Johnson make up her room. And would you and Sarah care to come here that night to dine? As Miss Colville knows you, it might ease things a little.'

'I feel it only right to warn you,' said the Bishop, 'that, in her conversation, Maud is inclined to be a little . . . forthright. One might almost say she thinks like a man. A gentleman, of course.'

'I'm quite looking forward to meeting Miss Colville,' said Lucy. 'I've never before met a blue-stocking, though George's Aunt Julia spoke of them in London. She seemed rather to admire them.'

I, too, was eager to meet the new arrival. I pictured her as a Romantic figure, lean and graceful, with a wistful expression and an air of unworldliness.

But, when the Bishop drew up in General Wynyard's borrowed carriage two days later, he handed out a short brisk lady who strode purposefully towards Lucy and me.

'Great Heavens,' whispered Lucy, 'she's wearing a turban and bloomers.'

The Bishop performed the introductions.

'How exceedingly kind of you to take me in,' said Miss Colville. 'I hope Gas didn't lean upon you too hard.'

Lucy looked puzzled. 'Gas?'

I saw the Bishop flinch.

'George Augustus Selwyn,' said Miss Colville. 'Hence, always known as Gas to my brothers and me.' She paused. 'As you see,' she went on, appearing entirely at ease in her new surroundings, 'I favour the bloomer costume. Most freeing to women, particularly in such a climate as this.' She gazed about her. 'I do hope you'll allow me to inspect your garden this afternoon, Lady Grey. And I'm most desirous of meeting Sir George tonight. I've read his accounts of his expeditions in Australia, and I understand he's compiling a study of Maori legends. I, too, am very interested in the study of indigenous races, in particular, the role of their women.'

Miss Colville appeared at dinner clad in a long red silk robe over an orange tunic. This bizarre ensemble was completed by a pair of embroidered slippers and a bandeau of matching silk wound about her hair, which had been scraped into some kind of topknot. I saw Mrs Selwyn start, then recover herself. The Bishop appeared not to find anything at all extraordinary in Miss Colville's attire, and was asking for news of her brothers when Sir George joined us.

'Ah, Sir George,' said Miss Colville, advancing upon him, 'this is such a great pleasure. I intend to quiz you later on land reform and colonisation. My brother, Frederick, is in the Colonial Office and he has spoken often of you.'

'Well, I trust.'

'Not always. But he has a high regard for your abilities, if not always your veracity.'

I saw the tip of Sir George's nose redden slightly, but he gave his arm to Miss Colville without further comment and led her into dinner.

There followed an awkward silence in which, to allay any further indiscreet remarks from Miss Colville, Lucy, Mrs Selwyn and I all began to speak together.

'You were saying, Sarah?' said Lucy.

'I was merely observing that it seems particularly humid today.'

'I imagine,' said Miss Colville, attacking her mutton with relish, 'that, in a climate like this, maggots are a continual problem.'

There was another silence, broken this time by the Bishop. 'You must tell us, Maud, what has brought you to New Zealand.'

'Well, you are aware, Gas'— the Bishop winced — 'how very much engaged I am in the betterment of the lot of women, and I determined upon coming here to see for myself the part played by females in the shaping and establishing of a new colony.' She looked expansively at us. 'The true scholar must see for herself. Would you not agree, Sir George?'

'Er, naturally . . .'

'And my principal interest is the enfranchisement of women.'

'That's quite ridiculous, Maud,' said the Bishop. 'You are not seriously suggesting that women should have the vote?'

Miss Colville turned to her host. 'I understand that in your dispatches, Governor, you argue that the natives here should be enfranchised? Is that not so?'

'Yes, but how—?'

'You will find me very well informed on these matters. Now, if a Maori should be allowed to cast his vote — and, here, I am in complete agreement with you, Governor — why should a woman not do so?'

'Woman, Maud, is the weaker sex. She must rely on the judgement of her husband or father.'

'The weaker sex? In what way is woman weaker?'

'Why, in every way. Even the Holy Book tells us that it was woman who succumbed to—'

Miss Colville gave the table a sharp rap. 'You're a Puseyite, Gas. I'm ashamed for you. What ridiculous notion is this, that woman in 1850 should be held accountable for the purported sin of Eve, set out in some Hebrew or Greek translation that—'

'I must stop you, Maud. Remember you're speaking of God's Holy Word.'

'My dear Gas, I can't believe that Frederick and William haven't told you I've long been a Freethinker.'

'It may have been mentioned . . .'

'Now, how is it logically possible that a woman should be speaking with a snake? It defies reason.'

Sir George leaned forward. 'We are talking here not of reason but of belief.'

'Ah, there we come to a topic on which I'm most desirous of interrogating you, Governor. From your study of Maori lore and legends, have you, yourself, taken on any of the native beliefs?'

'Of course not. They are, in the main, mere superstitions.'

'And no more logical, then, than the story of Adam and Eve?'

'They are *native* beliefs, not Christian.'

'And therefore inferior? I have lived among the Mussulmen in Turkey and I assure you they are quite as adamant as any Christian that their creed is the true one. But any opinion founded on lack of evidence is merely a form of superstition or a belief in magic.'

I thought guiltily of the spells and potions of my childhood. 'But, surely,' I ventured, 'if belief provides comfort or a sense of security, it should be encouraged?'

Miss Colville smiled warmly at me. 'Bravo, Miss Thompson, for entering our argument. I agree with you that there is a place for belief in human life, but it shouldn't be confused with religion. It's not belief I'm against but the dominance of the practitioners of religion over the credulous. Now, Lady Grey, do you support the enfranchisement of women?'

'I've never yet considered it.'

'Were my wife to have the vote,' said the Governor, 'she would, of course, cast it as I instructed her.'

'As would my dear Sarah,' said the Bishop.

Miss Colville spent much of the next week in conversation with Sir George. Leaving them together in the drawing room one morning, Lucy and I escaped into the far reaches of the garden.

'What do you think of her?' she asked.

'Well, I began by finding her quite horribly overbearing, but the more I see of her, the more I find myself warming to her.'

'And I. She's very strange, but I believe she has a good heart.'

'And she's as committed to her own ideas as the Governor or the Bishop. Has she told you that she's taken up land about ten miles south of here and that she plans to farm it herself?'

'She'll have to have some help.'

'She intends to employ a few men but still to do much of the work on her own. She says that after her experiences in the East End clinic, delivering lambs will present no problems for her at all.'

'Well, I commend her for it, though I hope she didn't say it to my husband or the Bishop. Godfrey, of course, finds her most original and entertaining.'

'She most certainly is. But, sometimes, she makes me feel rather uneasy.' I hesitated. 'Do you recall her speaking about magic?'

'Yes.'

'Well . . . Te Toa once told me that his tohunga could make the gods speak.'

Lucy glanced around to make sure we were not overheard. 'You must *on no account* tell my husband I've told you this, Fanny, but I know that to be true.'

'*You* know it? How so?'

'If I tell you, you must swear that you'll never speak of it to a living soul.'

'Of course not. But I thought you'd deem it merely the conviction of savages.'

'No, never. I have seen it for myself.'

'*What*? When?'

'Do you remember that when we were first at New Plymouth, Sir George became unwell?'

'Yes, you wrote that you were seriously alarmed at his condition.'

'The doctor feared for his life. Well, during that time, a tohunga from the local tribe came to me, saying that Sir George was at the point of death and claiming that he could call on the gods to help him. For all that he holds the natives in esteem for their intelligence and statesmanship, my husband, as you heard, professes that in their beliefs they are but as children and derides their reliance on spirits. I knew he would never consent, but the doctor could do nothing and, as Sir George was too ill to be consulted, I thanked the tohunga and asked him to do whatever he could to restore my husband.

'The tohunga then asked for a green chair for the god to sit upon. As the only chairs to be had were black, I offered a black one, but he was adamant it must be green. "The god tells me," he said, "that in this house there is a green chair and it is only on that chair he must sit."

'I'm sure the servants thought me quite mad. I set them to searching the place and, finally, in the attic, a dilapidated green chair was discovered and brought to me. The tohunga took it and entered the room, indicating that I might sit at the threshold and observe him.

'I must tell you, Fanny, I was assailed by the strangest feeling — somewhere between doubt and fear. He muttered and murmured for some time, then cried out in English, "I see the gods ascending!" And then, from every corner of the room, came strange whistling sounds, like winds howling, which swirled about us and rose in pitch until the noise was almost unbearable.

'Eventually, they died away and the tohunga rose and asked me to take him to my husband. I demurred, but he insisted. He laid his hand upon Sir George's left side, made some sort of incantation over him in his own tongue, then said that within three days he would be well again and at that time he must ride on horseback to the tohunga's pa.

'And, Fanny, on the third day, my husband was, indeed, almost completely restored — to the amazement of his doctor. And, very unwillingly, since he purported to disbelieve such nonsense and wizardry, he rode to the pa, where he found the tribe gathered for his arrival because the tohunga had told them he would be with them on that day.'

'But that is quite astounding . . .'

'If I had not witnessed it, I should have said it was the stuff of fairy tales.'

The longer Miss Colville remained with us at Moleskin Hall, the more I began to realise that it was only in Te Toa's company — and hers — that I felt myself truly free to think, to speak, to act as I believed, untrammelled by the strictures of polite society. I longed for Te Toa with a physical, corporeal intensity which frightened me. When we two were alone, it seemed as though we constituted the whole world but, hedged about by the need for secrecy and caution, these interludes were stolen and infrequent. I dreamed of some nameless place where we might openly meet, and was seized by a burning need to share the intensity of my passion, to make it somehow solid and real, a fact not an illusion. But I dared not yield to it.

I found myself slipping Te Toa's name into my conversations with Lucy and Lady Martin, even with Miss Colville, but guardedly, so that it seemed no more than a casual remarking. And the pleasure it afforded me to hear others speak warmly of him or praise him was a secret joy that I clutched greedily to myself.

Behind his whare at Waikanae, Mr Hadfield had a little yard where he tied up his two horses on which he travelled all the time to Otaki and back. When he rode along the sands to Otaki, and stayed in his hut among the bare dunes, he was obliged to tether them to a hook in the side of his potato store there and carry their water from the pa across the sand-hills.

I remembered our mother's words: 'Disgraceful that such a man as Harawira should be forced to fetch water like a common Maori. Here at Waikanae, we respect our missionary.'

And whenever Mr Hadfield was back with us, she had set Hone and me to brushing the horses and bringing them water in a Pakeha pail.

Hone and I longed to ride them but, said Mr Hadfield, 'I depend on them for my journeys, so I am obliged not to work them too hard.'

'But when you are sick,' said Hone, 'I could take them for a gallop along the sands at low tide. Just to exercise them a little.'

'That is very kind of you, Hone,' said Mr Hadfield, 'but Te Ahu, who helps me here with my Mission work, has promised to take care of them. And he needs them for his own journeys to and from Otaki.'

It was Te Ahu who had taught Mr Hadfield to speak the Maori tongue. Although he was from Ngatiawa, he had been with Mr Te Kara Wha Williams in the North where he had learnt to read and write the words of Te Ariki. Then, Te Kara Wha had sent him back home to assist Mr Hadfield.

'Te Ahu,' said Hone to me later, 'knows nothing about how to ride a horse properly. Whereas I often used to ride our stepfather's horse and I—'

'Wish to parade on a horse before the other boys on the sands,' I said. 'Think of what our mother said to us.'

'Our mother is gone now,' said Hone, 'and you had better run away now, too, Makareta, before I lock you in the hen whare.'

AUCKLAND, 1851

'Come and help me, Fanny,' said Lucy. 'It's the placement for tonight's dinner. I think I shall have to select Miss Colville's partners at table with great care.'

'So do I! But surely she'll be on the Governor's right.' I laughed. 'Poor Sir George. She does quiz him quite harshly. Why not place General Pitt on her left? He'll enjoy her forthright manner.'

'That's an excellent idea. She is rather like a soldier.'

'Not entirely, but you must own she speaks her mind, and so does the general.'

Miss Colville made her entrance to the dinner in an even more flamboyant silk bloomer costume than usual.

'Hand-dyed,' she explained to Lady Martin, 'by the Turcoman women. It's their speciality. You see the delicacy of the colours.'

'Indeed, I do. You've spent time among the Turcomans?'

'Two years. My youngest brother, Septimus, and I travelled widely in the Persian and Ottoman territories.'

'But, surely,' said Mrs Rough, 'it was extremely dangerous?'

'By no means. We bought camels on our arrival, hired an experienced guide and I wore the robes adopted by Septimus. We passed an immensely fascinating time there. It is always surprising to me how much simpler it is for a member of the female sex to penetrate the interior of such societies.'

'How so?' enquired Sir George.

Bishop Selwyn assumed an air of pained expectation.

'Why, Governor, the hammam. Possibly one of the most refreshing experiences of the Orient.'

'Hammam?' asked Mrs Wynyard.

'The Ottoman steam bath and massage.'

'You mean,' said Mrs Selwyn, 'you partook of . . . of . . . er . . . a communal bath with the infidel?'

'With their women. Yes, of course. I must tell you it is one of the most civilised experiences one may undergo. For their own women, it is generally a form of restraint since, as I'm sure you know, they may not have any bodily hair before they present themselves to their husbands so they must undergo a most painful process of waxing and plucking, but I, being European—'

I saw Mrs Rough exchange glances with Mrs Selwyn.

The Bishop drew breath. 'Ah, Maud, do please excuse my interruption, but am I not right in thinking that Septimus has lately been appointed Prebendary of Lincoln?'

'You are correct. And he is much engaged in the study of the images of the Green Man there. Quite pagan, of course.'

'Now, what *I* wish to know,' said Lady Martin briskly, 'is how you are enjoying life in Auckland.'

'Very much. I am quite committed to making a home here. I've begun to study the Maori language and, now I am more settled, I would like to offer my assistance at your little hospital.'

'We should be most grateful for your help. I understand from Sarah that you have had . . . nursing . . . experience at Home?'

'Quite so. As you may imagine, I was met with fierce opposition from most of my family.'

'Well, it is not exactly the calling that gentlewomen at Home generally—'

'You are right, Sir William. And conditions in the hospitals there are even worse than is commonly believed. The nurses are frequently drunk, and share wards, and often even beds, with the patients. But I was less interested in hospital work than in assisting the women of the poorer classes in their own homes. And when my father saw that I was entirely determined upon my course, he assigned two of our burliest grooms to accompany me about the East End.'

'I take it,' said Sir George, 'that you were you motivated by a spirit of Christian endeavour.'

'It was my intention, Sir George, to be useful. I have no time for the common lot of women sitting at home sewing or lying about with the vapours. I have noticed that many of the pioneer women in this colony seem to enjoy a more active form of existence than their counterparts at Home.'

'I have observed to Miss Thompson that it is a feature of life here,' said Lady Martin, pleased.

'The brutality of the lives of those poor East End women was appalling, but in my work among them I was constantly struck by how the lack of constriction of the female body by lacing ensured simpler deliveries of their infants, in the manner, no doubt, that God intended.'

The Bishop shifted uneasily on his chair. Perhaps he divined what was about to come.

'So I, myself,' continued Maud, apparently oblivious, 'have entirely abandoned lacing. I regard it as a modern form of the chastity belt.'

'I cannot suppose, Maud,' said the Bishop, 'that if Her Majesty sees fit to lace, it is for the females of the poor to take it upon themselves to set an example to their sisters.'

'The Queen laces? I think not, Gas,' retorted Maud. 'Have you seen Her Majesty at close quarters?'

'Miss Thompson, a word, if you please?'

'Why, certainly, Miss Colville.'

'Let me begin by inviting you to call me Maud and I shall call you Fanny. It seems so much friendlier.'

'Thank you . . . Maud.'

'You know I am soon to take possession of my farm and its cottage?'

'Yes, and I hope you'll be very happy there.'

'It's my earnest wish that you and Lady Grey should come to visit me as soon as you may. But, Fanny, I should like to talk to you of other topics. I observe you are an exceedingly pretty young woman but you appear to have no suitor.'

Fearing she might somehow have guessed of Te Toa's existence, I blushed.

'Is it that you wish to remain unmarried?'

What I wished was that our conversation should be over swiftly before I in some way betrayed myself. 'Why, no, not at all.'

'I understand from the Bishop that you're in possession of independent means.'

'That's true.'

'Then I beg you to allow me to advise you, my dear. In my own youth, I contracted a marriage with a young man, a charming rogue, penniless but with a silver tongue, who swept me quite off my feet. And, by the time I'd come to my senses, I was married and all control of my considerable fortune, indeed all power over my own life, had passed into his hands. My husband treated me with contempt, dismissing my ideas as worthless. Having studied with my brothers' tutors I am exceedingly well educated, but to him this counted for nothing.'

'So how did you free yourself from him?'

'By the greatest piece of good fortune, within fifteen months of our marriage and before I had borne any children, he succumbed to the cholera.'

'Would you not have liked children?'

'No. They don't interest me in the least. I'm not at all fond of children.'

'But surely you were a little saddened by his death?'

'Not a jot. For me, it was a merciful escape and I learnt from it a most valuable lesson. Until we women have control of our own money, after marriage as much as before it, we will forever be no better than slaves at the mercy of any fortune-hunter. You, my dear, must take the greatest care in your choice of a husband. You're a thoughtful young woman and you might do much good with your fortune. When you and your sister come to visit, I shall show you some pamphlets I've written regarding women's place in society and you must tell me, honestly, what you think of such ideas.'

'Thank you. I should like that very much. And so, I think, will Lucy.'

She shook her head. 'Too late. Lady Grey married when she was far too young and unformed.' She paused, then she said with sudden ferocity, 'It's the greatest pity.'

'I believe she married in order to escape life in Albany,' I said. 'But I'm sure that, at the time, she believed she was in love . . .'

'Which she is clearly not now, though she remains entirely dependent on the Governor, reinforcing his view that woman is a chattel granted to man by God.'

'He is not alone in that.'

'Alas, no. And though he's a clever man of great ability, if I'm truthful . . . Sir George lacks decisiveness. And, of course, his addiction makes his behaviour unpredictable.'

I stared at her. 'His *addiction*? What do you mean?'

'My dear Fanny, you've been living so long in this house, surely you're aware that the Governor, like half the population, is addicted to laudanum.'

'I'm sure you're quite wrong.'

'Not at all. Have you not observed how often he requires your sister to bring him the medicine for his hip wound?'

'But that's a cordial, prescribed by—'

'It's laudanum under a different guise. And laudanum is opium.'

'Are you saying that Sir George is *an opium addict*?'

'Hardly in the sense that one generally uses the term. But his irritability, the erratic changes in his moods, all these speak to me quite visibly of a dependence on laudanum.'

'He has a hip wound. It's natural he should seek relief from—'

'And how was this hip wound occasioned? By his own recklessness in mounting such an ill-conceived expedition in hostile territory of which he had no knowledge at all.'

'I thought you esteemed Sir George.'

She re-adjusted her turban. 'In very many ways, I do. But it is his scholarship I admire, not his skills of governance.'

'Fanny, the most terrible, terrible news! Godfrey is to *leave* us. You remember Mr Domett, the Colonial Secretary here? You met him at the investiture. Well, my husband has found a post for Godfrey in his office. In *Wellington*.'

'And what does Mr Godfrey say to this?'

'He says he will miss us all so much but he's delighted to have been offered such a position. Oh, Fanny, it's so utterly wretched. What shall I do without him?'

'But the Governor is obliged to spend more and more time in Wellington now, so surely you can accompany him and see Mr

Godfrey there. It's not as if he's going Home.'

'Oh, Fanny, you don't understand *at all*. Godfrey and I . . . I . . .' She stopped herself. 'How will I bear it without him?' She began to weep uncontrollably. 'Oh, Fanny, what shall I do?'

Since Mr Godfrey's departure Lucy had barely left her room. The food Johnson took her on a tray was returned untouched. All my efforts to interest her in any sort of activity or pastime were futile; she seemed unable even to engage in conversation with me.

'Come now,' I said, 'and try to rouse yourself a little. Here is a letter for you. From Wellington.'

She sat up at once and snatched it from me. 'It must be from Godfrey. Yes! I recognise his hand. But why did you not give it to me before?'

'It has only just arrived. '

To my consternation, she began to smother the letter with kisses.

'You must open it,' I said, 'and see what he says.'

She tore at the envelope with her fingers. 'I *knew* he hadn't forgotten me.' She scanned the paper. 'Let me see. He says already he misses us all and he sends his warm regards to you, Fanny.'

'Is he enjoying life in Wellington?'

'It seems so. What does he say? Yes, here it is. *Domett is quite the man about town. George has always spoken highly of his qualities and I see for myself every day how valuable a service he performs for the Government.* But he makes no mention of any parties or balls.' She twisted a piece of her hair around a finger. 'It seems such a wretched bachelor life he's leading.'

'I'm sure you'll see him again before too long and then you'll be able to judge for yourself.'

But any hopes I had entertained of Lucy's spirits reviving after the receipt of her letter were unfounded. Although she had left her bed, she spent most of her time lying on the sofa, tired and listless, uninterested in anything around her. Since she refused to go out, I was left to amuse myself and, as it was well known that I liked to ride, no particular importance was attached to my setting off alone on Tsarina each day.

I had donned my riding-habit and was about to set out in my usual fashion when Sir George came in.

'Eliza,' he said, 'I've received a message from Mrs Godley.'

Lucy sighed. 'Another? What misconduct in the colony is disturbing her now?'

'It's about Mr Hadfield.'

'But Mr Hadfield is the very model of respectability. I don't see how *he* could have upset horrid Charlotte G.'

'She's concerned about his living arrangements. Some time ago he took two young orphans into his own house, a boy and a girl, and she doesn't feel it right that the girl should be there still with no woman present.'

'She's always interfering. If she feels so strongly, why doesn't she take in the children herself?'

'She asks if I would call on Mr Hadfield at Otaki when I'm next in Wellington and see what arrangements can be made. She wonders if I might bring the children to the Bishop and see that they're educated at his new Mission school. But I thought, perhaps, that we might have them here for a time. You know how fond you are of children.'

Lucy appeared to brighten a little. 'Well, I suppose it would do no harm to consider it. And if they are orphans . . .'

As had become my custom, I rode to the Domain, tied Tsarina and continued on foot to the little slave settlement that had become our regular meeting place. Te Toa was generally there before me, having taken the precaution of leaving his stallion in a different place entirely. It seemed that the slave settlement was known only to him, for I had never seen anyone else in the vicinity, but I was careful to check about me before disappearing into the bush that surrounded it.

He was standing, looking round for a sign of me. I ran to him and he clasped me against him.

'Come,' he said, 'let us go into one of the huts.'

Since being with Te Toa, I had, for the first time in my life, become conscious of my own body as a source of pleasure. I craved Te Toa's presence with a physical longing. When I saw him, I felt a throbbing excitement in my breasts, in the privy parts of myself I had never before dared to contemplate. I warned myself against showing any sign of my feelings for him when he came to visit the Governor. But how can it be, I thought, that no one else is aware of the agitation of the very air between us? I was alive to the tension of desire, the hunger to be alone with him, to press myself against his body. When I saw him with others, I felt my eyes brighten, my skin glow, so that I was obliged to cast my eyes down, to deflect the slightest hint of any existing intimacy between us.

Lucy was still laid low with a fatigue and spent most of her time resting in her room, writing endless letters to Mr Godfrey. This allowed me the freedom to ride unaccompanied to the Domain whenever I might wish. Should I see Te Toa's black stallion tethered in his usual place, I would carry on my way, tying Tsarina so far distant that no casual observer would suspect a connection, then make my way to the slave settlement.

We lay entwined, he stroking my hair and murmuring words of endearment, I with my head on his breast, before we were obliged once more to don our clothing and return to our separate mounts and separate worlds. I could not allow myself to think of the future, any future, since I knew we could have none, yet I could not bring myself openly to acknowledge such a thing. We existed out of time, within our own world together, in the wider world apart.

'Makareta' said Mr Hadfield, 'Mrs Godley has spoken with me in Wellington.'

I frowned. Mrs Godley's nose has become long and narrow from sniffing into the business of others.

'She has written to Te Kawana. She says she has asked him to find you and Hone another place to live.'

'But why should we leave you?'

'Mrs Godley feels that it's time you experienced more of the world beyond the pa. So Te Kawana, when he is next in the south, will come to visit us and we will talk of it again at that time.'

I did not wish to leave Mr Hadfield. I was afraid. Every night now, I sang my mother's karakia silently to myself for protection. Then, afterwards, I recited the Lord's Prayer, the most powerful of all Te Ariki's words. Or so said Mr Hadfield.

Hone and I packed our belongings in a box.

'I have spoken with Te Kawana,' said Mr Hadfield. 'Very soon he will come to take you to your new home in Auckland.'

Perhaps he saw my expression.

'Te Kawana is a good man, Makareta. You have nothing to fear.'

Nothing to fear but myself.

And so he came and took Hone and me away with him. Mr Hadfield was most delighted for us. 'Now that you are under Te Kawana's protection, you will be educated and guided in the Christian way of life. It is most generous of him. He is a good man of high principles.'

So, I thought, Mr Hadfield has seen nothing. It is my own guilty imaginings.

'And what of Waka Nene?' I asked. 'Now, I am moving closer to his lands.'

'You will be quite safe. Te Kawana's mana will protect you. Nene will not complain of such ancient wrongs and Te Rau-paraha has passed from this earthly life.'

So, with many tears, my brother Hone and I left that good man, Mr Hadfield, and paid our last respects at the graves of our mother and Mr Nicoll.

I did not know then that I would never return to my ancestral lands.

AUCKLAND, 1851

'Fanny, you must come at once. Ingrams says the Maoris are invading. There are more than three hundred of them in a fleet of great war canoes.'

'What, here, in Auckland?'

'The Fencibles are massing on Constitution Hill above Mechanics Bay. My husband has put on full dress uniform and ridden to command them. Ingrams says that the Governor has ordered us to go to Colonel Wynyard's house and remain there until he sends for us, but I don't see why we shouldn't ride to the hill above the harbour and see for ourselves what's happening.'

Lucy and I reined in our horses at a spot from which we could observe events without being seen. Below us, drawn up on the sands were at least a dozen huge war canoes, their high wooden prows elaborately carved and decorated. Two others, each manned by forty or fifty paddlers, floated in the harbour.

'Look, beyond the canoes, there's the *Fly*,' said Lucy.

Fully rigged, the government frigate lay further out in the harbour, commanding the entrance to Mechanics Bay.

'She has her guns trained on the canoes,' I said, trying not to sound as alarmed as I felt.

'And do you see there, on the beach? More than three hundred natives. And they are working themselves into a frenzy. Fanny, if they attack, which way shall we flee?'

Gathered in a large group, the Maoris had indeed begun to stamp and dance, brandishing their weapons with great ferocity and emitting blood-curdling screams. A number of chiefs, distinguishable by their ceremonial dress, were mounting Constitution Hill where the Governor stood, flanked by Colonel Wynyard and Captain Oliver, behind them, the lines of the 58th and the Fencibles standing to attention with their muskets. Clad in short feather cloaks and bearing long heavy wooden spears, two of the chiefs now advanced in a sort of dance which ended with the taller flinging his spear into the ground in front of the Governor. There followed some kind of angry parley, during which the Governor seemed to be issuing an ultimatum, for there was much head-shaking from the chiefs and more chanting and stamping from the warriors below on the sands. Some of these began to advance up the hill but, at an order from one of the chiefs, retreated again.

At length, some kind of agreement seemed to have been reached. The chiefs returned to their tribesmen and, after more shouts and clashing of weapons, the Maoris dragged their canoes across the mudflats, exposed now by the receding tide, and paddled away.

'And we must ride back at once,' I said, 'lest the Governor spy us.'

'I shall tell him we were too afraid to continue to the Wynyards' so we turned for home,' said Lucy.

'But why did they invade?' I asked the Governor, as we sat at dinner.

'A Hauraki chief, who was under tapu at the time, came to Auckland to ask about the arrest of one of his tribe, and a local Maori constable laid hands on him, breaking the tapu. That is a deadly insult and they came here to avenge it.'

Lucy frowned. 'How could the constable know that the chief was under tapu?'

'He's a Maori himself. He should know better than to lay hands on a chief at any time.'

'We saw . . . you said . . . the *Fly* was in the harbour with her guns trained on the canoes. How did she manage to arrive so quickly?'

'I was warned of the invasion. Te Toa sent a messenger yesterday.'

'But were you not a little frightened that they might attack you, Governor?'

'Not at all, Miss Fanny.' He smiled. 'I had the Colonel, the Captain, the 58th *and* the Fencibles to defend me. And it is not the way of the chiefs to launch an assault during a parley.'

'I confess I am surprised at the ease you display among such warlike people.'

'I daresay, at times, they might consider us to be warlike towards *them*.'

'Tomorrow,' said Lucy, 'the Governor will return from the south and he intends to bring the children with him.'

'Children?'

Lucy looked at me in exasperation. 'You remember. From Mr Hadfield's pa.'

So occupied had I been with my meetings with Te Toa, I had forgotten all about the children. 'I daresay they will be a little shy at first,' I said quickly, to cover myself.

'Possibly. Now, come and see the room I've prepared for them.'

She led me into one of the guest rooms which opened onto the garden.

'There, you see. I've put the toy chest between their beds and some books and games on the shelf for them. And we have Midget ready for them to ride. Once they're settled we can always get another pony if we should need to.'

'Fanny, have you *seen* the children Sir George has brought from Otaki?'

'Not yet.'

'They're not children at all. The boy is at least eighteen and will be taken tomorrow to board at the Mission school. We will pay for his education there.'

'And the girl?'

'She's about sixteen or seventeen years old. Quite grown, and beautiful after the native fashion, though very sullen. It seems she's been spoilt by Mr Hadfield. Since the death of her parents, he's indulged her too much. It's quite disgraceful of Mrs Godley to send them. And so very disappointing.'

I lay in Te Toa's arms.

'Have you seen yet the girl from Harawira's Mission?' he asked. 'Te Kawana is making a mistake. This girl is dangerous.'

'I agree she seems surly and most ungrateful, but my sister says she won't be with us for long.'

'There, I fear she is wrong. The girl is of chiefly blood. She will not easily relinquish such a position in Te Kawana's household.'

I had barely had time to observe whether Te Toa's judgement was correct when the household was thrown into utter disarray. Feeling unusually exhausted in the oppressive heat, I was resting on the veranda of Moleskin Hall when Lucy appeared, red-eyed and with her clothing in disarray. I roused myself from my lethargy. 'What is it? What's happened?'

She held out a letter. 'Something quite terrible. Sir George has had . . . a communication. It's Godfrey.' She burst into tears.

The Governor knows about Lucy and Mr Godfrey! I thought.

'I simply can't believe it. Oh, Fanny, he's been utterly base. He's *betrayed* me — betrayed us all. This letter is from a clergyman in Nelson, a Reverend Cole. He says that several days ago Godfrey called on him in the middle of the night and with him was a girl . . . a *servant* girl! And Godfrey said he had . . . formed an . . . attachment with her in Wellington but found she was already married.'

'What are you saying?'

'She was expecting soon to have a child, which Godfrey owned was his.' She sobbed harder. 'I can't believe that *Godfrey* could be so duplicitous.'

'Nor I. Are you certain?'

'I assure you, it's true.' She turned to the letter. 'Reverend Cole says, *Mr Thomas, infatuated with the girl, spoke of his prior engagement with her, her situation, her dislike of her husband, of how Mr Thomas's having brought her into trouble constituted her morally his wife.* And read the postscriptum. It's that which has particularly enraged Sir George.'

'I should have thought the intelligence contained in the letter enough for that.'

'Read on and you'll see.'

I took the paper from her. '*P.S. Private and confidential*,' I read. '*I should fail in faithfulness to Your Excellency if I omitted to say that it is my belief that this sad, sad affair is no unnatural consequence of the contamination into which Mr Thomas has been thrown by Your Excellency's most unhappy selection of persons to fill some of the most prominent public offices . . .*

'*Your brother, Mr Thomas, will lose his berth. Why? The Sheriff, the medium of communication between the Government, the Public and the Natives, grieves the natives by debauching the girls at the pa, but is kept in office. Yet why should the Sheriff lose his berth when Domett publicly keeps his woman (and that woman a "Neighbour's Wife")*?'

I looked up from the letter. 'That's all. It appears to end there.'

'Isn't that enough? My husband is apoplectic with fury. I can't believe that *Godfrey*, of all men, could be so vile.'

Remembering the scene in the stables, I tried to choose my words with care. 'This must be so distressing for you. I know you regard Mr Godfrey as . . . as a brother.'

She turned on me furiously. 'I thought you loved me, Fanny. How *dare* you call him my brother?'

'But surely his conduct towards the young woman shows he has a genuine regard for her?'

'She's a *servant*, Fanny. Why are you defending him?' Her sobs increased. 'How can Godfrey have deceived me so?'

To my consternation, she sank onto the veranda seat and began to gasp for breath.

I ran indoors, returned with wet cloths and laid them on her brow. She opened her eyes briefly. 'Go away, Fanny,' she said. 'I feel too ill to talk. Even to you.'

From the moment he brought us back with him, she did not like me. I remember how she looked at me. 'This is not a child,' she said. 'She is fully grown. You must send her back.'

But he overrode her objections and he kept me, as I always knew he would from the first moment I saw him again at Waikanae.

The next day, he took Hone to the Mission school and I was left with Mata Kawana and her sister. She did not offer me tea or speak to me, but gave me into the care of a servant woman, Johnson, who seemed to think I had been hired to assist her in the kitchen.

I waited for Te Kawana's return.

'If you wish me to become a servant in your house,' I said to him, my eyes cast modestly down, 'then I will be so. But, in Mr Hadfield's home I—'

'What is this talk of being a servant?' he asked, so I told him of Johnson and how she had set me to menial work. As I expected, he strode immediately to the kitchen and berated her for being ungracious to an honoured guest.

Then he came back to me where I waited in his study. 'Sit down in this chair,' he said, 'and we will speak together.'

I told him of my early life and of my father and Te Rau-paraha and my mother's fabled journey under the protection of the god, Tangaroa. And when I had finished, I allowed my eyes to lift and seek his. He gazed at me for a long time and I saw how his hand flickered and he was forced to restrain it from stroking my hair.

And so, you might say, I was reborn again and entered into yet another life on this earth.

I waited for Te Kawana to approach me, for his shyness to crumble. For I knew that the more mighty a rangatira, the more is his need for the solace of woman. But Mata Kawana, herself, demanded constant attention. Her constitution was weak, and every day she became more tired and discontent, more querulous and demanding. And so, every day, he turned from her a little more. It was clear to me that he did not go to her bed. This was my power. I knew what she did not.

He took me to him; *he* chose me. *I* am not to blame. Consider my fate had I stayed where I was.

It was not simply a matter of the fulfilment of desire. In all of the time I knew him, I do not think he felt the passion of the body. With him, it was a craving for a meeting of spirits; if you like, a fervour of the mind. He would stroke my hair, run his hands across the smoothness of my skin, lay his head upon my shoulder or in my lap and cast from himself, for a brief time, those heavy burdens of rank and state that distanced him, in his own mind, from the common man.

When first he touched my hair, I flinched. Even among the lower caste of Maori, to lay a hand upon the head, the most tapu part of the body, is forbidden. But though he might speak our tongue, collect our legends, treat with our great chiefs, he did not truly believe us his equals. He was not Mr Hadfield for whom Maori were as himself. Our legends Te Kawana thought imaginary and fanciful; he did not see the truth of them. He respected our tapu but he did not understand it, and our beliefs, our magic spells and chants he dismissed as the prattle of children. *This* was his weakness. *This* was what sealed my power over him.

AUCKLAND, 1852

I rode the ten or so miles to Maud's farm, grateful for the chance to leave the heavy atmosphere of Moleskin Hall. For some time, Lucy had lain in a state of severe melancholy. Earlier, driven by a sense of increasing urgency, I had gone to her room. 'I *must* speak to you, Lucy. Without delay.'

But she had turned her face from me. 'Go away,' she whispered. 'Leave me. No one can help me now. Not even you.'

Maud's cottage was set on the top of an incline, with a small orchard to one side, a garden before it and fields adjacent and below. Two of these, I noticed, had been ploughed in readiness for crops. Behind the house, I glimpsed the shimmer of the sea where the land ran down to the shore. Had I been about less desperate business, I should have stopped and looked about me to take in my first sight of the agreeable aspect of Maud's new home.

At the sound of my approach, she came out to greet me, wearing a strange combination of what seemed to be a labourer's overall and a felt hat.

'Fanny! I'm delighted to see you, of course, but whatever has occasioned this visit? You look quite exhausted.'

Her friendly concern overwhelmed me. I dismounted and broke into weeping.

'Quickly, we must get you inside,' she said. 'I'll call Tamati to see to your mount.'

A young Maori appeared from an outbuilding and led Tsarina away.

The cottage had already been set to rights. Even in my wretched state, I noticed the pleasing effect of the large collection of books, the fine furniture and silverware. Maud set me on a chaise and brought me a glass. 'Drink this brandy. It will help to restore your equilibrium.'

She waited till I had finished it. 'Now,' she said, 'tell me what has brought you here?'

'Oh, Maud,' I said, through tears. 'A calamity. Lucy refuses to speak about it and you are the only soul I could think of to turn to for help.'

Maud crossed to the sideboard, opened a box of Turkish cigarettes and lit one. She regarded me keenly. 'Then you must speak to me entirely frankly.'

Maud continued drawing on her cigarette. She blew out a smoke ring. Then she said, 'You have not been wholly open with me, Fanny. You have not yet told me the name of the father.'

'I give you my word, I cannot,' I said. 'Believe me, Maud, I beg you, it would cause such scandal if it became known.'

'No one would ever hear of it from me, I assure you, but I understand your hesitation, so we will let it rest. There is one part of the Good Book with which I have always concurred. *Dust thou art and unto dust thou shalt return.* And while we're not yet dust, it behoves us to grasp life and, provided it hurts no other, to live as our own consciences may dictate.'

'I fear this would hurt many others.'

'That is generally the case. And, in truth, I have not been entirely frank with *you*, either. When I spoke to you of my own ill-starred marriage, I omitted to tell you that, for many years after my husband's timely death, I carried on a liaison with an already married man, the father of a family, and a figure well known in British public life. Indeed, he is a confidant of two of my brothers.'

'They condoned such a thing!'

'They had no knowledge of it. But had they been aware of it, no, they would have been horrified. He was, he *is*, the passionate love of my life.'

I looked at Maud, still in her workman's garb and felt hat, and struggled to see in her any marks of the ardent lover. 'And . . . his wife?'

'Is an invalid. She has suffered for most of their married life from a series of *crises des nerfs* that no medical man has ever been able to cure. Like your sister, she married when she was only sixteen and believed she was in love.'

'And he?'

'Fell in love with her youth and beauty, quite overlooking her lack of serious education or interest in the world outside the domestic sphere.'

'But, if you love him, why did you leave him?'

'Because I knew that, sooner or later, gossip about our situation would leak out and ruin his career. My own reputation is of no consequence to me and I am, to a considerable degree, protected by the wealth and power of my family, but he . . . he would be utterly disgraced. So I decided to end our liaison and remove myself entirely from the temptation for either of us to see each other again. I have come here to New Zealand and begun a new life.'

Even in the midst of my own concerns, I was moved by her words.

'So you see, Fanny, as I know for myself, one cannot make a dispassionate decision about the person with whom one falls in love. But I tell you, I would rather have known my own dearest love — and been forced to relinquish him — than to have settled for one of those arid unions, formed for security, money or family alliance.' She lit another cigarette. 'Now to the situation you have laid before me. Let me tell you that I see no benefit in charity if it is not practised first at home.'

'You mean you will . . . help us?'

'My dear, of course. How could you doubt me? But we must make very careful plans to allay suspicion from any quarter. And in that I include the Governor, the servant Johnson — and the native girl, Makareta.'

It was now many days since I had last seen Te Toa. Despite the muggy heat, I had managed to excuse myself for a short time almost every day to ride to the Domain in hopes of finding the familiar black stallion in its appointed place. But there was no trace of it there, nor at any other spot it might possibly have been tethered, and though I continued to expect him every day, Te Toa did not come.

I found myself watching out for him as I toiled up Queen Street, feeling faint in the continuing summer heat. Once, I caught sight of him in conversation with two Englishmen outside the dry goods store. I lingered further down the street, gazing into the haberdasher's window, until I they exchanged farewells and I saw Te Toa enter the shop. As casually as I could, I slipped into the dark cool interior only to find, as he turned about, that it was not Te Toa at all but another, unknown, chief.

Te Toa has forgotten me, I told myself sadly. He no longer wishes for my society.

'Miss Colville!' said the Governor. 'Such a pleasant surprise.'

'I was obliged to come into Auckland town for supplies, so I have taken the liberty of calling on you uninvited.' She laid down several bundles. 'Now, Governor, I have here some anthropological journals I feel may be of interest to you.'

He took them up. 'Why yes, they are. How very kind of you.'

'And for your ladies' — she smiled at Lucy who was sitting with me on the veranda seat — 'a selection of apparel ideally suited to this apparently interminable heat wave.' And she drew from another bundle several loose-fitting, layered silken garments. 'So much cooler and healthier, I consider.'

Sir George looked without enthusiasm at this offering. 'Er, perhaps . . .'

'I realise, of course, that to the inexperienced eye such clothing may be considered a little outlandish, but to an informed anthropological historian such as yourself, Governor, its adoption in extremes of weather can, I am sure, be recommended, rather in the manner of the wearing of fur in inclemently cold temperatures.'

'Ah, yes. I am sure you are right.'

'And if you will permit me, and your ladies are in accord, we might repair now to some private room where I shall instruct them in the correct manner in which such clothing should be worn.'

'I am aware,' whispered Maud, 'that your situation cannot be easily concealed for much longer. You must both insist on adopting these clothes for the next few days to combat the heat, and I will speak now to the Governor and beg him to allow you to pay me an extended visit.'

'You think he will agree?'

'I have reason to believe he will.'

Mata Kawana went away with her sister. Every day, in his study, I assisted Te Kawana with his great work. He was writing a book, an important book of Maori lore and language, and, since he could not ask the chiefs to speak of such secret matters, he wished me to tell him all that I learned from my mother, Kahe. I was his 'native secretary'. 'Secretary', 'secrets' — a very proper choice of name.

I had spent all my life thus far in Waikanae and Otaki where Mr Hadfield and my own people spoke the Maori language but, because I had a Pakeha stepfather, I could also speak almost perfect English. I knew only the legends of my own people, Ngati Toa, and those spells my mother had taught me: how to turn away the wrath of the gods, protection against illness and cruel weather, the charms for a safe journey, the magical incantations to launch and guard a new canoe, how to ensure a long life for a newly born infant. But all of these Te Kawana took down from my words and wrote in his large bound notebooks.

And still nothing of what lay so palpably between us had been made manifest.

AUCKLAND, 1852

Leaving Lucy resting in Maud's cottage, I went alone down to the coastline and saw, beached there, a Maori canoe and, walking along the sands, a familiar figure. Though I had yearned for so long to see him, I turned away as he approached.

'Why, Fanny, what is it?'

'I don't understand why you left me for so long. I heard no word from you. Your horse was not—'

'Fanny, my dearest, dearest Fanny, I am more sorry than I can express.'

I looked at him. 'Is it that . . . you have no wish to see me again?'

'How can you say such a thing? All this time, I have been longing for you.'

'Then why didn't you come?'

'Because I could not leave my pa. Some women of the tribe trespassed where they should not go and, to appease the gods, my tohunga placed me under tapu.'

'But, surely—?'

He shook his head. 'Even for you, Fanny, I cannot break sacred law. But I came here as soon as the tapu was lifted.'

'How did you know I was here?'

'When I saw that you were not at Moleskin Hall, I thought most carefully where you would be most likely to go. And why you and Mata Kawana might have gone so quickly and quietly from Auckland.'

I leaned against him. 'I fear if we're absent too long from Auckland the Governor will suspect something.'

'Te Kawana will guess nothing. On the contrary, he will be very happy at your absence. Tell Mata nothing of it but, as both Mata Colville and I know well, Te Kawana is, at this moment, most preoccupied by the girl from Mr Hadfield's Mission. Very soon, he will leave to go south and you may be sure he will take her with him.'

I know what some thought, but I learnt to ignore their icy looks, their glances of disapproval. Why should I care? I had the prize for which I had so patiently waited, which the gods had always intended for me . . .

Te Kawana came home from a visit to Mata Colville where he had gone to see Mata Kerei and her sister. But when he arrived he found Mata Kerei in her sickbed, not well enough, said Mata Colville, to accompany him on the long trip he must make to Nelson in the South Island, Te-Waka-a-Maui.

'So, Makareta,' he said, placing his arm about me, 'it seems *you* must accompany me instead. We shall travel together on the government brig, and you will entertain me with your songs and legends for the long weeks we must be away.'

AUCKLAND, 1852

And, finally, came the day of birth. The pains rolled in waves, like the sea and, amid the mounting screams, Maud set calmly and competently about what needed to be done.

'This is women's work,' she said. 'And why, whatever men may say, we are certainly not the weaker sex.'

While Maud set about delivering the child, I clutched Lucy's hand in mine and prayed for strength. For what seemed an eternity, she and I breathed together in deep, panting gasps. As the screams filled the room and soared around my head, I understood how powerless I was to intervene, to stop the agony. And then, another shriek and, beneath it, a thin wailing cry, and the child was born. A fine, beautiful boy.

As we gazed at him, I saw his tiny chest rise and fall.

Tihe mauri ora.

The breath of life.

'You must return to Moleskin Hall as soon as possible,' said Maud. 'I had a message yesterday from Gas, asking if he might call on me the day after tomorrow. To stay here now would be far too dangerous for you.'

'But the boy . . .?'

'We need an ally in this,' she said. 'We can no longer manage things alone. So, yesterday, after I received the Bishop's communiqué, I took the liberty of speaking in closest confidence to Te Toa.'

'Te Toa!'

'I could see no other option. He's agreed to take the boy tonight to his pa and to find him a wet nurse. He promises to tell no one and I believe him to be entirely trustworthy.'

'But . . .?'

'Despite the fact that the Governor is still in the south, Te Toa tells me he returns very soon. You must understand the absolute necessity of returning home immediately, of being at Moleskin Hall when he arrives in Auckland. Te Toa has assured me he will guard the baby. And he suggests the boy be named Hori Kerei.'

'Surely not! In Maori, that is . . . George Grey.'

'What will flatter the Governor more than a child named for him?'

'Lucy we *must* go. We have no option. If anyone discovers our secret we will both be utterly ruined.'

'The situation is not nearly as desperate as you believe,' said Maud. 'When I spoke to Te Toa, he agreed to ask the Governor to adopt the boy.'

'*Adopt* him? The Governor? That would be quite wonderful. But how will Te Toa persuade my husband to accept him?'

'He'll say that the infant is the fruit of a liaison between his kinswoman and a Pakeha soldier.'

'But the baby's so fair . . .'

'Look at the offspring of such relationships between Maori and Pakeha. Some are dark, looking entirely like natives. Some are fair. Some have the components of both races. There's nothing to fear on that score.'

'When will Te Toa take him?'

'Tonight.'

'*No*! So soon? How can we bear it?'

'You must both be strong. For the child's sake, it's better so.'

'We must try to appear delighted by the Governor's return,' I said.

Lucy shrugged. 'I will do what I can, but you know it will be only play-acting and a sham.'

'But think of what is at stake, I *beg* you. We should in no way antagonise him at this juncture.'

'Fanny, the most wonderful, wonderful news. Maud has sent a note. Te Toa has seen Sir George who's agreed to take the boy.'

'I thank God! May I see the note?'

'I burnt it immediately after I read it. But she wrote that she was present and that Te Toa was very distant, almost as if he didn't want the Governor to adopt him but felt it would be only to the infant's advantage. A very clever ploy, I think, because my husband was at once interested in him.'

'I'm overjoyed. But we must remain calm. Even a little indifferent. We can't afford to have anyone guess his identity.'

'I'll prepare his nursery and you must help me. You must be his godmother, of course, and what do you think of asking the Bishop and the Martins to be his other godparents?'

'I think it's all one could desire for him.'

'Oh, Fanny, you can't believe what this means to me. At last . . . after all these years . . . to have another child.'

AOTEAROA

Te Kawana chose *me*. In return, I gave away to him our songs, our spells, our secrets. Perhaps it is for that I am condemned now and not because of *her*. He wished me to tell him the ancient stories, to sing, to dance ('but cover your breasts, Makareta, cover your breasts'). When he was troubled, he loved to brush my 'blackbird' hair. That is what he called me, his 'blackbird'. I never saw a blackbird, though he promised to show me one. Like a tui, he said, but with no missionary's white collar at its throat . . . And yes, I thought, I *am* a bird, but without wings.

AUCKLAND, 1853

'My dearest, beloved Fanny, you see that I am weeping. I can scarcely bear to bring you and Mata this dreadful intelligence. Te Kawana has changed his mind. He refuses now to take the boy.'

'But *why*, Te Toa? Only three days ago he spoke of it as if it were about to happen.'

'I do not know. But I know the mind of Te Kawana. If I persist now, he will become obdurate and he will never agree.'

'That's true. And it may even rouse his suspicions. I dare not tell Lucy this terrible news. Oh, Te Toa, what can we do?'

'The boy is safe in my pa. He is under my protection and he is healthy.'

'But we *must* see him. It's been so long, and we haven't seen him since he was eight days old.'

'I know this and I am truly sorry for the pain it causes. But to gain Te Kawana's consent, it is a necessary thing.'

'I don't understand why he's changed his mind.'

'Nor I, but be sure, I shall try again.'

'In the meantime, I implore you to let us see him.'

He put his arm around me. 'That is impossible. I beg you, listen to me, Fanny. I am more sorry for this than I can say, especially as he is the most fine lusty boy and all he lacks is his mother, but we must remain steadfast. I am a warrior. It is the first rule of battle that, to succeed, you do not rush at your enemy but wait patiently for your opportunity.'

'Te Toa has tried again to persuade the Governor. He's even suggested that, as the child has been named for him, he should bring the boy here to Moleskin Hall for him to see . . .'

'Oh, Fanny, he continues to refuse?'

'He won't countenance it. And it's very strange. In general, the Governor wishes to please the Northern chiefs and he has a high regard for Te Toa.'

'Then what shall we do?'

'What *can* we do? Wait and pray.'

'Things are not working out as we hoped. Te Toa still hasn't managed to sway the Governor and I dare not, for my life, mention it.'

'Don't think of saying a *word* to your husband. It would be disastrous.'

Lucy flung her arms around me. 'And I have even more distressing news. We have very little time to lose if we want Sir George to change his mind. He heard this morning that he's been recalled Home by the Colonial Office. We sail for England very soon.'

'*No*!'

'And, Fanny, he says he's taking Makareta with us.'

'Makareta! What is he thinking of? She'll never be accepted in polite society at Home.'

'You don't know all of it. He intends to adopt her.'

'*Adopt* Makareta? He can't possibly.'

'It's his intention to do exactly that. He says she'll help him with his Polynesian researches into lore and language.'

'I suppose—'

'Fanny, she's been brought up at Mr Hadfield's Mission. Her stepfather was an Englishman. Look at Sir George in her presence. I believe he's in love with her.'

'Can't you speak to the Bishop?'

'The Selwyns wouldn't — couldn't — believe such a thing as that he might have an . . . unfortunate . . . interest in her.'

'Well then, Lady Martin?'

'Even *she* would think it a figment of my fevered imagination. It's only Maud who says she believes what I say.' She looked at me beseechingly. 'Fanny, I have never felt so alone — so bereft. I *beg* you, come Home with us.'

AOTEAROA

I have cried to Tangaroa, god of the sea, to carry me back to my own lands. Only he, who controls the waters, can give me safe passage, can calm the ocean and command it to be still. Mr Hadfield told us that it is Te Ariki who directs the waves but I know in my heart it is Tangaroa. It was he to whom my mother prayed to save our lives, he who heard her entreaties and spared us. But now I have committed evil, I have embraced what is forbidden, I have broken the scared law of tapu, he is angry, and I fear his vengeance against me for the wrong I have done.

In the waters between my birthplace, Kapiti Island, and Otaki, the mainland pa of Te Rau-paraha, lived the mighty she-taniwha, Awarua. At the bidding of Tangaroa, she rose from his deeps to capsize the canoes of those who offended her master. Her wrath was terrible; the heaving and lashing of her great body caused the waves to swell and churn and crash upon the shore. To appease her, said my mother, Kahe, the fishermen offered the first of their catch to Tangaroa and the second to Awarua. Only the most revered of the tohunga could lull her into quietness, and even this was only a respite. 'She is ever vigilant,' said my mother. 'You must on no account anger her or, for utu, she will destroy you.'

Now that the time is near when I am to go with Te Kawana on this great voyage, I can longer sleep in the night. Perhaps Awarua has a sister-taniwha in the vast ocean that we must cross; perhaps there are many such. And how will I, who have no fishing net, placate them?

AUCKLAND, 1853

'Oh, Te Toa, how is the boy?'

'Strong and healthy. A magnificent infant. But I have news that will distress you very greatly. Te Kawana is resolute. He entirely refuses to change his mind.'

'But *why*?'

'I do not know. I cannot understand it.'

'I'm in despair. What can we do?'

'There is only one thing possible to do. The boy must remain with his wet nurse under my protection.'

I could not speak for some time.

'Fanny, my dearest, beloved Fanny, I am more sorry than I can express.'

'This is a truly unhappy day. There is something *I* must tell *you*, Te Toa. I am leaving.'

'Leaving Auckland?'

'No, New Zealand. I am going Home.'

He drew me to him. 'You cannot leave now.'

'Sir George has been recalled to England. How can I remain here?'

'You have very many friends in Auckland. It would be a simple matter to acquire a house and—'

'Without the protection of my being under the Governor's roof, it would be almost impossible for us to meet. What pretext would you have for visiting me? Where could we find privacy in Auckland? And it's certain I can't come and live with you at your pa.'

'Mata Colville is most free-thinking. And she is your good friend.'

I laid my cheek against the smoky-purple moko of his shoulder. 'Even she couldn't conceal our situation for long.' I paused. 'And you couldn't . . . you wouldn't . . . come to England?'

'How can I leave my people?'

'Your wives . . .'

'Not merely my wives and children. All my people. I am their chief; I cannot desert them.' He pressed my body against his and I saw he, too, was weeping. 'If it were myself only . . . you must believe me, Fanny . . . I have never in my life felt for anyone as I do for you, but how can I leave Aotearoa?'

'We could live in my house in Lyme.' But, as I spoke the words, I knew how futile they were.

'I should like so much to see your house and its mulberry tree like Pihopa's. If I had only myself to consider, if I could be like a bird and fly wherever I might, away from my own flock, I would go with you wherever you went. But I am not a bird. I am born to my rank and I cannot abandon it. If I were to desert my tribe, every member of it would be shamed. Forever.'

'So,' I said, through my own tears, 'just like any Englishman, you must do your duty. Ah, Te Toa, I see you are as *proper* as I am.'

'I fear you are right.' His hand caressed my hair. 'Will you cut for me a piece of this so that I may remember you always?'

I nodded. 'And the boy? Lucy and I . . . We must see him for one last time.'

'That cannot be. He is no longer at the pa. I have removed him to a safer place.'

'But, Te Toa, you *promised*.'

'And I will keep my word. I have taken him away for a short time only, to protect him. Pihopa has returned to Waimate and he is often now at my pa. Despite what you think, such a light-coloured infant among the dark ones might excite his interest.'

'So we can't even say goodbye to him?'

He shook his head.

I hesitated. 'For the first time, I'm unable to say what I wish to you, Te Toa.'

'There is no need. I know already what is in your heart. And mine.'

He leaned his forehead against my own. I felt the warmth of his breath across my face. 'Tihe mauri ora,' he said. 'And as you cross the ocean, look up at Te Punga, your Southern Cross, the anchor of the waka of the Maori warrior, Tama-rereti, and remember me.'

VI

LYME REGIS, 1858

And so I left Aotearoa. At every port on our voyage, I thought of how I might ease my burning misery, my desperate longing, simply by leaving our ship and waiting for another to bear me back to where I most yearned to be. Though I knew this was an entirely foolhardy dream, at night when visions of Te Toa haunted me, my desire to be back in Auckland was like a hunger that nothing could assuage. Lucy and I, mutely wretched, tearfully parted at Portsmouth with promises to meet soon, and I returned to Lyme.

For all of my adult life, I had held a vision of Lyme, its churchyard, its markets, its crooked streets, the Walk, the Rooms, the Cobb . . . And now, as the dogcart bore me into Church Street and I saw the two steps leading to my own front door with its black knocker shaped like a gloved hand, my heart began both to ache and, briefly, to lift. I could not bring myself to knock, but asked to be set down by the gate where, at once, I was confronted by the branching green span of my mulberry tree. I laid my hand on its gnarled trunk, then skirted the side of the house and, to the consternation of the servant, entered by the kitchen door. The smell of wax polish, the sight of the hearth with its fire, stirred a sense of familiarity in me. I was conscious of the roots of the mulberry spreading beneath the floor on which I stood, of the faint sound of the sea slapping the shore of Lyme Bay, the bark and bustle of my new servant, Jane, who resembled Martha in her stance and the set of her hands on her hips as she watched me invade her domain. At last, I had come home, but, with all my heart, I wished only to be back in New Zealand.

The pain of loss did not diminish. Every morning, when I woke, I could scarcely bear to find myself still alive, the fiery ache in my chest seeming too much to endure for even one more day. Feeling myself no more than a phantom in my own house, I took to wandering in St Michael's churchyard, tracing the names on the gravestone where my family lay, but the old grief for them seemed to have dissolved in the ferocity of my current anguish. I inhabited a town peopled with ghosts. Forgotten costermongers haunted the market, invisible bathers screamed as they were dunked beneath the waves, spectres played at cards in the Assembly Rooms. On the Cobb, long-dead traders loaded their wares on the backs of unseen pack-horses and, when I finally forced myself to walk to Cobb House, I barely recognised it.

Lucy had written that they were now in London at the house of Mrs Martin, Sir George's Aunt Julia. In my letters, I did not dare to ask if Makareta was with them, nor to mention the boy left behind with Te Toa. Like me, Lucy must surely think of him daily, but I could not set down a word about him lest someone else have the intelligence of it. She had promised to visit me in Lyme, but then came a note saying that Sir George had been posted to the Cape Colony and they were to leave within the fortnight. To this, she had added a postscriptum: *And Makareta is, of course, to accompany us. I only would it were you, dearest Fanny.*

In my waking hours, I dared not allow myself to think of Te Toa. But at night I dreamt of green bush, the starry fronds of the great tree ferns, the lesser white stars of the clematis, the scrubby kanuka, the spreading canopy of southern stars in a low black sky, their clarity making them appear within reach of a human hand, and of the long sandy beaches where, in these nightly reveries, I galloped with Te Toa. It was five years since I had seen him. Did he, too, still dream of me?

Over the past two years, Lucy's letters from the Cape had become more and more infrequent, and it was possible to glean from them only that the climate did not suit her and that she was increasingly unhappy. Her sole activities appeared to be some occasional riding, and the collection of rare bulbs and plants, though it was clear that her health did not permit her to engage often in either. Of Sir George she said little except that affairs at the Cape occupied him constantly and, as a result, his health was suffering and his old wound was troubling him.

Then, unexpectedly, I received a letter from Sir George's aunt, Mrs Martin, informing me that Lucy had returned from the Cape suffering severe nervous prostration, and was staying with them in London. *But,* she wrote, *her progress is slow and we, and her physician, are alarmed at the weakness of her constitution. She speaks of you constantly, but is far too unwell to contemplate a journey to Lyme. I wonder, therefore, whether you would consider paying a visit to us here in London where you and dear Eliza might be reunited. I believe this could do much to lift her from her present low state.*

Within days, I was in London at the elegant house in Eaton Terrace, where I was warmly greeted by Mrs Martin. 'I cannot tell you how grateful we are that you've come. Eliza is worse and no physic seems to improve her health. Before you see her, we'll take tea together and I'll tell you what little I know of what has taken place at the Cape.'

We sat in the drawing room before a leaping fire.

'Eliza travelled Home with Bishop Gray and his wife, who are currently on furlough here,' said Mrs Martin. 'She's too ill to quit her room, but today, because you are coming, she has insisted on leaving her bed and is sitting in a chair for the first time. You'll find her room overheated, but she's so thin and feels the cold so greatly I've been obliged to order that fires be kept burning at all times. I won't attempt to keep from you how worried I am.'

'I only hope your confidence in my restorative abilities isn't misplaced. Was she ill at the Cape?'

'From what I understand, she had various *crises des nerfs* but nothing quite as serious as her present illness. In her letters she seemed unhappy, and I fear that my nephew behaved very thoughtlessly towards her. He was away for months at a time, and didn't trouble himself to write to her and let her know of his progress about the country or even of his impending return.'

I thought of saying that he had done much the same in New Zealand but held my silence.

'There's no doubt George is a brilliant man and very much tested by his present office, but I fear he has displayed an indifference to his wife's natural feelings that falls below the standards I find acceptable. I have written to tell him so.'

'I see,' I said. 'And at present he remains at the Cape?'

'He must. He has troubles on every front. He writes of tribal battles among the Zulus and of famine gripping the Xhosa people. And now, even though he has not enough troops to hold the precarious peace at the frontiers, he's obliged to send soldiers from the Cape to swell the forces in India . . . But I must cease talking of his affairs and take you to Eliza. I should warn you that she looks . . . rather altered.'

Wrapped in rugs in a large armchair in front of a blazing fire, Lucy turned towards me as I entered and made to rise but could not find the strength. Despite Mrs Martin's warning, I was shocked. She was emaciated; her hair hung limp, her eyes, their blackness emphasised by her pallor, lacked animation, and her speech was hesitant and wavering.

'Oh, Fanny, how I've *longed* to see you. I can't believe you're here.'

'She is indeed here,' said Mrs Martin, 'and very glad I am to meet her at last.' She drew up a chair at a distance from the heat of the fire and motioned me to it. 'And now, I'll leave you together. If you should need me, Eliza, you have your bell.'

I looked at Lucy and saw she was weeping. 'Come and kiss me, Fanny dearest.'

As I put my arms about her, I felt the angularity of her body and saw that her wrists were translucent and as narrow as a child's.

'Will you stay here for a time?'

'Your kind aunt has asked me to remain for several weeks.'

'You see that I'm not in the best of health.'

'I do. What has happened?'

She sighed, lay back and closed her eyes. For several minutes she did not answer, then she whispered, 'That I can't say, not even to you.'

'Why not tell me about Cape Town? Did you find congenial friends there?'

'None so dear as those in Auckland. Very soon after we arrived, we met Bishop Gray and his lady, and we've become quite well acquainted with them.'

'Is Mrs Gray agreeable company?'

Lucy's eyes were open now. 'I know one shouldn't criticise the wife of a bishop, but, Fanny, she's a most difficult woman. She's the driving force behind her husband — everyone in Cape Town says as much. She keeps all the accounts and minutes for the diocese, and rides vast distances throughout the country with her husband.'

'Clearly she has no children.'

'That's just it. She has four, and when the youngest, Florence, was still a baby, Mrs Gray set off on a five-month trek on horseback with the Bishop, leaving Louisa, the eldest, in charge of Florence and the other children *and* the church affairs. She's quite a . . . domineering woman, nothing at all like dear Sarah Selwyn. But you'll meet her for yourself. And the Bishop. Aunt Julia has invited them to tea the day after tomorrow. And since you are here, dearest Fanny, I shall make every effort to come downstairs and join you all.'

Mrs Gray, a small forceful woman in drab black silk, burst into Mrs Martin's drawing room ahead of her husband, whose air of misery was heightened by his sombre black bishop's apron, breeches and gaiters. As he uneasily paced the room, his wife settled herself on the edge of a chair and held court in the manner of one who was in no doubt that her presence served to elevate the moral tone of the company around her. I disliked her instantly and so, I suspected, did Mrs Martin.

'We must thank you,' said Mrs Martin, 'for your kind attentions to dear Eliza on the voyage Home.'

'As to that,' said Mrs Gray, 'since we were returning Home in any event, it caused us very little inconvenience.'

'And your children? Have they all accompanied you?'

'Good gracious, I should think not. I've left them in Cape Town in the charge of Louisa, our eldest.'

'And how old is Louisa?' asked Mrs Martin.

'Why, let me think . . .' Mrs Gray turned to her husband. 'Is Louisa eighteen or nineteen, Robert?'

'She's just seventeen,' put in Lucy.

'Ah, yes, I suppose she must be. I don't really care at all for children, Mrs Martin. It's only the Bishop who misses them. He writes to them almost every day that we're away, but he dotes most particularly on babies. He's always kissing and dandling them.' She smiled fondly at her husband. 'The Bishop's constitution isn't strong and it worries me that he can never find the solitude he requires in Cape Town. We're hoping that here, at Home, he may replenish his physical and mental strength.'

For the first time, the Bishop spoke. 'Bishop's Court, you see, is always overrun with visitors. There's no chance of seclusion there. And we've been obliged to set up a native school which merely adds to our burdens.' He turned to Lucy. 'I am, of course, at one with the Governor's Christian endeavours, but—'

'It must be said,' interrupted his wife, 'that the blackies are a most trying race.'

I saw Lucy's expression and said quickly, 'It sounds a little like Bishop Selwyn's Auckland Mission.'

'I think not,' said the Bishop. 'We maintain an episcopal carriage, you know.'

'And I understand you travel with your husband on his parish visitations to the most inaccessible and dangerous areas, Mrs Gray.'

Mrs Gray looked pleased. 'That's quite correct, Miss Thompson. And, if I may say so without appearing conceited, I've designed most of the churches built in these remote places.'

'Even to the calculation of the number of bricks required for their construction,' said her husband.

'Goodness,' said Mrs Martin, 'you are a helpmeet indeed.'

'I see assisting Robert as the principal duty of my life. Now, last year, we made a visitation to the Bishop's most far-flung parishes. We had a cart to carry our possessions and the Bishop's robes—'

'And they rode more than two thousand miles over the most inhospitable terrain you can imagine,' said Lucy. 'At one point, the cart was submerged as they forded a river and all poor Mrs Gray's clothes were utterly ruined.'

'I own I was exceedingly cross. One of them was a new silk gown I'd ordered just before we left, so I didn't have the pleasure of wearing it even once.'

'You must have great fortitude,' said Mrs Martin.

'Our strength comes from doing God's work. On an average day on our visitation, the Bishop and I maintained a pace of between fifty and sixty miles' hard riding.'

'I'm quite astounded,' said Mrs Martin. 'Are you never ill?'

'Only from headaches brought on by all the copying of the Bishop's documents. For want of time during the day, I'm often reduced to doing them by candlelight at night.'

'Well,' said Mrs Martin, when the Grays had finally departed, 'I'm sure Mrs Gray is a most admirable woman in her way, but she's scarcely the most sympathetic of creatures. One feels for her children.'

'Louisa and I have become close friends,' said Lucy. 'She's not a bit like her mama. She's very sweet-tempered but entirely put upon.'

'Tell me something about South Africa, Lucy. I've heard it's very beautiful. Did you visit much of the country?'

She shifted uneasily in her chair. Something about her demeanour perturbed me. 'A little,' she said, 'but it's even more difficult to traverse than New Zealand. The sea voyage around the Cape is quite terrible. It's one of the most perilous stretches of water in the world, you know, so, as the Grays said, a lot of travel is by land — on horseback or in bullock carts.'

'It sounds very similar to New Zealand.'

'The terrain is far worse. The mountain passes are much higher and very narrow and tortuous. It was quite terrifying crossing them.'

'And Cape Town?'

She wound a lock of her hair around her finger. 'It's much larger and more populous than Auckland. It lies in a bowl at the foot of a steep escarpment called Table Mountain because its peak has been quite worn away and the top of it is entirely flat.' She shivered. 'It has a very . . . ominous . . . appearance, and next to it is the most sinister place of all, Devil's Peak. The natives say it's inhabited by Satan.'

'There are many such legends, even here in England.'

'Ah, but if you were to see it for yourself, Fanny, you would understand how menacing it is. Whenever I glanced up at it, I couldn't help but shudder. It's as if an evil cloud hangs about it. Makareta is terrified of it. She refuses to look at it.'

'Is Makareta still in Cape Town?' I asked cautiously.

'Yes.'

'But surely she didn't stay with Mrs Martin or the Governor's family in Bodiam when you were here at Home?'

'No, not even Sir George would have dared suggest that. He sent her to Mr Grant of the Church Missionary Society, saying she was an example of how well the church was succeeding in its conversion of the New Zealand natives.'

'And she agreed to go?'

'She didn't want to go at all, but what choice did she have? And Mr Grant and his colleagues took her about in London and Cambridge where she was made much of. Sir George saw her from time to time but always in the company of others. Then, when it was time to leave for South Africa, he announced that she would accompany us to help him with his Polynesian researches and to serve as an exemplar to the natives there.'

'I see.'

'But things in Cape Town are very different from New Zealand. In South Africa, Makareta is treated with great scorn; she's regarded as a "blackie" and, therefore, a servant.'

'By the Boers?'

'There are very few Boers in Cape Town. No, it's the English settlers who hold such views — led, as you heard, by Bishop and Mrs Gray.'

'Eliza has just received a letter,' said Mrs Martin, 'and its contents seem to have severely depressed her spirits again. Might you speak to her?'

I went at once to Lucy's room. She was lying back in bed, silently weeping.

'What is it?' I said. 'What's happened?'

'Oh, Fanny, you know I've been low-spirited, but since you've come, things have seemed so much more hopeful that I really believed . . . And now . . .

'Now, what?'

'I've had a letter from Gussie.'

I felt sudden dread. 'Is she ill? Are the children?'

'No, but it's about the children that she's written.'

'And what does she say?'

'Fanny, you remember my husband refused to adopt the boy?'

'How could I forget it?'

'Ever since, I've longed . . . Fanny, I need . . . I *must* have a child. If my husband and I had children, I'm certain our dissentions would be resolved. That lies at the heart of all our difficulties.'

'Perhaps you're right . . .'

'I'm *certain* it's so. Did you know that when I arrived here, Gussie and Egerton-Warburton were also at Home, visiting his ailing mama?'

'Yes, I met them very briefly when they paid a short visit to Lyme. I was delighted to see them again.'

'They were due to sail for Australia shortly after my arrival, and they came to see me two days before they left. It was twenty years since I'd seen them. Then Gussie came alone the next day for a final farewell . . . I'm almost thirty-seven now, Fanny, and the physician in Cape Town says it's an impossibility for me to bear more children. But Gussie has nine. *Nine*. She has no need of *nine* children. So, when she was here, I asked her if my husband and I might take one or two of them and bring them up as our own. I assure you, Fanny, we'd give them every advantage Sir George's station affords. I begged her, as my dearest sister, to spare us two, and she agreed, though reluctantly, to discuss it with her husband. "I will love them as my own, with all my heart," I said. And she said she was in no doubt of it and that she would write to me once she and Egerton-Warburton had had time to think about my proposal. And now, she has sent me this letter . . .' She began to weep again. 'It says that . . . that . . . she and her husband have spoken at length of it but — and they regret it most profoundly — they love all their children so dearly, they can't bring themselves to part with a single one. So, you see, all my hopes are utterly dashed.'

She paused. 'It's a punishment, Fanny, for my wrong-doing.'

'It's no sort of punishment at all. It's entirely natural that the Egerton-Warburtons should find it an impossibility to relinquish any of their children, even to you.'

The following morning, as I sat with Lucy, she asked suddenly, 'Do you remember the tohungas in New Zealand?'

I nodded.

'Fanny,' she said quietly, 'if I were to tell you what is ailing me, will you give me your solemn promise never to breathe a word of what I've said to a living soul?'

'You have my word.'

'And will you also promise that you won't . . . sneer at me?'

'Surely you know I've never in my life seen fit to sneer at anyone, least of all you.'

Tears flowed across her cheeks. 'I wish so much to speak of it and yet . . .'

'You *must* confide in me.'

'Fanny, I'm ill — dying, I think, because . . . because I've been bewitched.'

'*Bewitched*. But when? By whom?'

'By Makareta.'

She was crying in earnest now and I put my arms about her. 'Listen to me, Lucy. This is madness.'

'I'm not mad. It's true. Makareta has placed a spell on me. In her tribe she was a prophetess and—'

'Who told you this? *She* did, I have no doubt.'

'Yes . . .'

'She didn't even live with her tribe. You know that. She lived with a Maori mother and an English stepfather near the house of Mr Hadfield, the missionary. Do you think *he* would have permitted her to practise witchcraft and spells?'

'She says she's of the blood of Te Rau-paraha and—'

'Her entire tribe is of the blood of Te Rau-paraha. That doesn't make her a sorceress. Don't you remember Maud Colville saying such prophecies are merely superstitions believed by the credulous?'

'But the Maori tohungas *could* make the gods speak. You know what I saw in New Plymouth when my husband was so ill.'

'That's quite different from Makareta's threats. The tohunga came to heal Sir George, not to destroy him. And, if Makareta is such a powerful sorceress, why hasn't she bewitched the settlers of Cape Town and caused them to admire and accept her? She's unhappy and she wishes to inflict her own misery on you. Isn't that so?'

'It may be. She hates Cape Town.'

'She's angry at her lowered status and seeks to blame you for her troubles. And you must not allow her to succeed in this. She has no power over you except for what you, yourself, permit her to exercise.'

'You don't believe I'm bewitched?'

I took hold of her shoulders and stared full into her face. 'I *know* you are in no way bewitched. You must stop this at once. No one can conjure spirits. Think of what Aunt would have said to such nonsense.'

'But what of that fortune-teller in Rio? She caused you to faint.'

'Lucy, I was a ten-year-old girl, grieving and confused.' I searched for an adequate lie. 'I was overcome by the oppressive heat. No more than that.'

Lucy clung to my hands. 'Do you swear to me you don't believe I'm under a spell?'

'On my life, I do not. And, tomorrow, you must leave this room and come downstairs again to the drawing room for an hour or two to profit from the company of your aunt. It's not good for you to stay brooding up here alone.'

'Fanny, I promise I will. I can't tell you how much . . . safer I feel. But there's one more thing I must confide to you. It's difficult to tell you this, but I must. I'm guilty, too. I . . . I'm jealous. Of Makareta. I'm often quite consumed by hatred of her.'

'That's hardly a sin.'

'But I detest her, Fanny.'

'Perhaps with good reason.'

'I *do* have good reason. In private, she usurps my place in the household. It's she my husband consults on everything. It's as if they exist only for each other and I'm of no account. And she's cruel and venomous to me. She exalts in her position.'

'However much she may have commanded his private heart, you

are his wife; your position is unassailable. And surely Bishop and Mrs Gray, from what I've seen of them, would never approve of such a liaison.' And as I said this, a vision of Te Toa rose before me. Why should not the Governor, too, be enchanted as I had been — as I remained?

'You know, on several occasions, I've discovered them . . . embracing. Once, I found them with her head against his shoulder as he stroked her hair. And when I confronted them, she looked at me with such an expression of mingled defiance and triumph, I could scarcely bear it.'

'And what had Sir George to say for himself?'

'He told me that I had been a neglectful mother and now I was a neglectful wife. That it was my own doing that he'd been forced to seek comfort where he might find it.'

'He said this in front of Makareta?'

'Yes. And I felt so torn between pain and fury I wanted with all my heart to destroy them both. I even thought . . . of killing myself.'

'But you haven't killed yourself. To think of a deed is not the same as committing it. And Sir George has behaved shamefully. If his aunt were to know of it—'

'She mustn't. Think of the distress it would cause her.'

'Has no one in Cape Town observed his conduct?'

'Only Dr Bickersteth. He came out from Oxford to the Cape and, one day, he called at Government House to speak with my husband. Sir George was not at home, so I offered him tea and he said he felt unable to take tea in a house where *certain goings-on* were condoned by the mistress of it, no matter that that house be the highest in the land.'

'He blamed *you* for the Governor's wrong-doing?'

'It seemed so.'

'A pity this doctor did not see fit to speak directly to Sir George. Is he a physician?'

'No, a clergyman.'

Lucy became strong enough to walk occasionally in Hyde Park. As the days passed, I increasingly longed to speak to her of the boy, of

Te Toa, of New Zealand, but could not find a way to approach such a delicate topic. Then, quite by chance, she herself provided me with my opportunity. Mrs Martin was out for the day and Lucy and I were seated in the garden. 'It's so very peaceful here in England,' she said. 'I've become used to living in countries where there are continual wars and skirmishes. And, of course, there are no native races here, unless one counts the English themselves.'

'That's true.'

'Since I've been Home, I've often thought of how, wherever we go in the service of the Empire, the people hate us.'

'The Maoris didn't hate us.'

'Not all of them. But they didn't love us either.'

I was silent. Then I said, 'Do you remember Lady Martin's little hospital?'

Lucy nodded. 'Oh, Fanny,' she cried, suddenly. 'Do you ever think of him — the boy?'

'Always. And you?'

'Not a single day passes without some thought of . . . what might have been.'

We sat silently and I became aware we were both quietly weeping.

As Lucy continued to improve in health I grew more confident of her eventual recovery. Mrs Martin had spoken of making a visit soon to their country house in Herefordshire and we were both looking forward to the possibility. Then came a setback.

'I've received a letter from my husband. Will you read it, Fanny? You'll see he begs me to go back to him. He says he can't live without me, that he is sunk in bleakest despair . . .'

'What . . .?'

'He means it. I'm certain of that. He says he's cast aside Makareta, that he'll send her back to New Zealand, if only I'll agree to return.'

'And if you do return, and she doesn't leave, how long will it be before she once again reduces you to misery? Are you certain he doesn't simply require you as a chaperone? He can scarcely keep her in Government House without you there.'

'But he says he's sunk so low that, if I don't come, he'll take his own life. You see, he loves me after all.'

'That's not love, Lucy. It's blackmail.'

'You're wrong. You misjudge him. Ah, Fanny, do you remember I spoke to you once about the Xhosa, an entire South African tribe that was dying of hunger? That's how I've felt, ever since Makareta — before Makareta even — but after she came it was worse. When she told me I was cursed, I felt like those poor famished people, only it was not my body but my spirit that was starving and withering to extinction. And now . . . now that I see my husband loves me after all, I must go to him.'

'No, you must *not*. You must wait for his next letter.'

We had not long to wait. Sir George's second letter arrived within a week.

'He's even more desperate for my return, Fanny. Look at what he says — that everything in Government House reminds him of me and emphasises his loss and desolation. You can't believe how long I've waited to hear him say such things.'

'Lucy, if Sir George is truly sincere in what he says, I'm glad for you, but I find it strange that he's conceived these sentiments for you only in your absence. When you were with him, he treated you with cold indifference. I saw it myself in New Zealand.'

'He says he can't set himself to the task of governing; his thoughts are all of wretchedness and extinction. He prays several times a day for my return.'

'And has he asked you anywhere in either of his letters about your own health?'

'Why, no, but that's because he's so cast down.'

'It was ever in his nature to be selfish. Even his aunt says so. Do you think the leopard can so easily change its spots?'

At first, Lucy's letters after her return to Cape Town were full of the pleasures of her reunion with Sir George. Louisa Gray, she wrote, had been delighted to see her again, large numbers of people had welcomed her back, and she had even found some new rare plant specimens. Of Makareta, she made no mention.

Then, in the next year, came a letter:

. . . How right you were in your surmise that Sir George wanted me to return only so that he might keep Makareta with him yet present a respectable face to the world . . . Despite all his promises, she remains here in Government House.

Her letters became more infrequent, and then came a short note to say only that Sir George had been recalled from South Africa and they were about to leave for Home. She asked if, after her arrival, she might spend a little time with me in Lyme. I wrote immediately, care of Mrs Martin, telling her she must come whenever she wished.

For the first few days of Lucy's visit to Lyme, I asked her nothing, and she ventured not a word about Cape Town, her husband or herself. She looked stronger than when I had last seen her, but I was concerned that her spirits seemed low. Drifting about the house, she resembled nothing more than a wraith, the shell of what she had once been. She sat at table with me, eating almost nothing, she stared from the windows for long periods, and frequently retired to bed. She could not be coaxed to walk about Lyme or to visit Cobb House, and any suggestions of a stroll on the Cobb she refused to countenance, saying she was 'too tired today'. When we sat together, I noticed how her hands plucked ceaselessly at her skirts, brushing away invisible particles from the fabric, and how she constantly twisted the same lock of hair behind her ear.

Though at first merely exasperated by this, I gradually became alarmed, and resolved to engage her in some kind of discussion about her true situation. I was still contemplating the best way to approach this when I was woken one night by a presence in my room and was startled to see Lucy, in her shift, standing beside my bed.

'What is it?' I said, sitting up and trying to collect myself. 'Are you ill?'

She shook her head.

'You're shivering. What's happened?'

'Someone is crying. A baby. Do you hear it, Fanny?'

I cocked my head. 'That's just the wind in the chimney. In these old houses . . .'

'No, it's a child. Or perhaps a young woman.' She began to wring her hands. 'We must find her, Fanny.'

'Come,' I said, fully awake now. 'It's after midnight. We can't search tonight. Climb into bed beside me and sleep. In the morning we'll see what can be done.'

'The morning may be too late. It's only at night that she comes. She brings the child with her. For me to take care of, I think. Though I hear her quite clearly, I can never find her.'

But she slipped into bed beside me and lay back on the pillows. In the faint moonlight, I saw the marks of tears on her cheeks.

She was silent, and I thought perhaps she had fallen asleep, but then she spoke again. 'Do you remember how we shared a bed at Strawberry Hill?'

'Yes. And the room was so small there was only space enough to dress ourselves one at a time.'

'We were happy, then.'

'Yes, we were.'

'Are you happy now?'

I thought of Te Toa, whom I had not seen for so long, whom I would never see again, of New Zealand, of . . . 'I have had my share of happiness,' I said. 'And you?'

She did not answer this. Instead, she said, 'Do you recall the old woman in Rio? The fortune-teller.'

'You've asked me about her before. And I've told you she was simply a blind old woman.'

'Fanny, do you believe our lives are preordained? That everything that happens to us is merely Fate and that we are powerless to change our destinies?'

This was the most she had spoken since her arrival and I wished to encourage her to continue. I said guardedly, 'I think some parts of our lives are guided by Fate, or even by Heaven, but we also have the power to shape our own destinies.'

'I have sinned,' she said suddenly. 'And God is punishing me.'

'I'm sure we've all sinned at some time, and you no more than I or any other.'

'You don't understand, Fanny. I've done very wrong. I've forfeited my place in Heaven.'

'I can't believe such a thing,' I said soothingly. 'Only God can judge that and, if you truly repent of what it is you've done, you'll be forgiven.'

'You've heard of Godfrey's situation?'

'Why, no.' Since leaving New Zealand, I had not thought at all of Mr Godfrey.

'His father, Sir John, my husband's stepfather, you know . . .'

'Yes, I remember.'

'. . . Soon after we arrived at the Cape, he died and Godfrey succeeded to the baronetcy. He's Sir Godfrey Thomas now. He's in very poor health and my husband is visiting him at Bodiam at present, but I have refused ever to meet him again.'

I said nothing.

'He's entirely base. When he succeeded to the title, he left his mistress, that dreadful servant girl, with their daughter in New Zealand, saying he would send for them. But, Fanny, within a year of his arrival here, he had married someone else. She's extremely respectable, from a good family, we're told. And rich . . . And now, he has four other children.'

I thought carefully of how to reply. Finally, I said, 'And what does Sir George think of all this?'

'I have no idea.'

'But surely he's discussed it with you?'

'Not once.'

'I daresay he's been much occupied with government business.'

Her eyes were closed now. She said sleepily, 'Do you remember the poisonous snakes in Albany? And how the Aboriginal children carried them about on sticks? In Cape Town there are venomous snakes, too. The puff adders hide themselves in logs and crevices in the rocks, but the Cape cobras come right inside the house to escape from the heat. And their poison is so deadly it's fatal almost at once.'

'Well, there are no snakes in this house,' I said, 'so we have nothing to be alarmed about.'

'I hope it doesn't sound vain,' Lucy said as we sat together in my garden in the sunshine, 'but I must tell you that I've had a South

African town named after me. Lady Grey it's called. It's just a small place in the north-east, in the Southern Drakensberg. Sir George and I made an expedition there and the townspeople asked if they might name their settlement after me.'

I thought that she seemed calmer, though I could not help noticing how she still plucked and picked at her skirts. 'What an honour,' I said. 'They must have liked you very much.'

'It's a strange thing but, somehow, when I returned to South Africa, even though I was often lonely, Sir George and I found ourselves extremely popular. When we left for England, we held a farewell levee at Government House and thousands of people came from all over the country, even from as far away as Durban. And when the carriage took us from Government House to the wharf, our route was lined with crowds of people, shouting and applauding, and suddenly, a group of men surged forward, unhitched the horses and pulled the carriage themselves all the way to the port captain's boat. Then, once we were aboard, all the ships and small boats in the harbour formed a sort of procession, and the crowd on shore cheered and cheered us, and when we finally appeared on the ship's deck, we were so overcome by emotion that even my husband wept. It seems so odd to think of it now. I felt exactly like a queen.'

And, for a chilling instant, I caught the echo of the words of the fortune-teller in Rio. *You will reign like a queen . . . and slink like a cur.*

'Fanny? Are you awake?'

'I am now,' I said, a little crossly.

'Can I climb in next to you? I've tried my best to sleep in my own bed, but whenever I close my eyes, my sins come crowding in on me and I'm afraid.'

Sighing, I sat up against the pillows. Lucy settled beside me.

'What is it that you're so afraid of?'

'I fear for my immortal soul.'

'Lucy, you surely know that's only because it's night. In the darkness, such terrors assume an importance beyond their daytime reality.'

'No, even in the daylight I'm obliged to stave them off by forcing my thoughts elsewhere. That's why I like to sketch. It takes my mind from my fears.'

'Then don't you think it may be time to confront these fears?'

'I can't. I daren't confide what I've done to a living soul, not even you, Fanny.'

'Whatever you've done, I'm your dearest sister. I will always love you.'

'Not if you know the terrible nature of my sin.'

'Lucy, I want you to tell me what it is you believe you've done.'

'It's not a belief, Fanny. It's a reality. *I have done those things I ought not to have done*. And now, as the Confessional Prayer says, *there is no health in me.*'

'And what does the Prayer go on to say?'

'I've forgotten,'

'Let me remind you. *But thou, Oh Lord, have mercy upon us, miserable offenders. Spare thou them, Oh God, who confess their faults. Restore thou those who are penitent*. Aren't those also the words of the Prayer?'

'Yes.'

'*That we may hereafter live a godly, righteous and sober life*?'

She burst into a storm of weeping and I forced myself not to lose patience with her. The time has come, I thought, when the only way I can help her is to make her confront those demons which appear to possess her.

'You must tell me now,' I said, and I heard the severity in my own voice, 'everything about this imagined evil you say you've committed. I tell you honestly that I don't believe in it.'

For a time, she was silent, but she ceased weeping and seemed to gain some control of her emotions. She pulled nervously at a strand of her hair. 'Do you remember when Sir George begged me to return to him, that you said Makareta might refuse to leave the Cape? Well, you were right, Fanny. She wouldn't be unseated from Government House. And then, one day, she came to me and said . . . said . . . she was carrying my husband's child.'

'*What*? Surely not? Did you confront Sir George?'

'How could I? Supposing he said it was true? What would I have done then?'

'Sir George is at Bodiam now. Is Makareta with him?'

Lucy turned to look directly at me. In a voice barely her own, she said, 'Makareta is dead.'

'*Dead*? Makareta? When?'

'A year ago.' She covered her face with her hands. 'And now, I am even more jealous of her than when she was living.'

'Then you're jealous of a ghost.'

'You don't know, you can have no idea . . . the effect her death has had on Sir George. Every day he was in Cape Town, he went to her grave and wept. I followed him secretly, Fanny. I saw it for myself.'

'Did she die in childbirth?'

'No.'

'Then, how? What happened to her?'

'She . . . met with an . . . accident. She died very suddenly.'

'Lucy,' I said, consumed with sudden alarm, 'what are you trying to tell me?'

'You asked me, Fanny.'

'I did. And now you must tell me. I swear I will never divulge a word of what you say to any other living being.'

Again she tugged urgently at her hair. 'I don't know what possessed me, but I suppose it now to have been the Devil.'

'What are you saying?'

'At Government House, we had a native houseboy. To the natives, snakes are sacred; they leave out food and drink for them. But they terrified Makareta. She said the Cape cobra was the Serpent which beguiled Eve in the Garden, that it was entirely evil. You know that in New Zealand there are no snakes of any kind, so before she arrived at the Cape she had never seen one.

'Shortly after she'd told me she was with child, when she was out somewhere with my husband, I called the houseboy. Since, at the Cape, cobras frequently enter houses to seek relief from the heat, every day it was his duty to rout them out and dispose of them. Such snakes are very dangerous but, like the Minang, he had no fear of them.

'I told him that I wished the holy presence of a cobra in my house. For his race, this is customary. "Yes, Lady," he said. "So," I said, "you will not expel them. You will leave them to seek comfort here." I indicated Makareta's bedroom. "Place a saucer of milk outside that room, on the veranda.' Cobras love to drink milk. They are almost blind, but I knew they would be lured by the smell.

'The boy said, "Very much luck to have snake in house, Lady." And with great reverence he laid out the saucer of milk.

'My husband and Makareta came home. Neither of them spoke to me, but they walked together to his study, and then she left him and went to her room. My heart was hammering as I sat pretending to read. At last, there came a scream and then a dreadful shriek. Sir George rushed from his study. Feigning alarm, I ran to join him. "What is it?" I cried. "What's happening?"

'He flung open Makareta's door. She lay on the floor, her eyes closed, her lips blue and her limbs jerking. "She's having some kind of fit," I said.

'Sir George raised her. "Makareta. Makareta, what is it?"

'"Look out!" I shouted. "Behind you. A cobra."

'The snake hissed, a sign it was about to strike. "Get out!" he ordered me, and I ran. But as he dragged Makareta from that room, I saw the cobra spread its evil hood, lash itself forward and strike her again on the leg.

'"Send for the physician," he cried. "At once."

'I did, but it was too late, as I knew it would be.

'As soon as Makareta had been pronounced dead, my husband entered that room with his service pistol and shot the cobra. Not once, but four times. It was dead with the first bullet. The others were simply a punishment, a statement of his hatred for the creature that had robbed him of what he loved most in this world.

'I have killed her, I thought. And, Fanny, that is why I will be denied eternal life . . . Because I am not repentant. My heart rejoiced — and is still rejoicing — because, at last, she has gone.' She looked at me and I could not decipher her expression. 'I willed it,' she said. 'I met witchcraft with witchcraft. *That* is why I am condemned.'

Lucy did not speak again of what she had told me about Makareta and, in truth, I did not know what I could say to her. Then, a week later, she came to me.

'I have a letter from Sir George,' she said. 'He writes from Bodiam to say that, as we returned Home, we passed the *Phoebe* bringing word, too late, of his reinstatement as Governor of the Cape. He must sail for the Cape within the fortnight . . . and he has begged me to accompany him.'

'I see.'

'And with his letter he enclosed something very precious for me from Aunt Julia Martin. Look.'

She unfolded a piece of watered red silk, revealing a small square envelope. 'She says I'm to have this as a memento of her.'

'What is it?'

'Aunt Julia is a great friend of Mrs Browning — they've corresponded for many years. This is one of Mrs Browning letters . . . in her own handwriting. You may read it in a moment, but first, lift up the flap on the envelope and see what's written there.'

I peered at the minute scrawl. '*Pen has just come in . . .*' I stopped. 'Pen?'

'Her son. She dotes on him.'

'What a very strange name. *Pen has just come in with his little friend,*' I continued, '*who asked him, "Why do they call your mama Ba?" And Pen said, "I am not sure but I believe my mama is called Ba because she is as good as a lamb." No compliment I ever received touched me so much. You see I am conceited and tell it! Now write, to prove you forgive me — and tell me of your dear husband, of both of you — how you are, what you do. Robert's love—*'

'That's Mr Browning,' put in Lucy.

'*And I am ever, my dear friend, your affectionate Ba.*'

'It's hard to believe I've been given something so precious. I shall cherish it forever.'

'How very kind of Mrs Martin. It's a mark of how fond she is of you.'

'I believe she thinks it will help sustain me if I return with my husband to the Cape.'

I could not help but think Sir George required Lucy to accompany him merely for the sake of propriety, but I said only, 'And will you go?'

'I don't want to. I feel it's my duty, but . . . I'm terribly afraid. I . . . Fanny, *please*, dearest, dearest, Fanny, I implore you, come to Cape Town with me.'

VII

JOURNAL OF MISS FRANCES THOMPSON

30th April 1860

Today, we set sail from Plymouth for the Cape of Good Hope. Sir George's recall to the Cape was at such short notice that hasty arrangements have had to be made to accommodate us on the *Forte*, the flagship of Admiral Sir Henry Keppel, who is going out to take command of the Cape Station. He has relinquished one of his pair of connecting cabins to Lucy and his stateroom to Sir George, while an ante-chamber from Captain Turnour's rooms serves as my cabin. We are not the only passengers; with us are the explorers, Mr Speke and Mr Grant, on the first leg of their expedition to discover the source of the Nile.

Lucy thinks Mr Grant most unprepossessing but considers Mr Speke quite dashing. She intends to quiz him about his expeditions.

I warned her to be careful that Sir George does not become jealous, but she merely shrugged and said that perhaps it is only justice that he, too, should be made to suffer the pangs of pique.

Though I rejoice to see Lucy in higher spirits, such talk makes me uneasy.

5th May 1860

The sea is calm — not even Lucy is troubled by the motion of the vessel — and my initial annoyance with myself for allowing her to persuade me to undertake this voyage has lifted. Each evening, Mr Speke and Mr Grant play at whist with Sir George, who reminisces with them about his (greatly embellished) early exploits in Western Australia, while Lucy and I promenade about the decks, taking advantage of the clement weather. Tonight, after supper, we were joined in our stroll by the Admiral, who pointed out various features of the *Forte*. We parted from him at about nine o'clock.

6th May 1860

The Admiral again joined us on our evening promenade. He is very small — at least a head shorter than Lucy — and has bright orange-red hair, but he makes up for these deficiencies by being most entertaining and agreeable. He has travelled all over the world in his naval career, including to New Zealand, and he knows Cape Town very well.

'Now, as you ladies have spent time in New Zealand,' he said, 'I must tell you of an incident that occurred when I was posted aboard the *Rainbow*. The master, Captain Haus, was a great collector of curios: there were game-cocks secured by the leg to alternate gun-carriages on the main-deck, two Bengal tiger whelps, a ferocious-looking bull-dog as gentle as a lamb, and a monkey free to go where he chose. She was quite the oddest vessel on which I ever served. She'd been on the Australian and New Zealand stations and, on my first night aboard, when I dined with my new Captain, on the removal of the dish-cover I was confronted with the tattooed head of a Maori chief.'

I know that the Admiral meant this only for our amusement but, while Lucy laughed greatly, I was forced to turn away and make an excuse to go below.

12th May 1860

To a thirteen-gun salute, *Forte* put in at Funchal Bay in Madeira.

'You're looking at the top of a huge volcano,' said the Admiral as we stood at the rail, marvelling at the steep green mountains before us. 'We'll be here for three days, so you'll have time to explore a little. It has unique plant life which may interest you, Lady Grey.'

20th May 1860

We met up on deck with Admiral Keppel, who tells us we are about two weeks out from Rio. I am hoping that the leg of our voyage from there to Cape Town will be as calm and mild as this, but he says it is unlikely.

As we promenaded, the midshipmen gave us their customary salutes and waves. 'I see,' said the Admiral, 'that the picnic hamper you ordered for the middies in Madeira has entirely won their hearts,

Lady Grey. Your enthusiastic admirer over there is my young nephew, my namesake, Harry Stephenson.'

'They remind me of my brothers,' said Lucy. 'Always hungry.'

'That's boys for you,' he said, laughing.

'Do you have brothers and sisters, Sir Harry?'

'My poor mama died in childbirth delivering her sixteenth infant, Miss Thompson; only eleven of us survived to adulthood and now we number a mere eight. But young Harry's mother, Polly, has always been her brothers' pet. My oldest brother, Albemarle, still seeks her counsel in all things.'

'Is His Lordship also a naval officer?' I asked.

'No, he oversees the estates. He's as unlike me as it's possible to imagine. First, he's tall and lean where I'm short and round. Then, I'm a keen hunter—' He broke off. 'Do you ladies hunt?'

'I love to ride,' I said, 'but I don't care for hunting.'

'I enjoy it greatly,' said Lucy, 'but it was impossible to engage in it in New Zealand. There wasn't a pack of hounds in the entire country. And, when we were last in Cape Town, my health wouldn't permit it.'

'Well, there's ample horse racing in South Africa,' said the Admiral, 'so, sooner or later, it should be possible to organise a hunt. I love the chase but Albemarle is of exactly the same mind as you, Miss Thompson. Hunting, he says, is merely "a fool in a red coat chasing after a rogue in a yellow one".'

We laughed.

'How does it come about that you and your brother are so very different?' asked Lucy.

'Now, as to temperament, I couldn't say, but I believe the difference in our size is due entirely to the circumstances of my own birth. I was such a sickling, I was given up for dead. I was born unexpectedly, a six-month infant, and as it was high summer and no coffin was ready, my father ordered some receptacle provided in which they might bury me speedily. I was brought, washed and shrouded, to the library where my father and his clergyman cousin were waiting. My father said he folded back the cloth and observed that I was so tiny I resembled a manikin, the smallest of templates for a nine-month child, my head the size of an apple, my tiny buttocks no bigger than damsons. And the only coffin that could be found, late at night and at such short notice, was an old handleless warming-pan . . .'

'A *warming-pan*?'

'Yes, indeed, Lady Grey. It was polished and brought to my father by two of the household servants. He rested it on the library table, lifted the lid and placed me inside.

'But the maid noticed my little chest moving. She screamed, crossed herself and cried out to the steward that I was still alive. My father snatched me from my brass coffin and instructed his cousin to baptise me at once. I have other, more illustrious, godparents, but my original sponsors were Cooper, the household steward, and Sanders, the second under-nursery maid.'

24th May 1860

The further south we sail, the more I feel the pull of the other side of the world and the harder I find it to turn my thoughts from Te Toa. At night, the stars hang low and dazzling in the canopy of the inky sky; the Southern Cross has replaced the North Star now, and I feel it drawing me back to the Antipodes . . .

To escape from such idle fancies, I left the deck and returned to my cabin where I was roused from a light slumber by Lucy's tapping at my door. It was just after ten-thirty but she seemed in unusually high spirits. She said she had had one of her headaches and had been unable to sleep so she had taken a turn about the deck for some fresh air. And, as she stood at the rail, the Admiral had passed by. 'I've been talking most delightfully with him, Fanny,' she told me. 'He's fifty-one years old and his situation is so similar to my own. He's childless, too. He lost his only little boy seventeen years ago but he says he feels the loss as keenly today.'

'Your situations are not at all similar,' I said very firmly. 'You're only thirty-seven years old and you have a husband.'

'I have a husband in name only. You know yourself he has no love whatsoever for me. It was all lavished on Makareta.'

'Makareta is dead,' I told her. 'You must put her from your mind.'

'I cannot because *he* has not. That's why he's so gloomy, so withdrawn . . .'

'He's always retreated into black moods from time to time. He'll recover.'

'How can he recover? We're going back to Cape Town where she's buried. He will mourn at her graveside.'

'You're being dramatic, Lucy. He can't possibly be seen to make such a pilgrimage. Think of how people would gossip. He would be ruined.'

'I promise you, Fanny, I long to forget but I can't. Such humiliation. To be put aside for a native mistress . . .'

Briefly, I saw Te Toa before me. 'I don't see why the fact she was a native should influence your feelings.'

'But she wasn't even beautiful or accomplished. What did he see in her?'

'I can't say, but you must lay aside these thoughts. You're pitting yourself against a ghost.'

'A ghost who has devoured Sir George.'

25th May 1860

I have just bid Lucy goodnight for the second time today. I am not at all easy in my mind. After dinner, when I was almost composed for sleep, she rapped on my door and came in flushed, her manner over-bright.

'You'll never guess, Fanny. I went out to the deck for a little air. It's close in my cabin, you know — and there was the Admiral. He detests card games and prefers to be outdoors, he says. He asked to accompany me and we talked most agreeably. I told him Papa was one of Nelson's captains and he said his greatest pride is that his first commission was signed by Admiral Hardy. Only think of it, Fanny! And your papa, too, knew Admiral Hardy, did he not?' She sat down on my bunk. '*Now* say that the Admiral and I are not alike, if you will?'

'You may be alike in some respects but not as much as you believe.'

She stood up and moved about restlessly. 'It's such a beautiful evening — the moon is throwing a path right across the sea. I told Sir Harry of the Maori belief that the souls of the dead walk along it to their final resting place.'

I remained silent.

'He said it comforted him to think of his little boy on such a path to Heaven. And then, he recounted to me a most wonderful legend of the South Seas. He said the natives say that in the Pacific Ocean, far below the reach of the sun-shafts, lurks the giant octopus, a hideous thing with a beak of iron and tentacles half as long as the top-mast. It's sightless and tracks its prey by scent alone, releasing a spray of blinding ink through which it seizes its unwitting victim.'

'Has he seen one?'

'No, but he's often heard tell of it. The natives say that in springtime, on just such a soft night as this with scents drifting over the sea, the octopus rises from its dark lair, up through the moonlit water. It glides towards the seashore where the sweet-smelling breadfruit tree, the pandanus — you remember, Fanny — bends its blossoms to touch the ocean's surface, and there . . . the horrid thing is lured, crazed, by the fragrance of the flowers. It hauls itself from the water, lumbers to the trunk of the pandanus, entwines itself around her and . . . makes . . . love to her.'

I sat speechless.

'And after it is . . . spent, it falls exhausted back into the sea and doesn't rise again for a full twelve-month. Isn't that a remarkable story?'

'Lucy, you're speaking to the Admiral much too intimately for such a short acquaintance.'

'You're quite wrong. He was entirely respectful and polite. I can see you disapprove but, after all, my husband himself collects such legends.'

'So you'll recount this story to Sir George?'

'Of course not.'

'And why not? Because you know very well his jealousy and fury would be roused. Listen to me, Lucy, I *implore* you. You're in grave danger if you continue to allow even such a harmless light-hearted dalliance with the Admiral to continue.'

'My husband has no idea of where I am.'

'The *Forte* is a very small community. People will gossip.'

'They have no reason to. And why should my husband deny me the simple pleasure of congenial company? *You* know how cold and uncharitable he is to me, Fanny, and I promise you he has no cause whatsoever to reproach me. All I am guilty of is conversation.'

'Sir George may consider it criminal conversation. I think you should meet Admiral Keppel again only if you're accompanied.'

'Then I must ask you to accompany me tomorrow evening. I've promised to join him on a perambulation about the deck. He will leave a note at my door as to the time and place. His cabin abuts mine, you know.'

'I'm pleading with you, Lucy. Be sensible. Don't antagonise Sir George.'

'Well, since it pains you so, I'll be prudent.'

At the cabin door, she paused and turned to me, her eyes still bright. 'Have you noticed, Fanny, the daintiness and delicacy of the Admiral's hands?'

1st June 1860

As we approach Rio, my old feelings of apprehension are mounting. This is ridiculous. I am being fanciful. Have I not travelled a large part of the globe and come safe home? What are the silly fancies of an old blind gypsy woman?

3rd June 1860

This morning, under steam, we put in to Rio. The salutes from the other vessels in the harbour seemed endless and continued to echo about us as we disembarked for Petropolis.

7th June 1860

I was foolish to be so worried about returning here. We passed a most agreeable time ashore, the Admiral having persuaded Sir George, Mr Grant and Mr Speke to join him in hiring two open carriages in which we made several excursions. I saw no grotesques, was accosted by no one, and even the flamboyant colours of the plants no longer seemed menacing. I understand now that my fantasies were, indeed, merely the imaginings of a distressed child.

Earlier tonight, we all crowded on deck for a last sight of Rio.

'They say the *Flying Dutchman* haunts the South Atlantic,' said Lucy, 'trying still to round the Cape.'

'Merely a sailor's tale,' said Admiral Keppel, joining us, 'isn't it, Sir

George? We seamen are known for our superstitions.'

'That's true,' said Lucy mischievously. 'Papa always said it was considered bad luck to carry a woman aboard ship.'

'Hush, Eliza.'

'Nonsense, Ma'am. Many captains' wives accompany them on voyages. And how would you ladies traverse the world if no ship would give you passage?'

9th June 1860

The weather remains fair and the ship steady. Lucy and I are engaged to play together at cards.

10th June 1860

I now set down a most frightful turn of events which must be revealed to no other living soul.

Yesterday evening, after our card game, I bade Lucy goodnight and retired to my cabin. As usual, Sir George, Mr Speke and Mr Grant were engaged at whist in the saloon. I was woken by a tremendous commotion, a woman screaming and the thunder of what I recognised as Sir George in one of his rages. Another male voice appeared to be remonstrating. I rose and hastened towards the hubbub.

As I approached Lucy's cabin, the clamour increased, Sir George's voice dominating the din, 'I tell you, I *will* have satisfaction, sir!' He was standing outside the Admiral's door, his face puce, saliva frothing at his mouth. With a shock, I saw that his arms were pinioned on either side by Captain Turnour and the ship's surgeon. In his left hand he clutched a scrap of paper and, in his right, his army pistol. His struggles to free himself were so intense that, as I watched, the Captain and the surgeon were forced to grapple him to the floor.

Lucy stood pressed against the door of her cabin, staring in horror at her husband as Admiral Keppel attempted to remonstrate with him. 'I assure you, Sir George, you're entirely mistaken in what you surmise. There has been no hint of impropriety in your wife's conduct. She has borne herself at all times as a lady should. I swear it on my honour.'

Sir George strained against his captors. 'Release me at once or I'll have you court-martialled!' He turned his head to Keppel. 'And you, you vile seducer — I'll shoot you like the dog you are.'

Lucy moved a little towards him. 'George, please. I beg you, listen. Things are not as you think.'

'Get away from me, you Serpent, you . . . you *Part Sinister*.'

'But George—'

'Lady Grey,' said the Captain, panting from his attempts to contain Sir George, 'it would be better — and safer — for you to retire at once to your cabin.'

Lucy began to weep and I saw the Admiral make a slight movement towards her before he checked himself.

Drawn by the uproar, others were now congregating. Sir George commenced again to roar and rave. 'Let me *go*! I *command* you to release me. I am Her Majesty's representative. In laying hands on me, you desecrate the person of Her Royal Highness Herself. You are committing an act of high treason.'

'If I were to release you, Sir George,' puffed Captain Turnour, 'I should be court-martialled for being even guiltier of an act of gross folly. I cannot condone murder aboard my ship.'

The surgeon looked about him and spied Mr Speke. 'Mr Speke, I must ask for your assistance.'

Sir George gave a bellow of fury. 'Don't dare lay a hand on me, Speke.'

'You know my cabin?' said the surgeon to Mr Speke. 'Go there at once. Open the sea-chest you will see in there and bring me the . . . the garment you'll find within. But *hurry*, man.'

Sir George, writhing, began to drum his heels against the floor.

'I need a chair from your suite, Sir Harry,' said the surgeon. 'A plain upright one, and make sure it's stout.'

As the Admiral returned with a chair, Mr Speke ran back flourishing a white garment. Never for a moment releasing his grip on Sir George, Captain Turnour looked up at the small assembled crowd. 'What the *devil* are you ratings doing here? Who ordered your presence? Get below to your quarters, at once, the lot of you, or I'll have you all whipped. And you, sir' — he inclined his head towards Mr Grant — 'be good enough to assist us.'

'I must ask you again, Sir George,' said the surgeon, 'to drop your pistol if you wish us to allow you your freedom.'

'I shall *never* relinquish my weapon.'

'It would be better for us all if you were to comply,' said Captain Turnour.

'Never!'

The surgeon looked towards the Captain, who gave a complicit nod.

'Mr Speke, Mr Grant,' said Captain Turnour, 'as commander of this vessel, I order you, whether you wish or no, to assist the surgeon and me with the restraint of the Governor. Lives are at stake here and I must do my duty.'

The two men edged towards the prone figure of Sir George.

'Give me that garment, Mr Speke, and hold his arm here, so.'

The four of them hauled Sir George to his feet, his arms still immobilised.

'How *dare* you . . . what the devil . . .? Turnour, I order you again to release me!'

'And now, onto the chair,' directed the Captain. 'Keep hold there, Mr Speke. He has the strength of ten men.'

As the surgeon and the Captain forced first one of Sir George's arms, then the other, into the strange white garment, the pistol tumbled from his right hand, the paper from his left. With great speed, Mr Speke crossed one arm across Sir George's body, while Mr Grant bent the other above it in the opposite direction. Then, Captain Turnour deftly wound the strings at the front of the garment around and across Sir George's body, passing them to the surgeon to secure at his back.

Half-inside her cabin, Lucy passed a hand across her eyes.

Rocking on the chair which now held him secure, Sir George attempted vainly to free himself. His complexion was so apoplectic I feared he might have a fit and so, I suspect, did the surgeon, for he spoke to him soothingly.

'I've brought brandy and laudanum for you, Sir George, and you'll be kept in this condition only for as long as is necessary for your safety. When you've recovered your senses, you'll see the wisdom of our actions. We wouldn't wish you hanged for a precipitate murder.'

'I am quite within my senses and I order this ship be turned about for Rio.'

'I don't understand what's happening here,' said Mr Speke. 'Has Sir George suffered a brain fever?'

'Thank you for your assistance, gentlemen,' said the Captain. 'I'd be grateful if you were now to return to your cabins.'

'But you surely can't be intending that Sir George should remain in this corridor, restrained in a *strait-jacket*?'

'By no means. I shall order the mate to provide assistance to carry Sir George from this corridor to the surgeon's rooms, where the surgeon and I will remain on watch until he's convinced Sir George no longer poses a danger to himself or any other. Goodnight, gentlemen.' His eye fell on me. 'Miss Thompson, I'm so very sorry you've witnessed this. Would you attempt to provide some comfort to Lady Grey?'

'Willingly.'

Sir George let out a roar. 'I forbid you to enter Eliza's room. You are as guilty as she. You've encouraged her in this folly.'

'Come, Sir George,' said the surgeon quietly, 'you are not yourself. Go in to the lady, Miss Thompson. She'll be in need of her friends. I'm sure the Governor doesn't mean these harsh words against you.'

'I mean every word I say. They are *Jezebels*, both!'

'But what has happened?' I cried, as soon as we were both safely in Lucy's cabin. 'What have you done?'

'I've done nothing.'

'It can't be *nothing* to bring Sir George to this.'

'I give you my solemn word that I'm innocent of any wrong-doing. You saw the paper my husband was grasping? It was the note . . . He came back from his game of whist . . . I didn't expect him. You know it's always far into the night before they finish their evenings together. And he's never before come to my cabin at such an early hour.'

'Lucy, you *must* tell me. What was in the note? Who wrote it?'

'I did . . . *We* did. It's been my habit to talk — that's all we do, Fanny, I promise you upon my honour — to talk with the Admiral in the evenings. You know how I can't sleep . . .'

I sank my head into my hands. 'Have you been meeting in secret with Sir Harry?' Even as I said it, I had a vision of myself urging Tsarina on towards the Domain, to my own clandestine meetings with Te Toa. I felt again the surge of excitement, the reckless desperation of love, the heedless courting of danger . . .

'Not in secret. In his stateroom.'

'Lucy, are you mad? Are you telling me you've gone alone to a gentleman's room, and in the evenings?'

'We've done no wrong. Harry would never do anything to cause me harm.'

'It's entirely wrong for you to have been alone with him. If he cared for you, he would know that, and seek to protect your reputation.'

'It wasn't he who wanted our conversations. It was I, *I* who begged him to see me. Don't look at me so, Fanny. Why shouldn't I speak alone to a gentleman of things which interest me?'

'But what did the note say? And where did Sir George find it?'

'He must have been watching me for some time.'

'I've warned you often that he's a jealous man. But tell me the contents of the note and where he discovered it.'

She pointed towards the door which linked her cabin to the Admiral's stateroom. 'You see that little aperture there, in the middle of the door? On Harry's side is a small box. If you insert your fingers, it's just possible to pick up a paper deposited there.'

'And you were in the habit of leaving notes in there for each other?'

'Sometimes.'

'And tonight?'

'It was the greatest ill luck. As I was slipping in the note, my husband entered, gave a great bellow of rage, and seized the paper from my hand. I tried to snatch it back but he was too quick for me.'

'And the note said?'

She did not look at me. 'It was a reply to Harry. There were two messages on the one paper. He wrote . . . he wrote . . .'

'Go on.'

'*I . . . I hope and expect to see my own darling. I am too deaf to hear.*'

'And you replied?'

She hung her head. '*You must clear the door, dearest, and leave me to come when I think it safe. Lucy.*'

My darling. My dearest. And she had signed it *Lucy*, not Eliza. What utter foolishness. 'Have you been to Sir Harry's room before?'

'Twice . . . three times only. He has boxes stacked against his door but he puts them to one side to allow me freedom of entry.'

I could think of nothing to say, nothing to do, that might in the smallest degree alleviate the situation. 'There is one piece of advice you must heed absolutely,' I said. 'After what has happened tonight, if you wish to protect yourself, and the Admiral, you must never again in any company but mine refer to him as Harry.'

'I *must* see him, Fanny. I *have* to speak to him, whatever the cost. Since he's going to command the Cape Station, he'll be from time to time in Cape Town, and we've agreed we'll ride together. He's a keen horseman, you know.'

Great weariness engulfed me; I felt anger welling. 'Don't you *understand* what forces you've unleashed against yourself?' I cried. 'And the Admiral? And me?'

She stared at me. 'Against *you*? How so?'

'Sir George has just been confined against his will in a strait-jacket such as is generally employed for lunatics. In this mortifying condition he has been seen by the surgeon and the Captain, by his friends Mr Speke and Mr Grant, some of the ship's crew, and by the man he now hates more than any other in the world — Sir Harry Keppel. And by me. As they carried him to the doctor's cabin, he accused me of being complicit in your deception. He said I encouraged you and was the instrument of your downfall.'

'But that's wholly untrue. You knew nothing of it and I'll tell him so.'

'Do you think he will listen to you? I'm a witness to his utter humiliation. Don't you see that he'll detest me forever?'

Lucy began to move agitatedly about the stateroom. Though I wished more than anything to escape to my own cabin and sleep, I dared not leave her alone.

'Why doesn't Harry come?'

'He can't, you stupid goose.'

'Then I'll pass quietly into his room by this door. I *must* speak with him.'

As she placed her hand on the knob, I caught her arm and pulled her away roughly, forcing her to sink onto her bunk.

'No,' I said. 'You can't. You mustn't.'

She rolled onto her front and, sinking her face in the bedcovers, began to weep loudly. 'You don't understand, Fanny,' she choked through her sobs. 'I have no wish to be selfish. It's Harry . . . the Admiral . . . he's kind, you know. He speaks to me so gently. He tells me I have a fine intelligence . . .'

'Which you are in no way employing at this moment.'

'He saw . . . he couldn't help but notice the manner in which my husband addresses me, his coldness to me . . . the . . . Ah, Fanny, just the smallest modicum of tenderness from Sir George would have sufficed, but it has never been forthcoming. I don't know how it happened.'

'*What* happened?'

'No, no, not that. You're mistaken. I found myself . . . Harry's so sympathetic, you see. I told him of what had transpired in Cape Town between my husband and Makareta. Fanny, since I've been in the company of the Admiral, I haven't once suffered one of my nervous attacks.'

There was a tapping at the door.

Lucy started up. 'He's come. I knew he would.'

But it was the surgeon who entered. 'I've come to enquire after your state of health, Ma'am, and yours, Miss Thompson. I've brought something to help you both to sleep.'

I did not return to my cabin but lay down beside Lucy and endeavoured to rest. Some time later, I heard a scrabbling, and a man appeared in the connecting doorway. I was awake in an instant and, having ascertained it was not Sir George bent on vengeance but the Admiral, I made to arouse Lucy who had fallen into an exhausted sleep.

'Leave her to rest, I beg you,' said Sir Harry. 'I was apprised of your being with her, Miss Thompson, and I ask to speak briefly with you about the events of tonight. First, I give you my word as a gentleman that nothing criminal has occurred between us.'

'I understand how the situation between you came about but—'

'The fault is entirely mine. You know of her sad situation so you'll understand that I felt — I feel — the greatest pity for her. She's treated by her husband as less than his horse. I don't consider Sir George a gentleman. My greatest error has been that, in sympathising with the misery of a wronged wife, I've allowed myself to expose her to harm.'

'Sir George is not in his right mind.'

'On the contrary, I believe him to be entirely in his right mind. For his own ends, he's playing very cleverly the part of the wronged husband. I greatly fear he's seen his chance to cast off his lady while appearing in the eyes of the world to be the injured party. No madman is capable of the arguments he's advanced to us tonight. He claims that if he is forced to carry on to Cape Town on the *Forte*, he will murder Lu— Lady Grey or shoot himself. I don't believe for an instant that he'll do either, but Captain Turnour and the surgeon certainly take him at his word, so, under the most extreme pressure from them both, I've instructed the Captain to return the ship to Rio.'

'And Sir George remains confined?'

'Yes, and must be so for the two or three days it will take us to get there. What will happen then, I simply don't know. The Governor will speak to me now only through the agency of a third party.'

'But he may murder Lucy in Rio . . .'

'He's a wily fox. He won't place himself in jeopardy by murder. I assure you that if I believed for one second he would harm a hair of her head, I'd shoot him myself.'

13th June 1860

In a dark silence, accompanied only by young Harry Stephenson, Sir George, Lucy and I were disembarked from the *Forte* in Rio. A trap deposited us at the Rio Hotel.

'Midshipman Stephenson,' said Sir George, 'you are to tell Lady Grey I shall organise new passages for her and Miss Thompson. She will be informed of the arrangements in due course. Meanwhile, they are to remain in the hotel unless told otherwise.'

'Aye, aye, Sir. M'Lady, His Excellency requires you to remain here until such time as he has procured new passages.'

Lucy merely looked at the midshipman, expressionless.

'Thank you, Harry,' I said.

'Since this message was not intended for you, Miss Thompson,' said Sir George, 'there is no cause for you to respond.'

I felt a hand press into mine, and the cut of a scrap of paper. With the most imperceptible of movements, Harry Stephenson nodded towards Lucy. I slid my hand into my reticule, lodging the note safely out of sight.

15th June 1860

No amount of effort will rouse Lucy from her listlessness and I have begun to fear for her health. She spent most of today and yesterday occupied at her writing case.

Young Harry Stephenson has just appeared, begging leave to send his uncle's kindest regards to the ladies and to bid them be strong. I have not yet dared to pass the note he gave me to Lucy for fear of some unquenchable outburst, but for the first time in many hours, she spoke. 'Please to tell your kind uncle I will never forget him.'

'I shall, Ma'am.' He hesitated. 'Ma'am, I've been instructed to inform you that the Governor is re-embarking on the *Forte*. She sails again for the Cape tonight.'

'Rejoining the ship! But it was *he* who ordered her turned back, who swore he would kill the Admiral if he was obliged to—'

'My uncle says they've come to an arrangement in which each will entirely avoid the company of the other. Any essential orders will be conveyed through Captain Turnour.'

'But I don't understand why Sir George leaves us here . . .'

'Lady Grey, you've been so kind. All the middies are most warmly disposed towards your ladyship, and I would that some other, not I, had been sent with this intelligence. Ma'am, it is my . . . painful duty to . . . Ma'am, you and Miss Thompson will not be embarking on another ship for Cape Town. You are going Home.'

LONDON, 1860

Upon our arrival, I took lodgings for us in London. 'And, next month, when my tenants have vacated,' I said, 'we will go to Lyme.'

'It's very dear of you, Fanny, but I can't possibly retire to Lyme. If I do, all the world will believe me guilty of what Sir George claims. No, I must go directly to Oxford and lay my case before Bishop Wilberforce. He's Papa's cousin; he's certain to exonerate me from my husband's charges.'

'But if you see the Bishop and become . . . upset or . . . emotional, you might very well undermine your own position. Wouldn't it be better to write to him?'

She brightened a little. 'Yes, you're right. Will you help me with the letter?'

'We'll compose it together tonight.' I hesitated. 'Have you heard anything yet from Sir George?'

'Not a word. It seems he feels no duty to maintain his wife. Without your charity, I'd be entirely destitute.' She clung to me. 'Oh, Fanny, I'm so afraid he may be intending to divorce me.'

'He has no grounds for a divorce.'

'He has the note.'

'But even if he tries to use the note to show you intended . . . criminal conversation . . . that's not the same as proof of such an act. He cannot divorce you.'

'I most sincerely pray that's so.'

Lucy ran into my room, waving a letter. 'A reply from Bishop Wilberforce. And so quickly. I'm *vindicated*! With him as my supporter, my honour is safe.'

'This is excellent news.' I looked at the letter. 'But, Lucy, the seal hasn't yet been broken. How can you know what he's written?'

'A bishop is God's minister on earth, and, as God Himself knows I've done no wrong, how can Bishop Wilberforce fail me?'

'Open it,' I said. 'At once. Let's set our minds at rest.'

She left it to me to break the large red seal, revealing the letter and two others enclosed within it. I passed them to her, but she handed the Bishop's letter back to me, indicating I should read it aloud to her.

'*Cuddesdon Palace*,' I began.

'But what does he *say*?'

'Patience, I'm coming to that. '*My dear Lady Grey, it is not without great hesitation that I write to you. It is so painful to write what must give you pain*' —I paused — '*especially to one in many ways so crushed already. Yet if I am to do you any good I must speak to you with entire openness. I have received two letters from Sir George — one sent to me by the Bishop of Cape Town*—'

'That odious man.'

'*—the other an answer to the Bishop of Cape Town on his repeating to Sir George some remarks of mine as to his present duty towards you.*'

Lucy clapped her hands. 'He means to have my husband take me back.'

'*You have wished me to advise you . . . but before doing it I ought to say One; that whilst I do not admit for an instant that the Sin of infidelity in the wife is altered by the want of chastity in the husband, I do not believe the charges you have brought against Sir George.*'

She stared at me. '*What*? The Bishop doesn't believe me?'

'Lucy, I'm truly sorry. He says, *That you were second in Sir George's house, that he with cruel neglect of you maintained a mistress in the house etc. I am bound to say I do* **not** *believe.*'

'But, Fanny, I swear it's the truth.'

'Hush,' I said. 'There's more, much more. He writes, *You named Dr Bickersteth as one who knew the evil rumour*—'

'He did! Indeed, he did.'

'*I sought out the Doctor . . . and so far from confirming your statement he distinctly affirmed that had such a state of things existed he must have known it and that he never, amongst the scandals of the small Cape community which made free with Sir George riding with young ladies and so on, he*

***never** heard a whisper imputing to him infidelity to you.'*

At this, Lucy broke into loud sobs. 'He lies,' she cried.

I placed an arm about her shoulders. 'He's protecting Sir George. And himself. How could he say now to the Bishop what he knows in his heart he should have said months before? He'd be accountable for the sin of complicity.'

'And, as a result, *I* am to play the guilty part.'

'Tear up this letter,' I said. 'It's clear the Bishop won't plead your cause.'

'No, I must hear in full what he has to say.'

'If you insist. He goes on, *I believe you then . . .*' I stopped. 'Lucy, I beg you, let's not continue. Its contents will only distress you further.'

She shook her head. 'No, read it all. I must know how the world intends to view me now.'

'*I believe you then, under the influence of jealousy first and recrimination since, to have allowed yourself to exaggerate (to say the least) so as to really state untruths in this matter.*'

'He says I'm bearing false witness.'

'I fear so.'

She clutched my arm. 'Tell me, Fanny, please. Do *you* believe I am lying?'

'No.'

'Then I am satisfied. Please to read on.'

'*Now the light that this throws on the reality of your penitence before God is very fearful and if there be not penitence what security is there for the future if guilty sympathy is offered to you? I do beseech you for your Soul's sake to think and pray this deeply over. And now for the rest. The letters I enclose show, first, the depth of Sir G's affection for you . . .*'

Lucy spread her hands in a gesture of despair and resignation.

'*The Bishop of Cape Town says, "He will talk to me for hours of Lady G, weeping as an heartbroken man."*'

'I told you he was a hypocrite.'

'And you were right.' I resumed reading. '*They show secondly that*' — I paused — '*his mind is made up as to a permanent separation.*'

'No!'

'*You should write to him — fully — freely — affectionately — penitently. The Bishop of Cape Town says in his letter, "Sir G. would be glad if she went to live near his Aunt and Uncle; they are very fond of her." This should be your first course. But the root of your peace must be in deep real true penitence — and oh, my dear Lady Grey, does God see in you a penitent? Or an angry self-justifying, self-deceiving Spirit? What more can I add? Do not let this post go without its bearing to Sir George the wail of a penitent heart and self-reproaching wife. I am ever most sincerely yours. S. Oxon.'*

I laid down the letter. Lucy, her face blotched with weeping, crossed silently to the shelf, took up the blue vase which had been given to her by Sir George's mother, and smashed it to the floor. Then she took down her bound volume of Sir George's handwritten Australian journal, tore it into pieces and threw them onto the fire. A stray sheet fell next to me. Picking it up, I flung it into the flames after its fellows.

'There is only one good aspect to this whole dreadful affair.'

I frowned. 'Which is . . . ?'

'I always believed that some day I should see poor Mama again, and it has been the greatest source of sorrow to me that I was never able to do so. But now I feel it's a mercy she has not lived to have to endure my public shame.'

'Aunt would never have believed ill of you.'

'No, but she would have had to suffer knowing I shall be ostracised by everyone in England and be the butt of gossip everywhere. And so will you, Fanny, if you associate with me.'

'What nonsense.'

'And unless Sir George agrees a settlement on me, I'm utterly destitute.'

'Come back with me to Lyme. I have more than enough for us both.'

'I can't run away to hide in Lyme. Everyone would believe it was a sign of my guilt.'

'We can face that together. After a time, people will lose interest.'

She shook her head.

'Well, you could certainly go to Aunt Julia Martin. It would be impossible for Sir George to refuse you an allowance if you were under her protection.'

'That's true.' She sighed.

'Is something else troubling you?'

'No — well, perhaps . . .'

'Yes?'

'I thought that possibly, by now, I—'

'—would have had some communication from Sir Harry?'

She nodded.

'But, Lucy, how can he write to you? He can't afford to arouse Sir George's venom and spite.'

'Do you believe he ever thinks of me?'

'I'm sure of it. He's a good, just man, and it's clear from the note he asked young Harry to pass to you in Rio that he's very troubled by your situation.'

'Ah, his dear note. It's my only keepsake of him. I have it by heart.'

'Then tell it to me again,' I said, in hopes of deflecting her a little from her low state.

'He wrote, *Would that I might have spared you the agony of what has transpired and that I could rescue you from the wretched state into which I have unwittingly plunged you. I believe you know the true nature of my feelings towards you; it would be folly to state them here, but be assured that I pray for you and that you are ever in my thoughts. Until we meet again, may the Lord keep you. H.K.*'

'There. It's scarcely likely that he's forgotten you.'

A few days after this conversation, out alone on an errand, I was accosted by a well-dressed stranger. 'Excuse me, Ma'am, I believe you are Miss Frances Thompson.'

Taken aback, I did not immediately answer.

'I beg you to excuse my forwardness in speaking to you, but please be assured I mean you no harm. *Are* you Miss Thompson?'

'I am.'

'And are you cognisant of the whereabouts of Lady Grey?'

Though something in his manner made me feel I might trust him, I hesitated. 'Before I answer, you must tell me the reason for your question.'

'Ma'am, I know where you are lodging but I dare not risk calling on you. Sir George has set spies to report upon his wife.'

'I have no trouble in believing that. But what is your interest in this matter? '

'Ma'am, I am Arthur Stephenson, the older brother of Harry, the young middy on the *Forte*.'

'The Admiral's nephew?'

'Yes, and I am charged by my uncle with the delicate matter of passing correspondence to Lady Grey.'

'That may be very dangerous for her. If Sir George becomes aware of any communication between them, it will exacerbate her position.'

'My uncle is all too aware of that. Are you privy to the fact that Lady Grey sent him a letter from Rio?'

'I have no knowledge of any such letter.'

'By some means, Sir George learned of it. It was the greatest misfortune. So I imagine you have no idea either of how things stand at the present time?'

'None whatsoever.'

'Regrettably, the incident aboard the *Forte* has now reached the newspapers, which are fuelling the scandal daily. Miss Thompson, I've been entrusted with communiqués for you and Lady Grey but I am known in London. If I'm seen to deliver anything to your lodgings it will arouse immediate suspicion. I have already had to wait several days for this opportunity to speak with you. Is it possible that you could pass exactly this way again tomorrow and at this time?'

I nodded.

'Excellent. As you reach this spot, a woman carrying a basket of apples will bump into you. Her apples will fall, she will apologise to you profusely and, as she brushes down your cloak, she will slip into your pocket a small bulky packet containing correspondence from my uncle and others.'

'And if Lady Grey should wish to reply to this correspondence?'

'It would be far too unwise to do so. She must protect what remains of her reputation.'

'Which appears to be even less than we presumed.'

'I fear so. Sir George is a relentless enemy. He wishes to damage both my uncle's character *and* his wife's.'

'But Lady Grey has none of your uncle's powerful friends and connections.'

'My uncle is not concerned for himself. He wishes only to preserve what he can of the lady's honour. It is not he but *her own husband* who has spoken publicly of events aboard the *Forte* and has set out to ruin her.'

I retraced my steps of the previous day but saw no woman, only a man, loitering opposite our lodgings. Remembering Arthur Stephenson's talk of spies, I recalled I had seen this same fellow several times, always apparently idling nearby. Could he have been set by Sir George or his agents to witness our movements? I passed to the shop where I had completed my errands the day before and set about for home. Then, as I turned the corner before the lodging-house, a woman darted across the street between two hansoms, colliding with me as she gained the pavement. Apples flew from her basket. While she helped me to my feet and brushed down my cape, I felt the thrust of something into my pocket.

'I beg your forgiveness, Ma'am,' she said loudly, as concerned passers-by began to gather. 'I pray you're not hurt.'

'No. Just a little shaken.'

'Be careful,' she whispered, apparently smoothing my bonnet. 'We are watched.'

And, as I made to walk away, I saw that the loiterer had joined the small knot of people forming around us.

In the privacy of my bedroom, I sat before the fire and undid the package. Wrapped about its contents was a letter:

My Dear Miss Thompson,

I thank you for being the bearer of this package. May I beg you to read the contents and pass to Lady Grey only those to which you feel she should be privy? It grieves my uncle greatly that, in order to try to preserve her honour, he must eschew all contact at the present time. His fervent wish is that it had been possible to spare her the cruel injustice of what has transpired.

I remain, Miss Thompson,
Your obed. Servant,
Arthur Stephenson.

Unfolding the contents, which included newspaper clippings and copies of letters, I began to read.

. . . an unfortunate incident that took place on the <u>Forte</u> between Sir H. Keppel and Lady Grey . . .; the honour of an English gentleman, who had the misfortune to be the guest of . . . a dishonourable English Admiral . . .; the greatest injury a man can suffer . . . inflicted before his eyes . . .

Horrified, I consigned *The Times* to my bedroom fire. The next item was a copy of a letter from Sir Harry to his brother:

5th July 1860

Last evening, we anchored at 8-00 PM in Simon's Bay intending to put ashore next morning when . . . the Governor would have been welcomed under a salute with manned yards. But His Excellency was in such a hurry to convey to Sir Frederick the fact of his arrival that, unseen, he dropped himself into a short boat and landed at Admiralty House . . .

I did not pay my own respects to Sir Frederick until July 5th when he received me distantly and informed me that Sir George had apprised him of my 'dishonourable conduct towards his wife aboard the <u>Forte</u>' . . . The Governor is a very devil, wily and conniving . . .

10th Nov. 1860

I now know that, three days after I had sailed in July, Sir George wrote to the Duke of Newcastle, claiming that, as Secretary of State, it was imperative he be apprised of what had transpired!! Need I say more about the character of the man! It will go some little way towards explaining how the whole sad business was spread so quickly and to such highest levels in England.

Filled with revulsion at Sir George's duplicity and cunning in the spreading of malice and gossip against his own wife, I nonetheless resumed reading.

In his letter to Newcastle, not only did that wretch enclose copies of the letters between us, further, he enclosed copies of the notes the Lady and I had so foolishly exchanged and his own — much-embellished — account of the incident with no mention of his own threats of murder and suicide . . . He went on to state that he had 'hoped the subject might not become a matter of public notoriety but I found that the matter had obtained entire publicity here at the Cape; moreover, I believe, upon evidence I cannot doubt, that this is, in a great degree, to be attributed to conversations of Sir H. Keppel, and to remarks of the most painful, and embarrassing kind, which he had made to other persons.' Such calumny! The sole person to whom I spoke at Cape Town was Sir Frederick so it evident that either he or the Governor alone can be responsible for the spreading of rumour and innuendo . . . That the Bishop of Cape Town felt it his 'duty' to intervene in a matter of which he had knowledge only from one party to the affair is not merely a matter for speculation as to his (the Bishop's) motives but has been the regrettable cause of the further spread of damaging gossip and defamation in regard to Lady Grey . . .

I felt such a surge of anger that, for a moment, I could not carry on reading. The next sheet was a clipping from a newspaper:

The Keppel Scandal
. . . It may turn out that Sir George Grey acted with unbecoming and causeless impetuosity, and that a British Admiral was removed from a valuable appointment at the request of the Home Secretary, because an irascible civilian Governor chose to pick a quarrel.

This was more encouraging. I looked at the next item.

From the Journal of Admiral Sir Henry Keppel, I read.

Nov, 1860

To Lady Grey.

If I say that I am and have been afraid to write it is not from anything that may befall me, but the further harm that my doing so may inflict on your comparatively innocent head. You are surrounded by spies. What Sir G's intentions are with regard to you it is impossible to guess, and although he believes in his heart (heart he has none) that you are innocent, he would sacrifice you to gratify his revenge on me. Would to Heaven that I could by any amount of suffering or misery on my part clear you from that which I have led you into. How painfully true is the simile with which you compare yourself to a climbing plant and in your ignorance clung to a support unable to uphold you. I dare not say what I feel for you, the injury my unfortunate feelings have already led you into is too painful to bear . . . For a long time I kept a diary for you but that you may never see . . . May God forgive me and help you. I will not trust myself to add more.

(Signed) H.K.

Is there a scar left on that poor little head?

So Lucy *had* written to the Admiral from Rio. How else could he have known of the injury to her temple she had suffered in a fainting fit there?

The next letter was marked *Secret.*

Lavington House,
Petworth.
Sep 3 1860

Sir:

I trust that I am not doing wrong in asking Your Royal Highness . . .

Your Royal Highness? To what lengths was Sir George not prepared to go?

. . . to read the accompanying most painful letter from the Bishop of Cape Town. I have two motives in venturing to take this step. First a sense of Justice to that great man Sir George Grey: and secondly; a

desire that all the circumstances of Admiral Keppel's shameful conduct should be known to Your Royal Highness: because I believe that your possessing that knowledge will greatly tend to enable in this Instance Her Majesty to maintain at the Cape the High Tone of Morals which through the Goodness of God to us She has been enabled to maintain at home.

I am, Sir,
Your Royal Highness's
dutiful & affectionate,
S Oxon.

Perhaps I may ask for the return of the letter here at the convenience of Your Royal Highness.

Bishop Wilberforce! No wonder, I thought in fury, as I tossed it onto the fire, that he is known to everyone in England as 'Soapy Sam'. I snatched up the document that had lain below it.

My dear Bishop

I return the Bishop of Capetown's letter which you have thought it your duty to communicate to me. It relates to a most melancholy affair, on which I had also seen reports from Sir Harry Keppel's friends.

Here are two of the most distinguished public Servants, within different branches, placed in antagonism where the Country had so much to expect from their united action; the one deeply offended and injured in his domestic life; the other exposed to public ruin.

I cannot conceive anything more painful.

As to the case itself, it appears to me that, if there be presumption of a crime having been committed, the legal tribunals ought to be left to adjudicate; if there has been only indiscretion, nothing more hurtful to the real interests of Sir G. Grey, & particularly to Lady Grey, could be devised, than by blind zeal for her welfare to make the Scandal of her shame more public in attracting general notice to it, nor could anything injure both men more than to encourage two parties to fight, each for their respective friend, in throwing most dirt on the other.

I can personally do nothing in the matter. Sir George Grey seems to have appealed to his chief the Duke of Newcastle. Sir Harry is under the command of the Admiralty; both Authorities are responsible in their departments.

Ever &c,
A.

If Prince Albert had been present I might have flung my arms about him, so exultant was I at the thought of Bishop Wilberforce's humiliation at this summary dismissal of his letter. But the growing evidence of the magnitude of the scandal appalled me.

I approached Lucy that same evening.

'From Harry! I *knew* he'd write, that he hadn't forgotten me.'

'Listen very carefully,' I said. 'Your entire future hangs in the balance. You cannot afford to be swept away by sentimental notions. If Sir George refuses you a settlement, what will you do? He won't want the scandal of divorce, but he will attempt to retain control over you. The Admiral knows that. His nephew was adamant that he wishes only for your honour to be protected insofar as that may be possible.'

'But why didn't his nephew call on us? It seems a little ungracious.'

'The Admiral believes Sir George has set spies to watch us and I'm certain he's right. There's a man constantly lounging opposite in the street.'

'*Spies*? What possible intelligence could be conveyed to my husband that could injure me more?'

'He suspects that the liaison between you and the Admiral continues.'

'Harry loves me, Fanny. I know it.'

For her own protection, I deemed it essential to show Lucy at least some of the cuttings and letters. Even with the worst of them kept from her, she was horrified at what she read. She was silent for some time, then she said, 'Why couldn't my husband have loved me just a little, Fanny? A small amount of kindness, affection — that was all I asked of him.'

'That he cannot give. Not to any wife.'

'Makareta . . .'

'Is dead, and she was his mistress, not his wife.'

LYME REGIS, 1864

I understood now that Maud Colville had been right. Woman is purely her husband's chattel and he may do with her what he will. Had Lucy been a widow she might at last have found happiness with the Admiral, whose concerns were all for her welfare and her honour. Sir George, however, was angered not by the alienation of his wife's affections but by the loss of his property; he did not want her yet nor he did he want any other to have her. But I was aware of my own double standards in this. What of Te Toa's wives? Were they any better off than Lucy? It was I, not they, whom he had treated as his equal, I in whom he had confided opinions and beliefs he would not have shared with even another man. And yet, I told myself, Te Toa has not written to me, has not kept a journal for *me*. He has forgotten me. I was merely a novelty, a Pakeha woman, of interest only for my difference.

In this way, I see now, I suppressed the pain of loss and made it possible for myself to continue living.

Lucy wrote regularly. Aunt Julia Martin had never alluded to her situation, and was so kind and attentive she fancied herself treated as a daughter. They were now at the Martins' country house in Herefordshire; a mount had been provided for her and she spent much of her time riding in the surrounding countryside, *so beautiful and tranquil, you cannot imagine, Fanny . . . And, in a month or two, I shall come to Lyme for an extended visit . . . I long to see you again.*

And then, I received a letter. I opened it unsuspectingly.

My Dear Miss Thompson,

Acting as his Solicitor and Agent, I write on behalf of His Excellency, Sir George Grey, Her Majesty's Governor at the Cape Colony. Following the unhappy separation of Sir George and Lady Grey, in conformity with his wishes, she currently resides with his Aunt but it has come to his attention that she intends to visit you at Lyme. Desiring that she should remain at all times under his Aunt's supervision, he has forbidden her to do so. Should she defy him in this, he will take steps to assert his authority over her, including the justifiable cessation of those funds he now supplies for her material wellbeing.

I feel certain, Madam, that you would not wish to oppose the wishes of His Excellency. Accordingly, I ask you, on Sir George's behalf, to desist heretofore from any further contact or correspondence with the Lady.

I remain,

Yr. obed. Servant,

Josiah Unwin, Esq.

I cannot recall at any time in my life feeling such rage as I did upon reading that letter. Not content with ruining his wife, Sir George was now set upon separating her from those few friends who still remained to her.

By the afternoon post, I received a communiqué from Lucy.

My dearest, dearest Fanny,

I write in haste. I dare not now dispatch further letters from here. I have been sent a copy of Sir G.'s solicitor's letter to you forbidding us contact. He knows how very dear you are to me and in this he seeks, as you envisaged, to punish us both. I may write now only to Gussie, and Aunt Julia is to have the reading of those letters, so I cannot even communicate with you by that circuitous route. I must tell you that with the solicitor's letter was an enclosure, a cutting of the announcement of the marriage of Admiral Keppel at the end of last month. My heart is entirely broken . . .

VIII

LONDON, 1867

21st March, 1867

My Dearest Fanny,

It is now almost seven years since last we were together and not a day has passed without my thinking of you and mourning our separation. I dared not write before but we have returned to Eaton Terrace and I have slipped out to the post while Aunt Julia is seeing her physician.

I am tolerably well and pass my days happily enough, in the circumstances. Aunt is very good to me, though her health is a cause for concern. I long to see your dear face again and pray that we may somehow, one day, be reunited.

I trust you are well and happy in Lyme. I should love to know all about your comings and goings, but please do not attempt to reply to me lest my husband should have knowledge of it. Fanny dearest, I am sure God will find a way to reunite us. I pray for it daily.

Believe me, ever,

Your most loving,

Lucy.

P.S. Do you, too, still think of New Zealand?

LYME REGIS, 1869

A letter arrived with an Australian postmark. It was from Gussie, who in all of our correspondence had never once alluded to the incident aboard the *Forte* or to Lucy's altered circumstances.

You may already know, she wrote, *that Sir George's aunt has died, and that Lucy has entered the lay branch of the Servite order . . .*

Lucy! The Servite order! Scarcely crediting this intelligence, I read on.

Might I beg you to consider visiting her at this address? My husband and I are anxious to ensure she is not in want.

I did not write to announce my coming, but called in person at the sprawling house in the dingy suburb of Fulham.

'I am her sister,' I told the stern nun who greeted me, 'in London for the briefest of visits. I beg you to allow me to see her.'

The nun left me in an austere sitting room on an uncomfortable upright chair set beneath a gloomy representation of the Crucifixion. On the wall opposite hung a large painting of a sorrowing Madonna, below it a cross adorned with a rosary. There was neither curtain nor carpet, merely one other chair and a bare deal table. The grimness of my surroundings lowered my spirits even further. It seemed impossible to imagine Lucy in such an inhospitable place.

At last, footsteps echoed in the corridor, the door opened, and the nun reappeared, shadowed by a white-veiled figure clad in a short-sleeved black tunic held by a leather belt. It took me several moments to realise it was Lucy.

'You have fifteen minutes, Sister,' said the nun, and withdrew.

I wanted to run to Lucy, fling my arms about her and kiss her cheek, but she stood motionless, then threw back her veil and looked at me with an expression I could not interpret.

'Ah, Fanny,' she said, finally, 'this is an answer to prayer. If only you could know how much I've longed to see you . . .'

I went slowly to her and embraced her. I could not speak for tears of happiness.

We clung together for some time, then she said, 'Sir Harry . . . he married, you know, Fanny.'

'Yes.'

'I heard he has two young children. I wonder often about what . . . but when such sorrowful thoughts engulf me, I pray to Our Lady of the Seven Dolours.'

'I—'

'I pray every day for you, too.'

'Lucy, come home with me, I implore you. Come back to Lyme. You needn't remain here. You have no more need of Sir George or his pittance.'

'I can't, Fanny.'

'You can. *Please*, Lucy. We don't have to stay in Lyme. We can travel anywhere you wish.' I hesitated. 'To New Zealand, if you want.'

She shook her head. 'Do you remember, so long ago, that fortune-teller in Rio? How she said I should reign like a queen and slink like a cur? That I should be pious?'

'I recall how we laughed.'

'But, Fanny, she was right. One cannot go against Fate. And, dearest Fanny, I told you how I ordered the servant to leave the cobra inside the house? How I rejoiced when Makareta was struck down?'

'And I said that did not make you responsible for—'

'I knew I would be damned because I was so thankful that she was dead I could not find it in my heart to repent. Then, after Aunt Julia died, I turned to the Roman faith. I am truly penitent now and my confessor has given me absolution.'

'If you've been absolved, you can return with me to Lyme.'

She shook her head. 'No. I will cherish your dear friendship till the end of my life, but I'm at peace here. I can never go back into the world again. I can't bear to reopen painful wounds.'

We were both silent. Then she said, 'Fanny, please, this is very hard for me to say, but . . . don't come to see me again. And don't write. You will always be my most beloved sister, but . . .'

Sorrow overwhelmed me.

'Don't cry, Fanny. Please. I know in my heart this is the right . . . the only . . . path for me.'

A hand-bell rang and the nun returned. I embraced Lucy and left, barely able to see my way through my tears.

AOTEAROA

I knew that, in time, the gods of my mother, Kahe Te Rau-o-te-rangi, would punish me for my wrong-doing. Every day, I felt the imminence of their retribution. And Te Ariki, Jesus, He, too, would avenge himself for my sins. *The Serpent beguiled me and I did eat.*

My bleaching, crumbling bones lie in a shallow grave far, far from Aotearoa. Though I seek it unceasingly, I cannot find the Broad Path of Tane that will lead me to Hawai'iki. There is no one from my tribe to call my spirit home; it is trapped forever, far from my ancestral lands.

I have looked for Mata Kawana here among the company of kikokiko, the ghost souls, but I have not seen her. It may be that she is not yet dead. It may be that the Heaven of Te Ariki is the true one after all, and she is there, while my restless spirit is condemned to wander . . .

LYME REGIS, 1872

At the kitchen fire, I warmed myself against the evening winter cold. Jane, called away to her ailing mother, had laid out my supper in the parlour before she left. As I sat, mesmerised by the orange and yellow flames in the grate, I had a sudden unwanted recollection of Rio and the blind fortune-teller. How had she known all our destinies? I fancied I saw in the fire the moving shapes of faces, heard in the crackling logs the whisper of voices. And, suddenly, there came a rapping at the kitchen door. I sat transfixed, unable to move or call out. The door was on the latch, unlocked. I had a vision of phantoms crowding outside, about to swirl inside the safety of my kitchen and overpower me. Forcing myself to look up, I caught a glimpse of something peering in at me through the window. The contorted mask from the hovel in Rio! I screamed and it withdrew; the door opened and a man entered.

So tall he could barely stand upright in the room, his light-coloured hair swept into a topknot, his face heavily tattooed, he moved towards me. 'Kia ora,' he said. For a moment I thought he might be Death, come to claim me. Then, he leaned towards me and pressed his forehead to mine in the long-remembered Maori salutation.

He moved a little towards the fire and I saw he was shivering.

'Please to sit down and get warm,' I said, recollecting myself, 'and then tell me the purpose of your visit.'

'Mata, I have travelled a very long way to this cold country. From the other side of the world I came to seek my mother.'

I could not take my eyes from him. I tried to speak, but for some moments I was mute. Then I said, 'What is your name?'

'I am Hori Kerei, the adopted son of the Ngapuhi chief, Te Toa.'

My heart hammered at my ribs. 'Hori Kerei . . . George Grey,'

I said. 'You are named for the Governor.'

Outside, the snow fell thickly. I struggled again to find my voice. 'Te Toa . . . Tell me, is Te Toa . . . still living?'

'Yes. And when he knew that I was determined to find my mother—'

I heard my voice break. 'Has he . . . told you about your mother?'

'No. He has always forbidden any talk of her. To protect her, he refused to disclose her identity. For many years, I had no idea of who she might be, but one day my grandmother called me to her. "You are a grown man,' she said, "and I see how strongly you desire to know your parentage. This is something your father will never reveal to you. Even for me, he will not break his silence. Now, every child has the right to know the name of his mother and, as I am near to death, I have decided that I must tell you this. Listen carefully," said my grandmother, "but swear that you will never disclose to your father that I have spoken to you of it."

'"I swear it," I said.

'And then she told me that, when I was an infant, shortly after my birth, Te Kawana and his wife agreed to adopt me. "And it would not be the first time a baby had been introduced in this fashion by its mother to its rightful household," said my grandmother. But then Te Kawana refused the child. Te Toa, who had named the boy for Te Kawana, was most troubled, but Te Kawana remained adamant. So Te Toa took the child himself. That child was me, and my mother was the sad and headstrong young wife of Te Kawana.'

I stared at him, unable to speak.

'Mata,' he said, 'I saw in your garden a most splendid tree.'

'That . . . that . . . is a mulberry tree, more than two hundred years old.'

'In the garden of Pihopa Selwyn's old house at Waimate there is just such a tree. Mata Pihopa wished to take it with them to Kohimarama, but Pihopa would not permit it. Such trees, he said, are like certain people. They can never be transplanted. I think perhaps the same was true of my mother.'

I took in the colour of his hair, the lightness of his skin, the regularity of his features. 'Why do you say that?'

'Mata Kawana could not be planted in one place. England,

Australia, Aotearoa, South Africa — she was without a turanga-wae-wae.'

I looked at him blankly.

'A standing-place. Somewhere to lay down roots as a tree does. But more than just a dwelling place — the mountains and the sea, the land that claims your heart.' He gestured at the garden. 'That great tree there, I think it is part of your turanga-wae-wae, Mata. My mother, I believe, had nothing such to hold her fast to one home.'

'I . . .'

'I arrived in this cold, frozen England, seeking my mother, Mata Kawana, but I was unable to find her. And then I remembered the friend my grandmother said had been always with her. I determined to find this lady and ask her about my mother, so, many weeks ago, I wrote to Mata Colville, a Pakeha friend of my father, and she has sent me a letter from Aotearoa, telling me where I might find you. Mata Colville says she is not at liberty to tell me of my parentage, but I think that you will help me to find my mother. I believe you are that friend of Mata Kawana.'

'I am . . . I have always been . . . her dearest friend. I love her as a sister. But after . . . after her return to England—'

'After Te Kawana sent her away?'

'*You* knew? Even *the Maori tribes* knew of her disgrace?'

'Of course. It was carried to us from everywhere on the winds. But my father would not allow any mention of it. It was my grandmother who told me why Te Kawana had put away his wife.'

'And why was that?'

'Mata, it was because of my own existence.'

AOTEAROA

Before he left Aotearoa, Te Kawana took me with him to the pa of Te Toa, the Northern chief, to make a formal farewell. This chief was a favourite of Te Kawana, but he looked at me with eyes of frost and I saw that he despised me; he scorned me, but Te Kawana's mana obliged him to welcome me. There, I could not share lodgings with Te Kawana. They placed me in the whare of the chief's mother. And in that dwelling was a tiny baby who gazed directly at me, then turned away his head, a certain sign of displeasure from the gods.

The chief's mother told me that the child was to be adopted by Te Kawana. I stared at the infant, at the lightness of his skin. I remembered the absence from Auckland of Mata Kawana and her sister. I remembered the desperation of Mata for the orphan . . . and, suddenly, I understood.

That evening, I whispered into the ear of Te Kawana. I told him that the chief's mother, herself, had told me of the boy's parentage, that his mother was Mata Kawana.

And, as I said it, the flame of triumph flared in my breast, blazing throughout my body. I knew it was certain now he would refuse to take the boy.

But, in the night, in that strange whare, I was assailed by evil dreams, beset by ghostly howls and whistling winds. I woke to find the chief's mother beside me.

'What is it?' she asked. 'Why is your soul so violently distressed?'

In my confusion and fear, I confessed to her that I had discovered Mata's secret and betrayed her. 'And now,' I cried, 'the gods will punish me. I will die in a strange country. My bones will never lie in the soil of my ancestors.'

'The closer one is to death,' said the kuia, 'the more wrong-doing eats the soul. You must go in the morning to Te Kawana and pretend to him that you lied.'

But how could I do that? Words cannot be recalled to the mouth. Forever now, Te Kawana would have the knowledge of the guilt of his wife.

LYME REGIS, 1872

We sat by the dying fire. I stared at Hori Kerei. 'Are you saying that the Governor believed you were the child *of his own wife*?'

'Yes, but for true utu, sometimes one must wait very long. It was so with Te Kawana. He waited many years to punish my mother.'

'To *ruin* her.'

'My poor mother . . .'

I saw that he was weeping. I went to him and put my arms around him. 'Hori Kerei,' I said, 'you are not the adopted son of your father. You are Te Toa's true son. And it is I who . . . *I* am your mother.'

CAPE TOWN

Te Kawana and I rode together in the carriage from Government House into Cape Town and, as we returned, I saw before me a portent of death. A small dark cloud, a funeral wreath, encircled the head of Devil's Peak. My heart filled with dread. I turned to Te Kawana. 'Look,' I said. 'What do you see?'

Te Kawana glanced upwards. 'Why, only the mountain-top.'

'And round about it?'

'The blue of the Cape Town sky.'

The cloud-wreath swelled and grew until the mountain was entirely hidden in the sinister grey mist swirling now behind the House. I thought of the dying words of my mother, Kahe, as she looked towards Tutere-moana on Kapiti Island in far-off Aotearoa.

My terror increasing, I climbed the staircase and entered my room. The weather was muggy; the servant boy had left the balcony windows ajar to air the room. I stepped towards my bed. I will lie down, I thought, and rest until I am calmer.

And then I heard it. The softest, slightest sound, as if a stockinged sole slid across the floor. I looked into the dark corner, and saw, rising from the gloom like a pillar of fire, the sinuous shape and swollen hood of the Serpent, come to claim me. I felt the child leap suddenly in me. And I heard again Mr Hadfield's voice: *Thou art cursed above all cattle, and above every beast of the field; upon thy belly shalt thou go, and dust shalt thou eat all the days of thy life . . .*

Hypnotised, I stared at the Serpent's small black eyes, the dark flicking fork of its tongue. *Dust thou are, and unto dust thou shalt return*, said Mr Hadfield.

The creeping fog outside now filled the room, covering the

windows, the walls, the bed, everything but the fiery column of the Serpent's body. And from within that cloud of mist rose another sound, an eerie hissing, a whistling, like the howling of the wind — the voice of my gods. As it utterly enveloped me, it soared to a pitch so intolerable that I screamed aloud and felt, as I did so, the poisoned thrust of the flaming sword of the Serpent. *Vengeance is mine, saith the Lord. I will repay.*

Utu.

LYME REGIS, 1872

Hori and I sat silently for some time, our foreheads gently pressed together. Then, he drew back and gazed at me.

'Mata,' he said quietly, 'there is something I must tell you. After my grandmother died, as I had promised, I did not reveal to my father what she had told me, but, secretly, I determined to travel to England to seek my mother. My father was opposed to my leaving Aotearoa but he saw I was set upon it. And as he bade me farewell, I asked him one last time, "Tell me the name of my mother." He looked at me and I felt his steadfastness waver. "I shall seek until I find her," I said. "Let me know her name." He was silent for a long time, then he said, "My son, I cannot. Long ago, I gave my word. But I bestow on you a father's blessing. And, if you should find your mother, I charge you with a message for her."'

'A message? Tell me, I beg you, what is it?'

'Mata, I *have* found you. So here is the message from my father, Te Toa. "*Tihe mauri ora.*"'

'The breath of life.'

'Yes, Mata. And I am to say that he wishes her — he *implores* her — to return to Aotearoa.'

NEW ZEALAND, 1875

My life has been bounded by the sea. Now, whenever my thoughts drift back to Lyme, it is always late spring or early summer. I know very well that it rained, was dreary, sometimes biting cold with gales from the east, that the frost crunched underfoot and the snow lay deep in winter, but when I look away from this southern landscape of mountains and bush, rainstorms and blinding sunlight, and re-inhabit that other northern world, above the pink blossom of my mulberry tree the sun shines perpetually in an eternally cloudless blue sky. I stand again on the shore near the Cobb, the sea curling up towards me, its bubbling white froth vanishing into the shingly sand. Strands of bladder-wrack lie beached, their fat greenish-black grapes waiting to be popped later before the fire. As the foam sinks, ribbing the grey Dorset beach, I see again the sea behind it, shallow ripples giving way to the slate colour of the deeper water stretching far away to Rio, South Africa, China, Australia and, furthest by far, New Zealand . . . And there we sail, all of us, Papa, Uncle, Aunt, the Admiral, the Governor, Makareta, Maud, Lucy, Hori my son, and I, forever crossing and re-crossing those hidden pathways on the vast expanses of the world's oceans.

AOTEAROA

There is a want of intellectual apprehension of the vast difference that necessarily exists between the civilised man, brought up among a people who have been for many generations civilised and Christian, and those who, however sincere in their religion, still bear about them the marks of that barbarism and that heathenism which they have inherited from a long line of ancestors, and from which it is so difficult to divest themselves. But the Christian should endeavour to overcome such prejudice, and to emancipate himself from its deadening influence. Englishmen are apt to speak of these people as men of an inferior race, unfitted for civilisation, forgetting that a Greek — Aristotle, for instance — spoke in the same contemptuous way of the race from which we have sprung, as irreclaimable barbarians.

Octavius Hadfield.
Anglican missionary
Bishop of Aotearoa 1890–93

AUTHOR'S NOTE

This novel is a work of the imagination, but its plot and characters draw on historical as well as invented sources. While Fanny Thompson and her family are entirely fictional, the Great Storm did, indeed, shatter The Cobb at Lyme in November 1824, and Sir Richard and Lady Spencer and their family lived in Cobb House, Lyme Regis, from whence they emigrated to Albany, Western Australia. Dates for the voyage vary and since naval records before the later part of the nineteenth century are often arbitrary, I have taken 1835 as the date for the *Buffalo*'s voyage. The Spencer's former cottage, Strawberry Hill, is now a national monument. Sir Richard was one of Nelson's captains and his youngest daughter, Eliza Lucy, known to her family as Lucy, married Grey at the age of sixteen, shortly after he had succeeded her late father as Resident in Albany. In places, I have drawn on Lucy's letters and her Australian journal; in others, I have invented her correspondence.

Grey's Aunt Julia Martin was a close friend of Elizabeth Barrett Browning and I found the quoted passage on the flap of an envelope containing one of her letters in the Sir George Grey Special Collections in the Auckland Libraries. Godfrey Thomas, Grey's half-brother, is described in contemporary accounts in Australia and New Zealand, and I have drawn also on his Australian journal. The letter from the Rev. Coles to Governor Grey is taken directly from his letter in the New Zealand National Archives. Godfrey's later abandonment of his mistress and daughter, and his return to England and subsequent marriage there, are factual.

The Selwyns, Roughs, Martins, General Pitt, Miss Cockcraft and other Auckland characters, including the redoubtable Mr Outhwaite who took his wife to a ball in a wheelbarrow, were all known figures in early New Zealand and feature in Una Platts's *The Lively Capital*, which I have used for source material and background. I have also drawn on Lady Martin's *Our Maoris* for her account of the incident with the Watsons at Tauranga and other material. Henry Williams and Octavius Hadfield, the St Hills, Mrs Godley and Mr Nicoll, Eyre, Petrie and Domett are all based on real people. The Gilfillan massacre was an actual event, as was the fire at Government House, but, for the purposes of the narrative, I have sited the fire after Grey's investiture, not before, as was really the case.

Among the Maori characters, Te Rauparaha, Te Rangihaeata, Te Mamaku, Wiremu Kingi, Heke, Hongi, Harata and Waka Nene are based on real people, but Makareta and her immediate family, and Te Toa, are fictional. There has long been speculation that Grey had a Maori mistress whom he took to South Africa, but no evidence has ever been found for this, though Lucy Grey mentions it in her letter to Wilberforce, who dismisses it as a figment of her imagination.

Willie Selwyn's voyage alone on the *Dido* to England at the age of six, the taking of Te Rauparaha, and other events are based in reality, although I have largely re-imagined them in this narrative. Mr Gladstone was, in reality, the godfather of one of the Selwyns' children and a family friend.

Events aboard the *Forte*, the subject of a great scandal in Victorian England, are drawn from an account, first brought to my attention by Edmund Bohan in his biography of George Grey, *To Be a Hero*. The widespread interest in this incident is reflected in newspapers and journals of that time when 'criminal conversation', a euphemism for adultery, was a serious offence, and any woman who was divorced by her husband, no matter the degree of his own guilt or neglect, was automatically a pariah within society and regarded as the guilty party. After Grey's discovery of notes between his wife and the Admiral, Sir Henry Keppel was the subject of a vendetta by Grey, and though Keppel lived to be ninety-four and ultimately rose to become Father of the Navy, his mid-life naval career was seriously hindered by this. His letters from Cape Town and his journal entry to Lucy are authentic. Other letters relating to this affair, including those between Prince Albert and Bishop Wilberforce, are held in the Royal Archives at Windsor, as is the letter from the Maori chief Tutukaka to Queen Victoria.

Maud Colville is entirely fictional, though her opinions and views of women's enfranchisement, their rights and their station were prevalent among certain women of her class in contemporary England. Her observations on the perilous situation of women of large fortune married to husbands who misused their money, and on women's inability to control their own wealth, mirror the contemporary situation before the enactment of the Married Women's Property Act in 1870 and 1882.

The love affair between Fanny and Te Toa is entirely imagined, but the problems within the Greys' marriage have been well documented and appear to have arisen after the death of their only child as an infant. Te Toa's observations and concerns about the New Zealand Company and others seeking to obtain Maori land are based on contemporary disquiet about this from both Maori and Pakeha sources. Hadfield's life at the pa in Otaki and Waikanae is drawn directly from the letters of his contemporaries, and from his own journal and letters in the appendices to Barbara MacMorran's biography, in which he relates how he managed to win favour with the chief at Otaki when he first arrived there. It is Hadfield, too, who documents how Te Rauparaha wished to learn to read and write and occasionally attended services at Otaki because he was fond of an English breakfast.

Lucy Grey did enter the Servite order for a brief period. In reality, she and Grey later reunited after thirty-five years of separation, but it was a disaster and they separated again, and died within ten days of each other. The unhappy state of their marriage has been noted by contemporary observers.

Governor Grey was, and remains, a complex character, one of the main reasons for my wishing to portray him through both actual and fictionalised sources.

Judy Corbalis
May 2015

ACKNOWLEDGEMENTS

I am very pleased to be able to express my profound gratitude to the following: Her Majesty the Queen, for permission to use the letters between Prince Albert and Bishop Wilberforce, and the letter from the Maori chief to Queen Victoria, all held in the Royal Archives at Windsor; Archives New Zealand: Te Rua Mahara o te Kāwanatanga; National Library of New Zealand; Alexander Turnbull Library, Wellington, New Zealand; Sir George Grey Special Collections, Auckland Libraries; The British Library; The National Maritime Museum; The Public Records Office, London; The Philpott Museum, Lyme Regis; Albany Historical Society, Western Australia.

⋆

I am enormously indebted to Edmund Bohan for his generosity in allowing me to draw freely on the material in his biography of Sir George Grey, *To Be A Hero* (Harper Collins, 1998) and for his kindness and patience in giving me information and advice about incidents in the lives of the Greys. It was he who directed me to the Newcastle Papers, and to B.J. Dalton's *Historical Studies* for further information and source material of the Keppel Affair aboard HMS *Forte*.

I have also drawn on nineteenth-century sources that are not only relevant to my story but contemporary with it, including:

Elsdon Best, *The Maori Division of Time*, Government Printer, Wellington, 1922

—*Some Aspects of Maori Myth and Religion*, Government Printer, Wellington, 1922

Harry Bioletti (ed.), *Reminiscences of Sarah Selwyn Wife of Bishop Selwyn*, Auckland, 2002

Historical Studies vol.16, no.62, pp. 192–251, B.J. Dalton, 1974

Sir Henry Keppel, *A Sailor's Life Under Four Sovereigns*, 3 volumes, Macmillan & Company Ltd., New York, 1899

Letters and Journal of Godfrey Thomas, National Archives of New Zealand

Letters of Lady Eliza Lucy Grey, National Archives of New Zealand

Barbara Macmorran, *Octavius Hadfield*, David F. Jones, Wellington, 1969

Mary Ann (Lady) Martin, *Our Maoris*, published posthumously, The Society for Promoting Christian Knowledge, 1884

Una Platts, *The Lively Capital, Auckland 1840–1865*, Avon Fine Prints Ltd., Christchurch, 1971

William Swainson, *Auckland, the Capital of New Zealand, and the Country Adjacent: Including Some Account of the Gold Discovery in New Zealand*, Smith, Elder & Co, 1853

The Letter-books of Samuel Wilberforce, Bishop of Oxford, 1843–68, transcription R.K. Pugh and J.F.A. Mason, Buckinghamshire Record Society and the Oxfordshire Record Society, 1970

The Newcastle Papers, University of Nottingham

Contemporary reactions to the incident aboard the *Forte* are taken from *The Times* of London, the *United Services Gazette* and the *Army and Navy Gazette*, while the account of Grey's investiture is based on the report of the ceremony in the 1848 editions of the *New Zealander* and the *Sydney Morning Herald*.

Every effort has been made to trace and acknowledge the holders of material which is still in copyright, and to credit and acknowledge source material. Any inadvertent mistakes or omissions can be corrected in future editions.

*

In particular, I want to acknowledge the huge debt I owe to my publisher, Harriet Allan, whose constant sound advice has been invaluable and whose unwavering belief that I would, eventually, deliver this manuscript gave me the impetus to keep going. I really appreciate her resilience, forbearance, patience and expertise.

I wish, too, to thank Paul Lynton for his valuable and unstinting assistance with New Zealand history and the geography of early Auckland; Ronda Armitage for her many readings of the text, her useful suggestions, and for accompanying me to Lyme Regis; Win and Bruce Lynch for all their help with information about Waikanae in Hadfield's time; and special thanks to Penelope Hoare for her generosity and friendship.

Very grateful thanks for help and advice are due, too, to the following: Roger Cazalet, Graham Davies, Alison Derrett, Jillian Ewart, Vivien Green, the late Janet Hicks, Witi Ihimaera, Donald Kerr, Phillip King, the late Margaret Mahy, Neel Mukherjee, Rose Walker.

Enormous thanks to Jane Parkin, Kate Stone and Anna Bowbyes at Penguin Random House for all their careful work on the manuscript, and for being so patient and helpful.

Last but not least, I gratefully acknowledge the assistance of a Hawthornden Fellowship in the writing of this novel.

